MW00533993

The *Sunshine Shenanigan*

A Novel

John M. Whiddon

DORRANCE
PUBLISHING CO
EST. 1920
PITTSBURGH, PENNSYLVANIA 15238

The contents of this work, including, but not limited to, the accuracy of events, people, and places depicted; opinions expressed; permission to use previously published materials included; and any advice given or actions advocated are solely the responsibility of the author, who assumes all liability for said work and indemnifies the publisher against any claims stemming from publication of the work.

The Sunshine Shenanigan is a work of fiction. Any resemblance to actual events or persons, living or dead, is entirely coincidental. The Florida Medicaid program was/is obviously real and at one time there was a Department of Health and Rehabilitative Services. The fact that fraud and abuse has been historically present within the Florida Medicaid program is well chronicled and documented ad nauseam. For the purpose of the story, I may have rearranged some of the historical events either intentionally or by accident and I feel certain that I may have possibly condensed several time periods in unrealistic ways. Certain long-standing institutions, agencies, and public offices are mentioned, but the characters involved are wholly a creation from the bowels of late age memory. The thing I have learned about fiction and storytelling is that one does not have to be real careful with the truth!

Dorrance Publishing Co
585 Alpha Drive
Pittsburgh, PA 15238
Visit our website at *www.dorrancebookstore.com*

ISBN: 978-1-6366-1510-3
eISBN: 978-1-6366-1681-0

Foreword
by Dominic Calabro*

Florida's phenomenal rise in population has brought immense economic prosperity, unbelievable opportunities as well as extraordinary challenges for the Sunshine State. And while Florida slightly more than doubled its population, the Sunshine State witnessed a meteoric forty-fold rise in Medicaid spending during these past forty years (1980-2020). With that exponential growth came unprecedented opportunities for fraud, waste, and abuse.**

That target rich environment and incentive for fraud, and the state's efforts to fight and control it, provide the backdrop — and thus the theme — of this novel.

While fiction, the story is told in very vivid, real-time, penetrating, colorful, and emotional detail. The characters and events jump out at you as if you were right there —experiencing each frustrating failure, conversation, laugh, and exhilarating accomplishment.

In my experience as President and CEO of Florida TaxWatch these past four decades, the unparalleled growth of Medicaid payments and its potential scope of fraud is often beyond the proficiency, proper incentives, and tools of the massive state bureaucracy then The Florida Department of Health and Rehabilitaive Service, (HRS) overseeing and regulating this multi-billion-dollar game. I have known John Whiddon for over forty years as a graduate school professor, academic advisor, senior Medicaid administrator, health care regulatory consultant, and successful entrepreneur. The author of this intriguing tale, *The Sunshine Shenanigan*, was at the helm of Florida's Medicaid regulatory oversight for a decade during the 1980s and '90s and is credited by many with numerous innovative and creative detection strategies, including the application of some crude forms of artificial intelligence. John's real-life experience allows him to show that despite being outgunned, out-incentivized, and with less-than-ideal technologies, good public servants working with integrity, competence, innovation, and excellent teamwork can still make a difference.

John Whiddon's novel will take you for a jolting ride with highly colorful, eccentric characters, fascinating places throughout Florida, dramatic twists and turns, and an incomparable surprise ending. While this is John's "first formal attempt at fiction," I sure hope it will not be his last, and I think you will very much agree.

Dominic M. Calabro

* Dominic M. Calabro has been President and Chief Executive Officer of Florida TaxWatch since 1980. Florida TaxWatch is a public interest, non-profit, non-partisan taxpayer research institute and respected government watchdog.

**The federal Centers for Medicare and Medicaid Services (CMS) estimated an improper payment note of 15.83% for Medicaid spending nationally in 2019 (November 18, 2019).

The Sunshine Shenanigan

A Novel

Introduction

Unlike Medicare, which is strictly a federal healthcare insurance program and is universal throughout the country, Medicaid is a federal/state partnership, and each individual state participates uniquely. No two states use their matching federal Medicaid dollars alike. For almost two decades during the 1980s-90s, some growth states, like Florida, for example, viewed Medicaid as an "entitlement program" and seized the opportunity to expand numerous state-budgeted healthcare programs through an array of innovative intergovernmental financing strategies. The result was that the Florida Medicaid program became a "cash cow" with a premium on enrolling providers/practitioners, paying claims quickly while rapidly expanding optional programs and recipient eligibility groups. The consequences were both predictable and bittersweet.

Florida received a significant amount of additional financial resources via these strategic maneuvers, but in the process created an environment for unscrupulous individuals to falsely and greedily siphon off vast amounts of illegitimate payments for personal gain. After several egregious healthcare fraud horror stories were exposed, lip service *related to oversight entered the conversation. As of 2020, there is still an enormous amount of health care fraud and abuse nationwide.*

It was a time of transition. It was a time when computer dinosaur mainframes were being challenged by smaller, more compact data processing machines. It was a time of technological explosion that rendered state-of-the-art computer products and programs obsolete by the time they reached the end of the assembly line. It was a time when few individuals possessed personal computers. It was a time when crude mobile cell phones were being used by only a select few. It was a time when theorists and systems experts were well ahead of the curve and could envision computer applications that would leave "Future Shock" in the dust. It was an exciting time for those with insight and resources to facilitate that insight. It was also a time when "political correctness" peeped around the corner every now and then.

1

APRIL 19, 1994

Rural area, West Gadsden County, Florida

The next wave of nausea produced nothing but dry heaves. The small, wiry-framed, adrenaline-drained man struggled with all the strength he had left in an attempt to raise and brace himself with his elbows to keep from strangling from the mixture of blood and vomit. The paramedics attempting to start IVs were making futile efforts to keep an oxygen mask attached. Between the wrenching and subsequent gagging, the man lying on his back, with two paramedics swarming over him, kept frantically grasping and clawing empty handfuls of air while languishing over and over indistinguishable audible pleas.

Deputy Sherriff Waylon Griggs, a veteran officer with the Gadsden County Sheriff's Department, was one of the two uniformed officers perched on the overpass at County Road 270A overlooking Interstate 10, just off the Chattahoochee Exit #166; a rural area often referred to by local residents as the Sycamore Community. Geographically, the exit, situated approximately four miles due east of the Apalachicola River, is about forty miles west of Tallahassee in Gadsden County, Florida.

It was a few minutes after sunrise and a humidly cool thirty-nine degrees. Griggs's fleece-lined windbreaker felt comfortable and welcome in the early-morning chill. It would be in the eighties by two o'clock, which was quite typical for this time of year when temperatures could easily range fifty degrees during the day.

Until he was joined by the Highway Patrol officer, Griggs had been in deep thought for several moments and was well beyond bewildered. He had been one of the first to arrive at the designated rendezvous provided by the 911 dispatcher and made the scene almost in unison with one of the EMT units. Within two minutes after his arrival, a black GMC SUV, with hazard lights flashing, came sliding to a sideways halt on the overpass. The driver opened the door, emerged from the vehicle, attempted to take a step, and collapsed face-first onto the asphalt below without seemingly any attempt or ability to break his fall. It was immediately ascertained that the backseat contained another severely injured individual, with a massive head wound of some sort which required immediate emergency lifesaving medical attention.

Griggs was a well-trained veteran law enforcement officer with a degree in criminology from Florida State University and in no way a country bumpkin. He had worked his share of various kinds of crime scenes and realized this one appeared uncommonly different. Once it was determined that neither of the two men had any identification on their person, and the initial triage of their physical conditions revealed that nothing would be gained by devoting any additional attention to either of them, Griggs turned his entire concentration to examining the physical evidence available. Using crime scene gloves, he checked the interior of the vehicle for registration and anything else that might assist in identifying the vehicle's recent occupants. The vehicle search yielded what appeared to be a strange-looking mobile phone and a set of car keys, and not much else. Griggs wrote down the tag number, went back to his patrol car, and ran the plate numbers. After calling in the tag numbers and receiving the results, he returned once again to the vehicle for another closer inspection.

The Life Flight Helicopter from Tallahassee had just set down on the north end of the overpass, and a beehive of activity was in progress. The two law enforcement officers ignored the rubbernecks in both east and west lanes below on the interstate and concentrated their attention on the man that the paramedics were attempting to assist. It was impossible to hear any sounds whatsoever coming from the man's persistent, discordant, and incomprehensible pleas over the insistent roar of the Life Flight copter's deafening rhythmic rotor blades, which were at least serving to keep the tribes of marauding mosquitos at bay.

The Highway Patrol officer, who had just arrived on the scene only seconds earlier and was standing next to Deputy Griggs, cupped his hand toward the ear of the county deputy and practically hollered in order to be heard. As Griggs had anticipated, the officer wanted to know what he knew about the situation. Griggs's mind had been racing, and he was totally preoccupied with his own thoughts. Based on the circumstances, he was bothered by his peer, considering him a nuisance, and was in no mood to be cordial or engage in social intercourse, although professional courtesy dictated such decorum. In summary fashion and in all honesty, Deputy Griggs revealed a sharing of ignorance! He had more questions than answers. There were very few facts at all. He shared the general substance of the 911 call that he had listened to several times that was practically incoherent, as he displayed the bagged and tagged plastic evidence bag containing a small instrument, reminiscent of a Star Trek device, for the other officer's inspection. He neglected, or possibly on purpose, did not mention that the number from the phone received by the 911 dispatcher was apparently unknown and untraceable. Without waiting for questions, he continued with the phantom vehicle, complete without a legitimate license plate, registration, or locatable VIN number. Next, he speculated the possibility of a hunting accident, albeit with reservations. In summary, the situation was: there were currently two unidentified individuals at death's doorstep, one with wounds that he probably would not recover from and the other who was apparently having a coronary on the spot and who had seemingly bit half his tongue off. In addition, there was a vehicle that had been driven to this spot from the twilight zone after a strangely bizarre 911 call from an extremely unusual mobile phone. Griggs felt an immediate sense of relief when the highway patrolman indicated he needed to attend to other matters out on the interstate. Griggs wished him well, bid his comrade *adieu*, and ratcheted up his thoughts to another gear.

Griggs was intelligent, but he also worked very hard and took nothing for granted. He had that rare overachiever drive that set him apart from his peers. He had been a walk-on as a freshman at Florida State's football program, earned a spot on the scout team, eventually was awarded a scholarship, and won a starting role for several games as a senior. Griggs was extremely popular on the force and had aspirations to run for sheriff one day if things lined up just right.

To Griggs, right off the cuff, this would normally look most likely to be, or at least initially or appear to be, a potential hunting accident. And, in most instances, it would have been his initial hunch that the little fellow in obvious distress, possibly experiencing a coronary, had more than likely shot his buddy. Based on what Griggs knew from experience and with some degree of expertise, this kind of thing can happen sometimes to these spring turkey hunters. Griggs, including himself in the fraternity, had long ago concluded that turkey hunters in particular were somewhat bat-shit crazy to begin with! Who in the hell in their right mind would ever voluntarily get up at four-thirty in the morning and subject themselves to bloodsucking mosquitos, vampire-assed ticks, and those sociopathic "no shoulders" things sporting baby rattles on their tails? Only die-hard turkey hunters! Turkey hunters aren't like other hunters; they don't wear orange, and when things start to get exciting, they're just as liable to shoot some kind of a sound or a blue jay as a real love-sick gobbler.

Based on his experiences, he would normally have concluded that this case ought to be cut-and-dry, but his gut kept telling him that this one had some hiccups. The 911 call was bizarre as hell; he had listened to the tape several times, and it sounded like one of the damn patients from the State Mental Hospital over there in Chattahoochee calling it in. He was pretty sure the call came from the strange kind of mobile phone he had in his possession.

The deputy continued to fixate on the little man still heaving and struggling against the attendants trying to affix the oxygen mask as he continued thinking about the phone. It was strange to begin with, not too many folks had mobile phones and especially one like this! According to the 911 dispatcher, the number that the call was received and recorded from had no service origin, account code, or registered number. The deputy continued through the various mazes of his thought process. The phone wasn't the only freaky thing either; the damn GMC vehicle they materialized in didn't have proper registration or an identifiable tag he could locate in the database, even though it had a Florida plate. The most perplexing thing yet was that he had been unable to discover even a trace of a VIN number, although he knew exactly where it was supposed to be!

As he approached the vehicle once again, the tow truck driver he had summoned earlier was affixing straps to the underneath of the SUV in order to wench it on to the truck. Griggs had already decorated the vehicle in yellow crime scene tape, which the tow truck driver had worked around to take the car out of gear in order to begin the process of loading it. Griggs glanced again over at the little fellow fighting with the EMTs and thought to himself that he was probably the only living soul that might possibly be able to shed some real light on the situation, but he was not communicating coherently, and it was impossible to understand what he'd been trying to say, anyway, because it appeared he had bitten off half his tongue when he fell face-first onto the highway. Griggs concluded it probably wouldn't make any difference, at any rate, since shortly they would have him sedated, and he would reside in another world for quite a while.

Based on the 911 call, the direction from which the vehicle came, and the time the call was initially recorded, Griggs cataloged the current situation into three groups: one, things he knew; two, things he could make educated guesses about; and three, things he might wildly speculate on. He immediately put number three on the back burner and began concentrating his efforts on number two, educated guesses. The best he could figure, it seemed like things must have started going south just before daylight down off the big river. He could not imagine there could be any kind of mobile phone reception down there in the river ridges and mud swamps. As upset and as inaudible as the caller had been, it was an absolute wonder they were able to get enough of a fix on them in order to set up a staging area at this spot. He had to give that little bastard credit, though. It took a hell of a man and some kind of a heroic effort getting his buddy out of the swamp in the condition they both were in. If he'd tried to stay put and wait for someone to find them, it would pretty much be guaranteed they'd still be waiting for help to arrive! Griggs was somewhat familiar with the general area where he guessed they might have been and suspected that they had been in some extremely treacherous terrain. Some of the ridges in the area were dang near forty-fives, and it was easy to get disoriented in a heartbeat and stay turned around in there for a spell if you weren't real damn careful.

The story Griggs pieced together so far was completely unintelligible. At least three times during the 911 recording, the caller seemed to be referencing some other third person's involvement. What he had been saying, or attempting to communicate, made no sense at all, and now, obviously, he was in no shape to even talk, much less show anybody anything. Most people would have more than likely reached the conclusion that without him to take them to where everything went down, it would be pointless to even begin trying right now. Griggs, however, was not most people!

Griggs was no medical expert, but it appeared to him like the little fellow might possibly be suffering a life-threatening coronary. He had a gut-wrenching feeling this thing was going to turn into a cluster-fucking mess before it was over. It was a frustrating and helpless feeling.

Eventually, Griggs turned his attention to the second victim. Through all his law enforcement experience, he had nothing in his frame of reference or archivable repertoire for comparison. Shaking his head in resignation without even realizing it, Griggs was thinking to himself that it looked to him like half the man's face was gone, and what could be made out resembled three-day-old bloody hemorrhaging hamburger meat. The man had lost one hell of a lot of blood; the paramedics couldn't even find a blood pressure when they started working on him. Griggs saw nothing positive about the man's medical condition and could not possibly see how in the hell the man was going to make it. Hell, he wasn't even sure if he'd want to if the choice was his. The poor bastard had to have some kind of brain damage with all that head wound stuff.

Griggs, with his thoughts in overdrive, just stood where he was, swatting at renegade mosquitos that braved the insect repellant and watching the paramedics prepare both men for transport. He continued to observe as both men were eventually loaded onto the helicopter to be airlifted for the short trip east to Tallahassee Regional Memorial Medical Center. As the aircraft departed, Griggs turned his attention to the tow truck driver, who was in the final stages of loading the vehicle for the trip to Tallahassee to the Florida State Crime Lab. Griggs was working the graveyard shift, and normally his tour would soon be ending; however, not today, he opined. Armed with the knowledge that a reception committee of county investigators were already waiting at the hospital for the arrival of the Medevac helicopter, Griggs waited until the tow truck driver had finished up and was just getting ready to pull out. Griggs gave a thumbs-up salute toward the driver as he entered his car, immediately left the scene, and headed toward

Aunt Susie's Diner for some fresh smoked sausage (special home-made from scratch), cathead biscuits, and sawmill gravy. Griggs, with food as a priority, was well out of sight as the tow truck pulled out and headed down the east bound ramp to merge onto I-10.

Griggs had an initial report to write, two mysterious hunters to identify, and a phantom vehicle, as well as a strange mobile phone and a set of car keys in his pants pocket that he had forgotten to give to the tow truck driver. Over the past few minutes, the germ of an idea had begun to emerge from deep within the bowels of Griggs's hunch, but first, food was a top priority at the moment, and he intended to eat before he began attending to any of those other work-related endeavors. It had occurred to Griggs that there was really only one main artery road heading west toward the river that hunters would most likely use, which dead-ended on a high ridge before reaching the river. All the side roads, primarily old logging roads off this main road, were gated or chained by the hunting clubs or landowners when they were not using them. Griggs felt pretty confident he might be able to identify the gate the little fellow had used because, in all probability, it would certainly not be locked. The fellow had obviously left in a hurry, and locking a gate would never have been any kind of consideration. He had a plan, but he needed a little help. He had someone special in mind to call, but it was a bit too early for that call yet.

It had the makings of a long day, and he knew the High Sheriff was not going to be happy with any of this. With any luck, he was thinking maybe the case would get transferred to one of the department's special investigators, and he wouldn't have to go tromping around in that mosquito-infested mud swamp. Something told him, however, that the prospects of that kind of luck were pretty damn unlikely. He had no idea!

2

SS Death Reported In Spain

On June 20, 1987,
the following article appeared in the Miami Herald:

"Accused Mega-Fraud Physician Reported Dead in Spain"

Spanish authorities in Valencia confirmed today the death of Dr. Luis Renaldo, age 59, formerly of Miami and accused U.S. Medicare scam artist, who has been residing in Spain for the past several years while fighting extradition back to the U.S. Renaldo, accused of fleecing the federal Medicare coffers of an estimated $238 million, was previously the President and CEO of the now bankrupted PLATINUM PLUS PPO, Inc. Few details or circumstances related to Dr. Renaldo's death have been released. The latest information available from Spanish officials is that the doctor was discovered dead on a yacht owned by a close friend, where he had been residing for several months. An inquiry related to Dr. Renaldo's death is ongoing.

To the uninitiated, Luis Renaldo, M.D., was not a scam artist; he was a flamboyant, charismatic charlatan in a league all by himself. A snake oil salesman in scrubs, who was also known as *"El Leopardo"* (The Leopard) to those who had various business associations with him. Through numerous questionable federal/state grants and a multitude of private entrepreneurial venture capital credits, Dr. Renaldo set the stage for a host of schemes that would henceforth define health insurance fraud in a manner that only David Copperfield might comprehend. In the heyday of this charade, he was able to unwittingly solicit and enlist some of Hollywood's most glamorous and recognizable celebrities to volunteer their advertising endorsements in marketing strategies for the doughnut. Dr. Renaldo perpetuated his grand hoaxes to the tune of millions of dollars of fraudulent health care third-party insurance billings. For almost a decade, he successfully maneuvered the safe harbors of professional self-referrals, medically unnecessary procedures/services, kickback strategies, illegal solicitation, and clever and completely unlawful old-fashioned phantom billings. He was the master of setting up out-of-country catastrophic health crises for those Medicare recipients traveling abroad that resulted in huge medical claims for medically unnecessary services. Many of these coincidently occurred in Nigeria, Africa. For years, Renaldo was able to fly under the radar based on his coding expertise and diagnostic billing profiles that escaped detection from the automated Surveillance Utilization Review systems. He understood what many attempting to cheat the federal insurance systems did not; it paid to be strategically less greedy. Dr. Renaldo might have continued the deception much longer if it had not been for some incompetent overzealous billing agents trying to hustle a buck for themselves on the side. His illegal operations came to an abrupt end in the spring of 1985 when Platinum Plus, Inc. received notice of a special audit to be conducted by a team of special agents from the Atlanta Regional Department of Health and Human Services, Office of Inspector General. It also indicated that the team would include agents from the Federal Bureau of Investigation (FBI). Renaldo's transgressions had finally caught up with him, but he had always anticipated that they would, so he just went to his well-rehearsed exit strategy. For a while, it seemed as though he had completely disappeared off the face of the earth. Then, just as suddenly, from out of nowhere, he seemed to be everywhere simultaneously. On certain dates, in South Africa, while reliable evidence on the very same date placed him in the Netherlands. He traveled under numerous alias and passports. Eventually, Renaldo settled in Spain as his final roosting spot for a variety of good reasons; first and foremost, dual citizenship.

When the dust finally settled after the audit and the finger-shaking and pointing were done, the white-collar forensic accountants, so late out of the gate that the gate was gone, with much pompous ignorance determined that Dr. Renaldo had personally absconded with somewhere in the neighborhood of $238 million of American taxpayer dollars. What these bean counters were really saying, specifically, was at the end of the day, there was at least $238 million unaccounted for. Their calculations did not in any way begin to identify exactly how much revenue had actually been billed via Renaldo's various schemes, which were wholly fraudulent but resulted in massive stolen funds in his pockets. In actuality, it was impossible for them to have achieved any realistic final number, anyway, due to their lack of knowledge of the tangle of relationships and billing associations that created near-duplicate fraudulent records. This maze that Renaldo built would most assuredly escape detection via almost all quantitative methods. In reality, Dr. Renaldo hightailed it out of South Florida with almost one billion dollars, which was cleverly deposited in clandestine bank accounts throughout the world.

Renaldo was obsessive regarding many aspects of his daily life. He was vain when it came to his physical appearance and kept himself in great shape. He maintained a vigorous exercise regimen that included a daily five-mile jog, weight training, competitive tennis, and recreational golf. Within a month before his 1987 death, his annual physical revealed that he was in the 95th percentile for men his age. At the time of his death, both his parents were still alive in their nineties, in good health, living active, independent lifestyles. When it came to nutrition and lifestyle, Renaldo was a man of moderation. He did not smoke or use recreational drugs, and alcohol consumption consisted primarily of wine and an occasional after-dinner liqueur. If he had any vices, it would have been the numerous skirts he chased — and being rich and fit, that chased him. After the initial autopsy, various pathologists and forensic experts were brought in for consultations and specialized testing. The Spanish authorities, as a courtesy, allowed the FBI to bring in a team of experts for its own independent assessment, including forensic and clinical autopsies. When it was all said and done, the conclusion without dissension among authorities was that Dr. Renaldo apparently died of natural causes. In the harsh reality, Dr. Renaldo had been assassinated, and there were at least one billion motives. The 600-pound gorilla in the room was; where was all that money? There was someone that knew!

3

July 24, 1987

A small upscale café in Little Havana, Miami, Florida

Jorge De Valle turned off West Flagler onto 27th Avenue. Miami traffic was always the same. "Hurry up and wait," De Valle muttered to himself. He knew that he had time to spare. He had planned it that way. He always planned things that way. De Valle was obsessed with punctuality. He had no patience for those that practiced being fashionably late or adhering to so-called "Latin Time." He was of a firm conviction that punctual people are the foundation of the consistency required for trust. To many of his friends and business acquaintances, he was referred to as *"el hombre de la reloj"* or "The Clock Man". It was a nickname that fit, and one that De Valle did not particularly mind. Today, he was preoccupied with other things. Something real special was apparently about to happen, and the juices were flowing. Today, he was not going to leave anything to chance, and one thing was for sure, he was going to be on time for it. At the next street, he turned left and deliberately drove completely around the block and circled back in the direction from where he had come.

Jorge was pleased to notice that the Lexus he was driving would not be conspicuous in comparison with other cars in the parking lot of Perez's Cubano Café. To his relief, there were several automobiles of equal vintage already parked in the nicely landscaped and recently manicured lot. De Valle registered a little surprise to himself that he had never been to, or even heard of, this particular place previously. Although he spent the better part of his working day in Hialeah, in his main pharmacy, he enjoyed many evenings in Little Havana, having dinner or drinks with business associates, friends, and various civic groups. It registered as just a little strange to him that he had not frequented this little establishment before.

Jorge De Valle was a member of many organizations; he was extremely popular and politically active. Although never an office-holder or any ambitions toward that end, both newcomers and veterans alike sought out his advice and blessing before launching a political career or an election campaign. It was thought to be a real advantage or insurance of sorts to have Jorge De Valle in your corner. One of De Valle's primary activities outside his business was his role as the President of the Cuban Pharmacy Association in Exile. This was an extremely prestigious organization with powerful influence. His leadership of this group was all the more impressive since he was not Cuban but Dominican. Due to his civic-mindedness, community involvement, professional status, and familial background, Jorge De Valle was a respected member and a major player in the Latin community in South Florida.

Making his way inside the establishment, De Valle was greeted by an energetic and seasoned *maître d* with a curled and waxed handlebar mustache, sporting a bright crimson cummerbund. De Valle palmed the little man a twenty and told him he was meeting someone and would prefer a remote spot with a little privacy. He was quickly ushered to an agreeable, isolated cubicle toward the rear of the cantina, which provided excellent surveillance opportunities for a good portion of the premises and an unobstructed view of the front entrance. He ordered a *Cuba Libre* with *Brugal Añejo* and extra lime, one of his real weaknesses, along with at least 17 cups of Cuban coffee each and every day of the world. Once the cocktail arrived, he settled in and began his anticipated wait.

He was early for his appointment, but of course didn't mind. He was used to waiting on people. *Merengue,* the native music from De Valle's homeland, was playing in the background, and he took note that it was quite impossible for the shapely young woman to perform waitressing duties without incorporating a little extra hip to the tantalizing rhythm. "You just can't help it," De Valle mused while keeping the beat by tapping his ring finger on the glass.

To entertain himself during his self-imposed impassive wait, De Valle glanced down at his *guayabera,* standard everyday attire, and pondered if an expert forensic scientist might conceivably retrace and time his sequential trail during the day's events from the stains and signs displayed on the shirt. Probably wouldn't be all that difficult, he finally resolved. De Valle's thoughts wandered from his shirt to his pending appointment. He had been excited when he received the call from his old friend Marcus Manasa. It had actually been almost two years since he had even heard from him. De Valle was accustomed to long intervals without contact, and he had long ago accepted the fact that, due to the kind of work his friend was involved in, it made it impractical for them to be in regular contact, if at all. He possessed no phone number for his friend and no address. De Valle had been instructed years earlier that in an emergency, he could always take out a classified ad in the *New York Times* with a coded acronym, and he would be contacted within twenty-four hours. He had never used or even really considered using this method of contact over the past twenty-five years.

De Valle had no idea what Marcus really did professionally, or who he actually worked for, but he knew it was important, highly sensitive, maybe even somewhat on the dark side, and probably dangerous at times. Manasa's work, or what he did, was an area that was more or less acknowledged with a wink and a nod between the two, and something De Valle knew intuitively that "you just don't go there."

The two had met for the first time in the early '60s at Charlotte Hall Military Academy in Washington D.C. as high school freshmen. They had been assigned as roommates and immediately became good friends. The real common denominator had been baseball. Both were good players, students of the game, and big Yankee fans. Their differences brought them closer, as well. Marcus loved the academy structure and discipline and military demeanor and was eager to attend. De Valle simply tolerated it as a temporary rite of passage, having been sent to a military school as many young Latin males from upper-class families often are, to add some discipline and structure to his life. De Valle excelled in the hard sciences, while Manasa's talents were more towards the social sciences. Each prospered from one another in the academic disciplines for four years and graduated magna cum laude. After graduation, Marcus was accepted at The Citadel in Charleston, South Carolina, and De Valle did both his undergraduate work and master's program in pharmaceutical science at the University of Miami.

The two of them stayed in touch regularly during their college years and made it a point to meet at least once annually. It had actually been Marcus that introduced De Valle to Myra, a Cuban Diplomat's daughter, at the Commandant's Ball while on a visit to the Citadel. That introduction resulted in a love affair, a thirty-year marriage, and four children. Once Marcus left The Citadel, contact between the best friends became increasingly scarce.

In addition to being introduced to his wife by Marcus, De Valle would always be indebted to his friend in a manner for a favor that he could never repay. It had happened during an extended period of political upheaval and several thwarted *coup d'états* during the '70s in the Dominican Republic. De Valle's parents had been targeted by one of the interim groups as political radical supporters. Several of the husbands of his parents' closest friends had been arrested and interrogated. A few were actually awaiting some form of mock military tribunal. His father had realized this and had relayed the fact to his son that it was just a matter of time before he met the same fate. Both parents wanted to leave and escape to the States, but it was impossible for them to obtain the required authorization and passports for even a brief visit. There was absolutely nothing Jorge could do but sit and wait for the inevitable. It was the most helpless and excruciating experience of his life. It happened, coincidently, that Marcus was making one of his rare appearances in Miami to visit briefly with his friend when he learned of the situation.

Marcus Manasa's only comment to his friend once he had listened to the problem and realized his friend's agony was, "Jorge, don't worry. Everything is going to be fine." De Valle would never forget the reassuring smile and nod accompanying the statement. To De Valle's total bewilderment and disbelief, within seventy-two hours, both his parents, along with their pet and most of their prized possessions, appeared at his front door. They each possessed international passports, green cards, and permanent US visas. They also had a key to a storage unit that they had been informed contained all their furniture and worldly possessions. All their financial assets, including the sale of their home at an extremely inflated price, had been converted to US currency and deposited in Bank of America account in Miami. From that moment forward, De Valle knew that he would do anything ever asked of him by his friend Marcus Manasa.

Jorge recognized his old friend immediately when he entered the café and raised his arm. Marcus immediately saw the signal and charged directly toward the table to embrace his old friend. "Qué tal, hombre?" Manasa laughingly bellowed as he bear-hugged Jorge. Unbeknownst to De Valle, Marcus could have muttered the same greetings fluently in at least five different languages. Most of the time, their conversations were in English, but from time to time, they spoke in Spanish or at least integrated Latin phrases or colloquiums. Although De Valle was sure about his own Latin heritage, he was not sure if Manasa himself was totally cognizant of his true lineage. Marcus had been orphaned and adopted as a baby by a military family. He claimed to have no idea who his real parents were or where they were from. He did believe that he was actually born in the United States. He had moved many times during his childhood and continued to do so until his adopted father was killed in military action during the early days of the Vietnam War. Not long after, his mother, who Marcus claimed to adore, discovered she had breast cancer and died the following year. His parents had planned well for Marcus's life, and when the time came, his future was secure financially, and the military simply became his family. The exception to this was Jorge De Valle. Due to their friendship, and because there was really no one else, De Valle's family had become Manasa's surrogate family. Although there was not regular contact with one another, there were periodic surprises that arrived unannounced, like the World Series tickets on Jorge's eldest son's sixteenth birthday, or full clubhouse privileges Masters tickets for a week for Jorge and his youngest golfing son, which not even members of Congress could obtain. These kinds of generous feats just added to the family's enchanted "Manasa Mystique."

The waitress who was serving the two men decided to herself that the two middle-aged men who shared many of the same physical characteristics had to be related, probably brothers, concluding that the early bird with the stained *guayabera* was the older by several years. She would have been wrong. Manasa was six months older than Jorge, but had maintained a physical fitness regimen that had apparently allowed him to cheat some of the aging process often associated with middle age. It was true; however, they could easily be cast as brothers. Both featured prominent noses and olive complexions, were bald on top with thick black hair on the sides, along with thick dark mustaches. They both had similar somatotypes and probably not a centimeter difference in height. Jorge probably bested Marcus by twenty pounds above his fighting weight.

During the course of the evening, the waitress served several *Cuba Libres* to one of the men and at least a half dozen stems of a rather expensive port to the other. She observed that the early part of the evening was mostly lighthearted, and she picked up on some baseball lingo from time to time. In the last hour and a half, the conversation had apparently become serious, with the late arriver doing most of the talking. "Must be serious family business," she had concluded to herself.

When the two called it an evening, De Valle had imbibed considerably more than he needed to drink and decided to finish the night with a couple of strong Cuban coffees. The earlier discussions with Marcus had been sobering enough, but he knew he should not drive without a little time and some expresso insurance. He sat in thoughtful silence and reflected on the things that had been shared with him tonight for the first time. Jorge realized that he had just learned more about his friend in an hour and a half than he had in his entire lifetime. He was somewhat astonished that he had not been more shocked by some of the revelations. None of it mattered anyway; he had convinced himself. He was committed to a cause; Marcus required his help, that's what really mattered, and he would provide all that was required, regardless of the costs. From this night forward, he would not look back. He could not afford to second-guess.

As Jorge left the café, he discovered a taxi — actually a chauffeured Lincoln town car — waiting for him outside. *The maître d* informed him that his Lexus had been delivered to his home and that he had been instructed by the gentleman who he had dined with earlier to inform Mr. De Valle that his wife, Myra, had been notified that he would be returning late and not to worry.

4

February 8, 1993

Tallahassee, Florida

There were only the sounds produced by the constant hum of the water cooler and the occasional kicking on and off of its compressor. It was Webb Espy's favorite time of the day, any day, even if it was a workday. He had long ago determined that he possessed most of the stereotypical characteristics customarily associated with a lark and therefore structured his life accordingly. Most of the time, he was at the office well before seven o'clock, and normally that afforded him at least forty-five minutes of uninterrupted, concentrated work time. Webb Espy could do a lot of work in forty-five minutes. Most days, Webb used this particular time to work his inbox, which involved reviewing correspondence, making assignments, forwarding memos, and making notes for follow-up questions. Usually, he finished going through this daily ritual before staff began to stagger in. This work habit was one that carried over from his earliest Air Force experiences and evolved through other administrative positions he had held. Espy, with a Doctorate in Public Administration, a title he rarely if ever used, was a disciple of the new public administration that held to the principle that it made no difference as to the level, quality, or competence of staff; sixty percent of an administrator's time during a routine work day was going to be spent dealing with some type of personnel issue. To date, nothing had convinced him otherwise.

As Bureau Chief for Florida's Medicaid Regulatory Office for almost four years, Espy had grown with the job. The specific type of work itself, coupled with previous academic teaching experiences and published research at two major state universities, provided a unique opportunity to be on the cutting edge for developing insights and specialized expertise on issues dealing with healthcare fraud and abuse and other types of Program Integrity inquiries. Espy had grasped early in his tenure that aberrant practices in the health care arena were significantly unique from other forms of white-collar crime and therefore required innovative approaches and strategies for dealing with them. He had also concluded, much to the chagrin of some others, that it was big business. As a result of his published opinions and outspokenness on the subject, he was often asked to appear at various national symposiums and conferences or serve as consulting contributor to "White Paper Commissions." It often was suggested by peers and colleagues that Webb probably fostered more of a national reputation than he did within his own state. While popular with the insurance industry and other numerous government regulatory groups, there were other medical and health care associations that did not share an enthusiastic appreciation or endorsement of Espy's work. It would have been unlikely to ever find his name as a keynote speaker for an American Medical Association convention or conference.

There had been several life-altering events in Espy's adult life that defined his present state and extraordinary position. The first had come during his academic tenure at Columbia University

with the back-to-back publications of two revolutionary intro-
ductory textbooks and a simulated learning exercise concept,
which he had sold to a group called Microsoft. The other had
been the tragic death of his wife and two children in a freakish
electrocution accident on a faulty grounded tarmac connection
in a small airport in the Midwest. Webb had been devastated and
had taken an extended leave of absence and fought depression for
over a year. Following the tragedy, he had been in such a mental
state that he had not even consulted with any personal injury legal
experts that were drooling to represent him and allowed an old
family friend attorney to negotiate and settle on his behalf. As a
result, he accepted an extremely generous insurance settlement
with little enthusiasm. Consummate with these situations, Webb
Espy found himself as one of a select few of multi-millionaires
working in public service.

After a year's hiatus and living abroad much of the time, Webb
found himself uninspired and had no real interest in returning to
the academic world. Eventually, he succumbed to the relentless
recruitment of his old childhood friend, David Baswell, Secretary
of the Florida Department of Health and Rehabilitative Services.
Webb was offered his choice of numerous upper-echelon positions within the organization, several of which he immediately
declined. David Baswell's motives were not for the sole purpose
of assisting with rehabbing his old friend's mental state. He was
eager to bring Webb's talents into the fold because he realized
Webb had skillsets that were extremely rare and would fill a significant void within his management team.

Today's inbox exercise yielded only three exceptional issues
and one primary routine matter that required some additional
personal attention on his part. The first was an unusual request

for an ad hoc report from the archive files related to pharmacy claims for several providers for specific time frames over the past few years. The second was a summary of some curious irregularities on an MIS Report relating to the top Medicaid providers. The third issue was a note from Precious, his obsessive/compulsive and protective administrative assistant, regarding a call from Department Secretary David Baswell. Webb knew from experience; when Precious left a note in his inbox, he needed to put it on the top of his priority list, and more importantly, he needed to talk to her first, and he intended to do just that. The final routine matter was a phone message from his close friend Max Bloodworth, which might represent the highest priority!

The sounds of the office coming to life began to filter into Webb's awareness. He enjoyed deciphering the noises, and even more attentively, who was responsible for them. Appreciating that people are creatures of habit, Webb had become extremely proficient at predicting the sequence of arrivals and the ritualistic routines associated with his staff. At his office, there was an open-door policy, and Webb Espy's office was legendary for early-morning skulduggery and frivolity. It was not for the weak of heart, and you had to be able to give and receive. Sexual harassment was rampant in the office, and even the fellows had an opportunity to participate occasionally. Female staffers in MPI were ruthless and gave no quarter. It was claimed by most of the female employees, especially the nurses, that they had no intentions of reporting sexual harassment; they rated it, and with much vigor. If one entered, one had to be prepared that few things were off-limits. Most of the personalities were strong enough to weather the inevitable torment and harassment when it was their time in the stocks. Webb, just like the rest, took his share of harassment as well. There were some ongoing classic duels between certain staff, and most everyone, especially Webb, enjoyed the witty repartee.

Of the fifty-five permanent career service staff assigned to Espy's unit in Tallahassee, all but about seven had been either personally selected or approved by Webb during his tenure. The staff represented a unique combination of talent, skill, and competence. The professional backgrounds were varied and included nurses, pharmacists, investigators, systems specialists, coders, statisticians, and even a former music professor. One common denominator was that they were all as smart as a tree full of owls and good at what they did. There were also several other characteristics that made this group somewhat unusual. The first was the continuity produced by longevity, which was uncommon in state government. For the most part, this staff simply enjoyed the work that they participated in. Espy felt it was probably the proclaimed "Thrill of the Hunt." Another group trait was that there was little absenteeism, maybe for the same reason. The final feature of the group was that many of the staff had become extremely close friends over the years and yet were able to maintain healthy professional objectivity related to work matters. Espy himself set the standard for this kind of demeanor. He possessed an uncanny ability to participate on a personal level with his staff and immediately change course and become all business without the slightest hint of intimidation. It was this ability, more than anything, that had earned the complete respect and dedicated loyalty from the entire staff. The staff did not work for Webb Espy; they worked with him. He made it a point not to surround himself with "Yes People." He expected to be tested, and he rewarded unorthodox and innovative suggestions for problem-solving. He went out of his way to hire individuals that exercised initiative. He could forgive errors of enthusiasm much easier than those of complacency or procrastination. The office was an enjoyable place to work, and this atmosphere was created, for the most part, through Webb Espy's leadership style.

5

February 8, 1993

Tallahassee, Florida

Marsha Kaye McLean, known throughout the Florida Department of Health and Rehabilitative Services as "Precious," made her way through the MPI security system's checks and headed toward her office in the rear of the building. She already was aware that her boss, Webb Espy, was there well ahead of her. He always was. Precious, a 1950's Watermelon Queen and a valedictorian from neighboring Jefferson County with the most tantalizing, syrupy southern drawl (at least three syllables in the word "and"), had done an exceptional job of taking care of herself over the years and could still turn a few heads after raising two grown children, and she loved it. Some were accused of calling the office just so they could listen to her answer the telephone. It was something special and considerably better and certainly cheaper than a 900-number call. She was a widow, having lost her husband to liver cancer several years previously, and seemed content to live for her work and her grandchildren.

Precious was efficient and the consummate perfectionist when it came to an organized office, correspondence management, and office protocol. After finishing high school, she eschewed several potential scholarships offers to several out-of-state universities and opted to marry her hometown sweetheart and start a family. She attended a local trade school for business services and was ultimately offered an entry-level teaching position with the institute, which she inopportunely declined due to the long daily commute required. Precious had a Ph.D. in the real world of hard knocks and exploited it to the hilt. Marsha Kaye was intelligent and possessed uncanny technical skills, and Webb Espy was the main beneficiary. Above and beyond all her intellect and skills, she had style and matching charm, which trumped everything else.

Marsha Kaye was completely devoted to Webb Espy, and protectively smothered him like a ferocious mother hen. The two had met several years earlier while he was at the university and engaged in research for one of his books. He had needed someone to type his manuscript drafts, and she was in desperate need of some part-time work. Espy had realized immediately that she was much more than a typist or secretary. He grasped the fact from the beginning that she possessed exceptional editing skills and an eye for continuity to detail, something sometimes lacking in his own writing style. Espy sometimes wondered, deep in his gut, if some of his work would have been published to date if it had not been for the persistent and insightful editing suggestions and resourceful research initiatives from Marsha Kaye. Since the first time they worked together, they had established a mutual admiration society, and from that time forward, wherever Webb Espy worked, Marsha Kaye Mclean was positioned in some capacity in close proximity.

Since the tragic death of Espy's wife and children, Precious had become even more attached and devoted to him. She assumed more of a mother (although she preferred big sister) role than ever before. She suffered his loss and felt his pain. She assumed the roles of protector, facilitator, and sounding board, although he kept many thoughts and feelings to himself. It was her inherited role in this life to support both his personal and professional well-being. There was also another reason that her allegiance was so die-hard. When her husband died, the insurance did not take care of everything. His illness, fortunately, was not long and drawn out, but the last few days of his life required intensive care due to other medical complications. As a result, she was left with astronomical medical bills, forcing her to face overwhelming financial obligations. Although accomplished with absolutely no fanfare and quite anonymously, she knew that she would be indebted to Webb Espy forever. Not only had the medical bills been taken care of, but the mortgage note with nineteen years remaining had been satisfied, as well as all existing debt. For kickers, she discovered that $200,000 had been deposited into her savings account and a special 401-K had been set up for her, with generous monthly installments paid from a blind trust. Her future had been secured, and she knew who was responsible.

As Precious went through her office arrival rituals, which of course started with building herself a serious cup of coffee, she realized that there were at least two other early birds in Espy's office. One was Jim Harbone, the administrator of the Surveillance/Utilization Unit; the other was Ed Shanks, in charge of the Special Investigations Section. Precious finished making her coffee, smiled to herself, took a deep breath, adjusted her posture, and proceeded confidently into the inner sanctum.

"Well, good morning, Precious," the trio chimed in harmony.

"G-u-d mo-aning yur-selves, you great big 'ole boys," she parleyed back with all the southern emphasis and sultry haughtiness that she could put into it.

"Oh shit, I can tell it's going to be a hell of a day around here; she's already started," moaned Ed Shanks.

"Why, whutever do you mean, Mr. Shanks?" she protested, conjuring up her best Melanie Wilkes impersonation.

"Damn telephone be jumping off the hooks around here today, once word gets out that you in one of your playful moods," he mused.

"Well, whatsa girl to do? You 'ole boys cain't jus havve all the fun to yurselves."

"Precious, do you know what they call ex-lax in Holland?" Jim Harbone queried.

"Why, no, I don't know if I've ever heard it referred to, one way or another," she bit.

"Dutch Cleanser," said Jim, holding back a laugh while the other two spectators snickered.

"You know, that reminds me, Jimmee — now, you don't mind if I call you Jimmee, do you, sweetie?" whispered Precious. "I've been meaning to tell you how absolutely fascinated I am by those big brown cow eyes of yours," she said while drawing herself closer to him. Jim, totally aware that he was being set up but unable to avoid it, just sat tight, gritted his teeth, and got ready to take his medicine. Precious, now with her face just inches away from Jim's, reached down and tenderly grasped his hand while breathing in a heavily seductive manner. "You know what they say about men with big dark brown eyes like yours, don't you, Jimmee?" she murmured enticingly, directly into his ear.

"Why no, I can't say I do," Jim stammered as he confessed.

"Well, it means, big boy, that a man with those kinds of eyes is simply full of shitttt up to here!" she exclaimed provocatively while simultaneously taking his hand and wiping it across his forehead. Jim just shook his head while Webb and Ed roared.

"Now, gentlemen, if you both would be so gracious enough as to allow Dr. Espy and myself a little time to ourselves, we would be most appreciative," ordered the belle of the moment. Both men, realizing that playtime was over, for now, took the hint that Precious wanted the boss's complete and undivided attention and made their hasty exit. They both knew what Precious wanted, Precious got.

About the only one that addressed Precious as Marsha Kaye was Webb Espy. In groups or when horsing around, he might sometimes refer to her as Precious, but when it was business, it was always Marsha Kaye.

"I assume you saw the message I left for you regarding Secretary Baswell," Marsha Kaye quizzed, the syrupy drawl completely missing and replaced by an all-business tone.

"Yep, got it right on the top of my priority to check with you first. What's up? But first, let me ask, was the call from him directly or was it from his office?" he asked, making direct eye contact.

"Come on, Webb, give me a little more credit; you know better than that! I would never have left you a message like that if the call had come from anyone else but him." She feigned annoyance. "One of the reasons I wanted you to talk with me first is because a few of my feelers let me in on the fact all is not well with our fearless leader," she claimed defensively while pretending to straighten a stack of file folders on the edge of the desk. Webb suspected that Interpol's worldwide network failed in comparison with Marsha Kaye's so-called feelers. Like every other large organization, the Department of Health and Rehabilitative Services had its own informal organization, and Marsha Kaye was a significant linchpin in that chain of information.

"Seems as though he is getting more than just a little heat from the Gov's office regarding some Fraud and Abuse report that has been making the rounds through legislative staff's offices," she continued. "Webb, I understand the Sec had an absolute, plain old unadulterated conniption-hissy fit. Sources say they had never seen him in such a state. They say it was not pretty!" she emphasized.

"Wonder what he wants with me?" Webb questioned matter-of-factly with a straight face.

"Don't you be coy with me, Webb Espy! We both know what report got his dander up."

"You really think that's the one? I really don't think we got much to worry about." Webb shrugged, doing his best to suppress a smile.

"Well, I'm just overwhelmed with your abundance of confidence, Dr. Espy!" she retorted sarcastically.

"Well, just maybe, that's because you just might not necessarily know everything I know," he teased. If there was any one thing that really grabbed her goat, it was that there were parts of his life to which she was not privy. At the same time, that kind of mystique was one of his real charms. Sometimes she wondered what might be if she was ten, well, maybe fifteen years younger.

"Will you promise to tell me one day what you got on him?" she pouted.

"You're already too dangerous as it is," he snorted. "Did the Sec indicate what time my presence was required?"

"I believe he indicated ASAP or even sooner, if possible. He said you didn't need an appointment."

"Great, now I believe you said one of the reasons you wanted to talk to me. Is there something else?"

"Yeah, I got a call from your so-called Phantom Man. You know, he sounds kind of cute?" she parlayed curiously.

"Someday, tell me what cute sounds like, will you? Anyway, not your type, Marsha Kaye. What'd he say?" Webb asked.

"Nothing, except his special code I.D. and two names," she reported.

"Okay, tell you what. I'm going across the pond first thing and taking care of the Sec. Sure hope I don't have to give him his walking papers," he reported amusedly. "Give those names to M on the QT when she gets in. Don't tell her where they came from! Tell her I want our special research run on each of them and any links that kick out. Make sure she knows it is front burner. Please let her know I also need to talk with her as soon as I get back from dealing with the Sec. Next, if you will ask Jim to go back three months and check the Top 100 Report for each non-institutional provider type. I want a list by this afternoon, if possible, of every new one by specific provider type that did not show up on the previous quarter. Next thing, get on the horn and call Allen at home and see how he is feeling. Ask him when he thinks he will be ready to travel. Tell him I've got something potentially hot and right up his alley."

"Anything else?" she asked, writing furiously.

"Yeah, anytime you take a message for me from Max Bloodworth, that is front burner; top priority."

"How so?" she questioned.

"Because that's turkey business!" he laughed as he dodged her pen. "Yeah, and I guess you can also wish me good luck with Sec," he replied with a wink as he scampered out the door.

6

February 8, 1993

Tallahassee, Florida

The Florida Department of Health and Rehabilitative Services headquarters in Tallahassee consisted of several buildings built around a manmade pond located on approximately ten acres. The property was naturally landscaped, with dozens of huge live oaks, Formosa azaleas, and dogwoods. There was an asphalt walkway encircling the entire water area, which was a little over a quarter of a mile in distance. There was a patio dock built out over part of the pond, and also a fountain, which on those rare instances when it was actually working, was kind of spectacular for the setting. The reference to "across the pond," normally referred to any meeting outside the office, but it was usually reserved for meetings specifically with the Secretary of the Department.

Webb Espy was not particularly enamored with physical fitness regimens. He usually got a sufficient amount of exercise, but his weight could yoyo in a thirty-pound range from about 185 to 215 lbs. Webb would often joke about the Jackie Gleason wardrobe he maintained in three different sizes. Webb's culinary overindulgences and consumption capabilities at various lunchtime buffets were legendary. He could eat! When he went around the pond, he always took the long route to satisfy an unconscious guilt of

37

some sort to balance food and exercise. Today, as he headed in the direction of Secretary David Baswell's headquarters suite, he pondered if anyone really had any idea of what he had referred to earlier in his exchange with Precious, regarding his reference to the Secretary: "Because you don't know everything that I know."

Few people, if any, shared any notion of the relationship that existed between Webb Espy and David Baswell. Their association and friendship began many years before when they were sophomores in high school when they met as representatives from their respective high schools for a week at the state Capitol in a mock legislative session. As it happened, David and Webb had been assigned as roommates and had been selected on three of the same committees. It did not take them long to discover they shared much in common. They especially enjoyed chess and were competitively well-matched. After the week was over, they continued to correspond on occasion and then became reacquainted the summer after graduating from high school, when they both discovered they had enrolled for an early summer session at Chipola Junior College in Marianna, Florida, prior to their regular freshmen years at other major universities. Webb helped David get a summer job at the state mental hospital in Chattahoochee as an aide on the graveyard shift, and the two carpooled every day for their classes. They spent a lot of time together that summer, played a lot of golf, and even doubled-dated some.

Although their paths went in different directions after that summer, a lifelong friendship had developed between them, and a mutual respect for their talents and abilities had been established. They managed to stay in touch over the years and followed each other's professional careers and accomplishments. After the tragic death of Webb's family and during his reclusiveness and self-imposed exile, it was David that actually pulled him out of it by encouraging him to leave the academic community and come work with him in the Department. David's motives for this action were not altogether altruistic toward Webb. He was more than desirous of his talents and resourcefulness, and above all, he was desperate for someone he could really trust. Initially, David wanted and offered Webb his deputy position, but he declined due to the political requirements tied to the job. David Baswell was a political animal. Webb was not. David then tried to make him his Chief Inspector General. Webb again respectfully declined the offer, indicating that the job was really nothing more than a glorified internal snitch playing cops and robbers. Finally, it was Webb who convinced David that Medicaid was big business and that program and regulatory oversight would yield far more political dividends and public service rewards that accompany such modeling. Although David did not share Webb's vision and insights and genuinely felt he should aspire to a higher-level position, he nevertheless acquiesced and appointed Webb to head up Medicaid Program Integrity while promising to shield him from political pressure or interference, provided that Webb would allow himself to be unofficially used as a sounding board from time to time.

With regards to Precious's specific concerns and warnings, there were several things in this world that Webb was sure of; one was that he knew few people he felt had greater integrity than David Baswell; two, that David would never fire anyone, especially him, for telling the truth. And, finally, that his old friend was a hot dog, grandstander, and ham all rolled into one!

The Secretary's executive suite was impressive, not what one might expect in a public service environment. It was designed to deliver a message of power and subconscious intimidation. David was light years ahead of most in terms of psychological advantage and setting the stage for success. He did not believe in putting a mink in a brown paper bag and often went to extravagant lengths to accomplish this perception.

Marge, Secretary Baswell's staff assistant, greeted Webb warmly with an obligatory smile. "I believe he is expecting you," she suggested with arched eyebrows and shaking her head almost as a warning. Her expression said it all. "You're on your own from here on. He said if you showed up to just send you on in." She thumbed and head-gestured toward his office door.

Most of the time, David Baswell did not need any additional props to intimidate subordinates or peers. He was a mountain of a man with a deep bass voice that was well-matched with his mammoth frame. The Secretary was over six feet, six inches tall, and weighed around 280 pounds. David Baswell had attended Vanderbilt University on a scholarship and played offensive tackle. Few people other than Webb realized that he went on an academic scholarship and just happened to play football while he was there. David started out in pre-med at Vanderbilt, but soon discovered that his real talents and interests lay elsewhere. He found himself gravitating toward an interest in political science and industrial psychology and eventually ended up earning a master's degree in health sciences and hospital administration.

The Baswell family, no stranger to politics and government for over four generations, was well entrenched and schooled in Florida panhandle pork barrel politics. One of David's living uncles, Dawkins K. Baswell, was a retired Supreme Court Judge and another uncle, James T. Baswell, a former state senator during the Dempsey Barron regime, had been David's father figure and mentor since David's real father had been killed during the early advisory stages of the Vietnam involvement. The Baswell family was considered an old blueblood family with wealth and widespread influence and knew how and when to use it. David, as was the rest of his family, was a yellow dog Democrat, which spoke volumes about his political abilities since he was surrounded by an extremely partisan Republican Administration.

"The Sec," as he was most often referred to, was on the phone as Webb entered the office. He nodded an acknowledgment and motioned Webb toward a chair, which he intentionally ignored, and aimlessly wandered over to look at some framed pictures on the far wall credenza. He felt certain and smiled inwardly that the action probably annoyed David, who was accustomed to having others do exactly as he suggested. There had always been good-natured competition between the two that fostered a spirited repartee when in private, and Webb was mindful to exercise this sparingly and only when he was alone with his old friend.

Whomever David was talking to was getting the tactfully brutal treatment. David had the ability to change styles like a chameleon. When he finished, he yelled out to Marge not to be interrupted for the next ten minutes, finished writing a note to himself, and finally moved around his desk and plopped down in his big leather fat chair. "Come on over here and let me chew your ass out," he hollered playfully. "Need to make this sound good for my rep. I'm sure there are a bunch of ears waiting for an explosion in here after the little tirade I exhibited the other day over that damned report you circulated downtown."

"I didn't circulate anything downtown," Webb claimed defensively.

"Hell, you say; your damn name's all over the son of a bitch," David charged.

"Don't deny that I wrote it, just that I didn't circulate it."

"Well, if it wasn't you, then just who do you propose it might have been?" he questioned sarcastically.

Webb paused thoughtfully for a moment, looking up at the ceiling as if he was trying to contemplate the possibilities. "Well, let's see," he started. "There were only five original copies. I am confident that I know the whereabouts of three of them. I am also quite certain that there have been no copies made from them. Another copy went to the *St. Pete Times*. Reckon that could be it? Just kidding. No, the only copy I can't account for is the one I sent to you. What'd you do with your copy?" Webb asked in an incriminating tone.

"Hell! I don't know!" he claimed while jumping up, and began plowing through his in-basket like an aardvark in an anthill. "Don't actually even recall if I really ever saw it. Only thing I re-member is you telling me you were sending it," he responded somewhat apologetically.

"Well, let me assure you that it got here because it was hand-delivered, and my hand-deliverer don't make mistakes," Webb proclaimed with added emphasis. "Let me ask you a question?" Webb added in a challengingly manner. "Does that pompous nincompoop of a Deputy Secretary of yours have ac-cess to or work your inbox when you are out of town for a cou-ple of days?"

"Webb, come on, man, for crying out loud; give Skip at least a little room and respect, but to answer your question, yeah, he does, when I've done a delegation of authority."

"Well, in that case, I believe that's where I might start looking for the leak," he concluded somewhat smugly. "I can't, in my wildest imagination, figure how in the hell you ever allowed yourself to get attached to such a piece of work."

"If you recall, I offered you the job!" David replied with a scowl.

"If I'd had any idea there was such a yang-yang working in this place, I probably would never have ever considered coming here to begin with. He is the absolute antithesis of you. Have to admit, though, he's probably gone further on as limited an IQ as anybody I've ever known."

With that, David could not help but laugh. "His greatest admirer, huh?" he added.

"He is the most arrogant, condescending, manipulative individual I believe I've ever had the unfortunate pleasure of meeting," Webb overly dramatized.

"Yeah, but you know what? He'll do exactly what I tell him to do. He is the perfect hatchet man and don't mind one bit taking the blame for it. Never seen anything like it; hell, even seems to enjoy it. Makes me look like Mother Teressa. You got to know that is a legitimate role, Webb; got to have it in a large public service bureaucracy," David pronounced.

"True enough," Webb acknowledged, "but you don't have to get a born-again sociopath for the job."

"Okay, fine, what the hell, you don't like the son of a bitch. Maybe I ain't particularly fond of him, neither. Why'd you write the damn thing, anyway?" David cut to the chase.

"'Cause you told me to, asshole!" Webb stood his ground.

"I ain't done no such thing!" David challenged.

"Did I stutter? I don't believe I stuttered! You most certainly did, your highness. Do you not recall asking me to appear before

U.S. Congressman Town's subcommittee on Inter-government Relations and provide testimony at their little snowbird retreat down in Miami last February? The topic was Healthcare Fraud and Abuse. That's why you asked me to go. Well, that little appearance required written testimony, even if you chose to speak extemporaneously."

"Oh, shit! Really?" David practically answered himself.

"No shit! Really!" Webb gave no quarter.

"My fault, huh?" David began to cave.

"That's certainly my take on it." Webb held firm.

"Okay, don't tell nobody. Now that I've finished chewing your ass out, tell me about this infamous report," David demanded.

"Alright, but you got to promise to read it. It could be a major plank in someone's political platform if they wanted to run a campaign on a tunnel light," Webb offered.

"That strong, huh?" David asked with peaked interest.

"Yeah, I really think so. It represents some virgin territory that could be exploited by some insightful political wannabe," Webb said seriously. "At any rate —"

"Whoa, wait!" David interrupted Webb in midstream. "Don't tell me this was the testimony down in Miami? Oh, hell yeah, I heard about that damn thing. Didn't put it together until now and realize that was you. Shit, man, you're famous. Story I got was that they had invited several high-level muckity-mucks to testify, and they had this sassy-assed federal prima donna, some special expert prosecutor on health fraud. Way it was told to me was that some state person, which now I'm assuming was you, upstaged the whole bunch. Congressman D'Alemberte even interrupted her majesty's testimony to ask you several questions. Said the committee told her to get with you and utilize your blueprint for attacking the thing. I believe she was chewing ten-penny nails at the time. You didn't make no friends over at the Medicaid Fraud Control Unit neither, I understand. You didn't really say, please tell me you didn't say, that MFCU was as worthless as hip pockets on a hog?" he howled.

"No, as a matter of fact, I didn't. What I said was that the current criminal approach dealing with health care fraud and abuse was about as worthless as hip pockets on a hog," Webb declared, sticking his chin out in righteous indignation.

"And you see a distinction?" David inquired sarcastically, gesturing with palms held upright while shaking his head in resignation.

"Why, of course," Webb responded blamelessly.

"Never seen anybody could piss people off and act as innocent about it as yours truly," David charged. "Anyway, I'll read it, but in the interim, give me the short version."

"As you wish, sir. The abbreviated version goes like this. Health care fraud and abuse is invisible until you detect it, but if you decide to look for it, you find it. That's kind of it in a nutshell," Webb concluded.

"That's it?" David's deep bass voice boomed. "Maybe you better give me the next level then?" he suggested with some emphasis.

"As you wish, my friend. Criminal remedies have not worked, and when you stop and analyze the historical revelations, they suggest that those kinds of approaches cannot ever be very effective. We have the ability, or better, the capabilities to detect many more potential cases than we can muster the resources to work. Lots of folks, even in the regulatory business, don't grasp that. Detection is not the problem. We build a lot of great mousetraps and believe me when I tell you, we are on the verge of doing some things in that department that are going to blow the roof off. Right now, the real problem is getting the mouse out of the trap once he has been caught. In the report, I outlined a few potential strategies."

"Alright, I get the drift. Definitely want to spend some more time with you on this and get a handle on details. I think I see where you're heading on the political angle."

"Figured that might be of some interest to your highness," Webb crowed.

"Now let me suggest to you that you might as well get your ass prepared for an invitation to "The Hill" to provide some testimony on that little bombshell creation of yours," David chuckled.

"Always happy to be of service as your humble surrogate and human shield," Webb bowed mockingly.

"By the way, Mr. Comedian," the Secretary intervened, "I haven't seen you or talked to you since Dr. Pieo and that wild-assed Nigerian thing. Congratulations; damn good job!"

"I'll relay your feeling to the staff that pulled it all together. They will be pleased you noticed. Tell you the truth, though, that was actually an exception to what I just told you about criminal prosecution. 'Course MFCU wasn't involved. It went federal early on, and we set the table for them with our administrative hearings, without the FBI even having to get involved. The mandatory sentencing guidelines with the feds involved got the good doctor seventy-two months' hard time. It is a pretty good case study in state/federal double-teaming with administrative and criminal approaches."

"What was all that crap about his being married to more than one woman?" asked David. "Well, that's kinda how we managed to catch him," Webb replied hesitantly. "Apparently, under some type of African tribal law, a chief, which Dr. Pieo claims to be, is entitled to multiple wives, and it appears that he did just that; he had fourteen of them. He then proceeded to give them each a home healthcare facility for a wedding present. He followed up with a common list of Medicaid recipients for all his wives. Some Medicaid recipients were receiving home healthcare services from fourteen different providers!"

"Hell, I can't believe that didn't hit the papers," David winced.

"It did! I'm surprised you still have a job!" Webb deadpanned. "Well, let me tell you something that is going to excite you to death," Webb said, somewhat amused. "Were you aware that the department has been contracting with him for five years, to the tune of about 1.5 million, for special AIDS grants? No telling what the money really went for?"

"Oh, holy stinking shit, who I'm going to have fire for that?" "Don't know, that's your problem. Hope Skip was involved, though! 'Course, the best part is that after he was put in jail, he was brazen enough to keep on billing, and both the Medicaid fiscal agent as well as the Department of Grants Management were prompt and efficient enough to keep on paying him," Webb taunted while hiding a smile and heading towards the door.

"Oh, shit," moaned David as he buried his head in his hands.

If as an afterthought, once Webb had opened the door, he paused briefly, held it wide open, and turned back toward David and offered: "By the way, if you need any help cleaning out that in-basket, just give me a shout."

David roared a thundering **KISS MY SMELLY ASS!**" that echoed throughout the building and literally rattled windows.

Marge greeted Webb's exit from David's office with a horrified expression on her face. Webb gave her a fleeting glance.

"Bark is really a lot worse than his bite; just needs a little help with his in-basket, I suspect?" he suggested as he nonchalantly strolled out of the suite, laughing out loud.

7

February 8, 1993

Later the same morning

The meeting with Baswell had gone quicker than expected, and Webb decided to seize the opportunity to venture into one of his patented scrounge missions, a surreptitious administrative maneuver adopted from his Air Force tenure that linked personnel, personalities, products, and favors into an informal structure for cutting through bureaucratic red tape, thereby escaping the maze of official unwieldy routine protocols and procedures. Webb was a gifted horse trader and had an uncanny knack for recognizing some individuals' real needs, often before they did. Trivia and personal idiosyncrasies were not lost in Webb Espy's gray matter filing system. It was amazing to comprehend what a "You need to give so-and-so a call" or "Did you read the article/memo that some Joe Blow authored?" or "Give me a call and let's go to lunch" or an often "How 'bout them Noles!" Between Webb and Marsha Kaye's resources, there was not much that went on in the agency that they did not know about, or at worst, could not learn about if they really needed to.

Webb liked to use these impromptu scrounge missions to assess various talents and expertise and archive these observations for future reference. There were some very special and exceptional people currently working in Espy's shop that had been fingered and put in his inventory shopping list in this very manner. There were also some that, although he would have loved to have and would have made excellent additions to his team, were far more valuable to him remaining right where they were.

One such individual was Tim Fagan, a highly skilled investigator in the department's Office of the Inspector General. Webb had met Tim almost twenty years earlier, not long after the DHRS was created. At the time, both were young rookies in a staff division of the new agency, and often discovered themselves bottom-feeding on delegated tasks and gopher duties that the seasoned veterans funneled their way. In the vein that misery loves company, the two became very close friends, although, on the surface, it would appear that the two had very little in common. Tim was from north of the Mason-Dixon line, and Webb was from the South. Tim was a fundamental diehard GOP disciple, and Webb was of the other persuasion. Tim tended to espouse more conservative leanings, while Webb professed more progressive, eclectic-type tendencies. Tim was detailed-oriented, while Webb was a generalist. Tim had to always be doing something, while Webb was quite content to just sit and think about things for a while. Their differences, however, were overshadowed by their common passion for the outdoors and their admiration for one another's skills and abilities in pursuing these passions. Their obsession for feathers and their pursuit of feathers, especially turkey feathers, trumped all else.

From Webb's perspective, Tim possessed some truly uncanny talents. Nothing was ever too much trouble for Tim to tackle. Give Tim a pocketknife, some string, and a roll of duct tape, and he could fix or rig just about anything. Tim was one of the most methodical planners and proficient strategists Webb had ever encountered. When Tim set his mind on something, no plan conceived in the bowels of the Pentagon was better detailed.

Normally, on Webb's little scrounge missions, Tim's office would be on his itinerary. On this day, however, Webb was already aware that Tim was working an investigation in West Palm Beach and would be out for the entire week. Webb considered this unfortunate since he had several issues he really wanted to run by his special confidant. One in particular related to a personnel issue data/evidence-gathering inquiry that Tim had been pulling together for the past several months. Webb often used Tim as a sounding board because he could count on getting a straight answer without a punch being pulled. Tim was not cut out to be a "yes man" and was unequaled as a "devil's advocate."

Over the years, Webb noted that Tim possessed something akin to a vigilante gene that seemed to emerge from time to time when right didn't necessarily equal legal. Tim was prone to practice law without a license at times and had no qualms operating in no man's land without a shield. Although they had been separated over the years due to different professional career paths, they had managed to maintain constant contact, and several of their schemes were legendary. Their little "quid pro quo" arrangement had served them both well over the years, and they both realized that there was an unquestioned loyalty to one another along with their friendship.

Webb had wondered sometimes if he should offer Tim a position in MPI, but eventually concluded that he had the best of both worlds by letting Tim alone. It was like having extended staff beyond direct supervision, and besides, you should never put a plow line on a thoroughbred.

There was a certain mystique that accompanied Webb Espy when he ventured outside his little fiefdom at MPI. The players in the department seemed to be more than aware that he enjoyed some type of a special status with Secretary David Baswell, and therefore, in deference, gave him a wide berth and considerable leeway in his horse-trading escapades. Webb was aware of this fascinating perception and was careful not to overuse the privilege it provided. There were occasions, however, when he exploited it with great vigor!

8

February 8, 1993

Tallahassee, Florida

As Webb Espy retreated back toward his office after his amusing little encounter with The Sec and the subsequent visits with various and sundry Departmental personnel, he found himself going through a number of mental gymnastics, questioning if the time and climate were ripe to initiate several nontraditional shotgun strategies that had been germinating in his brain queue for several months. Webb had learned a valuable lesson early in his professional career progression: that timing could be everything. His meeting with Secretary David Baswell and their informal repartee, as well as some of the more serious exchanges, especially the political inferences, had almost convinced him that it was almost "go for it time!" Close, but not quite yet, he grudgingly conceded to himself.

As a student, and later as a professor, Webb had long ago come to the realization that he had colleagues, and eventually students, that appeared on the surface far more capable and brighter than he was. He was also aware, however, that he had other advantages over many of them, in that he was blessed with a couple of unique mental gifts and talents and extraordinary confidence to go with them that more than leveled the playing field. One of

Webb's most uncanny cognitive skills was the ability to identify and retrieve specific information from an abyss of unrelated data pools and synthesize these seemingly random pieces of information into problem-solving applications or conceptual testing models. Webb was practically unbeatable in Trivial Pursuit! These abilities, coupled with his knowledge and fascination with "systems theory," set the stage for intuitive curious inquiry, imagination, and creative problem solving. Webb had first been exposed to the concept of integrative systems technology and process applications during his tenure in the Air Force. Flight simulators were fascinating to him, and it did not take him long to realize that if you could learn to fly a plane in this manner, you could learn to fly a desk the same way. From those insights, it was just simple and logical progression for him to begin to make the transitional leap from hardware component relationships to more general social science configurations. These early fundamental building blocks in systems theory provided a foundation for new instructional designs and teaching methods in organizational behavior and public administration, and thus paved the way for his doctoral dissertation and several subsequent extremely lucrative publications. Webb Espy was credited by numerous scholars and academicians as one of the visionaries and initial pioneers of simulation training models for public administration. Prior to the tragedy with his family, he was in great demand as a speaker throughout the academic community and traveled extensively throughout the country and occasionally abroad to speak or participate on panels and conduct workshops.

Without realizing it, Webb had already made three unintentional laps around the pond and had commenced a fourth while completely engrossed in his sorcerer-like strategic concoctions. For over twenty minutes, he had been lost in his own cerebral wanderings and absolutely oblivious to his surroundings. As he returned to the real world from his creative stupor, he had a plan almost completely outlined in visual imagery, with most of the specific details in place. Now back to reality, a terrifying and horrible thought invaded his euphoria. Webb chuckled out loud to himself and considered that the only thing he did not have a handle on was what kind of story he was going to connive within the next five minutes to entertain Precious regarding his meeting with The Sec.

Each time Webb Espy entered the Medicaid Program Integrity Office, he brought a certain kind of energy with him. Staff knew almost intuitively that he was on site; of course, a lot of that, in all probability, might have had something to do with his thunderous bass voice and his contagious, vociferating laugh that routinely echoed through the halls. It was real easy to work in MPI with Webb Espy at the helm, primarily because you because you instinctively knew that he would never ask you to attempt something that he would not do himself, as he had demonstrated on numerous occasions by rolling up his shirtsleeves and getting down in the trenches with staff to troubleshoot unusual problems and meet critical deadlines or specific priorities. This point could not be illustrated more dramatically than what occurred not long after he took over as Chief of MPI after serving an almost two-year self-imposed hiatus. As legend has it, Webb was meeting with several staff members in his office when a ruckus outside his office interrupted the meeting. Webb got up to investigate to learn that one of the fellows from MPI was excitedly reporting to Marsha Kaye that one of the toilets in the men's room was overflowing and water was flooding out the door into the hall. Webb grabbed a vinyl file divider from atop the credenza and charged toward the rogue porcelain culprit. Without taking off his shoes, he waded into the current to the source and got down on his knees to turn the water off. Next, he created an impromptu plunger out of the vinyl divider and the palm of his hand. After almost a dozen thrusts, enough pressure allowed the water to begin a slow continuous drain. At that point, he reached down into the bowl with his fingertips and began gradually pulling enough toilet paper out to have wiped an elephant. Satisfied that things were now manageable, he turned the water back on and gave the perfunctory two flushes. Determining that all was well, without a word, at least out loud, he sloshed out of the men's room and down the hall, with water swishing in his shoes the entire way and with at least fifty sets of bewildered eyes witnessing the event. He exited the building and headed for his SUV, and moments later returned with Wet/Dry Shop VAC. At this point, most of the female employees were inwardly smiling with genuine admiration while the male employees were wrestling with some guilt and embarrassment. As Webb began the arduous task of siphoning the water into the Shop VAC, several employees began offering their assistance to which Webb responded, "Thanks, but no help required at this stage of the game. It's a one-man job. You all go back to doing whatever," he commanded dialogically, conspicuously glaring at them. That fabled glance scored volumes. In that swift instance, most of the female employees would have sworn that there was a mischievous gleam in his eye and a definite detectable wink. The male employees, on the other hand, detected nothing short of the proverbial "stink eye!" It made no difference; from that point on, there was not an individual working at MPI that would not follow their leader to the proverbial end of the earth.

Every employee of MPI knew Espy had their back and had

historically demonstrated that he would easily forgive errors of enthusiasm and initiative with genuine sincerity and candor. What he did not tolerate well was procrastination and a lack of personal accountability. When Espy delegated a responsibility to a staff member, he delegated the total enchilada, along with the specific authority to accomplish the requirement, and he held that specific staff member totally accountable for the completion of the delegated requirement.

As Espy entered the security code at the building and began to make his way toward his office, he frolicked with several staff members good-naturedly and made sure that Marsha Kaye knew he was about to make a grand entrance. As he exploded through the doorway into his outer office where Marsha Kaye reigned, she had a look of quizzical expectancy, which immediately turned to dismay as he canned any potential discussion of his encounter with The Sec with a hand gesture signaling dismissal, along with a directive to get M in his office for him, ASAP! Webb knew Precious was dying internally with insatiable curiosity, and that was just the way he wanted it for right now.

9

Later the Same Day

Tallahassee, Florida

A few minutes after Webb left for his meeting with the Secretary, Marsha Kaye slipped the names to M that he had indicated he wanted her to check out. She also put M on alert that he wanted to meet with her as soon as possible once he returned. M, in reality Peggy Melton, but referred to by a few friends and colleagues only as "M," a nickname bestowed on her by Webb himself several years earlier, admitted, mostly to herself, that she actually enjoyed. M looked forward to one-on-ones with Webb. More often than not, they meant she was about to be offered a challenge, and if there was one thing M lived for, it was challenges. She especially appreciated pulling rabbits out of a hat for Webb Espy.

M was Webb's pride and joy, his secret weapon of sorts. M, by most definitional measures, would not necessarily be considered a prodigy, but in Webb's mind, she was the closest thing he had ever been associated with in terms of her mathematical wizardry, coupled with her appreciation and knowledge of programming applications and theories. M's circuits were apparently just wired in a different manner than most people, and she was far more comfortable and happier solving a mathematical problem with multiple unknowns than she was with contemplating the literary nuances of the classics. She was by no means an "idiot sa-vant," but seemed to fit more succinctly in the category of being labeled top-shelf smart and socially introverted. M functioned significantly better in a one-on-one situation than she did in group settings, and an actual form of dysfunctional paralysis would set in if she was required to make any kind of formal pres-entation. On many occasions, she had overwhelmed Webb with ongoing recitations from memory of algebraic formulas, statisti-cal algorithms, and slide rule conversion tables. In fact, Webb at times thought her mind almost worked comparably to a slide rule. The bottom line was that in Webb's opinion, she was just flat-out smarter than a parliament of owls, with a memory like an ele-phant. Webb often joked that her 95 lbs. were mostly brain cells, all the way to her toes. M was petite, with dark red hair with the customary accompanying large, dark brown freckles. When M smiled, which she often did, she seemed to smile with her entire body, and displaying such a smile often resulted in oxymoronic signals to her colleagues, since she routinely deflected offerings to participate in various group activities. In fact, M was a mass of continuous contradictions. At 27 years of age, M maintained a rigid and seemingly monotonous routine each day, which began by running five miles, then eating a peanut butter, jelly, and ba-nana sandwich and several cups of strong black coffee, which she continued replenishing and consuming throughout the rest of the day. Lunch might also be another peanut butter, jelly, and banana sandwich supplemented with potato chips. If M had ever put any-thing in her mouth that was green, no one had every observed such phenomena. Although a social recluse, M dressed fastid-iously and was proficient in the use of makeup. Notwithstanding that, the word vanity would probably not be found in her vocabulary, even though she exuded such an impression. M outwardly demonstrated no interest whatsoever in social intercourse or any particular interest in the opposite sex. If she had ever had a boyfriend, nobody in MPI knew anything about it. A robot might fit the bill. She appeared perfectly content with her lifestyle, habits, and computers. M had an undergraduate degree with a double major in mathematics and statistics from Georgia Tech, and immediately upon graduation, moved to Tallahassee, and there earned a graduate degree in computer sciences from Florida State. It was there where Webb first met her when he needed some assistance for some statistical work related to one of his publications, and M had been recommended to him. A mutual admiration society began instantly between the two. M worked with Webb on several projects while still finishing up her graduate work. Just prior to the tragic death of Webb's family, she was offered and accepted a job with the Supercomputer Lab project, which turned out to be a bad fit, and M spent a miserable year of her life doing mundane data entry computations.

When Webb finally returned to the real world created for him by David Baswell, one of the first individuals he sought out was M. She leaped at the opportunity he outlined for her, which included purchasing, out of his own pocket, every state-of-the-art computer component that Radio Shack stocked at the time, along with computer programming books that would fill a semi. Webb also supplemented her state salary in a generous manner. M could not be more content in her own little isolated world. Neither of them had ever been sorry. M spoke several programming languages, starting with Fortran, evolving to Cobol, and more recently, several variations of Java Script. She had also developed her own unique version of a personalized program of data-based linkages, which M and Webb referred to as "The Thing."

Once Webb returned from his meeting with the Secretary and his little scrounge mission, and after taking care of a couple of in-house housekeeping errands, he asked Marsha Kaye to summon M if she was available. She arrived at his office before he made it back down the hall and made herself at home at the small con-ference table in his office. After a couple of minutes, Webb en-tered his office and sat down directly across from her, and thoughtfully leaned forward, resting his chin on his fists.

"Good morning, M, thanks for coming," he started. "I've been cogitating on something that I want to run by you," he said earnestly.

"That sounds as if it could be dangerous," quipped M, which was about as close to a sense of humor as she would ever display.

"M, there are 2,000 comedians without jobs, so please don't quit your day job!" Webb returned the favor. M presented one of those patented all-over smiles, and Webb continued. "But first off, before we jump into that, tell me, what did you find out about those two names I asked Marsha Kaye to give you to run?" Webb questioned.

"They appeared to be direct hits, and linked to several other related entries," she reported without hesitation.

Webb gave a fist pump in elation while announcing, "I had a feeling! Hot damn, M, now we're cooking with gas! Okay, next issue. It occurred to me over the last couple of days that you have created a two-step process at present to detect our targets for spe-cial medical review. Now, I'm not sure if you will agree with my supposition, but in one way, what you've accomplished represents a crude form of artificial intelligence, as I understand the concept," he concluded.

"Well, maybe in a long stretch, you might refer to it in that manner, but I just built it; it was your idea." she stated.

"Actually, M, you are being way too modest here. I say a lot of crazy things because I'm not sophisticated enough to realize they can't be done. At any rate, just humor me for a moment. Let's just try this on for size. Right now, what you have pulled off is linking two unique nonrelated databases and comparing selected fields, and sorting those matching entries into a report. At the present, we are using certain fields from the Medicaid provider files against certain fields from the corporate record files' database from the Secretary of State. Let me get your reaction to this. Do you theorize we could possibly incorporate an additional database, as well? I was wondering if it was possible to create another file and related reports if we linked another database, like a Bressler's Cross-reference Index, which links addresses to phone numbers and vice versa?"

M paused only momentarily. Thoughtfully, she began to respond, "Right off the top of my head, I can't see why the hell not. I believe there may be a couple of ways to approach it, but I tell you what, if you'll give me until bright and early in the morning, I can tell you the most efficient and quickest way to get there, if that will work," she answered rather excitedly. "Miss M, that will more than work," laughed Webb. "Another thing; let me plant the germ of an idea in that massive gray matter of yours. Currently, we are only dealing with pay-to-providers, and I have an idea that eventually the only way we are really going to be successful in attacking this thing overall is via the actual treating providers. Kind of let that idea fester and germinate for a while. For now, I would appreciate it if you did not mention any of this to anyone and play it close to the vest for a while."

"You got it, boss; M-M-M-'s the word," she stuttered deliberately, projecting initially a sly smile which evolved into another one of those spectacular, all-over smiles. Another decent attempt at humor, Webb had to admit, and just returned his own head-shaking approval in humble admiration.

"Go get 'um, special agent!" he concluded jokingly, as she began gathering up her various paraphernalia while continuing to expose that overwhelming smile.

10

September 30, 1987

Miami, Florida

Jorge De Valle and Marcus Manasa had met several times together since their initial meeting two months earlier. Most of their conferences now took place in an office suite in a bank building on *Le Jeune* Road, not far from Miami International Airport. The suite was sparsely furnished and decorated and was used only as a place to meet for the two men. Manasa had provided cash to De Valle for six months' rent and instructed him to write a business check for legitimate payment from his pharmacy's account for the deposit and six months' rent. Marcus had also provided Jorge with a small, special mobile phone-type device and a unique eleven-digit number, which could always be used to contact him. Marcus emphasized that although he would not be on the other end of the line when the call was connected, a return call would normally be received within three minutes, directly from him. Jorge was intrigued by the cloak-and-dagger routine and looked forward to their little private, surreptitious sessions. Life had been good to Jorge, and now he was involved in one of the most exciting things in his life.

Typically, the meetings between the two would not last very long. Today's get-together would probably be no exception. Marcus wanted to go over, once again, some operational procedures. Jorge had learned that Marcus was a fanatical stickler for procedures, and they had to be rehearsed and ingrained to memory. Nothing was ever to be written down. There was not one piece of paper in the office, and neither of the two possessed a pen or pencil when meeting together. Marcus taught Jorge how to remember many things by rote memory tactics. Jorge was completely astounded by how many things he now had recorded to memory that he could immediately recall and recite.

As Marcus entered the room and greeted his friend, he had a serious expression on his face. He got right down to business.

"We're going to have to up the timetable," he announced. "Things are now on a fast track, and we need to have the first phase operational within the next thirty days. I realize that's a lot to expect, and that's not usually the way we operate, but there's really no choice in the matter," he added. "In some ways, it may be better, anyway. In my opinion, we are well ahead of schedule, and, Jorge, I want you to know, it is mostly because of you. We could never have put this thing together or pulled it off under this tight of a timeline without you. The contacts you set up and the insights you provided regarding the players in the South Florida medical community were beyond my wildest imagination," finished Marcus sincerely.

"You are very generous to say such things, but I'm not quite naïve enough to buy all that. I may have set up some contacts, but it was you that had to meet with them and get them to play ball," he stated with sincere humility. "I have no idea how you pulled it off," Jorge admitted in honesty.

"First of all, just so you know, I didn't meet with them; let me repeat that! I did not meet with them, and, secondly, you have no idea how much integrity you can buy for $10,000," Manasa offered emphatically while laughing simultaneously. "Now, there are some issues that you and I need to talk about. I believe there are some things that you are entitled to know. You did not ask to be brought into this, and I took a lot for granted, getting you involved. You have no idea how much I appreciate what you have done and what you have risked for this," he said sincerely. "Obviously, there are some things that I cannot share in an official capacity, but on a personal level, I'll tell you what I can with certain discretions. Keep in mind, however, what you don't know probably can't hurt you, and also, what you don't know, you can't be forced to tell, and finally, what you don't know, you don't ever have to lie about. That being stated, let's play twenty questions," he finished.

Jorge was not prepared for the opening, but somehow managed to feign his surprise. Leaning forward on his elbows, he gazed directly into Marcus's eyes and simply stared for several seconds. "Actually, my good friend, I have thought this thing through as best I can, and based on what we have done so far, as well as what I can surmise are some potential outcomes. I am familiar with "the need to know" concept from our old military days. I don't feel a need to know specific details as to who or why. It is enough for me to know it is important, and I know you would never have involved me if you did not believe it was vitally important. One thing I am kind of interested in is, what kind of support can I, or we, expect once the project is operational?" Jorge paused.

"Good question. First of all, this project, as you refer to it, is not just a single operation. It is more of a component of a much more involved, larger mission. You really don't want to know more about that! There are a number of operatives; no, let's change that," he corrected himself, "to project support resources. The amount of resources to be called upon or that can be relied upon is opened-ended and is related directly to the specific solutions required. In other words, for all practical purposes, whatever it takes!" Marcus concluded.

"Fair enough," De Valle conceded. "I guess the real thing that stays in the back of my mind is, what happens if we get caught?" Jorge confessed. With a totally uncharacteristically spontaneous reflex, Marcus spat up the Coke he was drinking and almost choked, and began laughing uncontrollably. Jorge was more than a little confused and outwardly bewildered by Marcus's hysterical laughing attack. Marcus had a difficult time catching his breath, and it got to the point where Jorge suddenly got tickled himself and simply just began laughing along with him, even though he had no idea why; just seeing Marcus laugh so uncontrollably began to be really funny, for some reason, and became contagious. Finally, Marcus was able to stop long enough to catch his breath. Wiping his eyes on his sleeve, he cried, "Whooo, oh man; that almost cost me a heart attack! Oh boy, I needed that; been working way too hard," he grimaced, holding his side.

"Well, would you mind sharing what in the hell was so damn funny?" Jorge demanded, still giggling himself a little bit, somewhat.

"Well, first of all, you got to realize I was not laughing at you. I was really laughing at me and the situation. I guess I got so caught up in this thing that I just essentially forgot that you're not indoctrinated in this kind of business. There are a number of things that I assume that I shouldn't. It just struck me as funny, the way you said "if we get caught." The real question should be, when will we get caught, or maybe even more appropriate, why will we get caught?" Marcus grimaced while trying to suck more air in his lungs.

"You mean you anticipate getting caught?" Jorge exclaimed incredulously.

"Well, yes, of course, eventually," he answered. "Let me explain something to you," he began, still trying to regain normal breathing. "When you create something like this, it is normally time-limited, and you have various options along the way of shutting it down when you meet your operational objectives. Sometimes it gets shut down for you before you want it to. That's what you want to try to avoid at all costs. Now, in an operation like we have here, there is always the possibility that it could actually take on a life of its own and become systemic. You know, it's like an avalanche; it's hard to stop it once it gets headed downhill. I have a real hunch that's what is likely going to happen here. We've planted a seed, and that seed is going to more than satisfy our mission goals, provided enough time goes by. I anticipate some copycats very quickly, but that's not all bad, and, as we both know, there is a considerable amount of this kind of activity already in progress. As far as our personal liabilities go, and especially in your situation, there are really none to speak of. I have taken the precautions to insulate you completely, and as for myself, I practically don't exist, anyway. The only real thing that we have to be concerned about is getting compromised too early in the game and having the operation terminated prematurely. If that should happen, then I might have a professional liability to be concerned about, but that is of no concern whatsoever to you."

"So, in other words, what you're saying is that I don't have to worry about doing some time in the crossbar hotel?" Jorge asked, seeking verification.

"Yeah, that's about the size of it," Marcus confirmed.

"Well, I appreciate you sharing that with me," Jorge said with a sense of relief. Marcus finished the last of his Coke and turned his full attention to Jorge.

"Okay, Mr. Spook, this is what is required of you from here on out." He reached in his jacket pocket and pulled out two different keys and handed them to Jorge. "As you are aware, what kickstarts this whole thing off is going to be cold, hard, unadulterated cash, and a good bit of it. It's your job to start the process of handing it out. This thing is set up in way that you will have no personal or direct contact with anyone."

"Alright, wait a minute," Jorge interrupted. "So what you're telling me is that my role from here on out is basically that of a glorified bagman?"

"Cut right to the chase, did you?" Marcus chuckled. "You've picked up the lingo fast in this business for a rookie."

"Watched a lot of gangster movies when I was little," Jorge quipped.

"Whatever, wise guy; no pun intended," chuckled Marcus. "Listen, seriously, one of those keys is to a safety deposit box at the Ocean Bank at *Le Jeune* and 42nd Avenue; the number is Ty Cobb's highest batting average, 413. The second key is to a locker over at the airport located close to the American Airlines International gate area. The number is the year Babe Ruth hit sixty home runs, 1927. Got that?" Jorge nodded in the affirmative. "Good, now this is the way it will go down," Marcus continued. "You'll get calls from time to time from me on your special mobile phone. From the time the call comes in, you have a seventy-two-hour window to retrieve the largest of two packages you will find

in the box. Do not unwrap either package. You are to then immediately take the package to the airport locker, deposit the package
in the designated locker, and leave immediately," he concluded.

"What about the second package?' Jorge asked curiously.

"Had a feeling that might be on your mind," Marcus grinned.
"That package is for emergency purposes, and let's hope we never
have to use it," Marcus said in earnest. From time to time, you
will find a third smaller package. That package is for you. Do not,
and I repeat, do not deposit it directly into your checking account.
Take the cash and secure it into your own personal safety deposit
box, and over time, if you wish, buy U.S. savings bonds in small
denominations."

"Marcus, I can't do that! I never got involved in this for
money," Jorge protested.

"Jorge, I know that better than anyone in this world. At the
same time, you must be compensated, and believe me, you have
earned every bit of it. In my business, those who will not accept
compensation cannot be trusted," Marcus offered, grabbing his
friend by both shoulders and squeezing them affectionately.

"I don't know what to say," Jorge stumbled emotionally. "I already owe you more than I can ever repay in several lifetimes,"
Jorge continued, with tears swelling inside. "Doing what I am
doing for the operation is one thing, but receiving compensation
from the results seems to be quite another thing altogether."

Marcus tried to reassure his old friend. "Listen, few people
in my occupation have the luxury of a conscience. It's rare but
refreshing to be able to know someone with the kind of integrity
you possess. You took significant risks by helping to put this
thing together. You know I appreciate it, and there are others
that appreciate it even more. You can't afford to reject the com-

pensation because, whether you like it or not, you are already involved, and there are those that need to know that the commitment is secured and permanent. The only way that can be guaranteed is if you accept the compensation. Believe me, at this stage of the game, you really have no choice. You must accept it, my friend," Marcus said bluntly.

"*Coño*, Marcus, that sounds damn near like a threat," Jorge exclaimed in absolute astonishment.

"No, you know better than that. Think about it, Jorge; I'm just relaying or translating the rules for you. I got no voice or choice in any such matters. In this business, it's looked at as basic insurance. It is just a standard protocol, a simple fact of life. I have no control over it. That's just how it is and how it has always been," Marcus expressed both sincerely and sympathetically. Jorge looked shocked and felt somewhat betrayed, but momentarily regained his composure. Jorge did not doubt Marcus's friendship and loyalty. He was simply surprised by the bluntness, the absolute frankness, and the impersonal way that Marcus had presented the reality.

"You will have to forgive me. I'm new at this, you know. I have not gone through Spook Fundamentals 101," Jorge indicated, displaying an embarrassingly sheepish smile. "Back to business a minute, if I may?" he kept speaking. "Tell me, what happens once I make the drop at the airport?" he asked curiously.

"That, my friend, falls into the category that you really don't need to know," stated Marcus with a genuine smile.

"*Touché!*" conceded Jorge, expressing some degree of relief.

11

March 14, 1993

Flying between Tallahassee and Miami, Florida

Webb Espy would have been an enigma by almost any standard when comparing him to most other public service bureaucrats. The reason was simple: his individual wealth! Through a series of smorgasbord happenstances, Webb had accumulated a fortune via inheritance, hard work, good luck, and bad luck, and was no doubt one of a few multimillionaires employed by the state of Florida outside the legislative branch of government. Some of his financial stockpile was more than bittersweet.

Webb was not a frugal person and used his resources and the influence that came with such wealth in unusual ways at times. Webb could still recall his grandfather, Colonel Rob's, sage declaration: "Money don't talk son, it swears!" Webb had an entrepreneurial insight regarding money. Colonel Rob had instructed him dogmatically: *"One does not save his way to prosperity; one does not spend his way to prosperity; one invests his way to prosperity!"* Although Webb was not entirely sure that his particular approach was exactly what his grandfather had in mind, he enjoyed investing his money in certain people and their ideas and dreams, resulting in dividends multiple times over. He did not loan individuals money; he granted them money with no repayment requirements. He also made extremely generous anonymous gestures to select individuals from time to time, based on criteria known only to himself.

From time to time, Webb would not hesitate to infuse significant amounts of his personal finances into public service initiatives related to his overall responsibilities in order to accomplish things beyond what limited state coffers might allow, or simply to eliminate bureaucratic red tape and hurry things along. Webb paid very little attention to any restrictions imposed by public finance budgeting and appropriations and created numerous legitimate means for acquiring resources he deemed necessary to carry out his duties and responsibilities and go beyond exceeded mandates.

Webb closed his eyes as the aircraft taxied through the network of lights outlining the path to the final runway and eventual takeoff from Tallahassee to Miami. Unlike some others, Webb tended to enjoy his trips to South Florida. Webb Espy knew a different Miami than most people. His unique exposure and particular orientation to Florida's mystical multi-cultural mecca was the result of a number of lifelong coincidental relationships, experiences, and utter historical fate. Some of these associations occurred in Webb's early life and were simply carried forward by a form of social osmosis. Webb's mother, a genuine belle from the heart of Dixie, was the daughter of Arthur Robbins, an extremely prosperous general mercantile businessman and cotton futures investor/speculator in the south-central section of rural Alabama. Normally addressed as Colonel Rob, Webb's grandfather was far more interested in making money and hiring good, smart people to help him make money than he was about being concerned with anti-Semitism issues. After the war, Colonel Rob hired Aaron Rubin, a displaced European Jew, to help him in his store. Aaron Rubin took full advantage of the opportunities afforded him by Colonel Rob and learned from his mentoring. Aaron Rubin was a loyal and diligent employee, and with the influence and financial assistance of Col. Rob, became extremely prosperous in his own right, eventually becoming the largest single independent importer of ladies' fashion shoes in the southeast with over thirty major retail outlets and countless department store consignment accounts. Mr. Rubin had a son, Nathan, who was the age of Webb's mother, and the two became very close friends as youngsters, and remained competitive bridge players well into their college years. Their friendship endured their entire lifetimes.

As Aaron Rubin became more successful, he found that his business needs related to importing demanded more and more time in Miami. For several years, he maintained his home in the small town in southern Alabama, where his wife and children remained while he tended to business elsewhere. Once the children were grown and in college, coupled with the untimely death of his wife, there was really no legitimate reason to maintain a residence in Alabama. He eventually moved to Miami and remarried, but never forgot his indebtedness to Arthur Robbins and his family. As Aaron Rubin prospered during the years, Col. Rob lost a large portion of his fortune during the depression and later, due to poor timing of aggressive commodities trading, the inability to compete with large volume retailers, and an uncompromising, staunch commitment to long-term employees. Col. Rob lived into his mid-nineties and continued to open his totally outdated general mercantile store on the courthouse square every morning at 6:00 A.M., with a full complement of employees, up until the day he was stricken with a brain aneurysm and died in his sleep.

Aaron Rubin made sure that his son, Nathan, understood the history of his and the overall family's success, and made him promise to honor the ongoing debt of everlasting gratitude by maintaining a strong surveillance relationship with Arthur Robins's offspring and future generations. Nathan Rubin kept that promise in spades and passed it down to his sons and daughters, with the same expectations that his father had set forth.

Webb had spent a considerable amount of time with Nathan's family during his lifetime and had remained extremely close. When Webb's mother finally passed away at the age of 97, a full two years after Nathan had preceded her, the entire Rubin clan traveled from all over the United States to attend a small rural town funeral in the Florida panhandle.

Webb maintained contact with numerous family members and often visited them when in Miami. One of Nathan Rubin's grandsons was one of Webb's oldest and closest friends, and was an attorney of the silk-stocking variety named Mario Diaz. Webb planned to have dinner with him this evening if things went the way he planned.

Webb awoke from his mental wanderings as the plane touched down. One of the benefits of being filthy rich was that he did not have to rely on commercial flights and adhere to limited airline schedules. Webb had long ago realized that time was a precious and a limited commodity, and, therefore, had no qualms about spending his resources for convenience, comfort, and efficiency. He avoided lines at all costs! When it came to comfort and convenience, Webb was not frugal. The aircraft taxied into a hangar, and as usual, he could see a chauffeured limousine awaiting that Mario had arranged, which would take him to his condo in Miami Beach. As the driver pulled out into traffic leading to the causeway, Webb knew he was in Miami! His Miami! He really enjoyed South Florida, just as long as he knew he was there in a visiting capacity and could leave when he wished! His sentiments were exactly the same about Manhattan!

12

March 12, 1993

MIAMI, FLORIDA

Mario Diaz let the letter he had read for at least the sixth time slip from his large but delicate hands onto the giant mahogany, glass-protected desk, which, save for the letter, was the only item present on this expensive piece of furniture. The desk, absent of dust, was an indictment of the obsessive personality of its owner.

Although it was well before cocktail hour, Mario pushed himself away from the desk, got up and walked across the plush office suite to the credenza, flipped open the door to the bar, and methodically built himself a Long Island Iced Tea. Diaz had no appetite for straight whiskey and had decided long ago he would not pretend like he did when peers participated in such office rituals. Mario did not have an alcohol problem and, in fact, only drank socially on occasion. The drink he was currently holding, however, was for a different reason. He simply wanted a drink.

Seemingly without purpose, Mario wandered over to the window and gazed out over the scenic Biscayne Boulevard toward the Atlantic Ocean.

Even without his own prestigious law practice, Mario Diaz would have been envied by most for his business holdings and apparent prosperity. Part of that perception was purely a façade.

Based on an inheritance left to him by his parents, whose lives ended early as a result of a tragic automobile accident, Mario, barely twenty-one years of age, had parlayed the assets available to him, accumulated from trading sugar futures, into more conservative real estate holdings.

Most of Mario's inheritance was left to him in the form of trust accounts, with access at various age intervals. His parents needed not to have been concerned; Mario was a financial wizard by almost any standard, with a legal education safety net as a contingency. The very tall eighteen-story building in which he was standing, located on Brickell Avenue, was his without a mortgage, and all but his own entire eighteenth-floor office suite rented at 100% occupancy, with a waiting list for any square footage available. Most peers opined, at forty-three years of age, Mario Diaz was a poster child for Fortune 500 up-and-comings.

At one time early in his professional career, Diaz had dreamed of such success and luxurious surroundings. Now, seemingly to many at the top of his game, and with everything going for him, he searched relentlessly each day for fulfillment, challenge, and purpose. From the initial creation of his practice of law, Mario had tactfully shunned offers or mergers with other silk-stocking law firms and had established his practice without partners or assistants. He ran his shop with a small but talented cadre of personnel, starting with that of Harold, a middle-aged, speech-impaired, high-intellect and rehabilitated alcoholic with technical knowledge of the law unequaled by most legal scholars. There were also three paralegals, three secretaries, an office manager/accountant, and a private staff assistant. They had all been with him for some time and based on their compensation and benefits packages, they were not apt to ever leave his employ.

Since his divorce over eight years previously, for which he claimed full responsibility, Diaz had thrown himself into his work and had become one of the most sought-after healthcare attorneys in South Florida. He dealt primarily in civil medical malpractice cases and administrative law cases related to Medicaid and Medicare aberrant claim cases. Diaz had excelled in the specialization for these types of cases, and based on the demand, cherry-picked the most interesting clients and referred the less challenging cases to other attorneys in other firms.

Ironically, although not normally involved in criminal cases, Diaz had gained his real reputation by winning two back-to-back Medicaid fraud cases in which he demonstrated innovative strategic methods, uncanny knowledge of the specific details related to medical procedures, coding requirements, specialty protocols, and unparalleled courtroom litigation eloquence. Diaz was a brilliant composite of skills that participants in the legal profession recognized as the zenith in their chosen career field. Diaz's real ability to succeed in such a manner was really based on something else quite unique that could not be taught or learned from a classroom, book, or mentor. Although difficult to describe, Mario possessed an innate ability, or more aptly described, a mysterious knack to visualize situations from a "far side" perspective, apply logical consequences, and present these issues to the court in an extremely simplistic and convincing fashion. The result of Mario's mental gymnastics was a series of insidious strategic maneuvers that left prosecutors' cases in absolute shambles. Rival attorneys the state set forth to try their cases opposite him were severely overmatched and, for all practical purposes, were doomed before jury selection was even completed. Although Mario was already successful by almost any standard, however, two particular Medicaid fraud cases were the crowning anointment to superstar status, and provided the best advertisement that money cannot even begin to buy. Diaz was feared by most potential competitors and was despised by the upper echelons of various third-party payers, left in his wake of successful litigations and settlements.

What absolutely no one else knew, save possibly two other people on the planet, was that all of Mario Diaz's accomplishments and his prestigious legal credentials were nothing more than an elaborate façade. Mario Diaz had a hidden secret that would go to his grave with him, and surreptitious arrangements had long been set in place to continue to cloak a mysterious role that ruled both his personal and professional life.

Mario Diaz was bisexual. That eventual exposure had cost him his marriage and almost his professional career. If it had not been for an old family friend, Webb Espy, who timely intervened and foiled an extortion scheme associated with an indiscrete sexual encounter, Mario could not even begin to guess what might have happened to him and his life going forward. Mario had no idea how Webb had resolved the situation or what kind of price someone had to pay for such a resolution. He only knew that it had been taken care of. As humiliating as it was at the time, Mario had made an awkward attempt to thank Webb for getting involved and solving an extremely embarrassing transgression. Mario, until he drew his dying breath, would never forget how Webb had handled the occasion.

Webb had looked squarely into his eyes and stated matter-of-factly, "Let this be the last time we ever speak of this. As they say, he who is without and so forth, cast the first stone. Mario, I am old enough, experienced enough, and objective enough to know that we all are not built the same way. One way is not better than another, just different. The grass is not greener on the other side of the fence, just different sometimes. Rest assured, you are my friend, and I will never judge you. You are very important to me!" At that point, Webb hugged his friend and provided a reassuring smile that created a bond that would last a lifetime.

Mario was the son of Wendi Rubin Diaz, the youngest daughter of Nathan Rubin. Webb and Mario had known each other since childhood and had spent considerable time together with their families and played many competitive rounds of golf together as youngsters. Mario had been well indoctrinated as to the ongoing historical debt that the Rubin clan felt they owed the Robbins/Espy descendants.

When Webb began his publishing career, he approached Mario with a request for some legal assistance. Based on permissive initiative, not only was assistance provided related to the publishing aspects of his career, but his entire financial portfolio was under the complete discretion of Mario. Mario was far more anal, concerned, and astute than Webb was regarding money matters. Money, and more growth of money, was far more important to Mario than it ever had been, or ever would be, to Webb.

When Webb's wife and children died in the tragic airport accident, it was Mario who handled all the negotiations that led to a settlement which yielded more money than Webb would be able to spend in multiple lifetimes. Eventually, Webb handed over all of his financial obligations and transactions to Mario to take care of. Webb was essentially debt-free and lived off two major credit cards and a cash stash he kept in a gun safe at home.

Without an initial plan to move in that direction, an evolutionary osmosis occurred between the two men that allowed Mario to serve as a liaison between Webb and those with which he wished to share his wealth. Without realizing it, over time, Mario had become Webb Espy's personal valet, invisible procurement surrogate, and an extremely expensive bagman. Mario was prepared to do everything pro bono; however, Webb would not hear of it and refused to allow such an arrangement. Mario pretended to acquiesce, but knew exactly how to launder such fees back into Dr. Espy's financial coffers.

Mario took a long swallow of his concoction, felt the obvious effects, and moseyed back toward his desk in a thoughtful trance. Plopping down in his elegant leather high-back swivel chair, he picked up the letter and began reading it once again.

November 11, 1991
Mr. Mario Diaz, Esq
308 Brickle Ave., Suite 1800
Miami, FL

Dear Mr. Diaz,

First of all, let me congratulate you on your successful representation of your client Martha Vasquez, in the recent case Vasquez vs. McMann. Please accept this letter in the manner in which it is intended. It might easily be interpreted as sarcasm; however, I assure you it is not. I recognize excellence and proficiency when I see it, and you demonstrated an uncanny ability to integrate the law and procedural technical irregularities to your client's advantage. It was magnificent to witness such a choreographed proceeding based on research, due diligence, and rehearsed prep-

aration. My only regret is that I did not hire you before she did. I am confident that if you had represented my interests instead of hers, I would have prevailed in this particular dispute. The only real consolation that I have is the satisfaction of knowing that you know that I am really the victim in this instance, not your client. I will recover my losses over time and certainly survive, although it will require some serious sacrifices and a significant dose of intestinal fortitude. Once again, I hope next time I have you in my corner.

Sincerely,
Rachel McMann
Owner, Director
McMann's Home Health Center

After finishing the letter once again, Mario felt no different than before. The letter depressed him and caused an anxious, deep mental discomfort. What was most bothersome was that he could not, for the life of him, comprehend why. What was it about this particular piece of correspondence that was having this kind of impact on him? Mario was unaccustomed to not being able to understand things, or at least rationalize them toward some type of closure. This was totally foreign to him, and he was unable to come up with any type of a conscious explanation. It was not in his nature or his character to let something go without resolution. He knew he would not be at peace with himself until he had it figured out. He knew he would eventually discover what was unnerving him; yes, he knew it, based on historical precedent. Yeah, he would figure it out; he had to!

Later the same day, in the early evening hours after a full series of appointments, briefings, deposition scheduling, obligatory mundane Webb Espy requirements, and with the anxious uneasiness still gnawing away in his psyche, Mario reached for his phone and dialed a number from memory that he seldom had occasion to contact. The recipient on the other end was always there for him and was always reliable in terms of performing the tasks required. The call was answered on the second ring, instructions were given, and the call ended without any pomp and circumstance.

13

March 13, 1993

Coral Gables, Florida

Willie Diozos, or "Little Wille," as he most often was affectionately referred to in the vast networks in which he traveled in the South Florida communities, was finishing his normal daily routine by sending his end-of-the-day, greatly anticipated, erotic emails to those recipient members reserved for such consideration, when his phone rang. A call for him at this time of day was atypical, and as such, totally unexpected. He debated briefly about answering, then thought to himself, "Ah, what the hell," and grabbed the receiver.

Little Willie, age 52, a Cuban Jew, claimed to be 5'5" (maybe on tiptoes) and weighed 135 lbs. soaking wet. His nickname, however, certainly had nothing to do with his male anatomy and associated endowment. Some kidded that Mr. Dick was born, and Little Willie just grew to him. Willie relished the reputation and had no qualms about putting himself on display at almost any opportunity. For whatever reason, women were attracted to Willie like a magnet. He had a charming personality and a great sense of humor with resources to match, which he did not mind spreading around. He was not above paying for anything and often did just that. He possessed a harem that some sheiks might envy. Sex was the center of Little Willie's existence, and nothing else was even a close second. It was as simple as that. Willie was an eccentric. His daily attire rarely varied, which consisted of faded guayaberas, khakis, and an assorted variety of pastel tennis shoes.

Although Willie Diozos actually owned a small law firm, he was no longer a member of the Florida Bar, having relinquished his license as a result of a felony conviction almost twenty-five years earlier. Although Willie likely had done a number of things to do time for, this particular incarceration was probably not one of them. The charges had been vague and initially had not appeared really serious. On the surface, the case related to alleged fencing of stolen merchandise and apparent money laundering and was tried by an unamused judge lacking anything resembling a sense of humor. Considering the options available, Willie chose between the judge's sentence for a spell in the federal crossbar hotel or the consequences of exposing the dealings of some major players in the shadows of the Cuban mafia. Discretion being the better part of valor, there was really no choice whatsoever, and everyone knew it. As a result of keeping his mouth shut and doing his eighteenth months in the federal pen, Willie earned a special status and became highly regarded by certain elements in the South Florida after-hours establishments.

The hardest part of the confinement was the absence of sex, but Willie somehow set records for conjugal visits with multiple wives. Willie used his time in prison continuing to expand on his already vast inventory of international finance and resource-trafficking proficiencies. Although computer-proficient for the times and well ahead of the curve, Willie also honed some programming skills and expanded his research repertoire through jailhouse osmosis. Doing time in the federal pen was a productive period of time for Willie Diozos.

The bulk of the work conducted by the lawyers in Willie's little practice was tax law, with some family law and a few divorces thrown in. Willie was big on bartering and cash. He was extremely astute at using both to his advantage. Willie himself provided an array of extremely discreet and distinct services. Willie was conversant in five different languages and exceptionally fluent in at least three. He kept a bag packed at his office and could be prepared to fly out of Miami International at the next available opportunity. Willie did things other attorneys or prestigious law firms would not or could not do. Willie was a highly paid bagman! He delivered bribes and payoffs, and it did not bother him one bit. Willie was also a sleuth, a really good one, with surveillance as a specialty.

The caller's instructions were clear. Willie was given the name of a Ms. Rachel McMann, as well as other identifying information. He was to use his sources to find what debts she might have, choose one or several in the $62,000 range, and anonymously reduce such debts to zero. He would then deposit an additional $100,000 into her personal bank account in $9,000 cash increments over the next few months. Cash would be provided for satisfying these requirements, as well as an additional $10,000 cash for his services. This was right up Willie's alley. A piece of cake!

14
April 10, 1993
TALLAHASSEE, FLORIDA

It did not take long for Secretary David Baswell's gift of prophecy to come to fruition. Marsha Kaye, in her usual efficient manner, albeit with some additional fanfare, announced to her boss that a formal invitation from Senator Arthur St. John, Chairmen of the Senate Healthcare Committee, had been requesting Dr. Espy's presence to appear, provide testimony, and answer questions related to the current state of healthcare fraud and abuse within the Florida Medicaid program.

Under similar situations, Webb would not have welcomed such an invitation; however, for some reason, one difficult for Webb himself to comprehend, he was not annoyed, nor the least bit apprehensive about appearing before this particular committee. One of the reasons was the committee chairman, Dr. Arthur St. John. Dr. St. John, a fourth-generation Florida blueblood, like many prior relatives, refused to rest on the laurels of his family's well-chronicled contributions and instead preferred to build upon them. St. John was a renowned pediatric surgeon, prolific author, and contributor to the medical trade journals. He was also one of the strongest advocates for children's health services in the country. Last but not least, he was a shrewd politician and political strategist.

Webb had never met the man personally, but looked forward to the opportunity. Immediately upon receipt of the invitation, Webb contacted his invisible man Friday, Mario Diaz, and asked for a deep state dossier on the man. The information received was unremarkable. Apparently, no vices or skeletons to be found anywhere. St. John was a family man, married once, with two children. Webb was surprised to learn that St. John, at one time, was considered one of Florida's top amateur golfers. Based on his age, Webb was a little surprised that their paths had not crossed earlier at some point. If there was a knock on the seemingly "walk on water" persona, it was that most of the time, he was the smartest person in the room, but also wanted to make sure that everyone knew and was reminded of it!

Webb arrived in the Senate Committee room about ten minutes prior to the scheduled start time. After depositing his materials on the witness table, he took the opportunity to visit the men's room and grab a bottle of spring water. Returning to the room, there was still no visible evidence that a hearing was scheduled to commence in less than five minutes. Webb noticed that water pictures had been placed on the lengthy committee podium and information packets he suspected were relative to today's activities were also awaiting.

As if almost choreographed, doors at all sides of the room seemed to open almost simultaneously. The room began to fill, and Webb was somewhat mystified to observe that there were apparently far more visitors or spectators in attendance than he ever would have anticipated. Something atypical must be happening that he had not been made aware of. It all seemed very odd and curious to Webb. Several of the senators had already arrived and had taken their assigned positions and were engaged in conversations with their peers.

Presently, there was a stir behind the podium and a brief hush in the room as Senator Arthur St. John appeared, leading an entourage of select senators and legislative staff. There was a distinctive aura given off by the man. The senator was an impressive physical specimen, as well as mental giant. He was around forty-five years old (could pass for thirty-five), six feet, three inches, and obviously kept himself in great shape. He was a Cary Grant clone from another generation. From watching him work the various groups behind the podium, it was evident that he was polished, distinguished, and demonstrated a genuine graciousness towards everyone he came into contact with. Webb was in awe of the senator's overall charismatic effect over the entire room.

Everyone took their cue from him as silence took over the room as he sat down, organized some papers, took a brief sip of water, and adjusted his microphone. Once settled in, he flashed a brief hint of a smile in Webb's direction, along with a nod that signified that his presence had been acknowledged.

All of a sudden, Webb sensed something was strangely amiss. He had not picked up on it at first, but now, as his mind instantly shifted to fast-forward, he intuitively realized that the normal pomp and circumstances and courtesies usually afforded an invited guest to testify had been absent. Internal questions and defense mechanisms manifesting themselves on autopilot came to him fast and furious. Was this a set up? What was really at stake here? There had to be some hidden agenda! He pondered the possibility if his earlier testimony in Miami and the infamous report touched either a financial or political nerve somewhere. Webb resolved himself to the reality that it would probably not take too long to find out.

The chairman cleared his throat, glared over his reading glasses directly at Webb, and began with, "The committee and I want to thank you, Mr. Espy, for agreeing to —" Webb, recognizing the ploy, immediately interrupted St. John and apologetically alibied, "Please excuse me for just a second, but the caster on my chair apparently is not right, and I am listing to starboard here," bringing a series of snickers throughout the room. Webb immediately got up and swapped out the chair for the empty one next to him, and as he was readjusting himself, he continued the interruption, saying, "Please indulge me for a brief request on the protocol. I do not get down here that often, and I am not sure of the appropriate manner in which to address the chair. Is it Mr. Chairman, Senator, or Dr. St. John?"

"Mr. Chairman is fine, Dr. Espy. Title noted, as well as my apology. Certainly no disrespect intended," he responded, more tersely than he had actually intended.

"And certainly none taken. Mr. Chairman." Webb replied while smiling and making direct eye contact.

"We are going to proceed a little differently today than we normally would. With an earlier consensus from the members of the committee, I am going to make a brief opening statement for the record. Then I need to perform a little housekeeping of sorts. Once that is done, we wish to allow Dr. Espy the opportunity to make an opening statement in a summarized form related to this interesting report," he concluded, waving Webb's document in the air in an almost challenging manner. "Once that is completed, I will begin a prioritized series of questions for Dr. Espy. Depending upon his answers and responses, there may be follow up questions. I suspect that we will exhaust all of the time that has been allocated to us, given the detailed information presented in Dr. Espy's materials." Webb sat thought-fully, displaying no emotions whatsoever, and waited for the chairman to proceed.

The chairman's opening remarks provided a frame of refer-ence for the testimony from Dr. Espy and an overall orientation as to the significance of the information set forth in the report. From the tone of his remarks, as well as slyly-disguised elements of skepticism that bled through his presentation, it became abun-dantly clear to Webb that the senator was less than enthusiastic at this stage of the game for the content of the report. Webb be-came acutely aware that the senator was not a disciple or admirer as related to the findings and recommendations for corrective ac-tions as had been set forth in his work.

When he finished his presentation, there was a slight pause while he reached for another document. Securing the new doc-ument, he addressed Webb directly. "Dr. Espy, I've got to say, this is an extremely unusual, and let me add, concerning doc-ument to be found coming out of an agency like the Department of Health and Rehabilitative Services. I do not recall ever seeing anything like it since I've participated in public service. However, I'll get to that in a little bit. First, I want to get something out of the way that is troubling me. Please, if you will indulge me for a moment while I read certain excerpts from your report." He paused, opened the report, flipped to previously tabbed pages, and began reading into the record a number of selected portions from the report, citing lines and referenced page numbers for the record. Webb allowed St. John to go through this little exercise without any pretense, paying close attention, and displayed an unemotional air of indifference. Next, the chairman selected a second document he identified as "The Florida Task Force Report on Fraud Abuse in the State Medicaid Program." Finally, he produced a third document, a publication from Florida TaxWatch entitled "Fraud and Abuse: Issues and Answers," in which he duplicated the previous recitations.

As he finished, he laid down the last document, removed his glasses, folded his hands in front of him, and stared down at Webb. Then he began, "Dr. Espy, I know that you have previously spent part of your professional career as part of the academic community and have numerous notable publications to your credit. I am also aware that you are respected as an academic scholar, and that is why I am extremely concerned that you have not provided appropriate credit for work in your report that is not yours. I have to say, and let me assure you it gives me no pleasure to do so, that this transgression, in my opinion, and the opinion of this committee, raises serious doubts and concerns as to the credibility and the reliability of your work in this area, as presented in this particular piece of work," he concluded, shrugging his shoulders in defense of his accusations, and settled back in his seat.

The silence in the room was deafening. Webb played on the drama of the moment. Everyone on the committee was staring at him in total disbelief because Webb was grinning at them like an opossum.

"Do you find something amusing about this, Dr. Espy?" St. John asked disapprovingly.

"Yes, I guess; as a matter of fact, I do. Give me just a few seconds, please," responded Webb, laughing out loud as he began thumbing through some materials on his table. Finding what he was looking for, he got out of his chair, walked up to the chairman, and handed him a binder. Looking directly at the committee stenographer, he stated, "And for the record, my name is Dr. Webb Espy, and I have just provided Chairman St. John with a copy of a document I authored more than two years ago, dated April 1, 1991, along with a transmittal memorandum to DHRS Secretary David Baswell, dated April 5, 1991. The information compiled was based on a specific request by Secretary Baswell, and I believe, under close scrutiny, you will find that each and every excerpt identified by the chairman is represented almost verbatim in that original 1991 material. Also, please note for the record that the 1991 materials were almost a year and a half prior to both the task force and TaxWatch publications. Now, I know how TaxWatch got their information, because their director is a former student of mine, and I gave him explicit permission to use the information without restrictions. I gave no such permission to the task force, but I see no real point in trying to hold them accountable for such a public service breach," Webb let it sink in as he paused.

Webb continued, "Now, as I understand, Katie (as in Turabian) original work does not require that I reference or credit myself! The work submitted in the report in question is my own original work, and I had no intention whatsoever of footnoting it! You will note that there are, in fact, two specific footnotes in my report; the first is a direct quote from a top-level HHS OIG official, and the second is a paraphrased reference from a book called *Acts of Deception* by Milton Edwards. I take my scholarly responsibilities and integrity seriously. I must admit that I am somewhat dismayed that this matter proceeded to this point without legitimate verification of the materials and related details or appropriate vetting," Webb concluded.

The senator was absolutely stunned, and it showed. Beyond that, he was both ashamed and completely embarrassed at the role he had played in this fiasco. With a show of absolute class, Arthur St. John got up from his seat, walked around the back of the podium and his colleagues, and proceeded to Webb Espy's table. Webb could see that there was genuine anguish in the man's face, almost as if he had just lost a child on the operating table and was about to face the parents. Webb stood up and moved slightly toward St. John. Once the two men faced one another, St. John offered his hand, which Webb immediately accepted, and the senator stated in a voice that required no microphone for all in attendance to hear: "Dr. Espy, I owe you the sincerest apology. I am truly embarrassed over what has transpired here today under my watch, as well as my role in such a debacle. I am truly sorry. Please accept my personal apology."

"Only if you promise to let me play a round of golf with you sometime," responded Webb with a genuine smile, in an attempt to defuse the situation and allow St. John the opportunity to escape with as much dignity as possible.

"You have my word on it, and it will be a real pleasure. I understand you knew your way around the links rather well when you wore a younger man's clothes," St. John complimented, with a genuine smile of relief as he retreated towards the podium. It registered on Webb's radar that Arthur St. John obviously had a dossier on him as well.

Once the chairman returned to his perch at the podium, he was not through with the matter. He appeared thoughtful for an instant and then began an unrehearsed monologue. "To each of you here, committee members and others as well, I also owe and offer my deepest apologies. I am guilty of committing a cardinal sin in both prejudging and misjudging this truly academic scholar and gentleman, as well, based on acts of misfeasance and negligence that resulted in erroneous assumptions. These unfortunate circumstances occurred on my watch, and I am totally responsible. I can assure you henceforth that we are going to implement measures to ensure that something like this situation does not happen again going forward."

Webb smiled inwardly, thinking to himself that after his testimony was concluded, somebody better be wearing asbestos underwear! Webb's admiration for St. John had just magnified significantly. As Webb absorbed what was being said, he realized that this had nothing to do with being the smartest man in the room or being upstaged. It was a demonstration of legitimate innate integrity; extremely rare in the human race. Webb thought to himself that Arthur St. John was an individual he would enjoy getting to know and suspected they might become close friends if ever given the opportunity.

The rest of Webb's testimony went exceptionally well, with St. John asking questions and Webb responding extemporaneously. Webb's eloquent, sometimes folksy, oratorical style with anecdotal examples was both entertaining and educational. Webb provided for all in attendance a crash course in medical coding schemes and games, and outlined humorous examples of superbill upcoding, code explosion, and ping ponging strategies designed to enhance inappropriate billing reimbursements. He also outlined for the committee simple blueprints for provider self-referrals and the financial consequences associated with such practices. His finale highlighted various egregious solicitation models designed to bilk untold amounts of dollars out of third-party payers for totally unnecessary medical and related services.

There was one seemingly tense moment when the chairman was asking Webb about a particular detection strategy. "Dr. Espy, could you give me some more detailed information about how you set that up? I really would like to understand exactly how you did that," the senator questioned seriously.

"You and a lot of other people, I suspect," Webb responded somewhat flippantly, with a chuckle. "No, what I mean is, I don't believe I should answer that question, and I really doubt you want me to answer it either. As you know, we spend considerable effort in building mousetraps, but they become almost worthless once our methodologies are compromised. However, there is another reason I cannot answer your question. As you are aware, Florida Statute 409.913 states that a complaint or an investigation for fraud or abuse, or any information related to such an investigation, is exempt from the State Sunshine Statue Chapter 119 until several things happen or are in arrears. We currently have numerous investigative cases in the pipeline that have not met that criteria. Now, I realize that we have government in the Sunshine; I'm just not sure I'm authorized to be a "RAY" under the present circumstances!" Webb finally finished.

Senator St. John looked at Webb sternly, then began to smile, and then laughed out loud, and Webb joined him. The senator just shook his head in humble admiration. "That's a good one; I've got to incorporate that one into my repertoire," he continued, laughing.

"Please just remember to credit the source." Webb stuck it in and turned it. At that, everyone in the room was laughing.

When time expired, St. John had a different impression of Webb Espy altogether and was astonished to admit to himself that he had received an indoctrination to fraud and abuse nuances that had been well beyond the comprehension of the un-initiated. He had an instant trust for Webb Espy and would enjoy getting to know him better. He was looking forward to their round of golf.

Later that afternoon, after Webb returned to the office and was at his desk, Marsha Kaye informed him that Secretary Baswell was on line one. "Okay, thank you," Webb said somewhat casually. Webb pushed the blinking line button and said, "Yes, Mr. Secretary." David's unmistakable voice came thundering through receiver. Webb had to hold it six inches away to save an eardrum!

"What in the hell went on down at the Hill this morning? You ain't going to believe all the stories I've been hearing! You know how to stir up more shit than anybody I've ever known. Hell, I can't wait; give me your version?" David paused to catch his breath.

"Well, for starters, I believe it was extremely productive. I made a new influential friend, and as you know, any friend of mine is a friend of yours. Things started out a little rocky, as your sources have probably already briefed you, when the chairman and I had a little tit-for-tat sparring session over Katie Turabian, but once we got past that little obstacle, I had him eating out of my hand. You know what the best thing is, though; I parlayed a round of golf out of the senator," Webb crowed triumphantly.

"You're shitting me? Am I invited?" David asked, somewhat seriously. "Well, I don't know; how's you game holding up these days?" Webb laughingly challenged. "My game don't have to be good for us to get in their back pockets as long as I can ride on your coattails," David roared. "Let me see if I can make it happen?" Webb chuckled.

"Can you meet me a Porky's this afternoon so you can give me the real skinny on what went on down there today? Can't wait for details!" David concluded.

"See you there at 5:30," said Webb as he started hanging up the phone.

15

May 1, 1993

RETURN FLIGHT TO MIAMI, FLORIDA

The past 72 hours had been a whirlwind of itineraries for Marcus Manasa. Earlier in the week, the past Thursday afternoon, he had flown via a special charter from Fort Lauderdale, Florida, to Marsh Harbor in the Bahamas, then water taxied to Elbow Cay for a one-on-one dinner meeting with a prominent South Florida investment banker at a private residence. The next morning, he maneuvered his way via chauffeured watercraft to Great Guana Cay, to his favorite bar in the world, "Nippers," for another rendezvous with a CEO of one of the largest healthcare-managed care entities in the Southeastern U.S. Later, the same afternoon, he boarded a private jet flight that took him to La Romana in the Dominican Republic, where he was ushered to a seaside villa retreat within the compound of Casa de Campo as the guest of a major private entrepreneur and customs house broker from Central America.

The flight back to Miami provided Marcus with a rare opportunity to relax and think, something he did not typically do when he was focused on a mission. In reality, he actually wished he was flying the craft himself, which he easily could have done, along with at least a half-dozen other fixed-wing models, plus several whirlybird types.

There were very few people who knew much, if anything, about Marcus Manasa. For that matter, even Marcus knew very little about himself! From what little he did know, he admittedly considered himself a human enigma with an extremely mysterious past and interesting existence. Fate had dealt him a strange hand, yet it was one that he relished and had embellished. Marcus knew really nothing of his true origin or who his real parents might have been, although he had certain suspicions and theories on the matter. Based on what he had ascertained from various, somewhat reliable sources, he had been adopted before the age of one, according to records, although he was confident that such records had been altered and contained numerous fictitious entries, including his specific date of birth. Manasa's adoptive parents were apparently both U.S. citizens and possibly held dual citizenships. They both were working abroad in foreign service embassy posts for the State Department when he was officially adopted. One of the extremely curious things recorded in the adoption papers was that Marcus Manasa, for some reason, at birth had been afforded citizenship in the United States, Spain, and Austria. Although interesting to ponder at times, and would certainly provoke the curiosities of the uninitiated, Marcus had long since left his specific origins to someone that might care and fixated entirely on the life of privilege and opportunities that his situation and his adoptive parents had provided.

From the outset, it was obvious that Marcus benefited from excellent genetics. Mentally, he was a sponge, with untiring motivation along with the ability and will to absorb, explore, and excel. In the early stages of his life, his physical attributes were intuitively obvious, as he displayed incredible hand-eye coordination, uncanny reflexes, and matching quickness. Although Marcus did not spend considerable time with either of his adoptive parents, he never lacked for attention or quality nurturing throughout his childhood and was continuously surrounded by professional multicultural nannies, mentoring companions, and instructional gurus.

Living abroad for such an extensive period early in life, coupled with the exposure to various social and cultural experiences afforded via his parent's upper-echelon status in the foreign services, enabled Marcus to encounter a unique set of real-life experiences, thereby making him composed, confident, and comfortable in a variety of worldly settings and activities. By the time Marcus was sixteen, he was fluent in English and five romance languages and conversant in three others.

Although Marcus had traveled to the States numerous times and spent several summers there, his first real exposure to the country and the culture was when he attended Charlotte Hall Military Academy in Washington D.C. It was here where he had met and forged a lifelong relationship with his closest friend in the world, Jorge De Valle, from the Dominican Republic. Marcus was an excellent athlete, but his love was baseball, and he shared this passion with teammate Jorge for four wonderful years. His proficiency on the baseball diamond earned him a scholarship to The Citadel in Charleston, South Carolina. Or at least, he thought so. Unbeknownst to Marcus at the time, his education was completely secured, and he could have attended any college or university in the U.S. or Europe.

Marcus devoured the formality of the military academy and was perfectly suited to excel and achieve in an environment that demanded discipline and respect for tradition. Marcus was built for the themes associated with honor and all the ritualistic pomp and circumstance that accompany such military demeanor. At the beginning of his junior year, Marcus and five other cadets were asked to participate in a special study that would allow them to earn all their academic credits for the semester and would also provide them an additional stipend of $2,500 to be used at their discretion. It was obviously an extremely prestigious opportunity, and the $2,500 made any choice a "no brainer!" Marcus was surprised that the special semester consisted of constant bombardment of stimulus-response exercises, qualitative problem solving, focused observation experiments, and participant observation demonstrations. In addition, there were a number of memory gymnastic instructional requirements and developmental challenge competitions with both peers and unknown others. Marcus had never enjoyed anything as much in his life and thrived on the pressure created from these continuous challenges. It was somewhat anticlimactic when Marcus returned to his regular academic endeavors, but as usual, he immediately adapted and soon resumed the anticipated progressive path that would lead, at least initially, to a professional military career. Early in his senior year, he was summoned by the Commandant of The Citadel for "An Immediate Presence Required," a rare demand of unusual urgency, ordering the cadet to cease whatever activities were in progress and report in full dress uniform directly to the Commandant. These kinds of demand orders did not usually spell good news, and although Marcus Manasa was, for the most part, cool and collected under most situations, this request had unnerved him ever so slightly. To his surprise, he did not meet with The Commandant at all, but instead with gentleman claiming to represent the State Department, who flattered Cadet Manasa by indicating that he had been on their radar for some time and would like to offer him an immediate position upon graduation. He went on to say that during the initial period of employment, Marcus would be subjected to an intensive training regimen with various decision tree alternatives that would determine his ultimate utility and eventual assignments. For lack of a better term, he would simply be a special ops employee of the federal government and not specifically attached to the State Department. Although money was of little consequence whatsoever to Marcus (he already had more than he could spend in several lifetimes), and he was paying absolutely no attention to the compensation portion of the offer, the amount mentioned as initial salary during the training period would have stunned even him. The offer was accepted on the spot without hesitation, and the senior cadet, not having any idea what the future held, was on his way to a dark and intriguing professional career. Marcus was now headed down a path that would eventually lead him to what was traditionally referred to as "the invisible government!" No one could have been more suited and prepared for such a life.

For the next couple of years, Marcus was subjected and exposed to a variety of individualized and customized knowledge and skill development tutorials, known and utilized by only a select few. These training experiences were followed by practical applications referred to as "methods." Methods were concentrated upon "Access," "Identities," "Regress," "Weaponry," "Contingencies," "Decoys and Deception," "Operational Planning," "Logistical Support Assessments," and "Adhocracy," As a result of the culmination of these knowledge/skill developments and the applications proficiencies, Marcus Manasa was practically a walking/talking human machine with abilities almost unfathomable and inconceivable in a single human being.

Marcus always found it almost whimsical, sometimes, that he was in possession of over thirty different passports from over a dozen different countries that represented numerous identities as well as his own. He could secure others, if need be, in less than two hours and retrieve them at numerous deposit drops. Marcus had access to almost any kind of vehicle, complete with no VIN number or traceable license plate or registration. With a special driver's license and social security number, Marcus Manasa was simply a person that did not exist anywhere in this world. Individuals in his position and status could secure resources as required without question in order to accomplish their mission goals. Committed to memory were protocols for practically every situation that could solve almost any conceivable issue that might be encountered by an operative.

For his current assignment, although Marcus had no knowledge, or no need to know such information, he was almost certain that he had peers working in other states and locations with missions practically identical to his own. These kinds of operations were almost always one-man shows. Even though it was unspoken, there was an inherent understanding that there was ongoing invisible competition with parallel-type operations, with future assignment spoils being awarded to the highest achievers.

As the plane began its approach preparations into Miami, Marcus broke from his daze and refocused on the upcoming tasks ahead for the next few weeks. For the past several months, he had made commuting trips between D.C. and Miami on a regular basis, but now that several project trials had been initiated, evaluated, and smoothed over, he would be spending most of his time in Florida, particularly in the Broward-Miami areas, in order to oversee and monitor ongoing operations, troubleshoot aberrant consequences, and provide prescriptive contingency strategies. At this point, Marcus's eidetic memory materialized and projected an outline progression of a GNATT Chart format in significant detail. None of this was written down anywhere. The only place any of this information or any associated material existed was in the bowels of Marcus Manasa's brain. Marcus never wrote anything down. As a matter of fact, he deliberately did not carry a pen with him. Through a variety of memory tools/ techniques, enhanced rote and mnemonic learning strategies (incorporating multiplication tables through fifteen, the alphabet, a deck of cards, forty animals, twelve historical figures, the eight wonders of the world, and several others), Marcus could totally recall via association hundreds of phone numbers, bank account numbers, names, addresses, thousands of specific quotes, and complete details of almost any meeting he attended for the past several years.

As the special chartered jet taxied toward the hangar, Marcus was consciously distracted by a sign on the tarmac, "WEBB CONSTRUCTION." Through association, a reoccurring name that kept popping up in conversations among various key confederates over the past several months was an individual named Webb Espy. Marcus made a mental note to do some special due diligence on this particular individual.

16

May 7, 1993

LITTLE HAITI, MIAMI, FL

It was the third stop of the day in the sweltering Miami humidity for the large white-paneled van being chauffeured by Jacques Lafrance, a Haitian refugee who had resided in South Florida for more than a decade. The large, dark-skinned, muscular Haitian, attired in khakis, a sleeveless sweatshirt, and a St. Louis Cardinals baseball cap, leaned up against the van and haphazardly tossed out McDonald's kiddy packs as the dozen children passed single-file back into the van. Once the last of the children were back inside the vehicle, he locked the door, walked back into the facility, and returned with a sealed manila envelope. He deposited the envelope in the glove compartment with the other two from the previous stops and proceeded to his fourth and final destination with the kids for the day.

Every Monday through Friday for the past three and a half months had been just like the events of today. How long this could go on, Jacques had no idea, but he was loving this gravy train. He was pocketing almost $500 cash money a day with no expenses, and did not have to kill or strong-arm anybody to make such a payday. "Almost too good to be true," he continuously kept informing himself. The job was simple. All that was required was to recruit volunteers for free medical and dental care and pay them $10 for each visit and provide them a meal. Once the word spread in the neighborhood, he had parents waiting in line every morning with more kids than he could handle.

Jacques was referred to as a "solicitor," primarily for Medicaid recipients, for which he received handsome remunerations. "Life is good!" he mused. The best part about the whole thing was the fact that the van was rented for him, and he was provided cash for seed money, gas, and any other kinds of expenses. At the end of each day, he would call a toll-free 800 number and be provided instructions as to what was to be done with the collected envelopes. Usually, he would be directed towards some Easy Mail or mail box, etc. These drop boxes never existed for more than a week before he was instructed to go elsewhere. Each time he deposited the envelopes, he would retrieve an envelope which would contain cash for his services, expense cash, and a key or combination for the next mailbox that would be utilized. Although Jacques was acutely aware that the envelopes he was delivering to the drop boxes contained a considerable amount of paper currency, he had no idea how much and knew instinctively that it was smart not to be too curious about such things. One thing he was absolutely certain about was nothing should ever happen to any of those envelopes or what was contained in them. It had been made crystal clear that if, for some reason, anything happened to the contents of an envelope prior to the time it was delivered, it would result in something beyond bad, and there would be consequences more horrible than the human brain would be able to even imagine or comprehend.

17

May 1, 1993

LITTLE HAVANA, MIAMI, FLORIDA

Victor Hernandez pulled his late model, well-maintained, shiny black Cadillac into a designated space in the parking lot of Victor's Farmacia in the heart of Little Havana. Later today, while he was working, the car would be detailed as it was every week, rain or shine. Victor was a man of structured routines and was strict about appearances. He relished the status he enjoyed as a pharmacist, business owner, and civic leader in the Latin community in South Florida. As a self-proprietor, he had owned and operated his pharmacy, situated in the same location, for over a decade, and it had generated a rather tidy fortune for him.

Victor was euphoric; today was Christmas, birthday, Father's Day, Mother's Day, Easter Bunny, Tooth Fairy, and anniversary all rolled into one, and the best part about it was it happened twelve times a year. It was "Mici Day" (Pronounced "Mickey," as in Mouse). It was the day that each Florida Medicaid recipient received their monthly Medicaid Identification Cards, which included their approved current excess drug/prescription allocations. For Medicaid-participating pharmacies in Florida, it represented a goldmine, smokehouse, and gravy train simultaneously! It provided a license to steal, and there were some opportunists that yielded not from such enticement. Although the Medicaid Prescribed Drug program was ripe for the picking every day of the month, "Mici Day" was the big day, when a considerable amount of initial illicit activities was jump-started.

Victor was metaphorically licking his chops in anticipation of the day's yields. In the state of Florida, especially South Florida, "mom-and-pop" pharmacies," as opposed to big chain pharmacies, were able to survive and thrive, and it was due primarily to third party insurance participation, particularly Medicaid. Victor often pondered the policy absurdities and oversight laxness of the program; however, his ponderings were short-lived when he remembered how much money it was putting in his pockets. Victor's Farmacia yielded a net monthly income in the neighborhood of $135,000 taxable dollars, which in no way represented the real story.

Although some mom-and-pop operations attempted to disguise themselves as full-service pharmacies by representing a full array of legitimate, across-the-board pharmacological decoys while at the same time dipping into illegitimate Medicaid deceptions, Victor's Farmacia made no such pretense. Victor considered himself more of a professional sophisticated pawn broker than a traditional retail pharmacist. He had no illusions whatsoever about what he was doing. He enjoyed making deals, thinking on his feet, and bartering, and he welcomed competition from his peers.

There were some casual observers of the Medicaid program in general who espoused the notion that participating in unscrupulous Medicaid aberrant practices was far more lucrative and less risky in terms of getting caught and suffering consequences than trafficking in illegal street drugs and contraband. For the most part, their observations and overall assessment were absolutely on point.

Most regular working days, Victor's Farmacia had five full-time employees, not counting the proprietor himself. On "Mici Days," there was a full complement of seven from 8:00 A.M. to 11:00 P.M. There was always one extra pharmacist on the premises at all times. Victor compensated his employees well, and there was rarely any turnover. On "Mici Day," Victor was all over the store, filling scripts, brokering deals, romancing items, offering barter arrangements, and troubleshooting ad hoc situations. Some transactions required more inconspicuous negotiations and were therefore conducted in the privacy of a small office conveniently located for just such situations.

There were many ways to take advantage of the Medicaid opportunities afforded, and Victor did not shy from any of them, but there were those that he preferred due to their covert profitability-enhancing features. Victor catalogued Medicaid pharmacy deceptive practices into three moneymaking types of situations; one, those Medicaid recipients who had excess drug grants that actually required prescriptions; two, those Medicaid recipients who had excess drug grants and either did not need or want prescriptions and wished to barter their drug grant allocations for other merchandise in the store; and three, those that simply wanted discounted cash for their excess grant authorizations. Victor could accommodate all three areas, but he much preferred the merchandising/bartering opportunities and the ones where cash was desired.

Based on several years of experience and historical precedent, every pharmacist in the state of Florida knew that if they were in possession of a drug script by an authorized, prescribing Medicaid participating provider and they filled a prescription for an eligible Medicaid recipient in accordance with the specified allowances on the "mici," they would receive reimbursement the following week for the amount which was billed. There was no payment lag time! Medicaid providers in general rarely had a reason to complain about timely payments.

Victor enjoyed dealing with Medicaid recipients who preferred to exchange their excess drug grants for cash. It appeared to be a win-win situation for everyone, but in reality, the huge advantage went to Victor. When the pencil pushing and shell games were over, with everything being in the house's favor, Victor often made out with a 500 to 600% return on the deal.

Victor's next favorite scheme was what was referred to as "merchandising." Under this type of situation, a Medicaid recipient might elect to use their excess drug grant for some other type of merchandise that Victor sold in his pharmacy. This might be cigarettes, beer, wine, groceries, etc. On occasion, he might barter out a larger item on ninety-day time limit for a customer at a modest interest rate of 18%. He had regular customers that merchandised with him throughout the entire month in order to supplement their basic needs. For a select few regular customers, Victor ran his pharmacy like a "company store," and those individuals would never be able to get off the hook and would, in all probability, be indebted to him for their entire lives.

For those Medicaid recipients that required prescriptions for chronic medical situations or acute episodic illnesses, Victor was still in a position to pinch the system for some extra Medicaid sugar, which he accomplished with great gusto. Although not quite as lucrative as other drug diversion practices, it was still possible to easily generate additional illicit income through generic/legend brand substitutions, package-size differential price billing, and price scalping through the purchase and dispensing of both gray- and black-market prescription drugs.

Victor was watching the clock in eager anticipation. It was almost showtime, and he could sense the rush swelling up inside him. He could already hear voices outside the front door and caught glimpses of the willing sheep to be sheared. Special futuristic cameras might have been able to capture the invisible drools running down his grinning chin. Victor was cognizant that there were other pharmacists in close proximity that were going through exactly the same kind of emotions at this very moment.

18

March 15, 1993

TALLAHASSEE, FLORIDA

It had been almost six weeks since Webb had had his infamous meeting with Secretary David Baswell. Several things had come together in Webb's mind, and along with M's magic, he had determined that now was more likely than not the opportune time to pull the trigger. Webb asked Marsha Kaye to schedule a meeting with Kathryn Armstrong right after lunch, along with an order to immediately gather all MPI staff in "The Bullpen" ASAP! The Bullpen was the nickname for the large open room in the center of the building that contained the copy machines, network server, dumb terminals, and the only place large enough in the MPI complex for all the staff to gather at one time.

Webb Espy's other uncanny ability that more than leveled the playing field with others of suspected superior intellect and talent was simply the "God-given gift of gab." Webb was a poster child for Toastmasters International, the envy of political wannabes, and made seasoned evangelicals drool with his extraordinary extemporaneous monologues. Webb was accomplished in eulogies as well as standup comedy and could easily provide a completely unrehearsed impromptu recitation on just about any topic under the sun, whether he knew anything about it whatsoever.

Historically, students would never have considered missing one of his entertainment sessions disguised as college classes. Webb could integrate wit and humor into almost any type of scholarly or academic presentation. Whether telling a joke, participating in a bullshit session, or testifying before a congressional committee, Webb Espy was going to entertain you, and you were going to listen to whatever he had to say. Although under most circumstances, in most situations Webb would have defined himself as fashionably modest and humble; however, if you put a microphone in his hand or offered him a stage, a strange metamorphosis occurred that provided a glimpse of a ham gene in his otherwise well-rounded personality. It was Webb's gift for providing inspiration and motivation in his leadership roles that put him head and shoulders above his peers and colleagues.

Webb waited until he was sure that all MPI staff had assembled in The Bullpen. Precious had instructed all the sections to put all phone lines on hold status, ensuring that everyone in the building would be in attendance. There was not a soul in MPI who was not cognizant that Webb had a mandated one-on-one with The Sec a couple of weeks earlier, and their faces displayed a certain amount of anxiety in anticipation as to what was forthcoming. The rumors had been rampant; was Webb going to announce he had been asked to resign, had he been offered a promotion, was MPI going to be reorganized, or was there a budget exercise related to funding reductions that was going to force some overtime? Since it was learned that Webb had met with The Sec, the rumor mill was working in fast-forward and anxiety levels were at a feverish pitch!

As Webb sauntered into The Bullpen, his expression was deadpan, giving away nothing. He had no notes in his hands, and his only prop was an oversized golf umbrella. Every eye in the room was focused on him while he refused to make eye contact with anyone. For several seconds, he gazed upward, toward the ceiling, and after what seemed like an eternity, began to utter something almost to himself, "This morning, I heard a rumor that really frightened me." He paused for a millisecond, and after a dramatic, perfectly-timed pause, continued, "Until I remembered that I started it yesterday afternoon." With that, the room instantly erupted into a roar, and Webb's laughter along with them broke the ice, eliminated all anxiety, and set the stage for what was to follow.

"As a few of you might be aware, I had the privilege of going head-to-head with The Sec a couple of weeks ago. His Majesty obviously had no idea what he was getting into, because when I left him, he was struggling in a helpless heap after suffering the aftermath of what can only be best described as a plain old southern conniption-hissy fit, brought on by hysterical, gut-wrenching laughter as a result of what I mentioned I was going to do for him." There was another spontaneous wail of laughter from Webb's devotees.

"All seriousness aside, I do want to share what our little chat was about, but first, I need to convey his compliments to each of you, which translates to all of us, for the outstanding job on the Dr. Pieo case. I know David Baswell very well and have for a number of years, and I know when he is appreciative and sincere about something. There is no question that the positive outcome of that case, along with media and the blitz that accompanied it, paid huge dividends for him in his legislative budget hearings. He indicated that he will make it over personally and express to each one of you individually his genuine gratitude. I personally guarantee you that he will hold to that promise. I also promise that if he does not do that, I will go public with that last little visual scene I previously just described to you," he joked, yielding yet another wave laughter.

"Now, I want to talk to you about the meeting I had with The Sec, and I also want to delve into the topic of ignorance; let me hasten to add that there is absolutely no intended relationship or reference between the two," he proposed, eliciting still another howl from his audience. "However, as an aside, I did have some eloquent and complimentary things to relay to him regarding his Deputy Dog," Webb declared, once again bringing down the house.

"A very wise professor of mine once proclaimed that ignorance never solved any problems; education might. I believe at the time I heard him utter that statement that it might very well have been one of the most profound revelations I had ever heard. From that point forward, I began to look at institutional beliefs and acceptance of such views in a very different light. That seemingly simple, thought-provoking conception provided the springboard for an enlightened evaluation of issues and processes going forward in both my personal life and professional career. Ignorance is the antithesis to an objective, scholarly inquiry and progressive investigation. We are all familiar with the adage that a little knowledge is a dangerous thing; half of knowledge is knowing where to find it, but the most important half is realizing that we don't possess it to begin with! I love the story about the mouse that ate the elephant because nobody told him he couldn't do it. It is extremely difficult to break away from the bonds and security of institutionalized traditions, practices, and thinking, but I assure you that if you ever can, it will represent the genesis of new thinking and growth in each of your lives." Webb paused.

"There is some measure of truth to the stated belief that bureaucracy breeds mediocrity. Due to the division of labor and the specialization of functional processes that traditionally occur, bureaucrats more often than not operate with a degree of tunnel vision and protect their territories and functional areas of responsibility while neglecting the real goals of the organization. I would like to think that I am not the traditional or typical bureaucrat," Webb suggested, raising his eyebrows while gesturing and exposing a vulnerable and helpless pose with a genuine twinkle in his eyes, along with a definite wink. "Let me emphasize that is not going to be the case in our little corner of our little bureaucratic world!" he thundered, popping up his oversized umbrella for extra emphasis.

"Churchman, in his book on systems, made the claim that we have the technology to feed, clothe, and house every human being in the world today. The reason that we do not do this, aside from the fact that it is not our goal to accomplish such a feat, is the fact that we are not organized to do it. We have the talent, expertise, and personnel resources gathered in this room, right at this moment, to make a significant impact on fraud and abuse practices in the State of Florida. Why don't we do more? Well, I'll give you my take on the topic. I've allowed the constraints of bureaucracy, traditional methods, and archaic regulatory thinking to stand in the way of thinking smarter and utilizing our resources more wisely and to better advantage," Webb proclaimed, shouldering all the blame on himself.

"We are going to begin immediately to do something about that, but first, let me tell you about something I learned from my little tit de tot with The Sec. It seems as though our cops and robbers' relatives at the Medicaid Fraud Unit in the Attorney General's Office are sending signals that their puny fraud investigative results are due to our inability to send a sufficient number of substantive preliminary fraud referral cases. I suspect you probably don't need to let your imagination wander too far to predict my reaction to that suggestive absurdity." There was an instantaneous chorus of "BULLSHIT" that was intentionally solicited and anticipated by Webb at this juncture of the pep rally.

"Yeah, that's what I thought you might have to say. Hell, you guys work more fraud cases and recover more money by accident than they do on purpose. Tell you what we're gonna do right off. Ed, get with Phyllis; let's put a boilerplate together on thirty of the top sixty pharmacy cases; let's say, alternate every other one that we detected using the new formula and hand-deliver every single damn one of them this afternoon to those prissy-ass prima donnas."

"You got it, chief!" yelled Ed with the authority and confidence of being singled out.

"Then we are going to harass them every week for an official status report, indicating each time how much is continuing to flow out the Medicaid money faucet."

"Ditto!" confirmed Ed again, gesturing with a big thumbs up.

"Those yang-yangs don't know a NDC number from a 3-H enema," bellowed Webb, generating yet another guffawing response from his faithful minions.

"I guarantee they've got no clue how to work these kinds of pharmacy fraud cases, and I suspect this is going to get real embarrassing to them before it's over." By this point in Webb's little oratory, he felt confident that he had succeeded in creating the "them vs. us" challenge deemed essential as a foundation for the mutual support and protection of one another.

Webb escalated his rhetoric with volume and intensity. "That being said, hold on tight, gang; we're getting ready to shock the world! Over the next several days, I'm going to personally meet with each and every one of you and outline a number of progressive and futuristic detection and investigative strategies. By COB today, Marsha Kaye will have in your hands a schedule of times beginning at 8:30 in the morning. Don't be surprised if you find your name on the list several times with different groups. Let me tell you all right now that we are going to de-emphasize some federally mandated Surveillance, Utilization, and Review requirements and employ our own functional equivalents. I realize that there are a few internal gasps from some of you right at the moment, as what I'm proposing might, in fact, jeopardize our certification system percentage enhancement status for Federal Financial Participation (FFP). Let me worry about that. If we accomplish 10% of what we install, we will, in all likelihood, become the FMMIS prototype and recommended functional equivalent model for other state systems.

"My experiences in the public service arena have historically yielded consequences revealing that it is usually more prudent and effective to obtain forgiveness than permission. As far as I'm concerned, we are through in this office with the bridled constraints that have forced us to use obsolete methods that waste time and resources, just for the purpose of being in compliance with system certification requirements. We have already demonstrated over the last few months that we can build better mousetraps and recoupment strategies than the feds can even envision. Believe me, there are a number of other significant ones in the proverbial queue. In order to move on with these enhancements, we are going to use a variety of heuristic tactics and fly under the radar, employing something of an organizational adhocracy, along with a task force mentality, in order to achieve our purpose. So, get ready to do some uniquely different things with a variety of personnel. I can pretty much assure you, it is not going to be boring around here, and if my suspicions about you folks are correct, I fully anticipate that these new M.O.s are going to invoke a whole new meaning akin to the thrill of the chase!"

Webb could sense the mood of his mob and an elevation of emotion. You could see it in their facial expressions and body language. Although he had several more crowd-frenzy zingers, his intuitiveness told him that it would be overkill, and anticlimactic for the purposes at hand. He had achieved the apex of the *esprit de corps* for the group as a whole and decided to finish with a crescendo and motivational finale. After pausing briefly and making eye contact with numerous of those in the room, Webb continued, "I have worked in a number of places in public service, and I have served on a number of boards, task forces, etc., during my public administration career. Without reservation, I can honestly say that I have never had the privilege of working with a more diverse, dedicated, and talented group of peers. Generally, when I speak about what we do in MPI, I tell them that our mission is based on continuously asking the question, did we get what we paid for? I then go on to say that the first part of my tenure here with you guys at MPI was when we knocked on the door; during the next phase, we banged on the door, and now we are poised to kick that son of a bitch off its damn hinges. YES SIREE; that's exactly what I expect us to do! Thank you, each and every one of you, for your time and attention," he yelled at them. "You guys ready? Let's get started, then!" he challenged as he abruptly turned and headed out the door, banging his umbrella on the floor in cadence as he charged toward his office. The reaction was immediate and spontaneous, and the staff went maniacally wild while alternating between applause and high fives amongst themselves. Espy had fired them up, and he had their support, loyalty, and complete dedication to the task related to the missions ahead. He was their motivator and their inspirational leader! The metaphorical door that had just been referenced was "toast," and everyone in the room knew it!

19

March 15, 1993

Later The Same Day Tallahassee, Florida

As promised, by close of business, Marsha Kaye, in her efficient and perfectionist manner, had a schedule of meeting groups and times in the hands of all MPI staff for the next nine workdays. The first name on the list was something of a surprise to many and created quite a stir and numerous puzzled exchanges, as well as several quizzical innuendos. It was the only meeting that indicated a one-on-one with the Chief. That first name on the list belonged to Miss Kathryn Armstrong, an analyst in the SURS Section who had worked for MPI for a little over three years. She was one of the first hires that Webb made after David Baswell, apparently with some knowledge of her personal history and background, asked as a professional courtesy with no obligation whatsoever if there might be any place for her in Webb's shop. After some initial due diligence and an interview, Webb had concluded it was an absolute no-brainer and immediately put her on the payroll.

Kathryn Armstrong, on the surface, displayed a somewhat shy and introverted personality. After some amateurish detective work, Webb had concluded at the time when she was initially hired that she had apparently been dealt a pretty sorry hand, both in her personal life as well as her professional career. Just on the south side of thirty, she was a single parent with a five-year-old son, never married, and the legal guardian of her adoptive father, who was a resident in a local assisted living facility.

She earned her degree in English literature and journalism from Florida State University and worked for a couple of small newspapers in South Georgia following graduation. Small local newspapers in South Georgia, or in North Florida, for that matter, or possibly even in Berkley, California, were not prepared nor culturally ready for Kathryn Armstrong and concluded in short order that her editorials were on the far side of political correctness and delivered with what might best be described as the finesse of a hippopotamus in a bathtub. In short, her journalistic opportunities, based upon the geographic restrictions, limited her career progression, and she was forced to find employment elsewhere. She next became a paralegal for a large silk-stocking law firm in Florida's capital city and excelled in research and boilerplate template development. She also excelled in drawing attention to herself every time she ventured to the copy machine in her high heel pumps. Although not exactly movie star-glamorous, Kathryn, a legitimate strawberry blonde, was definitely not hard on the eyes and was a showstopper when assessed from the rearmost vantage point. In typical Harlequin romance novel fashion, she ultimately was unable to ward off all of the constant advances of ardent admirers, succumbed to delusions of living happily ever after, and eventually managed to have a fling with one of the upper-echelon attorneys in the firm. Believing his claim that he was legally separated, which ultimately proved to be something of a stretch, she learned in actuality that the wife was simply on an extended sabbatical with her convalescing mother, who was going through a long series of chemo.

Kathryn's scornful retaliation to her embarrassment and naiveté was a quick rebound with a younger attorney within the firm, designed to invoke a jealous response and an ultimatum toward the previous suitor, for a commitment that was not well-thought through. The results were pretty well guaranteed, with an immediate pink slip followed by morning sickness six weeks later. Kathryn was smart enough to realize she was outgunned by the firm and its resources to make real waves. She also was apparently too proud to allow them the satisfaction of being able to influence her life and her future in any manner. Although Kathryn was pro-choice to the core, she never considered an abortion. Several weeks after the termination of her employment with the firm, and learning of her particular situation after the fact, and in consideration of future potential repercussions that might be forthcoming, she received a generously-supplemented severance package which she did not refuse.

Since joining MPI, Kathryn had been more or less a loner and kept mostly to herself while performing her job and delegated responsibilities in an extremely proficient manner, requiring little, if any, supervision. Almost every day at lunch, she had errands to run, and therefore rarely socialized with her fellow peers. Kathryn was always cordial, friendly, and quick with a smile, but not a social mixer with her MPI coworkers. There were, however, reports from those who might have reliable insights into such things, that on several of those rare occasions when she had not been able to escape the social commitments and traditions associated with outside work activities, after a couple of adult beverages she became rather chatty, extremely witty, and had an extensive repertoire of stories and jokes that made her a main attraction.

At precisely 8:29 A.M., Kathryn appeared in Webb's outer office and was greeted professionally and courteously by Marsha Kaye.

She was gestured to a seat and offered coffee, which Kathryn respectfully declined. At that, Marsha Kaye advised, "Let me see if he is ready for you." Getting up from her chair, she reached around the door facing and announced that Miss Armstrong was here and asked if he was ready for her. Webb acknowledged that indeed he was. Marsha Kaye immediately turned to Kathryn and indicated that she was at liberty to enter. On cue, Kathryn entered the office and Marsha Kaye closed the door behind her.

Webb noticed that she was not in usual workday attire, and there was something different in her appearance, although he could not immediately put his finger on it. The only accessory in her possession was a leather-bound legal pad attaché.

Rising instantly in concert with her arrival, Webb impulsively motioned her to a seat, came around his desk, and sat in a comfortable side chair facing her. "Kathryn, thank you for coming, and I really appreciate your punctuality; we are really on a short rope here."

"Dr. Espy, the pleasure is mine, of course, and I, along with everyone else in this office, am acutely aware of your sentiments on tardiness," she responded, suppressing a sly smile.

Webb provided an accepting chuckle. "First off, it is not Dr. Espy; it's Webb," he interjected.

"In that case, then; first off, it's Kat. That's what I generally prefer, BOSS," she retaliated.

"Okay," Webb allowed, gesturing an acknowledging retreat with his palms facing out. "Now that we got that little bit of protocol out of the way, I assume you got to be a little curious about why you're here, huh?" questioned Webb.

"Not in the least," she responded, shrugging her shoulders and staring him straight in the face. "I'm a single woman, you're a single man, we've probably more in common than most, and I suspect you orchestrated this little ruse to hit on me without making yourself all that vulnerable to rejection under the pretext of work."

Rarely was Webb blindsided. To say he was stunned would be akin to the suggestion that Mother Teresa was, in reality, a closet whore! He was absolutely dumbfounded and totally incapable of a response. For what seemed like an eternity, she continued to glare at him with the posture of suggestive submission. With a perfectly-timed theatrical pause, she blurted out, "Gotcha, didn't I," accompanied with a good old-fashioned belly laugh. "Had that rehearsed pretty well, didn't I," she crowed.

Instantly relieved and simultaneously realizing that he had been the victim of a practical joke that he legitimately envied, he joined her with his own version of a "been had" belly laugh. Usually, Webb was accustomed to being the "getter" as opposed to the "getee!" "Yep, got to say, nobody has gotten me like that in a long time," he continued, laughing. "I've got to know. Did Marsha Kaye put you up to this?"

"Oh no, I concocted this little scheme all by my little old self," she confessed rather proudly.

"Well, I owe you a big one, but I'm not sure I can compete. However, remember I'm notorious for getting folks, and this ain't gonna be easily forgotten. Just remember, I invented revenge, so don't go sleeping too well at night," he warned as they both continued laughing.

"Now, Kathryn — uh sorry, Kat — the real reason I wanted to talk with you is because I need some very special assistance and expertise, and I suspect you might be just what the doctor ordered. As I'm sure you gathered from yesterday's little pow wow, we are going to be doing several unprecedented activities here in MPI, and, as I mentioned, some of those things are not currently in the feds' playbook. As you are aware, the current federal regulations require states participating in certified systems to have mechanisms for ex post facto review of potentially aberrant practices. No question whatsoever that this is an important and appropriate requirement, but there is little doubt in my mind that the primary SURS system is really nothing more than huge peer comparison and, in my opinion, the continuous application of these peer comparison models have become, for the most part, obsolete. Sure, we manipulate outliers and standard deviations and customize a few unique components in the reference file subsystem, but for the most part, it's like putting lipstick on a pig. You're following me so far, right?" Kathryn nodded an affirmative "yes."

"In order for us to accomplish what needs to be done, we have to convince the feds to allow the states greater flexibility for requesting waivers for functional equivalents to the requirements when states can demonstrate more successful mousetraps via a history of investigations and recoveries. That's kinda where I figure you might come in and can really assist us, if you are so inclined," Webb paused, looking directly at Kathryn.

"Go on. I'm listening," she said.

"This is what I have in mind. I would like to hit a sacrifice fly on these "less than sanctioned" little strategic adventures, if at all possible. By that, I mean that I want to delegate the responsibility lock, stock, and barrel to you to do whatever is required to request and secure those waivers while we are in the process of implementing and troubleshooting them, if you catch my drift?"

"Yeah, I believe I see where this is headed," she responded, staring thoughtfully toward the ceiling. "What else?" she immediately questioned.

"In addition, although your name does not currently show up on the group scheduling, I would like you to attend each and every one of these meetings and document the process we are going through. There are multiple purposes for this. One is to provide an ongoing orientation to you, which will assist you with your waiver requests. The second is the need for a neutral observer to the process who is documenting assignments and accountability. The third reason is, if my hunch is correct and we pull this thing off, there needs to be an objective basic case study of the entire process that includes those things that went right, as well as what went wrong. This annotated case study document will provide the primary catalyst for deploying fraud and abuse strategies for years to come. Assuming you are with me on this, I've had Marsha Kaye prepare a binder that includes a presentation I recently participated in down in Miami, which ought to provide a pretty good orientation as to what my overall thinking is regarding the state of fraud and abuse issues in the state of Florida and what might be done about them. In addition, there are reference materials related to federal waivers and some key contacts that you are free to contact as you deem necessary by just using my name. Also, there is an initial GANTT chart outlining what we plan to attempt here. Finally, there are some personal notes and themes that I have yet to flesh out," Webb finished, and leaned back in his chair in anticipation of Kathryn's reaction.

She did not speak immediately. Slowly and deliberately, Kathryn began to speak. "Before we go much further with this, I have to ask the obvious question; why me?"

"Legitimate question, Kat," Webb replied matter-of-factly. "Let's start with the simple reality that you are, at the present time, not working in a job or a position that you were educated and trained to do and that your talent and expertise are not currently being utilized in a manner commensurate with your skills. Next, I believe I have a good handle on what you are capable of, and I am in desperate need of those kinds of skills at this time. I cannot think of another single individual in MPI that can exceed your ability to do this."

"Go on, there's more, I suspect," she suggested.

"I have to admit, I've had the opportunity and also the pleasure of doing some due diligence related to your background, etc.; at first, of course, when you were initially hired, and then more recently, when I was scheming about this project." Kathryn remained stoic and expressionless, but Webb thought he might have detected a slight smirk emerging in her smile. "I have reviewed a number of things that you did in your professional journalism career, and one of your old bosses, John Conklin at *The Two Rivers News*, is an old friend of mine and shared several of what he considered to be some of your classic pieces of work. I also spoke with Professor Dr. Lester Hendry at FSU, an old colleague of mine, who I believe was not only your major professor, but also your advisor as well. He archives most of his students' work and selected a few examples for my review and amusement, including your award-winning essay on *The Octopus Syndrome*, which, I got to say, was certainly thought-provoking. Dr. Hendry was extremely complimentary and claimed that you possessed a type of creativity and imagination that was quite rare, and you had a most unusual ability and creative gift to embellish the most routine things into something beyond spectacular. I believe the example he used was that you could visualize a leaky, drippy faucet and make others believe it was the roar of the mighty Niagara. That is exactly the kind of thing we need to have happen to secure these waiver options, I suspect," Webb concluded, while noting something resembling a wicked smile beginning to emerge on Kathryn's otherwise expressionless face.

"I guess I also need to admit that I was able to pry a few tidbits out of David Baswell, who, for some reason, would not divulge why he holds you in extremely high regard. Although I know a considerable amount of what you have been through, I don't begin to pretend to have a frame of reference for everything you have had to deal with. I know you've had to suck it up big time, and you have apparently done so with dignity and with your integrity intact. That's just an observation on my part, and really, anything else is none of my business. I know that you visit your father three times a day in his assisted living facility, and that speaks volumes to me in terms of your sense of responsibility and unselfish loyalty. I know the single most important thing to you in this world is a little five-year-old fellow that calls you Kmaa. So there, what do you think?" Webb finally wrapped up.

Kathryn did not respond immediately and appeared to be staring blankly into space while concentrating intently on some fixed object. She seemed to be organizing her thoughts prior to putting her mouth in gear. Finally, she began to speak very slowly and deliberately while still continuing to stare away at some unknown object. "Hmmm, well, I guess before we go much further here, I suppose that I probably need to enter into a form of quid pro quo with you; my own little due diligence, if you will. So, boss, I suppose I need to let you know that I know you were born

on June 30, 1949, in a small town in North Florida. I know that
you were an underachiever in school and did not become aca-
demically motivated until you joined military service during the
Vietnam era. I know you fired "expert" and made rank very fast.
You finished your undergraduate work while you were complet-
ing your military obligation and had your entire GI Bill left to
utilize for graduate school, which you exhausted to the very last
penny. Enough of that, but I could go on. In graduate school, you
excelled and were viewed as an unusually gifted scholar and was
drafted to return to the faculty. Your pioneering into simulation
training in the "new public administration" arena and related
publications was financially lucrative by almost any standard, and
you continue to receive royalties related to the texts and case
study workbooks used in colleges both here and abroad. I also
have it on good authority that you authored or either coauthored
the novel *Orange* — which, by the way, I found entertaining and
insightful and which I suspect represents somewhat of a personal
catharsis — under the pen name William St. Marks; that also
added a tidy little sum to your net worth. You currently have a
net worth in excess of $30 million, which is projected to exceed
$80 million by the year 1997. I suspect I know more than you
might possibility imagine regarding a number of things you have
left in your wake, including, in all likelihood, Marsha Kaye's current financial stability. I am aware that after tragic events in your
life, you resigned from the University, even though they offered
you a year's sabbatical, became somewhat of a recluse, and exiled
yourself into a self-imposed hiatus. If it were not for David Baswell, you would probably still remain in that state. I know that
your favorite food is most any kind of crab, and you are wild about

Coca-Cola Cake, accompanied by Blue Bell Old-Fashioned Homemade Vanilla ice cream. And, by the way, your Florida Driver's License is due to expire in twenty-one days if you don't take care of it," she paused briefly.

For the second time in the past few minutes, she had completely stunned him, although he had accomplished (at least what he perceived to be) an Oscar-deserving performance deflecting his complete astonishment. While still staggered by what had just transpired, Webb was completely unprepared for what followed next.

In the blink of an eye, Kathryn Armstrong transformed herself into a southern belle in the fashion of Elizabeth Taylor's portrayal of one Maggie the Cat in Tennessee Williams' acclaimed play *Cat on a Hot Tin Roof,* and proceeded, with an admirably proficient impersonation of the star, to rise from her chair with the utmost grace and demeanor while demonstrating a flawlessly executed exaggerated curtsey, accompanied by drawling: "Why, Dr. Webb Espy, I would be most honored if you would allow me the privilege of accepting your invitation to participate in this worthy endeavor. However, I believe it proper that we commence an endeavor such as this on a level playing field, and therefore felt it wise to so inform you that there are others that know how to do research and personal due diligence as well. I suppose if I am to be cooped up with a bunch of old administrative terrorists for the duration, I must take leave at this point to build myself a serious cup of java and powder my nose." With her final words still echoing, she glidingly sashayed her way toward the door, swiveling her neck only once as she was opening it to deliver a direct final wink at a helpless heap of human protoplasm in the seat that once held a resemblance to Webb Espy. Kathryn vanished from sight, only to stick her head back around the corner to deliver one last parting shot. Grinning like the Cheshire cat, she announced, "Oh, by the way, you had me at Kathryn."

No sooner had she departed than Marsha Kaye stuck her head around the door jamb, just in time to hear Webb mutter to himself, "Well, that didn't go exactly like I thought it would!"

With all the mischievousness she could muster, Marsha Kaye innocently proclaimed, "Why, Webb Espy, you look like somebody jus walked over your grave."

Not quite under his breath as much as he intended, Webb retorted, "Holy shit, now I got to contend with two of them!" He could hear Marsha Kaye snickering in the outer office without the slightest bit of constraint whatsoever. There was one consolation, Webb thought to himself. "Well, she's not quite as informed as she thinks she is, because she doesn't know anything about my private stashes! There're 500 shares of privately-issued Coca-Cola stock that Colonel Rob secured in the early 1930s, which have passed through various safety deposit boxes and are currently now in my possession! Got to say, though, this gives a whole new meaning to 'Pandora's box!'"

20

March 15, 1993

Later The Same Day

Webb remained in a dazed state for several minutes, rehashing the bizarre encounter with Kathryn Armstrong, which had transpired only a few moments previously. It occurred to him in 20/20 hindsight that they had probably not had anything but casual greetings in hallway passing and possibly only a few generic work-related conversations, etc., since she had started working in MPI. All of a sudden, from seemingly out of nowhere, this mysterious creature had just erupted like a genie from a bottle. He simply could not believe what had just played out and what he had apparently witnessed. Replaying the earlier exchanges between the two of them, he kept thinking to himself, "What in the world just happened? Who in the hell was that? Where has this person, or more precisely this personality, been hiding?" It was almost as if he had come face to face for the first time with one of the personality characters from *The Three Faces of Eve*! He had no time to dwell on it right now, however, because his next group was due shortly, and he had an immediate phone call he needed to return.

The next scheduled group was composed of seven participants, including Webb. Four in the group were the section head administrators; Jim Harbolt, SURS Administrator; Ed Shanks with Special Review; Maria Morris, heading Peer Review; and Richard Andrews, who ran the Investigative Section. The other two were Peggy Melton, nicknamed and referred to only as "M,' a former computer programmer whiz and special projects analyst reporting directly to the Chief. Then, of course, there was the newly assigned Kathryn Armstrong.

Marsha Kaye announced their arrival, and he signaled her to send them in. At that, they all filed in and randomly selected themselves seats around the mini conference table. Kathryn was the last to enter, and Webb let her pass and closed the door. Webb could not restrain himself from casting a quick glance in Kathryn's direction. If she noticed, she gave no indication and had her legal pad opened with pen in hand.

"Okay, folks, let's see if we can get this show on the road. This kickoff session ought to be brief, but we'll take as much time as we need because it is imperative for us to be all singing out of the same hymnal. I've had conversations at various times since I've been here with all of you, both individually and collectively, and I believe if there is one common denominator we all share, it is the frustration with being forced to do things that we all know do not work as well as they could and that we are currently mothballed into utilizing institutionalized processes that are outdated beyond the current state-of-the-art. We are going to be requesting a number of waivers for functional equivalences, etc., but we are not going to wait for approval before implementing a number of them." Webb paused while collecting his thoughts.

"Just so you know, Kathryn Armstrong is taking the lead on that project, and I am sure that she is going to need to rely on your experience and expertise from time to time in order to go through that process. She has a general delegation of authority from me to go to each of you directly for assistance. If she needs something from one of your staff, she will go through you first. Although her name does not currently appear on all the group schedules, she will be attending each and every one of the scheduled sessions to document the entire process and provide an ongoing historical reference, as well as serve as a check-and-balance role for assignments and related accountability generated by yours truly. Are there any questions about that?" The administrators, with the exception of Dick Andrews, all nodded in acknowledgement. Webb quickly glimpsed in Kathryn's direction and received not the slightest hint of anything but all business as usual.

"Thanks, good. Now, first, I believe a little housekeeping is in order before opening the floodgates. As we have all discussed ad nauseam, and as much as we hate to admit it, human resource issues consume a large part of what we do as supervisors and administrators. Although we are truly blessed in MPI with personnel beyond comparison within other public service entities, we still have to deal with reality that comes with the territory. Anytime you take folks out of their comfort zones, you are normally going to get some pushback. Although I really don't anticipate much of a problem going forward with this, I believe we all need to be prepared and be on the lookout for signs of employee frustration and dissatisfaction related to the change of our direction and the accompanying roles and responsibilities that are bound to occur during this revolutionary process. Let me urge you all, at the first sign of anything that suggests this kind of anxiety or behavior, to send them individually and directly to me," Webb paused once again.

"Now, I realize I don't need to preach to the choir, but I want to make sure we are all operating from a common frame of reference. The Florida Medicaid program has a current budget over two billion dollars. I realize we all have our opinions about how much might be considered erroneous, and in my humble opinion, I don't believe we need to spend any time debating the percentage. I believe we can all agree that is bigger than a breadbasket. For a reference point however, assuming that 5% of adjudicated claims are considered aberrant payments for whatever reason, be it fraud, abuse, mistake, premediated carelessness, or whatever, which I know we all suspect is grossly underestimated, that represents a target of around a hundred million dollars. Since we recovered around only seven million last year, it becomes intuitively obvious to the casual observer that there is considerably more out there for the taking."

Ed interrupted. "Just based on inference alone, from the sample case study projects we have conducted and analyzed, I would not be at all surprised if we are talking about an 18-20% number. That would put us somewhere in the three hundred-million-dollar territory."

Webb responded. "You may very well be correct, but it really doesn't make a lot of difference as long as we agree that there is a hell of a lot more than we can detect and recover than we are presently doing."

"The six-hundred-pound gorilla in the room is, what in the hell are we going to do with SURS while pulling off this little clandestine maneuver?" Jim Harbolt chimed in.

"I was getting to that, but now that you brought it up, let's go ahead and deal with it right at the start," Webb acquiesced.

"Suits me," offered Jim.

"The short answer is, we are still going to use the damn thing, just not in the way we have in the traditional manner. Most of you were around when, right after I first got here, we decided to deemphasize the investigative portion of recipient side of SURS by agreeing that it made a lot more sense to go after a provider that might be treating, say, a hundred or more recipients, than to waste our time going after a single recipient. Assuming we go after a recipient, what are we going to be able to do to him if we catch him, anyway? Take away his benefits, lock him in, recover any money? Let me ask you a question, Jim. What are we currently doing on the recipient side of SURS right now, and how many staff do we have assigned to those functions?" Webb asked seriously.

"Hmmm, let me think for just a second. Okay, second part first; we have a total of eighteen analysts and professional staff assigned to SURS, and seven of those are assigned to the recipient side while the other eleven work on the provider side. Now, one of those staff on the recipient side does nothing other than those mandated sample surveys we send out to Medicaid recipients related to *Explanation of Medicaid Benefits (EOMBs)*."

"How's that working out, Jim?" Ed quipped sarcastically. The rest of the group were unable to restrain a chuckle; the inside joke being that everyone knew Jim's outspoken sentiments about the survey being about as worthless as a screen door on a submarine. Jim just slumped in his chair, looked down toward his feet, and simply shook his head in helpless resignation.

"Cheer up, Jim. Things are about to get better in your world! We are not going to be using the results from the SURS reports or EOMB processes as we have in the past, and we are not going to go through any pretext of modifying variables for subsequent runs, with the exception of the percentage of surveys based on recipient utilization. M has created a program that automates boilerplate files for EOMB recipients and initial contact letters and labels to both recipients as well as their respective assigned caseworkers identified on the recipient files. This ought to make your day! I have also just secured the services of an OPS (temporary employee) worker to handle all the clerical duties associated with dealing with all of that." Webb hesitated.

"As for the bimonthly SURS runs, M has also created a filter that sorts and eliminates any recipient that has been identified over the past two years, or any recipient which we have an open case on, or any that have been referred to our fraud friends at the Attorney General's Office. All remaining recipients will be dumped into a pool and sorted by "pay-to-provider," related to the overutilization that occurred under their particular watch. For starters, each of those identified will be receiving a cagily-worded, accusatory-toned letter that has been artfully crafted for their enjoyment. For emphasis, the letters will reference a potential peer review component that might be forthcoming, which ought to get their attention a while," Webb chortled.

"Man, that ought to create some stretching and fetching and tighten a few buns," cracked Ed, leaning back in his chair and placing his hands behind his head.

"If you think that's something, you're going to mess up your britches with a couple of other moves we have in mind," mused Webb. "But that's another rabbit hole that I'm going to reveal a little later. At any rate, the bottom line is that we are going to free up over 90% of the resources in the SURS Unit to concentrate on a totally other type of provider investigative protocol. Any comments about what I just laid out?" paused Webb.

"Well, yeah, I guess I'm going to have to be the one that asks the obvious question, although I'm sure you have thought this through far beyond what my mind is even capable of imagining; I have to ask, what are the consequences of abandoning the legitimately authorized SURS system for something totally different and unique?" asked Jim.

"Hmmm, I appreciate your concern, but I got to tell you, I'm really not all that worried. The main thing is, I am the only one of us that serves at the pleasure, so if everything goes south, I am the only one of us that is in job-jeopardy. Next, so you don't have to spend any time worrying about me, I have a couple of aces up my sleeve if that should transpire, and finally, I have a genuine "get out of jail free card" that I can play if I ever really need to. However, there is no need to worry, because this is going to work, I guarantee it!

Dick Andrews, which did not surprise Webb in the least, made a scoffing sound with a definite sarcastic intonation. Webb pretended that it went unnoticed but could sense an immediate tenseness infiltrate the room.

"Are there any other questions, and if not, in the familiar words of boxing's foremost barker and ring announcer, Michael Buffer, '*let's get ready to rumble*eeeee!'" finished Webb, pleased with his relatively proficient impersonation. "And they're off!" he announced to himself under his breath and as an afterthought continued, "And that son-of-a-bitch, Dick Andrews, just succeeded in royally pissing me off. I'm just gonna have to bite the bullet and deal with that situation sooner than later, I reckon."

22

March 15, 1993

Later In The Day

After Webb's meeting with the first group, he decided a clear head and some fresh air might be the prescription for calmness and restraint in anticipation of the next meeting he had scheduled, which he was really not looking forward to at all. In fact, he was actually consciously dreading it.

Webb exited the building and began wandering aimlessly through the mammoth live oaks cloaked with Spanish moss that haphazardly decorated the campus of the multi-office complex that constituted the Florida Headquarters of The Department of Health and Rehabilitative Services (DHRS). Absentmindedly, Webb kicked a pile of acorns, scattering them in all directions, and immediately realized that he had just managed to piss off a bunch of squirrels by invading their staging area, wrecking their stores, and wiping out several laborious hours of dedicated work. He could not help but chuckle, thinking about the names they would be calling him.

At that, Webb's mind began to focus on the situation at hand. Richard Andrews, Webb's administrator of the Investigative Unit and the focus of his next team meeting, in all likelihood, was the most unpopular individual in MPI, and Webb's least favorite employee. Richard (Dick) Andrews, almost three decades senior to Webb, was a cantankerous old codger he had inherited when he took over the Medicaid Regulatory responsibilities. Andrews was sour and bitter over a career of "what could or should have been" and had been put out to "the proverbial bureaucratic pasture" years ago. According to stories, Andrews had been a rising star in the reorganization of what eventually became DHRS but unfortunately managed to hitch his star to the wrong wagon during the transition to the controversial senior management system and found himself politically isolated in no man's land, on a career ladder progression that no longer legitimately existed.

According to some seasoned veterans of the times, Andrews might have easily at some point become the Secretary of the Department if the cards had fallen right. In his heyday, he had no equal in terms of talent, ability, and vision. The only real knock on Andrews's stock was a propensity during his career to give himself a little too much credit for the efforts and achievements of others, as well as an exaggerated arm length for patting himself on the back. The obvious irony, as observed by Webb and others, was that neither of these negative traits in his character were necessary whatsoever.

Andrews had no shortage of faithful admirers and those that were in complete awe of his skillsets and problem-solving insights. Dick could have retired several years previously, but exhibited no intentions to do so. Nothing ever came easy when dealing with Dick. It was always twenty questions, and Webb knew he played such games for his own amusement to mask his long-term resentment toward the system and symbolic personnel echelons that had betrayed him. Webb did not sense that Dick disliked him personally. Webb realized that Dick would have reacted to anyone that had been placed as Chief of MPI with equal disdain.

Dick seemed to know exactly where the line was and could walk an uncanny tightrope and not fall on the side of insubordination. Dick was unequaled in his knowledge of personnel rules, regulations, and employee rights and artful in his ability to cloak himself protectively behind the established precedents related to various personnel guidelines. Webb really appreciated and was desirous of Dick's expertise and experience with these upcoming efforts, but he was not prepared to sacrifice the time and energy required to nurse his historically wounded ego.

Webb's thoughts were interrupted by a squirrel's chattering. He found the aggravated little creature about twenty yards away on an oak limb next to an open knothole, letting him have it over his acorns. He laughed out loud, abruptly turned back to the office, and thought to himself, "Ah, hell, Dick, let's get it on!"

As Webb barged into his office right on cue, he couldn't help but notice the raised eyebrows Marsha Kaye threw his way, obviously suggesting something was most likely amiss and might be potentially upsetting to him. He was thoughtful for a brief second, shrugged it off, and concluded it really didn't matter; whatever it was, it was, and he was primed and ready for just about anything in his current state of mind. He had this! He grinned at her, acknowledged her signal with a detectable wink, and charged ferociously into the lion's den. As he entered, his awaiting entourage had all arrived fashionably early, and Webb instantly assessed and understood what Marsha Kaye had been trying to convey. There was no Dick Andrews sitting at the table or present anywhere else in the room. Instead, apparently one of his section supervisors, Charlie Mathias, had been sent as his delegate. The rest of the group consisted of Phyllis Newberry, a pharmacist who headed up the Pharmacy Investigative Section, and Virginia Miller, a seasoned old war horse nurse from the old school who had forgotten more about medical procedure coding than most physicians were ever going to know. Virginia had a voice like a screech owl, and when she got excited, the screech got progressively louder and was comparable to someone scratching their fingernails down a chalkboard. Of the remaining group in the meeting, there were the fixtures: Kat and M.

To the envy of every poker dealer in Vegas, Webb never missed a beat, greeted those present, and provided absolutely no indication whatsoever that the situation was anything but completely normal and totally copacetic. As he started to sit down, he immediately leaped to his feet, apologizing to the group. "Please excuse me, I forgot one little important thing I absolutely must do. It'll only take a sec. Be right back in just a jiffy." He left the office, closed the door behind him, and signaled Marsha Kaye to follow him out of the outer office so he could speak to her in private.

"Listen, need a favor. Call the Sec's office and tell Marge I need to speak to him via phone before the end of the day. Tell her it's important; it will take no more than two minutes, max," he directed. "Now, I want to know what Mr. Dick 'Big Britches' is doing right now and what he does to occupy his time for the next hour and a half. You handle that, all right," he grinned at her. Marsha Kaye nodded in the affirmative and Webb continued. "Also need for you to call Tim Fagan over at the IG's Office and tell him to be on alert to play that hold card for me. He'll know what I'm referring to. Tell him I'll call asap. Now, I'm going to dictate something to you right now. I want you to paraphrase it into memo form and have it ready for me by the time this meeting is over. That work for you?" he asked rhetorically. "My pleasure," she smirked sadistically. Webb knew without a doubt that Marsha Kaye could more likely write the memo better than he could and would enjoy every second of it! "Tell me what you got in mind, chief?" she questioned, grabbing a pad. "Well, for starters, he just served himself up on a silver platter, complete with an apple stuffed in his mouth," he gloated. When Webb finished his dictation, Marsha Kaye had tears in her eyes from hysterical laughter.

Webb reentered the room and could sense a degree of tenseness. To ease things a little bit, he leaned back in his chair, and with only a minimum amount of embellishment, told them about kicking the squirrel's acorn pile and how he had gotten the business from one of the little creatures. They all had a chuckle and then settled in and got down to business. "I would like to hear each of your individual opinions as to what you personally consider to be the current priorities of the unit," Webb threw out. He listened intently to what each of them had to say and scribbled several notes at random intervals.

After each had had their turn, Webb went in another direction. "Phyllis, let's start with the pharmacy component first because I believe it may be the quickest thing to launch right out of the hatch. Seems to me we have tested the formula enough now to put this thing on a fast track. What is your opinion; do you concur?" challenged Webb.

"Well, speaking as a pharmacist first and as a regulatory investigator next, I have to admit I was downright skeptical, maybe even something stronger, about the strategy, because I just couldn't bring myself to believe the detection and correction methodology could be so simple. I mean, I tried to shoot holes in it from every direction; however, after personally testing the model and analyzing the results via case study observations, I have become a disciple and advocate and believe we probably should have gone full-scale before now," she offered.

"Well, welcome to "the dark side," Phyllis," kidded Webb, eliciting several gurgles from the group, with Phyllis joining in. "Actually, it is a KISS (Keep It Simple, Stupid) formula kind of thin," said Webb, a little bit more seriously. Stands to reason if you didn't buy it you, you couldn't have sold it! What you may not realize is that the idea for this method initially came from you," Webb stated matter-of-factly. Phyllis gazed at him dumbfoundedly and finally managed her best intellectual "Huh?"

"Yep!" Webb began. "Not long after I got here, I was listening to you and the policy pharmacist, Roger Presley from the Medicaid Program Development, discussing the various schemes in the Medicaid Prescribed Drug Program that were being perpetrated to elicit aberrant Medicaid payments by enrolled providers. You made the profound statement that if there was a legitimate script from a legitimate physician for a legitimate Medicaid recipient, there were approximately twenty-six things that could happen, and twenty-five of them were bad! You were listing things like merchandising, magic marketing, package size differential, generic substitution, shells, slip and slides, black market purchasing, gray market purchasing, drug diversions etc., etc., etc. At any rate, that little exchange between the two of you planted the germ of an idea in the bowels of my haircut that just kept festering. I kept wondering; if they really were not dispensing the prescriptions and actual pharmaceuticals, then there was a good chance that they were probably not purchasing them at all. Obviously, if that were the case, the pharmacy would not be able to account for the alleged inventory purchases that had been billed to Medicaid. From there, it was just simply a matter of utilizing some queuing theory probability models to establish how much shelf volume inventory ought to be on hand at any given time in order to support or justify their gross yearly billings to Medicaid. We made it even easier by assuming that 100% of all their prescription billings were to Medicaid. The next issue was how we could do a fast-and-dirty without bogging ourselves down in long, drawn-out investigations. That's the birth of the three-drug sample audit. We charge in, guns-a-blazing, and inventory the drug volume on hand for those three specific drugs, and if the inventory on hand is less than what our liberal queuing norms have established, we then request that they provide all invoices for the purchases of these top ten drugs previously billed for Medicaid recipients. At that point, they are in the proverbial 'no man's land;' they can't lie and they can't tell the truth! What do you think they are going to do at that point? I got a real good idea," Webb finished, finally yielding to catch his breath.

"Don't you just love it when a plan comes together?" hissed Phyllis. They all cackled! "So, when do you plan to go live and full court on this, chief?" Phyllis asked frankly.

"Depends on whether or not you have completed that secret squirrel assignment I blessed you with about three weeks ago," Webb baited her.

"That's been put to bed for over a week, but you haven't been around for a report or briefing until now," Phyllis crowed, answering his challenge.

"Great work, Wonder Woman! Let's shoot for the weekend of April 4, then. I really want to hit them hard with their pants down.

How many teams do we have for the invasion?" questioned Webb as he doodled at note to himself.

"We have eleven locked and loaded," responded Phyllis.

"Then it's a definite go! I will get with you individually to go over some logistical issues you are going to get saddled with. Great work! Seriously, I sincerely mean it; you did a super job on this, Phyllis. Thank you! Okay, next victim," declared Webb.

For the first time, Webb noticed both Kathryn and M eyeing him somewhat curiously. "Hmmm, wonder what that's all about?" he pondered to himself.

Charlie was ill at ease, and it was obvious to everyone in the room. At this kickoff, this was the last thing Webb wanted. He felt bad for Charlie, because he knew Charlie realized he was in a catch-22 situation. Webb put his mind in overdrive as to how he could get Charlie to loosen up and not be worried about what Dick was going to think of him, and the anticipated debriefing that would obviously follow this meeting with his boss.

"Charlie, play along with me for a minute, if you will. There is a method to my madness. Just stay with me here," Webb started. "Let me ask you several questions based on your own personal observations and experiences, okay?" Webb nodded toward Charlie, signaling for concurrence.

"Sure! I mean, I assume then you're looking for a sharing of ignorance," Charlie joked, relaxing somewhat. "A little knowledge is a dangerous thing, Charlie," needled Webb. "Let's start the party like this. Assume you were king for a day, well, maybe for more than a day, and I asked you how to get the biggest bang for our buck out of your section; how would you respond?" asked Webb, appearing to be serious.

"Well, boss, that's normally your mantra. You're gonna make me have to regurgitate some of your pulpit rhetoric, and I'm going to feel like I'm preaching to the choir," he mused.

"Go for it," gestured Webb.

"Right after you got here and we implemented the TQM process, the first major insight was that given the history of resource allocations, it was going to be necessary to work smarter if post-payment review actions were to keep pace. After considerable turf battles amongst ourselves, we finally got to the mutual consensus that we needed an ongoing process and continuous assessment of where the biggest return for the investment was."

"Go on; you're doing just great. Keep going," urged Webb.

Charlie was gaining confidence and hitting his stride. "I believe there was pretty much agreement that quantitative strategies that would combine the analyses of multiple providers and emphasize such approaches would be the way to go." Charlie stopped to gather his thoughts.

"As you are more acutely aware than any of us, the TQM process provided the impetus for us to think outside the box, and as a result forced us out of our comfort zones, resulting in the development of several high-tech analytical, statistical, and heuristic models that we now use routinely for the targeting of aberrant practices and the recovery of dollars associated with such practices. I suspect that our early realization, that a qualitative approach to policy compliance violations was not practical, nor cost effective, necessitated the development of quantitative generalized analyses, which lead to large recoveries from multiple groupings," he concluded.

"Damn, Charlie, you go to the head of the class, big fellow," barked Webb. "So, now to the question; if you were king?" pressed Webb.

Charlie appeared thoughtful for a couple of seconds and then began a cautious and deliberate response to Webb's open invitation. "I guess, or rather I suppose, I would probably begin by assessing the current case activity in the process, and based on that assessment, begin to phase out the individualized qualitative investigations and begin diverting those freed-up resources to more of the generalized analyses. Deploying resources in this manner, I suspect, would be far more efficient and would generate far more recoveries, in my humble opinion, for what it's worth," declared Charlie in a tone that surprised everyone in the room, including Charlie.

"Exactly!" fist-pumped Webb. "Hell, Charlie, where you been hiding?" chided Webb in a playful, accusatory fashion. "I'll tell you what; as of right now, you are king, and I'm giving you a top-priority special delegation and assignment. Let me tell you what I want you to do. I want you to go back and look at all generalized analyses that we have conducted over the past twelve to eighteen months. As I recall, I think there were maybe seven of them. Then I want you to take the top thirty providers from each of them, and I want you to forget about who we paid the money to and look at who the actual treating providers were, and give those names to M. There ought to be at least 210 providers, if my math is right. Next, I want you to rerun all of those generalized analyses again, going back a full twenty-four months, and see if we pick up any stragglers. Remember, some of these folks are clever and realize that they have a year to adjust claims or submit a clean claim. We don't want anyone slipping through the cracks. That work for you, Charlie?" Webb asked, somewhat rhetorically.

"Uh, well, I guess," stammered a stunned Charlie. "Where we going to get the army to do this?" Charlie questioned, visibly shaken.

Webb stared at Charlie and deadpanned, "You just told me, Charlie!" Insight and horror immediately appeared on Charlie's face.

"Virginia, you feel somewhat left out," taunted Webb.

"Not just no, but hell no, especially if it's going to be anything resembling what you just bestowed on Charlie," she screeched. Everyone had to laugh out loud, not only at what she said but how she screeched it. Once the laughter subsided, Webb continued.

"At one time, you and I discussed a project you were working on that was kind of an inductive generalized analysis, which I thought was kind of unique but held out a hell of a lot of promise."

"Yeah, I remember you and I went back and forth regarding the fact that these kinds of analyses were not as clean as the deductive type; however, they might be more indicative of potential fraud," stated Virginia.

"For my benefit as well as the rest of the group, let me express my understanding out loud. As I recollect, a deductive generalized analysis is based on a premise like, if I was going to circumvent a Medicaid policy, how would I do it? At that point, we come up with potential ways it could be done, program those scenarios, and run them against claims history. The hits we get are direct, and we write those that participated in such egregious acts and request that they send the money back. You all agree with that crude representation?" Webb asked.

"Yeah, that's pretty much it in a nutshell," agreed Virginia.

"Good, now as I understand, the inductive-type analyses you and I were discussing are not nearly as clean, if I comprehend the way they work. For the most part, these types of analyses end up being a multi-part exercise. We start with an assumption that if we pay for a service, let's say a hypertension prescription or diabetics product, there is an inherent assumption that the individual patients involved must or probably have some history or diagnosis of these conditions. When those a priori conditions are not indicated in previous or earlier claims history, we have to ask a series of additional questions. Does that kind of sum it up in a general sense, Virginia?" Webb finished.

"Yep, pretty much," said Virginia, nodding her head in the affirmative.

"What I want to try as an experiment is simply this," offered Webb. "Let's run the initial programs, but forget about asking the additional questions. Instead, let's take the recipients that are identified, pull up their Medicaid payments profiles, and identify all the individual treating providers associated with these specific recipients. Again, let me emphasize, not the pay-to-providers, and let's send them to M, for her database. That make any sense at all to you?" questioned Webb.

"Well, that's sort of out of left field, but yeah, I think I see where you might be heading with this. You are taking a real shortcut here, but hey, why not; we ain't got nothing to lose. I say let's give it a whirl," conceded Virginia.

"Fine, then we all have our marching orders," declared Webb.

"Whoa, hold on just a minute," chimed in Charlie, "Curiosity killed the cat, boss, but I don't see us generating any recoveries off this kind of M.O., and our whole MPI measuring stick for zero-based budgeting growth strategy is based on dollars per investigator, so how we gonna justify this approach?" Charlie asked somewhat apprehensively.

"Charlie, if I gave you that answer, I'd probably have to kill you," Webb responded with a grin. "Tell you what; we are going to get the money, but we are going to calculate the amount via cost avoidance rather than by collections. If my hunch is correct, we are going to be so effective that no one is probably even going to believe us," Webb declared.

"A little history lesson for your entertainment, folks. During the Civil War, as the story goes, the Southern guerrilla bands apparently, at some point, became extremely adept at kidnapping Union generals and stealing Northern army horses. It was reported that President Lincoln was said to remark that he was far more upset about the horse stealing than the loss of his generals. He claimed he could always make new generals, but he couldn't replace the horses. I opine that the treating physician is the hammer that drives the nail. These solicitation scams can't work for the provision of any medically necessary services without a Medicaid-enrolled treating provider involved and attached to a pay-to-provider. There are only so many physicians to go around. If you stop a treating physician, there is no telling how many enrolled pay-to-providers we stymie and render sterile," Webb finished.

"That's absolutely fucking brilliant!" came a spontaneous outburst at the end of the table. Everyone turned to the source of this rapturous eruption, which came from the surprising form of Kathryn. With a simple shoulder shrug and up-faced palms, she said, "Well, hell, it was, is, whatever!" she emphasized by the tone in her voice and the unapologetic expression on her face.

Webb flashed a big grin in her direction and declared, "Now, hold on, Kat. We ain't walking on water here yet, but thanks for the vote of confidence. At any rate, you go to the head of the bonus list for my approval."

"Hell, in that case, I'd say it was double-fucking Nobel Prize fucking brilliant!" screeched Virginia. Everyone absolutely howled without restraint.

"Now that the fun stuff is over, let's get down to business," Webb said. They all gave him a bewildering glare. Webb punched the intercom and simply said, "Ready."

Immediately the door opened, and Marsha Kaye entered with fresh coffee and an assortment of goodies from Tasty Pastry, and the mood in the room became significantly more relaxed.

For the next fifteen minutes or so, the group chit-chatted about the logistics of several assignments and issues, and Webb had the definite impression that the group was energized. Eventually, he asked Phyllis if she could meet with him one-on-one first thing the day after tomorrow to deal with some specific logistical details related to her upcoming task force mission. Finally, he cornered both Charlie and Virginia together and asked them to go back to their offices, not speak to anyone, discreetly gather their stuff, and leave for the day. "If anyone and I do mean anyone asks or tries to debrief you on what transpired in this meeting, simply tell them you are on a very unique and special assignment from yours truly, and you are already late for a meeting," Webb instructed them. Both looked puzzled, but nodded agreement. Webb smiled knowingly at both of them and instantaneously witnessed an epiphany explode inside Virginia's intellect.

After the group finally dispersed, Webb left his office immediately and checked with Marsha Kaye on his requested Sec's call and the prized memo. She handed him the memo to review and indicated that the Sec had given instructions to be interrupted for any call from him. Tim Fagan said he is in launch mode. Webb glanced at the memo, smiled slyly, and blueprinted in detail, "Precious, my dear, you are about to participate in a form of bureaucratic vigilantism that is akin to a cousin of a *"lateral arabesque,"* as depicted in the satirical office management Bible, *The Peter Principle*, written by Lawrence J. Peter. Now, this is exactly what I want you to do. I am leaving the office for the rest of the day and will not be here at all tomorrow, but as usual, you know how to reach me if you need me." At that, Webb briefly returned to his office, made two calls lasting no more than three minutes each, grabbed his blazer, and exited the premises, casting a final appreciative acknowledgement in Marsha Kaye's direction.

Unbeknownst to Webb Espy and an unknown adversary at this point, the events, decisions, and strategies set forth in this meeting, on this day, were historic in the sense that numerous individual lives were about to be impacted and changed forever.

Later that evening, after a hearty bowl of chili over rice, Webb settled in for a relaxing evening of light reading and a Braves game with an expensive glass of tawny port. Simultaneously, 460 miles south, Marcus Manasa was enjoying a cold draft brew and a legitimate, illegal as it might be, Cuban cigar at a Miami Marlins' game in a breezy and humid Miami night. The two men had no idea they were on a collision course. Webb Espy had not the faintest idea of what he was about to stumble into based on the brazen innovative strategies he had unleashed on this day, and Marcus Manasa, although he knew of the existence of Webb Espy, had no idea of who he was dealing with.

22

March 16 and 17, 1993

Tallahassee, Florida

Dick Andrews was uneasy, which was an unusual state of mind in his traditional world. He was accustomed to making others uneasy and rarely found himself the recipient of such feelings. Things had not gone the way he had anticipated the previous day. Neither of his underlings had reported back to him and had left the premises without contact or fanfare of any kind. His bureaucratic gamesmanship antics to send a message to Bureau Chief Webb Espy instead had left him isolated and strategically helpless. He realized now that he had not analyzed the situation as carefully as he thought and, in all likelihood, had overplayed his hand.

Webb Espy represented an enigma to Dick, the kind of individual who was foreign to his experiences and bureaucratic stereotypes. His feelings about the man since their initial meeting ranged widely from outright admiration to competitive jealously. Dick's mind was racing as he drove to his office, thinking about how he might do damage control if things had really gone south. Try as he might, he was coming up empty. In most instances, he had contingency plans for everything.

He entered the building and noted that he was the first one to arrive in his section. He was extremely early, which in itself was unusual, but the anxiety had put him in high gear, and he was well ahead of his usual daily schedule. Dick Andrews was characteristically not an anxious person by any definition or historical precedent! Today, however, was uncharacteristically unique.

As he entered his office and hurriedly walked around his desk, he noticed it immediately; a standard #10 white envelope with the typed name "Dick Andrews" had been deposited in his chair. At this point, the anxiety simply overwhelmed him, and he vomited uncontrollably into his wastepaper basket. It was several moments before he could muster the energy or the courage to open the envelope. His hands began to shake as he eventually mustered the courage to claim entry to the envelope and began to devour its contents. The interoffice memorandum read as follows:

MEMORANDUM
DATE: MARCH 15, 1993
FROM: WEBB ESPY
TO: DICK ANDREWS
SUBJECT: SPECIAL ASSIGNMENT

By request of the Secretary of DHRS David Baswell, you are immediately reassigned work responsibilities in order to conduct a special assignment he has personally initiated related to the incidence of fraud and abuse associated with the Medicaid program within the State of Florida. As a result of your selection, you are henceforth relieved of all other previously delegated administrative, work-related duties, and responsibilities effective

May 30, 1992. You will report to Building 1, first floor, Room 118, at 8:00 am on May 31, where an office has already been set up for your personal use for the duration of this assignment. According to the Secretary, you have been specifically selected for the assignment based on your skills and experiences, as well as your proven historical record of analytical contributions for many years. This assignment requires initiative, creative independent modeling, and heuristic approaches in order to achieve the desired results. In my personal judgment, the Secretary could not have made a better choice.

I am not excited in the least about this reassignment; however, I understand the Secretary's needs related to this project. I wish you success. You are to contact Marge in the Secretary's Executive Staff Office for logistical support requirements.

Dick's hands were still shaking, but it was no longer from anxiety; it was from pure unadulterated rage! Most of the rage, however, was self-directed. "How could I have allowed myself to be so fucking arrogant and stupid?" he chided and cursed himself. At that, he catapulted himself out of his chair and charged down the hall toward Espy's office like a rhinoceros that had just been nudged unpleasantly in the gonads. Webb Espy's office was dark, and so was the outer office. Webb, normally the early bird, was not there, and Marsha Kaye had obviously not arrived on the premises as yet. He elected not to add insult to injury by making a spectacle of himself by just sitting there and waiting for someone to arrive. Realizing he was alone, he immediately turned on his heels and retreated to the solitude of his own office, which all of a sudden dawned on him, was no longer his office. That specific insight spawned a series of additional revelations that necessitated another trip to the wastepaper basket.

Marsha Kaye had premeditatedly decided to arrive fashionably late. She had a pretty good idea what was waiting for her, and she was determined to play her role to the hilt in Webb's little choreographed subterfuge. When she finally sauntered into the office, she went about her morning routine as she would on any ordinary day. She was making coffee when she felt his presence before he actually appeared.

"What time do you expect him?" asked Dick Andrews without even so much as a good morning greeting.

"Well, good morning, Mr. Andrews," Marsha Kaye replied with respectful formality. Her deferential demeanor and pretentious formality grated on him to his core, but outwardly he attempted to demonstrate civility and calmness.

"I thought you were meeting with Secretary Baswell first thing this morning?" suggested Marsha Kaye innocently.

"What do you mean?" asked Dick with a puzzled expression.

"Well, apparently, Secretary Baswell was supposed to go down first thing this morning to your new office and personally greet you and officially give you his formal marching orders," she replied with an Oscar-winning performance. Dick Andrews almost literally shit in his pants! Before he could say another word, she continued.

"As for Dr. Espy, I'm not sure if he will be in at all today. He had an unanticipated meeting down at the Capitol, and I know he also has a doctor's appointment around two this afternoon. He mentioned that he might not make it back to the office today. I feel sure he will check in with me, and when he does, I'll let him know that you would like to have a little time with him. I will call you at your new phone and let you know the first time it is convenient. Is there anything else I can assist you with this morning, Mr. Andrews? Would you like for me to call Marge at the Secretary's office and let her know that you had a previous obligation this morning and were unaware that the Secretary had plans to greet you?" Marsha Kaye requested, pursing her lips and arching her eyebrows.

"No, that won't be necessary. Instead, if you don't mind, please let her know that I am ill. Please be kind enough to call me at home when you speak with Dr. Espy." Dick requested, masking deflation.

"Why, of course, Mr. Andrews. I certainly hope you get to feeling better very soon," she drawled in a way that made Dick wonder if he had just been a victim of delicately delivered sarcasm.

The call from Marsha Kaye came at 4:30 P.M., just as Webb had previously instructed. Dick answered it on the first ring. After asking as to his health, she gave him the rehearsed opportunity to meet with the chief the next day at 5:00 P.M. due to the fact that he had a full schedule outside the office the following day but would make a special trip to the office to meet with Dick if that was convenient. With not much of another option available, Dick agreed, thanked her, and said goodbye.

Dick arrived at Webb's office at 4:50 P.M. He had spent another day at home after calling Marge in the Secretary's office to let her know he was suffering some form of stomach virus. Immediately upon arrival, Marsha Kaye informed Dick that Webb had just phoned and was caught up in traffic, but should be there shortly. Marsha Kaye asked if there was anything she could get for him before she left for the day and assured him that he should not have to wait very long. Dick thanked her, and she left him alone in a chair just outside Webb's office.

After waiting for about ten minutes, Dick heard the door open and immediately following, footsteps coming down the hall toward the office. Dick, for the first time in his professional life, had absolutely no real strategy or contingency plan for this situation and immediately suffered an anxiety attack. Webb entered the door, took one look at him, and realized what was happening, as well as why. He feigned concern, but held no sympathy or pity whatsoever for the man. Dick was like a turtle that had lost his shell and was ripe for the picking. Webb had already outlined in his mind two ways of dealing with Dick in this meeting, and now, seeing Dick in his current state, decided on the overwhelming one.

Taking the offensive, Webb did not give Dick a chance to speak. "Come on in here and have a seat," ordered Webb, as if Dick was a puppy in training, gesturing to a lowboy rocking chair directly in front of his desk.

As he was moving to the other side of his desk, Webb began his monologue. "Dick, just what in the hell are you doing here? I mean, really; you got nothing to say because you got nothing to say. Now, I could play out this little charade, claim complete innocence, plead ignorant or whatever, but I'm just not going to do that. I still have enough respect for your intellect to know that you know better.

We were probably never destined to be close friends, but I did grossly miscalculate that we could not be appreciative peers. For the life of me, I don't have a clue as to what you intended to prove by that disrespectful bit of grandstanding you pulled the other day, but it was insubordinate as hell, and as you can see, it accomplished one thing in particular; it pissed me off!" Webb paused, still standing and towering over a defenseless prey. "Let me tell you something else. Without knowing anything about me whatsoever, you resented my appointment to this job from the very first day I stepped into this office. You've attempted to sabotage several of my initiatives, and I let it go. The real irony here is that I was really excited to learn that I was going to have an opportunity to work with you. Your reputation preceded you, and I knew you were an extremely skilled and talented professional with innovative ideas. However, I found very quickly that you weren't a team player, that you stifled the initiative of your staff, and you took credit for things others had done. Why hell, you even tried to take credit for the pharmacy audit "didn't buy it, couldn't sell it," and we both know where that came from! Your exile was not without considerable thought." Webb paused momentarily.

Thinking out loud, he continued. "You may not have realized it up to this point, but there is a silver lining, and a real opportunity, in what you have been charged with in your special assignment. I'll let you figure that one out for yourself, and I have the utmost confidence that you will. That's all I got to say about that. Assuming you don't have anything else on your mind at the present, I need to be somewhere. You can let yourself out. Please remember to turn out the light," Webb concluded as he headed for the door. A speechless Dick Andrews remained seated in stunned silence for several seconds after Webb was out of the building.

Eventually, Dick mustered the energy to attempt an exit. As he began to rise from his chair, he felt the presence of another life force in close proximity. Standing in the doorway was Tim

171

Fagan from the Office of the Inspector General. Dick had no idea how long he had been standing there but was completely startled to discover that he was not alone. Before he could utter a word, his thoughts were interrupted by Tim.

"Mr. Andrews, I believe you know me. My name is Tim Fagan, and I am an investigator with the Office of the Inspector General. I need to speak with you regarding some potentially serious discrepancies with your time sheets going back over the past several months." And that is when Dick Andrews' day went from very bad to worse!

23

March 17, 1993

Tallahassee, Florida

It was 8:00 A.M.; Webb had already been in his office for forty-five minutes catching up on in-basket materials since he had been out the entire previous day. He heard Marsha Kaye greet Phyllis Newberry when she entered the outer office. Marsha Kaye had already briefed him on the MPI highlights of what had transpired during his absence, which was practically uneventful except for several persistent attempts by Dick Andrews to solicit an audience with him at his earliest convenience. As rehearsed, Marsha Kaye promised in earnest that she would convey his request to Webb, but relayed to him with the strictest pretense of confidentiality that she had gained somewhat of a definite impression that Secretary Baswell had been most adamant about this specific assignment, who he wanted to do it, and how he wanted it handled. According to Marsha Kaye, Dick's demeanor was a pitiful spectacle, but confessed that in her humble opinion, he had earned every bit of it all by his little old self. Marsha Kaye was never short on opinions!

Webb finished the last item in his in-basket and used his best bass intercom to invite Phyllis to join him. Webb genuinely liked just about everything about his lead pharmacist. She was intelligent, highly motivated, a natural leader, had a great sense of humor, and possessed an insatiable curiosity for things in the regulatory arena beyond just pharmacy issues. In his opinion, she was balanced in almost every aspect of both her professional and personal life. Phyllis had grown up as a pharmacist's daughter in a small community just outside Jacksonville, Florida, and spent many hours for many years working with her dad in their family business. In Webb's opinion, she probably knew more about how to run a pharmacy when she entered pharmacy school than most others did when they graduated. In addition, she had gained experience in a hospital pharmacy, had worked for a couple of years for a large pharmaceutical marketing firm, and just prior to her employment with Medicaid Program Integrity, had worked as a legislative liaison for the Florida Pharmacy Association. Phyllis was married with two young sons and was the prototype of a soccer mom. Phyllis demonstrated an excellent work ethic, an open mind, and a knack for improvising. Webb had complete confidence in her for the task at hand.

After initial greetings and small talk, Webb's demeanor became unmistakably businesslike, and he proceeded to provide specific information related to the upcoming "MPI South Florida Pharmacy Invasion."

Webb began, "Phyllis, as you are aware, what we are about to do is unprecedented. You obviously know the targets because you selected them. We have eleven teams, so if we do what we anticipate, we will hit at least sixty-six priority pharmacies in two days. We know that all of these targeted pharmacies operate seven days a week, so weekend closures should not represent a problem for our teams. As I understand it, you have already set up the order for each team, starting with the farthest away and working back, so in that way, if some teams finish ahead of schedule, they can move on toward their secondary targets. Are you on one the teams?"

"Absolutely," Phyllis replied categorically.

"Good, I'm glad, I was hoping you might want to lead the charge," said Webb.

"Wild horses or something like that," snickered Phyllis. "As a matter of fact, I have one in my personal crosshairs that I have been itching to have a go at for some time. The name is Victor's Farmacia, owned by a gentleman named Victor Hernandez. You'll note that I used the term "gentleman" rather loosely. He's managed to survive several of the historical traditional audits. The guy has impeccable prescription records and is a real smooth character. There is no question in my mind that he runs a Medicaid pill mill! I can't wait to see what happens when we serve up this curveball," she smirked.

"I almost feel sorry for him; I said, almost," Webb indicated with a straight face that turned into a huge merciless smile. "Okay, Friday afternoon, promptly at 6:30, have the teams report to the private charter terminal at the Tallahassee airport. Have you ever flown out of there?" questioned Webb.

"No, but everybody knows where it is; no problem," Phyllis responded.

"Good. When you land in Miami, you will be shuttled to Avis Preferred, and eleven rental cars will already be waiting for each team. You just need to find your name on the Priority Club board and then go directly to the assigned cars; the keys should already be in them."

"Yeah, know the drill; done it many times," Phyllis confirmed.

"From there, drive a short distance, practically around the corner, to the Embassy Suites, and there will be twenty-two rooms reserved and prepaid for each individual team member. As you know, they serve a full "ruin your day" complimentary breakfast for the big boys."

"Hell, it ain't just for big boys; have you ever seen me chow down, boss?" she challenged. "No, I must have missed that, but tell you what; I challenge you to a high noon buffet duel once you return."

"You're on, boss-man! May not win, but I guarantee I can compete. I may need a handicap, however, 'cause I hear that some of your indulging exploits they tell stories about at night around the campfires," she laughed.

"Okay, we got a date, girlfriend. Now, listen, I've had packages prepared for each team. Included in each are special IDs for each investigator, letters of introduction, assigned authority for these audits, and generous per diem vouchers for each that should cover at least six meals if necessary. There are also statutory references and specific authority for these audits and consequences for denying access to information requested by Program Integrity auditors. There are also several potential scenarios that the teams might encounter and specific contingency protocols to employ should any of these situations emerge. Medicaid field office directors in Dade and Broward have been alerted to contact me directly if they start getting any heat from anyone. I really don't anticipate that is going to happen, but it never hurts to be prepared," Webb concluded. "Oh, I almost forgot; payments for these OPS services are also in the packages. That's about all I got, Phyllis; you got any questions?" he asked.

"No, I believe you wrapped it all up with a neat little bow, boss. Well, wait a minute; maybe just one?" confessed Phyllis.

"Let's hear it, then," offered Webb.

"Will you please share with me just how we are financing this little mission?" she asked frankly.

"Phyllis, I believe that might fall under the category of "need-to-know," but in deference to your lack of military protocols, let me just say that I obtained a substantial private grant for this specific endeavor. That satisfy your curiosity for the time being?" Webb finished.

"I believe I catch your drift," Phyllis acquiesced with an approving nod.

"Well, in that case, Admiral Phyllis, I guess it's good hunting!" Webb said, smiling.

"Aye-aye, chief," she replied, matching his grin.

24

The Three Amigas

March 22, 1993 Tallahassee, Florida

It had been three days since Dick Andrews had been sentenced to exile in the basement cubicle of Building I. Due to some combination of morbid curiosity and self-satisfaction, Webb sought a personal glimpse of the dungeon and its new inhabitant. Under the guise of one of his patented scrounge missions, he made the rounds and eventually made a detour that granted a peep at his previous nemesis and his new digs. Satisfied that things were as they should be and that the punishment fit the crime, Webb began a retreat to the MPI sanctuary, back to the opposite side of the pond.

As he entered his office suite, Marsha Kaye greeted him flippantly. "Well, there you are. I thought you might show up here shortly. You have visitors. You didn't have anything on your calendar, so I suggested they just go on in and make themselves at home. They indicated some urgency, so I didn't believe you would mind," she finished off-handedly while stuffing some large manila envelopes.

"In-house or out-house?" he questioned.

"Webb, how in the hell could you possibly ask me such an asinine question? You know dang good and well that you have an open-door policy for staff. Do you believe it conceivable that I would ever allow anyone external to MPI to ever grace your office without your presence?" she protested with a provoked rebuke.

"Yeah, I know; just testing you. Don't want you going complacent on me. Need to keep you on your toes, you know," he toyed with her pretentiously.

"Webb Espy, I'm in no mood for your frivolity at the moment, and please just denote the sprig of mistletoe attached to my coattail, if you would be so kind," she emphasized with mock annoyance.

"I would be more than pleased to do so," he laughed as he entered his office.

As he stepped inside the doorway, he was a little surprised at the unique trio that had amassed to meet with him. The first thought that came into his mind was there were enough brains in his office at the present moment to give Thomas Jefferson a run. The little group consisted of M, Phyllis Newberry, and Kathryn Armstrong. "Well now, what is this? If it is some kind of *coup de tat*, I surrender and ask for terms," he bowed theatrically.

The group smiled accordingly at his playful gesture, but he immediately sensed that there were serious motives for this particular assembly.

"Okay, let's get serious. I know you didn't gather together for my amusement, although I know there is at least one legitimate practical joker amongst you," he stated while casting a discerning eye in Katheryn's direction. She had to laugh. It somewhat surprised Webb that Kathryn was apparently going to assume the designated spokesperson role for the group, but then just as suddenly, he realized that it more or less had to be that way.

"Boss, obviously we would not corner you like this if we did not believe there was a real serious reason to do so," Kathryn began.

"I am aware of that, and you have my undivided attention. Let's hear what you got."

"For the past several SURS runs, I've noticed a pharmacy provider named Fernando's in South Broward that flies just under the radar. Never seems to hit the outliers and therefore just falls back into the proverbial queue every run. I went back and checked, and this has been happening for several years now. He's punched Medicaid's ticket pretty substantially for some time now. At any rate, call it what you will, curiosity, intuition, or whatever; for motives unknown, I decided, based on what I picked up at the meeting with Phyllis the other day, that this might be an interesting candidate for her little task force invasion. I suspected it was probably not going to meet the criteria for a priority target unless there was something else in play. For some reason I just had a hunch, exercised a little initiative, and expanded my due diligence somewhat." She paused.

Webb, well cognizant of Kathryn's due diligence capabilities, braced himself for what he had a feeling was coming. He didn't have to wait long.

"Well, boss, I came up with several phone numbers and addresses, and don't even ask me where they came from, 'cause I'll lie, and you really don't want to know. I took the liberty of asking M if she would run them through 'The Thing.' In her defense, she was a reluctant participant up until the point that my hammerlock rendered her senseless."

Webb could not help himself and laughed out loud. "Damn Kathryn, get to the punchline; you're killing me here."

"Well, when the results came back, it provided a number of additional rabbit holes to go down. You know what; if you turn over enough rocks, you eventually find a snake or two. I believe we found three of them," she hesitated briefly.

"And? Wait, are you telling me you went bream fishing and caught a whale?"

"Yep, I believe that's a pretty good analogy," chimed in Phyllis. "Hold on to your ass for this," she said with a straight face.

"Okay, Kat, it's your show. Show your hand," Webb said seriously.

"I have no doubt that we have reliable and verifiable evidence that the District 10 Administrator, the District 10 IG, and a well-known state senator are dirty and are tied directly to Fernando's Pharmacy," she stated matter-of-factly.

Webb was stunned and was aware that it showed. He glared at each of them in turn and could tell by their expressions that they understood the seriousness of these revelations and accusations. In due course, he found his voice somehow. "I guess I don't need to tell you that what you have unearthed, if accurate, has extremely complicated consequences and tentacles that reach far beyond our limited perspectives. I can tell you one thing; I know somebody in particular that is not going to be pleased with this news, and unfortunately, I'm afraid I'm going to have to be the one to share it with him," Webb paused, shaking his head in resignation, "Yeah, none of us envy you, but that's why you make the big bucks," Phyllis interjected, "But let's move on for a moment. I assume, based on this new information, that you might want us to put Fernando's on the target list. I can actually do this pretty easily since I was going to have to substitute one anyway, due to the fact that we have learned that one of the providers on the list is no longer in business," she finished.

"Absolutely; put your strongest team on them for the first day. Not you, however; I want you to stay on Victor's."

"You got it, boss," Phyllis replied.

"Kathryn, I am more than to assume that you got this nailed down tighter than Dick's hatband, correct?"

"Yes, sir! I got the link analysis all gussied up, to the point that a first-grader could present it with confidence. Also got specific source documents, property tax records, and cross-referenced names, addresses, and linked phone numbers. Everything is in this tabbed binder," she confirmed as she held up a black loose-leaf binder.

"Now, I'm assuming that nobody outside this room knows anything about this except possibly Marsha Kaye, 'cause she knows everything that goes on around here anyway." He was sure he heard a definite cough in the outer office in reference to his remark and just shook his head. "For now, I want to make sure we all keep it that way. There are a number of ways to play this, but that's not going to be my call. I have a hunch which way the Sec might want to go, but due to some of the potential political ramifications, he might have some different ideas about which route he wants to take. One thing I can guarantee; there are several somebodies that ain't gonna be happy once the dust settles on this thing," Webb finished.

M had been sitting silently for the duration, taking everything in. She had not said a word, but her mind had been in "warp drive!" "Boss, this little exercise has been insightful. I've got an idea I believe you may eventually learn to love," she threw out thoughtfully. When M came forth with such a declaration, she had Webb's immediate attention.

"Dang, M, I was beginning to think you weren't paying attention. Now I can see smoke coming out of your ears. What's on your mind?" Webb proclaimed half-seriously.

"Will you purchase LexisNexis for me, uh, us, I mean," she asked a little sheepishly. Out of the corner of his eye, Webb caught a glimpse of Kathryn tilting her head back and rolling her eyes.

"Hmmm, well, let's see here. I have no doubt that you probably could put something like that to good use, and I'm not even going to ask what you're scheming, but I got to say, I suspect that's a pretty hefty ticket item right up front, and I would also assume there are ongoing fees associated with such a product. What makes you think we can afford this thing because you know we don't have any budget for something like this," he challenged playfully.

"Cause Kathryn said you could afford it," M answered gleefully. Webb could see Kathryn cringe, close her eyes tightly, and start shaking her head slowly.

"Well, I guess that settles that; doesn't it? You know, the one thing that gives me more pleasure than anything else about this job is being surrounded by a whole bunch of people that are a hell of a lot smarter than I am, are not afraid to exercise initiative, and make me look considerably better than I actually am," he finished, making direct eye contact with each of them. "Now if you will excuse me, ladies, I need to go witness a temper tantrum."

25

March 22, 1993
(Later The Same Day)

Tallahassee, Florida

Marsha Kaye phoned Marge in the Sec's office and inquired as to David's earliest availability related to a matter of extreme urgency. That little window of opportunity provided Webb just enough time to be briefed by Kat and go over the link analysis visual aid that had been proffered earlier. Webb agreed overall with the initial assessment that it was pretty much self-explanatory and, for all practical purposes, bulletproof. Next, he asked Kat and M to create a cheat sheet for his little chat with the Sec.

Webb considered his preparations more than adequate for the task at hand and felt confident that he was locked and loaded as he made his way around the pond toward David's office. This might go several ways, he thought to himself.

Webb entered the Sec's office suite, and Marge was on the phone. She gestured for him to go on in, even though the door to David's office was closed. Webb knocked lightly, waited a respectful perfunctory four seconds, opened the door, and entered. David was on the phone, but immediately signaled with wide-sweeping arm motions for Webb to come on in and make

185

himself comfortable. Webb was almost tempted to plop down in David's special fat chair as a joke, which would provoke just enough disrespect that would most certainly goad his good friend ever so slightly. In deference to his sense of humor, Webb selected another chair and waited for David to finish his call.

Shortly, David finished his call, made a few quick scribbles, and got up from his desk and headed in Webb's direction. It was always interesting and slightly humorous, watching and listening to David remove himself from a seated position. First of all, it took significant effort, which was a grunting noise accompanied by the sounds of athletic injuries and the calendar that was a combination of moans, groans, and inaudible muttering of colorful expletives.

"What the hell you doing here?" David barked as he found the sanctuary of his famous fat chair.

"Wish I could say I was just in the neighborhood and decided it might be nice for a chit-chat," Webb responded a little despondently.

"Can't be all that bad; tell old David all about it. He'll make you feel all better," his friend offered in jest.

"Ah, what the hell, I'm just gonna to cut to the chase. Unfortunately, you got some dirty laundry, and it's fixing to get hung out to dry. I am sure the whole thing has implications far beyond my limited scope of the political landscape, but I feel sure there are consequences and ramifications that you will seize on immediately," Webb paused briefly, collecting his thoughts.

"Proceed, my friend; you have succeeded in both capturing my undivided attention and piquing my curiosity," David said seriously.

"Okay, for starters, several members of my staff conducted a preliminary inquiry on a pharmacy provider in Broward county. The Medicaid provider is named Fernando's Pharmacy, and it has been in business for a number of years. It is a relatively large provider for a mom-and-pop type operation, and they have dipped into the Medicaid coffers for a pretty hefty sum over the past few years. They've been audited over the years and had a few minor paybacks, but nothing really big that we could make stick. We knew they were dirty, but up until now, we had to let them slide like all the other Micci pharmacy players. That, as you are aware, is going to change with our new innovative auditing strategy. Anyway, based on the initial results, my little elves decided to dig a little deeper and discovered a number of unusual things. First and foremost, it ain't Fernando that owns the lion's share of the pharmacy." Webb let it sink in.

"Ohh holy hell, something tells me I'm not gonna like this next part," David emphasized dogmatically.

"'Spect you're right, but let's try this. What would you say if I told you the District 10 Administrator and his District IG were two of the primary owners and that, for a kicker, State Senator Raymond Harris is the other," Webb laid out.

"You know damn well what I'd say; shit, shit, shit!" David bellowed as he collapsed back into the solace of the womb and security of the fat chair. He just sat there with his eyes closed for an unusually long time period, not saying a word.

To avoid the awkwardness of the silence, Webb decided to add a little more additional detail. "David, Here's the other—"

"Whoa, hold on a minute," David interrupted. "I'm processing some things here that I got to go through."

Webb had seen David in this state previously, and he wondered what electroencephalograph readings would look like with the things going on in David's head currently.

Webb was sitting there, waiting for David to emerge from his self-imposed stupor, when suddenly David returned to this world.

"Now, what was that you were about to say when I pulled down the blinds?" he spoke calmly.

Webb was absolutely amazed at how calm and relaxed David now appeared. "All I got to say is that must have been one healthy respite. Need something like that for me on occasion," Webb suggested, half in jest, and then continued. "What I was going to say is, there's no telling how many laws have been broken, to say nothing of the ethics violations. Let's also not forget that they are all probably guilty of Medicaid fraud as well. There are several questions of jurisdiction here, but I strongly recommend that we don't go the Medicaid Fraud Control Unit route." Webb stopped to organize his thoughts.

"Not even on my crumb list," David interjected with unconcealed prejudice.

"Now, I was going to let you in on this in a couple of days, but this revelation preempted my plans. So, I'll just go ahead and do it now. As you are aware, I have previously discussed with you the new pharmacy audit methodology we've been testing for a while now. Well, it's ready to go; we are set to launch Saturday week. We already have Fernando's targeted. I realize you have some personnel actions that need to go into the queue, but I believe you might want to wait to pull the trigger on that until after we conduct the audit. Knowing you as I do, I suspect there are some internal issues and human resource things that need to be addressed before we go halfcocked on this thing, anyway. On that note, let me suggest that since the IG's office is involved, I would not use the normal channels and solicit their official involvement. If I were walking in your moccasins at the present, I believe I would play this real close to the vest and limit information to as few people as possible," Webb concluded.

"Yeah, point well taken," David said, nodding his head affirmatively.

"How about this? Why don't we come up with a secret squirrel assignment for Tim Fagan from the IG's office, directly under your wing. Then you assign him to my little task force for the duration. There is precedent for this kind of unique approach," Webb suggested somewhat ardently.

"No problem; I can go with that, but why specifically Tim Fagan? I know him, and I also know he has been involved and solved some real complicated investigations over his career," David asked frankly.

"Because he has as much integrity as you do, has the pugnaciousness to see this through, is thorough to a fault, and is someone that I trust without reservation," Webb advised seriously.

"Consider it done, then. I'll call him down for a little chat in a few minutes, set things in motion, get a letter of delegation for special assignment, and send him over to you for his initial orientation," David said with resolution. "Now, I'll give some thought to the jurisdictional issues, but for now, you just do your thing, and we will head down that road a little later."

"Would you like to see the visual aid that was prepared for your perusal since I was pretty sure you wouldn't get it on the first try?" Webb said jokingly.

"That might not be such a bad idea, 'cause I've just taken everything you've told me *carte blanche* up to this point. Let me see that damn thing." David began pouring over the link tree, and it was obvious to Webb from his facial gestures that he was impressed. Finally, he looked up and asked, "Who put this thing together? This is pretty incredible."

"You ain't gonna believe it, and I guess in some ways, I owe my good fortune to you for this diamond-in-the-rough hire. This is Kathryn Armstrong's creation. Actually, she's the one that initiated this little search-and-destroy mission and was ultimately the one that sniffed it out, with a little help from M," Webb confided supportively.

A smile began to emerge on David's face, and he began shaking his head as if he were congratulating himself. "Well, I'll be damned; I knew I should have a head hunter for a Fortune 500! Please tell her I said really great work and bring her along with the team over here to see me once we get this thing put to bed," David said with a sense of pride and legitimate sincerity.

"Did I tell you about the practical joke she played on me? Man, she got me good; but later, that's a good Porky's story," Webb said, laughing at the memory.

"Can't wait to hear it," David said, obviously amused.

"At any rate, I will certainly relay your appreciation. Now, one more final thing. This is no joke. Seriously, I mean it. I want you to repeat verbatim after me the following statement," Webb said.

"What the hell are you trying to pull? I ain't gonna repeat nothing until I know what it is, you crazy son of a bitch."

Webb had to laugh, but said, "David, you got to trust me on this; seriously! It's simple, just repeat after me." Webb stated very slowly and specifically: "I am aware of a Program Integrity pharmacy audit in South Florida that is scheduled to occur the weekend of July 21, 1993, and this audit has been personally sanctioned."

David glared at Webb like he was insane, but finally acquiesced and regurgitated the statement in its entirety. "Is that all? Am I allowed to comprehend the purpose?" David questioned with sarcastic curiosity.

"Not just yet. Go over to your desk, grab one of the infamous daily note pads, and write it down like you do everything else," Webb instructed in earnest and then continued. "I can almost guarantee you that in the not-so-distant future, you are going to be asked about these audits and some of the consequences related to them. I want you to be able to have some bullets in your gun as well as an armor-piercing shield. Ultimately, I suspect you will thank me because you too will be able to state unequivocally that you were aware of this audit and personally sanctioned it."

"Hmmm, okay, I think I see what you're attempting to convey. Hell yeah, I'm with you. Thanks; you were ahead of me on this one. Now, talking about bullets; you probably don't realize it, but you already handed me a couple of the silver variety," he concluded, laughing out loud.

"I got to say, you took this considerably better than I ever would have anticipated," Webb remarked.

"Webb, you got to remember I deal with personnel issues every day, albeit not at this level or variety. Routine, my friend; just another day at the office. The trick is how to turn a liability into an asset, and in this situation, and I have a hunch if I play the cards right, I just may be able to pull it off in spades," he concluded with a wicked smile, intended specifically for Webb's benefit.

As Webb headed back to his office, he replayed the meeting several times. It had really gone better than he had anticipated. He had been a little worried that David might become explosive and exhibit one of his patented temper tantrums. For all practical purposes, the Sec had just given him a blank check to do what needed to be done. David had been "Mr. Cool."

26

Tallahassee to Miami and Return

April 4 through 6, 1993

Phyllis and her elite team of pharmacy auditors arrived in Miami on Friday evening around 7:40 P.M., took the AVIS shuttle to the rental lot, and secured the premium full-sized vehicles that were waiting for them. Once Phyllis confirmed everyone had been taken care of, the little troupe caravanned the short distance to the Embassy Suites hotel. After checking in, the group congregated for happy hour in the bar area before leaving for dinner. Two reserved hotel shuttle vans chauffeured them to Versailles in Little Havana for dinner. They were back at the hotel well before 11:00 P.M.

The group reconvened after breakfast the following morning, rehearsed protocols, and synchronized their watches. The teams then left for their previously designated staging areas. Each team was scheduled to enter their primary target pharmacy at precisely 10:00 A.M.

At the appointed time, each team entered the pharmacies, showed IDs, presented the pharmacist or pharmacy owner MPI business cards along with letters of authority for the audit, and indicated to each provider that this was the preliminary front-end audit component, which should be completed in a relatively brief period of time. They also invited the pharmacist to assist them if they chose to do so. A number of the pharmacists working Saturdays were fill-in part-time employees and were totally unprepared for their unexpected visitors. Their anxiety was obvious. Even the seasoned pharmacists were perplexed when the auditors showed no interest in prescription files or point-of-sale records.

Armed initially with a simple list of three NDC drug numbers, the auditors only wanted to inventory the current availability of those drugs in stock available for dispensing. After each specific shelf volume for each NDC number was inventoried and verified by each member of the audit team, the pharmacist was asked as a courtesy to verify the inventory count and offered an additional opportunity to produce additional stock if available. The pharmacist was then requested to affix his signature to each individual NDC count. Once the three NDC drugs had been inventoried, there was a brief caucus between the two auditors, and in almost every instance, an additional seven drugs were presented for inventory. The pharmacists were confused since they had never seen a pharmacy audit performed in this manner previously. Unbeknownst to the pharmacist providers, this audit was based on a very simple and basic premise; if you did not buy it, you could not have sold it!

The ten NDC numbers represented the most frequent drugs billed to Medicaid. A special queuing volume formula at the 95% confidence level determined that, given a certain volume of billing, a pharmacy should have available at any given time a shelf volume inventory sufficient to justify that level of billing. What the pharmacies did not realize, at this step of the process, was that if it were determined that the shelf inventories were deficient, they were then going to be required to produce evidence that these drugs had actually been purchased. Most pharmacies caught in this quagmire found themselves in something resembling no man's land; they could not lie, and they could not afford to tell the truth, and in most cases, they were going to be forced to accept their fate and simply pay the money back; a lot of money! They were certainly not about to admit they had committed fraud!

Phyllis entered Victor's Farmacia at 10:03 A.M., introduced herself and her audit partner, and stated the purpose of their visit. Since it was a weekend, Victor Hernandez did not keep routine hours but would usually drop in at various intervals. He was not at the pharmacy when the auditors arrived, but he was twenty-three minutes later, once he received the frantic call from his backup pharmacist/store manager letting him know that Medicaid auditors had invaded.

Victor displayed no sense of urgency or real concern and was in complete control of his emotions as he entered the parking lot on two wheels and skidded to an abrupt, unanticipated stop as a result of the brick retaining wall that some moron had obviously moved during the night. Victor deserved an Academy Award for his performance upon entering the pharmacy due to the agonizing mental anguish as a result of the injury to his Cadillac and his joy and delight of having two uninvited Medicaid pharmacy auditors in his pharmacy on a Saturday morning. Victor immediately introduced himself to the auditors, welcomed them, offered them coffee, and offered whatever assistance they might require.

Victor laid out the red carpet for them and provided an overall orientation to the pharmacy operations. He proudly exhibited for them his cross-referenced prescription files by name, physician, phone number, and birthdate. He was somewhat puzzled when they showed little, if any, interest in particular to these records and documents. He became extremely perplexed when he learned that they simply wished to inventory existing shelf volume for a limited number of prescription drugs. Victor became completely bewildered once the initial inventory for the three drugs was complete, and after a brief consultation between the two auditors, another seven drugs were requested for review.

Victor did his best to remain cordial and demonstrate complete confidence while the auditors were going about their work. His confidence was fading fast, however, due to their baffling approach, without apparently even being interested in matching drug scripts to patients and/or physicians and instead just concentrating on selected prescription drug inventory without any reference to a link to a specific Medicaid recipient.

Once the auditors had completed their tasks, and Victor attested via signature of the existing inventory results, he asked if there was anything else he might be able to provide them with. Almost as an afterthought, Mrs. Newberry asked if he maintained a "Cost of Goods Sold" that was most likely utilized for IRS purposes in relation to the completion of his federal income taxes. Completely blindsided, he mumbled something about having to check with his accountant. And that is when the "oh, shit moment" occurred!

Jorge De Valle received his first call before 10:20 that morning from the first of several anxious and somewhat hysterical pharmacists and pharmacy owners, and his phone kept jumping off the hook most of the day. His pharmacy had not been targeted for an audit, and he had no idea what was going on. It was afternoon when he was finally able to get his hands on one of the letters that the auditors had provided, along with a business card. After reading the letter and listening to what had transpired, Jorge was just as perplexed as the others as to what was going on. One thing that worried him above all else was this particular audit invasion, or whatever, was accomplished under the auspicious of Webb Espy's folks! That was not a good sign, and he began an attempt to contact Marcus Manasa.

That evening, when they all met back at the hotel for happy hour, there was a plethora of amusing anecdotes related to the day's adventures. Everyone had stories to tell. Most had to do with the antics of the owners and their frantic actions related to the unexpected audit invasion. Phyllis split off from the group with the initial inventory data sheets she had gathered and performed a cursory review of the findings. She had previously created a summary tally sheet, and by plugging in two numbers for each drug from each pharmacy, was quickly able to conduct a general analysis. Once she had accomplished this, she dialed Webb Espy's number.

Webb was waiting for the call and grabbed the phone as soon as it rang.

"General Espy, it's Admiral Phyllis reporting in, sir," she said formally, in a well-rehearsed, theatrical manner.

"Damn, Phyllis, I've been in suspense since noon. You could have caused me to start smoking again. Don't go beating around the bush now; what you got, girlfriend?" Webb demanded, holding his breath.

"Well, the short version is; I believe you might say, we caught 'um swimming naked! I did a preliminary analysis, and it would appear that over 90% of the initial three drug NDCs we inventoried were significantly short, even if we assumed 100% of their business was Medicaid. So obviously, we looked at the other seven," she finished.

"YESSSS!" said a fist-pumping Webb. "Phyllis, if you were here right now, we would be doing some serious partying! Thank you, thank you, thank you! You got no idea how much this warms the cockles of my heart. Tell me about your personal grudge match?" he questioned.

"Well, I'm probably going to have to recreate the scene for you in person so you can judge my impersonation abilities, but for now, let it be suffice to say that I believe I was witness to what might best be described as a "proverbial shitting hemorrhage!" she finished, laughing hysterically.

"Can't wait for that little demonstration. I'm going to fix myself a serious adult beverage and start a party right by myself," he exclaimed. Phyllis was not sure if he was serious, but it would not have surprised her if he meant every word of it.

"Oh, by the way, please relay to Kat and M that I said "BINGO" on Fernando's," Phyllis finished, laughing.

"You can bet I will. The Sec's going to enjoy hearing that as well. Tell all your stormtroopers how pleased I am and buy them all a drink on me. I'm really proud of all of you and what your little expedition has pulled off. I won't forget it; I promise. Now get back to the party and put a little extra step in that "victory dance" for yours truly. Thank you again," he concluded.

"You got it, boss, and I'll pass it along. We still got more to do," she reminded him. "See you tomorrow, and thank you. It was really a pleasure. Good night," she finished and hung up the phone.

The chartered plane touched down in Tallahassee at 6:30 P.M., and Phyllis did not know what her evening was going to entail, but it did not take long to find out. As she led her little invasion force into the small private terminal, she was greeted by over thirty MPI peers, who erupted with a cheer to the conquering legion that Patton most surely would have envied. She learned that this was just the beginning of an evening that would take them to Studebaker's for a specially planned party.

Once they arrived, it did not take long to figure out that Marsha Kaye knew how to plan a party, the nurses in MPI knew how to have a party, and a number of other MPI veterans demonstrated that they possessed significant proficiency in enjoying a party.

The liquor poured freely, all on Webb's tab, and inhibitions disappeared while dance moves rarely on display allowed the hidden hams to emerge. Webb, an excellent dancer with smoothness and rhythm, danced with every lady in the group and several others that were not even associated with their party. Marsha Kaye was a very good dancer, and after a couple of gin and tonics, showed off a couple of moves from earlier times that raised a few appreciative eyebrows. Webb even got M on the floor and was a little surprised that she acted like she had been there before and did an admirable job with the twist.

At one point, Webb had just completed a gut-wrenching boogaloo and was catching his breath as they slowed things down with what, at one time, was referred to as just plain old-fashioned belly-rubbing music. As he turned around, Kat was just standing there, and he instinctively grabbed her and made three waltzing whirls. She stayed with him and followed gracefully throughout the difficult maneuver. Her light-footedness and smoothness surprised him. She opened her eyes wide and looked at him suggestively as if challenging him to try something else. He bit and did his best to catch her off guard with an abrupt stop, followed by a stutter step and a dip. She proved more than up to the challenge. At that point, Webb realized he had a dancer in his arms, dropped his arm into a more comfortable position, complimented her silky smoothness, and just enjoyed the dance with an excellent partner. It was a hell of a party, and there were a number of serious headaches the following morning!

27

April 24, 1993

Doral Country Club, Miami, Florida

Two days after the Senate committee hearing before the Health Committee, Webb received a personal call from Arthur St. John himself, offering two potential dates for a golf outing. The earliest was in Miami at Doral Country Club, if by any chance Webb just might happen to be in the area at that time. The second potential opportunity was in Tallahassee at Golden Eagle a few weeks later. Without hesitating, Webb accepted the invitation to Doral. It was a course he had played numerous times years ago, but not recently. He liked the course layout, and the thought of playing there again brought fond memories from the past.

Webb flew into Miami the evening before they were scheduled to play. St. John had informed him that the tee time was set for 11:00 A.M. and that he would meet him on the practice green when he arrived. He suggested that Webb leave his clubs at the bag drop area, and they would load them on his golf cart prior to teeing off.

Webb arrived at the club around 9:45 A.M., left his clubs at the bag drop area, and searched for a convenient place to park. En route to the practice green, he stopped by his bag and retrieved his putter, a seven iron, and three golf balls. He was chipping with his seven iron at various pin positions at various distances on the practice green when he saw St. John drive up in a golf cart. From the sweat marks on his polo, it was apparent he had been at the range hitting some warmup practice balls.

The two greeted one another eagerly and in anticipation of Webb's question, let it be known that it was simply Art from here on out, unless another type of setting dictated otherwise. Art then introduced Webb to two other friends that would make up their foursome. One was a physician, and the other was an international customs house broker. Webb gathered from their ongoing conversations that they played together regularly and were all apparently low handicappers. He could tell by the way they practiced their putts that they were serious players and knew what they were doing on a golf course. There was the usual good-natured ribbing going on, and Webb was looking forward to a fun-filled day on the links.

As they arrived at the tee box a few minutes early, the serious business got started among the group in terms of how they intended to get into one another's back pockets. Webb was obviously the wild card. They had no idea if he was a pigeon or a sandbagger, so they were trying to hedge their sharking intentions for his benefit. Once Webb realized what was going on, he decided to intervene and make it easy on them.

"Tell you what, fellows; just play your normal games. I never bet if I can't afford to lose. However, let me suggest we do this; since I haven't been playing for a while, I suspect I'll be chasing balls all of the course, from one side of the rough to the other. I'll probably have a few decent holes, but I assure you there will be some of the other variety. So why don't Art and I take you two on in a low-ball Nassau, so I can pick my ball up and put it in my pocket without slowing us down too much on those real tough holes." He could sense that they were mulling over his proposal as if Scrooge McDuck was in their midst. Art never said a word. He just stood there, casually leaning on his driver with a slight grin.

Eventually, Ernie, the apparent designated spokesman for the opposing pair, questioned, "Well, what kind of Nassau did you kind of have in mind?"

"Well, pretty much anything from a candy bar to a Cadillac, but I'd hate to lose a Cadillac today, so how does a Jackson or a sandwich with a couple rounds of drinks sound? Webb offered, laughing.

"Sounds like you and Art are fixing to get your asses kicked!" Ernie answered the challenge, laughing manically. At that point, Webb knew he had passed the test, met their criteria, and was immediately one of them.

Since Webb had not warmed up earlier like the others, he pulled out four long irons and swung them lazily, stretching his lats and larger leg muscles. He noticed that all three of the group were eying him, somewhat suspiciously, as he went through the little warm-up routine. When it was time for the group to tee off, Ernie announced that he and his partner were conceding the honors to their opponents as a club member courtesy since Webb was a guest.

Webb responded with the old golf adage, "No honor among thieves, no virtue among whores! Show me the way, Art, since I'm your guest."

Art walked to the tee box, tossed a little grass in the air to gauge the wind, and teed up his ball. He walked behind his ball, stared down the fairway, and selected a reference point for his alignment. He then moved to his setup position and, without taking any additional time, initiated his swing. Webb immediately analyzed Art's swing as simple and efficient without any wasted motion. It was a mechanical swing, built by lessons at a young age, no doubt from a country club pro, and honed with hundreds of range balls. The ball came off his club hot but was pushed slightly right and, unfortunately, took a bad hop and ended up in the trap. Although the ball was in the trap, it was sitting up rather nicely and represented a not-so-difficult shot left to reach the green.

After watching Art's swing and the resulting shot, Webb opined they were going to make a formidable team. As long as Art could keep his ball in play, Webb could play extremely aggressive, gamble on practically every shot, and go for almost every pin. Webb had played a lot of match play golf over the years and early on learned the nuances of the risk vs. reward approach, especially when playing low ball partners.

Webb spontaneously decreed, "Nice drive partner, bad break. You keep hitting them to the right like that, and we aren't going to see much of one another today because I usually play on the left side of the world."

Webb teed up his ball, took a couple of lazy practice swings, and then went through pretty much the same pre-swing routine that Art had just performed. Webb's swing was a longer, flatter, and a more fluid swing, which was the same swing he grooved as a youngster and was thoughtlessly repeatable. As he predicted, the ball, solidly impacted, began hooking more left than he intended; caught a good break, however, and skipped by the trap and just kept rolling down the hill, leaving only a short-iron shot to the green. Webb was sneaky long, and the playing group had just witnessed a glimpse of it.

"All bets are off!" shrieked Ernie.

"Game on; that's my partner!" crowed an exuberant Art St. John.

Ernie was a big man with a big swing and could hit the ball a mile but had no idea where. However, as he demonstrated on several occasions during the round, he possessed an uncanny ability to recover from erratic shots and could seemingly get up and down out of a garbage can. His partner, Vic Seabolt, was a steady player from tee to green but struggled with his short game.

As Webb and Art drove toward their tee shots, Webb suggested a strategy to his partner. "Why don't you play as if this is medal play, and I'll approach it as match play. I believe we might keep the pressure on them that way. What do you think?"

"I think we are scheming exactly alike," said Art, chuckling as his competitive juices came leaking out. Webb and Art tag-teamed incredibly well together, and both won holes outright. Webb hit some great shots, as well as some really bad ones, and Art was always Mr. Steady. The match was over after the fourteenth hole, with five down and four to go. Everyone had had fun and had already begun debating on how things needed to be adjusted for the next time around.

In the nineteenth hole area, the group settled in, ate their sandwiches, and belted down a couple. They all talked about the round and other mundane things, and eventually, the conversation drifted towards other topics. Webb was really enjoying himself but was caught off-guard slightly by the overall progressiveness of the group. For some reason, he had anticipated a somewhat more conservative nature from these fellows. When it was finally time to leave, he walked out with Art and thanked him for a wonderful day. Art looked at him seriously and said,

"Well, don't think this is the last time. We really need to get to know one another a lot better, I think, and I sincerely look forward to doing so."

"The feeling is mutual," responded Webb.

As it turned out, that was not an idle promise from either of them. Over the next several months, the two played golf together several times, had dinner often in both Miami and Tallahassee, and during the process, Art was introduced socially to both David Baswell and Mario Diaz. The four actually played a round of golf together, and it was a bloodthirsty, cutthroat, no-holds-barred, and fun-filled event. David, Art, and Webb became somewhat regulars at Porky's when Art was in town and did not have other commitments. Quid pro quo was not on the table or under it either, for that matter.

On one occasion, at the senator's request, Webb set up a personal tour of Medicaid Program Integrity and introduced him to the unit's vast array of unusually talented characters. Webb sensed the senator was impressed with the potpourri of unique skills and expertise exhibited by this rare cadre of public servants. St. John had heard rumors and references of the legendary Precious's charming, award-winning, tantalizing drawl, and he was not disappointed as she had it on full display for his entertainment, and he was delighted!

28

May 14, 1993

MPI Office, Tallahassee, Florida

David delivered on his promise and had pizza delivered to MPI, and was thoroughly enjoying himself with Webb's cadre of merry little minions. Webb watched as David worked the room. He was good! He possessed an uncanny ability to integrate himself into the mix without the slightest pretense of superiority. David was a politician, but even better, he was a diplomat.

David had been right. Once the dust settled, the District 10 staff resolutions had ultimately turned out to be not much more than routine personnel actions. A considerable amount of that result and David's prophetic pontification was due to the investigative skills of Tim Fagan and Allen Freeman, along with supportive due diligence from Kathryn Armstrong and M.

Once Phyllis completed the task force audit of Fernando's, the coast was clear to initiate a number of actions on several fronts simultaneously. In a synchronized manner, the proverbial shit hit the fan. With departmental sanction authority and evidence in their possession, Fagan and Freedman interviewed both the district DA and the IG staffer separately within an hour of one another. Both lied initially, not realizing the evidence had already been obtained and verified. At that point, each was instructed to leave the building immediately under escort and that their personal items would be delivered to them forthwith. They were both informed that Secretary David Baswell had provided an option for each of them to submit a letter of resignation directly to him by close of business at 5:00 P.M. as of the current date. They both exercised the option afforded.

Unbeknownst to either of them at the time of their resignations, their lives would henceforth become legally challenging, to put it mildly.

In concert with departmental actions, Senator Raymond Harris was headed down another path. With the assistance of Senator Arthur St. John, an ethics complaint had been constructed and was in the queue, awaiting launch instructions for filing. In addition, a criminal referral, complete with all documented and verified information, had been presented to the Florida Department of Law Enforcement. Concurrently, a Medicaid fraud referral, complete with an exceptionally comprehensive investigation of Fernando's and the owners, was transferred to the Atlanta Regional Office of Health and Human Services.

Spirits were high, David was in his element, and Webb could not have been prouder of his staff and happier at the moment.

29

May 17, 1993

State Capitol Building, Tallahassee, Florida

Secretary David Baswell, the head of Florida's largest agency in state government, enjoyed the surreptitious subtleties of creating public service policy by tightrope-walking through the labyrinths of the executive and legislative branches of government. David was process-oriented and had the patience of Job. He also had a mind like a steel trap and a memory like an elephant. Aside from his in-depth knowledge of healthcare and human services issues, he was a skilled strategist when building coalitions for issue-specific outcomes. His approaches were KISS (Keep it Simple, Stupid) formula basic and centered around three primary postulates; one, the more you give, the more you get; two, almost everyone wants or needs something and is usually willing to concede something in order to get it; and three, the quickest way to kill a deal is to get too greedy! His good friend, Webb Espy, broke it down in more basic terms. He often said of David that he approached almost everything with a "plumber's mentality;" hot is on the left, shit don't flow up hill, and payday's on Friday, and everything else in David's approach was just window dressing!

Among David's peers, there were many new disciples of the "New Public Administration" approach that held to the premise that "compromise" was the worst decision an administrator could make; David eschewed that kind of thinking as highly idealistic and downright Quixotic. He was of the mind that everyone wanted something; the trick was discovering what it was and then orchestrating a way to get it for them. While many upper-echelon public service officials shunned the political aspects of their jobs, David thrived on them and was extremely comfortable with that role. David had never been intimidated by politicians or anyone else, for that matter, due in all likelihood to his massive size, and, in fact, was quite at home with them since his family had been consumed in pork barrel politics for generations. He had a knack for often realizing that somebody actually needed something before they did. David did not deny latent aspirations for political office, but he had decided years earlier that the stars would have to line up perfectly for that to happen and, if and when they did, it would be for a big prize.

On a more personal level, David was a mass of contradictions. Appearance alone enhanced part of the façade. His massive frame of over six feet, six inches, with a body weight of around 280 lbs., absent of much body fat, and a deep booming base voice to match, suggested something very different than the real person it housed. David was sensitive, cultured, progressive thinking, and much preferred brain over brawn. He had attended Vanderbilt on an academic scholarship and played offensive tackle as a starter for two years. He was an excellent player, but not due to his size; it was due to the fact that he was a smart football player.

People that were not within his inner circle would have never guessed that his pet, and his pride and joy, was a small six-pound Shih Tzu named Punz. David was an avid reader, a humanities buff, and an accomplished musician. He was also a gadget person and loved anything that required batteries! There was never a problem finding a gift for David! Another aspect of David's life was that he offered himself personally to several worthy endeavors. One in particular was providing hands-on assistance in a surrogate capacity as a mentor and male role model for single mothers with young sons. According to David's account and the public version, that was how he allegedly came to be acquainted with one Kathryn Armstrong and her specific plight.

There were some that perceived David as eccentric due to some of his more idiosyncratic and oxymoronic behaviors, but closer inspection, more often than not, revealed that some of these behaviors were nothing more than practical applications of sorts. For instance, with almost anything at his beck and call in the way of supplies, etc., he would personally cut discarded printer paper into quarters, staple them together at the corner, and write the date on the top. He would keep it with him for the entire day, scribbling notes to himself continuously. David was known as a notorious note scribbler, and these note pads had been dubbed "David's doodles."

David enjoyed being thought of as eccentric. On the dark side, David had an extensive repertoire of colorful expletives that he would employ when he deemed that the situation called for them, which was quite often! His temper tantrums were legendary!

Today, as David was wandering the halls of the Capitol, he was juggling several agendas, but his main priority, at the present, was centered around an idea of transforming the old state mental hospital at Chattahoochee in the Florida panhandle into some other use. When the federal government began withholding funds in the late 1970s related to the use of these kinds of facilities, it forced the state to begin a massive de-institutionalization initiative that left a significant economic void in the general area, an infrastructure underutilized, and a displaced and unemployed workforce. David felt there was considerable opportunity and incentive to rejuvenate these facilities and reinvent a mission that could create a win/win scenario for multiple parties. He just needed to find the right bait for the trap.

He had just left a meeting with two house members from that area and was now on his way to test the waters with Senator Arthur St. John in the Senate Office building. As he was passing through the Rotunda, he heard his name yelled, and he turned and recognized the Governor's Chief of Staff, Will Metcalf, hastily heading his way. David had few feelings one way or another about the Governor's Chief of Staff, other than he felt like he had probably reached his highest level of incompetence. He suspected Will probably did not care for him that much, primarily due to his political pedigree. In such a partisanship arena, it stuck in some folk's craw that a Democrat was heading up the largest state agency in a Republican administration.

Once Will caught up, he began, "Glad I ran into you. I was going to call you for a sit-down on a number of issues that would take more time than I've got right now, but in the interim, let me hit on a couple or so. You got a couple of minutes to spare?" asked Will.

"Sure, this way I'm kind of a moving target," chuckled David.

"Well, first of all, what do you know about this loose cannon over there in your Medicaid program floating all this nonsensical gobbledygook about massive amounts of healthcare fraud and abuse dollars flowing out of the state coffers?" Will more or less demanded.

David calmly took out his doodle pad along with a special pen he kept for certain situations and began scribbling something. "Go on to your next question; I'm going to have to do a little diligence on this one, I suspect," he said, lying through his teeth.

"Okay, somewhat related, I guess, is apparently this Espy fellow over there launched some kind of an ambush invasion on a bunch of pharmacies in South Florida a couple of weeks or so ago, and it appears several significant friends of the governor were accidently caught in the net, as I understand it. They are not happy campers, and therefore, the governor is not very happy." He paused.

"And I assume by significant friends, you mean financial donor-type friends?" David rhetorically questioned, smiling slyly while making direct eye contact with Will.

"Are there any other kind?" answered Will, more smugly than he probably intended.

David was still writing on his doodle pad. "Do you have names attached to these friends?" he asked without looking up.

"Well, I know one of them is a pharmacist named Victor Hernandez. I'll have them to you by this afternoon," Will stated, somewhat pleased with his progress to this point.

"Anything else you or the Governor need?" David asked, appearing serious.

"Yes, there is one other matter. There are two physicians that your man Espy has some kind of cases opened on. The governor knows both these gentlemen and personally will vouch for their integrity. He would like for you to personally have a look at these specific cases and see if there is some way to resolve or mitigate these situations," Will concluded.

David was still scribbling away and not looking up. "Names again, this afternoon?" he added. "And let's see, Will, Metcalf is spelled 'M-E-T-C-A-L-F,'" correct? And today is January 2,

1994?" he continued, almost as if speaking to himself and confirming his notes.

"Yes, on all counts," Will answered, shaking his head in disbelief.

David finished writing and put his pad in his pocket, but continued to hold his pen like a conductor would hold his wand. David looked sternly at Will and began speaking very slowly and deliberately, and his tone was not of a friendly nature. "Mr. Metcalf, on second thought, I believe no additional due diligence is required on my part to respond to your issues. Let me proceed in order as you presented them. First of all, the loose cannon you refer to is Dr. Webb Espy, who is probably one of the foremost authorities on healthcare fraud and abuse in the entire country. He has published extensively on the topic and is one of the most sought-after fraud and abuse consultants nationwide. Based on what the actuarial scientists tell me, it is not a matter of if he is right, it is only how right. I understand the political implications of having these kinds of revelations come to light on somebody's watch, but don't you think it might be better to have it come out in this manner, rather than that you knew, or should have known, and didn't turn off the faucet? If you question what I'm saying, I suggest that you pay a visit to Senator St. John. He was at one time a skeptic, but has done a complete 180, and as you know, he's not an easy mark!" David paused only briefly.

"Now, as to the second matter. For the record, I personally sanctioned that so-called pharmacy invasion, and I can assure you there was no collateral, accidental net-catching! Every single soul captured in that proverbial net was guilty of some extremely serious aberrant activities! The governor's special friend, Victor Hernandez, who I am well acquainted with, is running a Medicaid pill mill and, in all likelihood, will not be in a financial position to be able to continue any political contributions when the dust settles on this thing. My advice is that you recommend to the governor that he attempt to distance himself as far away as possible from this unsavory character. You might want to advise the governor to vet his friends a bit more carefully going forward, because with just a little closer scrutiny, those so-called "friends," as you refer to them, will, in all probability, be guilty of Medicaid fraud and be spending some warranted time in the crossbar hotel!" he asserted again, pausing only briefly, and then continued.

"Now, finally, I'm about to do you a significant favor and forget that you ever asked that last thing. Although we operate a government in the sunshine in this state, that particular sunshine is eclipsed significantly when it comes to complaints and investigations related to healthcare fraud and abuse. Whether you realized it or not, what you just did was an attempt to impede a formal investigation, which is an obstruction of justice and, under the federal mandatory sentencing guidelines, would put you in the federal pen for seventy-two months. Now, please tell the governor that I will be more than happy to brief him personally on these matters if he chooses to do so. Enjoy the rest of your day, Will," David concluded as he continued strolling toward his next stop at Senator St. John's office. Will was left alone, horror-stricken at what had just transpired.

When David returned to his office later in the day, he instructed Marge to give him five minutes of privacy in his office without interruption. Entering his office and sitting at his desk, he took the special pen from his pocket, unscrewed one end, and removed a small audio tape mini cylinder. Next, he retrieved a label, wrote Metcalf and a date, and affixed it to the tape cylinder.

He inserted a new cylinder into the pen and a new battery as well. Finally, he got up from his desk, walked over to a credenza, and unlocked one of the drawers, from which he took out a manila envelope. The envelope contained a number of tape cylinders and was now about to receive another. "Insurance for a rainy day! Well, maybe?" he chuckled to himself. David could not wait to share his Metcalf encounter with Webb. They met at Porky's later that afternoon for a complete debriefing, and they both laughed till they cried!

30

June 10, 1993

Miami, Florida

Marcus was passionate about baseball, and one of the fringe bene-fits of this South Florida operation that he particularly enjoyed was that it allowed him the opportunity to take in almost every Miami Marlins home game. He even attended a few Hurricane games, but could never seem to get used to the sound of the aluminum bats in college baseball. Marcus understood and appreciated baseball like few others had the capacity to comprehend. There was little doubt in his own mind that he could have been a successful major league manager if he had not chosen another career path in his earlier life.

It seemed to Marcus that his entire life was an ongoing list of "what ifs;" what if he had been at the plate rather than on deck at the Super Regional, in the bottom of the ninth with two outs and the tying and winning runs on second and third when his teammate took a called third strike? What if he had not developed turf toe as a senior at The Citadel while hitting over 400 and missed the final half of season? What if he had taken the scholarship offer to Florida State rather than The Citadel? What if Vietnam had not forced a series of premature career decisions on his part?

The "what ifs" were fun to ponder; however, Marcus had never regretted for a second the career path he had chosen.

217

Wherever his baseball skills and talents might have led him, he knew that he was made for the life he had chosen. The "what ifs" represented pleasant diversions for Marcus to escape the staunch realities of his world; what it would have felt like to drive in a winning run to win the pennant, play in an All-Star game, wear a World Series ring, or manage a major league championship team. Marcus had long ago rationalized that baseball, simply a game, could never have replaced the rush and the juices that flowed through his being when he was absorbed in an assignment. His line of work was not a team sport. He either succeeded or failed entirely on his own!

At this level in his professional career, he controlled the entire operation assigned to him from beginning to end. Pass/fail, as Marcus often joked to himself. In baseball, you got multiple at-bats in a game; it was easy to redeem oneself; there was always another game, an upcoming series, or even a next season. No such "nexts" existed in Marcus's professional world. He went at it alone, without a team, without a safety net, relying on his own honed skills after years of special training and unspeakable sacrifices. He was not ashamed to admit that he had savored each and every minute of it! Marcus was obsessed with the fulfilling pleasures yielded by the challenges and pressures that came with the territory, and he consciously welcomed it without the slightest hint of hesitation whatsoever.

The crack of the bat brought Marcus back to the game at hand. It was a line drive deep to the gap in right-center, with a man on first. Marcus knew instinctively, based on the speed of the runner and the renowned arm of the right fielder, there was probably going to be a play at the plate, the most exciting play in baseball! Along with everyone else in the stadium, he was on his feet, watching the play develop, screaming along with every fan in the park. It was going to be close. The right fielder retrieved the ball with his momentum going forward and fired an astonishing, jaw-dropping, missile-like strike to the cutoff man who, in turn, pivoted and made an absolutely perfect throw to the catcher blocking the plate. The runner barreled into the catcher, sending him somersaulting backwards. It was a bang-bang play, but everybody in the house knew he was out, everyone, that is, except the home plate umpire. When he gave the sign, both benches erupted based on both the call and the collision. Bedlam ensued, and Marcus laughingly predicted to himself it would take about ten minutes for the game to resume.

For Marcus, this was about as relaxing as it could conceivably get for him; at the ballpark, with the smell of roasted peanuts, an ice-cold draft beer, and an expensive illegal Cuban cigar. Everything would be about as perfect for him as was humanly possible as soon as his old friend Jorge De Valle arrived to join him, which he anticipated would be within thirty minutes or less. Jorge would always be on time! Marcus worked hard and was driven, but he also knew how to play hard and achieve the ultimate relaxation. In the melee interim, he allowed himself the luxury of some good old-fashioned, self-indulgent pampering while basking in the hot South Florida sunshine. As he closed his eyes and reflected on his current state of affairs, he concluded overall that things really could not be much better. His operation had been ongoing now for almost three and a half years and had exceeded even his own expectations. Things were practically on autopilot based on the initial comprehensive due diligence and a detailed series of protocols and contingency steps he had painstakingly initiated and put in place. Occasionally, there was a hiccup and a tweak had to be initiated; however, Marcus's forte was trouble-shooting, and he relished those special opportunities. Then there was this pesky Webb Espy character at the state Medicaid Program Integrity Office who was somewhat annoying at times, but Marcus figured, in due time, he'd eventually deal with that little matter. Marcus had long concluded that the Medicaid Fraud folks were going to be the least of his worries, based on their traditional law enforcement approach towards healthcare fraud. Webb Espy's group was somewhat different and posed a different kind of threat to his operations. In addition to the operational success, this assignment had added significantly to his already-existing coffers. Marcus was an extremely wealthy man, which was also a fringe benefit for those operatives like Marcus who took these kinds of risks and had sacrificed so much of themselves over so many years. Marcus had no idea how much longer this operation could go on unmolested, but at present, he saw nothing on his radar to suggest that it would not continue for some time to come.

Marcus was brought out of his daze by the boisterous greeting from his friend Jorge. The two men thoroughly enjoyed each other's company, and Jorge was one of the few individuals on the planet that Marcus actually considered a friend. As agreed to earlier, Jorge was to take a taxi to the stadium, meet up with Marcus, and afterward, the two would drive Marcus's car for a late dinner in Little Havana. The two spent the afternoon enjoying the game, talking baseball, and straying occasionally to discussions of world politics or current affairs. Jorge was a wonderful storyteller, with an ongoing repertoire of humorous antecdotes that could keep Marcus in stiches. Marcus had an excellent sense of humor and could hold his own with the best of them in the joke department.

Marcus encouraged Jorge to talk about his family. He was genuinely interested in all aspects of their lives and achievements.

At a very young age, Marcus had reconciled himself to the fact that he would never be a part of a traditional family, and that, in as of itself, did not concern him in the least. Marcus was an isolated anomaly on the "Maslow hierarchy of needs scale." His passion for life and his motivation for daily existence was controlled and fueled by pure and simple competition in almost every aspect of his physical and mental being. This competitive drive and the etiology of its source ruled his life and refurbished itself continuously via unconscious stimulation and rejuvenation.

As a young teenager, Marcus realized his mental makeup was unique and different from those of his peers. He routinely found himself in situations that provoked fear from those his age that he openly challenged and summoned. Later, he discovered that he was abnormally immune to fear and that legitimate situations of fear only enhanced an uncontrollable, competitive passion within his psyche. Under certain circumstances, he exhibited something akin to sociopathic approaches to problem-solving, as in any means justifies the end. In a fight, he was a ruthless adversary. Marcus could be completely indifferent to members of the opposite sex, yet heterosexual in every sense of the word. For reasons beyond explanation, on the surface, Marcus simply appeared to be incapable of an emotional attachment with a female, and beyond that was the fact that it seemed to result in no feelings of inadequacy, nor bore any negative consequences on him whatsoever.

Although not confirmed by those who had continuously evaluated his mental faculties over those many years of training, Marcus had concluded to himself that his unusual mental and emotional characteristics were, in all probability, a result of a combination of biological quirks within his DNA and various overzealous defense mechanisms in overdrive since an extremely young age during his formative years, as well as the intense mind growth and control strategies imparted on him over the years through research psychologists. Since Marcus had no traditional family of his own, he simply adopted Jorge's and fulfilled his own personal family void vicariously, and he took the role seriously. Although Marcus seemed devoid of love as an emotional expression, his protective emotional attachment to Jorge De Valle and his family came as close to love as was within his restricted capabilities.

Once the game ended, the two men drove to a popular little upscale cafe in Little Havana for dinner, complete with drinks, appetizers, full entrees with an excellent (meaning expensive) Argentinean Malbec, dessert, Cuban coffee, liquors, and cigars. It had been a wonderful evening, and they eventually realized that they were the last customers on the premises. Marcus settled the bill, and the two left the restaurant and headed to their SUV parked in the rear of the restaurant.

Marcus saw them first. There were five of them. He casually alerted Jorge and urged him to remain calm and follow his lead, reassuring his friend that he had this, all the while steadily advancing toward their vehicle. Marcus estimated the group to be Hispanic youths in their late teens. The group had picked their targets earlier; two older, apparently affluent gentlemen based on their dress, watches, and vehicle, which they had parked in a dimly lit parking lot in the rear lot of the restaurant.

As Marcus got within several feet of the car, the group swung into action, forming a semicircle around them. The spokesman for the group was brandishing an automatic handgun and excitedly began making demands. The youth seemed a bit confused, as Marcus did not stop immediately, as ordered. He was about to say something else when Marcus halted abruptly. With renewed confidence, the wallets were requested, and Marcus looked over toward Jorge and nodded, suggesting compliance while seemingly reaching simultaneously for his wallet to surrender. What happened next was a choreographed blur to Jorge. In one instant, Marcus was standing, facing a man with a gun pointed at his head, and in the next instant, Marcus was holding the assailant's gun in one hand and held another that had mysteriously materialized in the other, standing over a human heap of useless human waste sprawled heavenly with an open bloody pie hole, which, only milliseconds earlier, had contained teeth. As many times as Jorge hit rewind, he still could not reconstruct what had just happened. He was even more surprised when Marcus spoke calmly but frankly to the young hoodlums, displaying not the slightest bit of anger. Jorge was dumbfounded that Marcus had no intentions of calling the police. Instead, he requested that each of the young men produce their drivers' licenses, indicating that they would be returned to them in a couple of days, suggesting that he only wanted them for their addresses so he could visit them later if need be. He instructed them to take their used-up friend to the nearest urgent care center for medical attention while pontificating that he was, in all probability, going to need the services of an oral surgeon at some point in the near future.

As Marcus was driving him home, Jorge was still adrenaline-rushed and nothing short of stunned. Marcus seemed completely unfazed over the episode and was acting as if nothing out of the ordinary had ever happened. Marcus began talking about the earlier play at the plate that Jorge had missed. Jorge, for the first time in their relationship, had just witnessed another hidden component of his friend that he had no idea even existed. It was ruthlessness combined with a calm and detached demeanor, devoid of any real trace of emotion. It was nothing short of terrifying!

31

September 13, 1993

Little Haiti, Miami, Florida

Willie Dozios worked both sides of the moral and legal street, and individuals that retained his unique kind of skills and services were simply not concerned with his seemingly split division of professional oppositions. Willie possessed an uncanny ability to focus on each individual assignment with a tunnel vision mentality and rarely ever presented the results of his projects in less than a "baker's dozen" disclosure of specific findings above and beyond what was anticipated by his clients. He was good at what he did and enjoyed an established and well-deserved reputation.

What clients knew about Willie was that he loved cash, hated the IRS, and was wholly dependable. Willie was highly selective regarding the people from whom he would accept assignments and could afford to be because his type of discrete services was in high demand in South Florida. There were a select few long-standing clients who had been well-vetted over time to whom he owed special allegiance under his own code of respect and loyalty. These particular clients were given top priority and status in his project queue. Of course, a considerable amount of assignment status and loyalty was based on their past generosity.

One such client was an attorney, Mario Diaz. When Mario made contact, Willie quickly delegated what he was currently working on to one of his top-level subservient staff and concentrated entirely on Mario's request. Willie had been well-indoctrinated over time in his line of work that although a tunnel vision approach was customarily a preferable approach, and while unreserved initiative could lead to less-than-desirable consequences, it was his perception that a little peripheral peep outside the blinders often resulted in those "baker's dozen" insights.

Mario Diaz's instructions and orientation appeared clear cut and not overly complicated whatsoever, even though they were slightly unusual. He had been provided a surveillance target, with very specific deliverables. Each day, he was to report the precise progression of the target's activities to the extent possible and, based on immediate analysis of this information via his client, he would receive additional instructions for the subsequent day. On the surface, this appeared to be an easy assignment with an easy mark. Willie realized from real-life experiences, however, that appearances are quite often deceiving.

Willie was informed that the project would last at least four weeks and might be extended beyond, depending upon what transpired and was learned. Willie was more than pleased with that possibility, based on what Mario was paying him.

The following Monday morning, Willie, accompanied by his chauffer, Carlos, was staked out at their assigned spot in a late model GMC SUV with tinted windows in the heart of Little Haiti. Their set-up was located in close proximity to a dental facility with a sign signifying Poppa's Family Dentistry. They had reconnoitered the surroundings over the weekend, and Willie felt like they had selected an almost-perfect spot to observe the comings and goings of the clinic's activities. Willie had another two-man team parked about a block ahead, which could be deployed as needed.

Willie and Carlos had been in position for a little over an hour and began to watch the neighborhood wake up as routine traffic began flowing onto the narrow street and sidewalks. Willie, on his ninth cup of Cuban coffee, was wired and on high alert when he spotted what he suspected was his designated prey. He had been apprised that although it was not a certainty but a high probability, the target would be a white-paneled van with rental car barcodes in the rear window. The Florida license plate might end with the last four digits 955Z. The key identifier was that, in all likelihood, the vehicle was going to be driven by a large, muscular Haitian, and the van's cargo was more than likely going to be of the human variety, to the tune of approximately eight to twelve little youngsters.

"Bingo, got you, you predictable son of a bitch!" Willie exclaimed, with dollar signs flashing in his brain. There he was, no question about it. It was the big fellow that had been described to him, with the St. Louis Cardinals baseball cap as the distinguishing feature, herding his little troupe into Poppa's. Willie immediately began snapping pictures with his expensive Nikon equipped with a long-range telescopic lens. After the entourage had disappeared into the building, Willie ordered Carlos to casually get out of the vehicle, go get himself a cup of coffee, and reconnoiter the van for any markings that might identify the rental agency that was leasing the vehicle, and then secure the entire license plate number since the angle of the vehicle did not allow his camera to capture the plate number in its entirety. There were other ways to ascertain this information, but this represented the quickest and easiest method. Carlos returned shortly, indicating that there was nothing visible on the van that identified the specific rental company, but handed Willie a small slip of paper yielding the full license plate number. Now it was just wait-and-watch time. It did not take as much time as they anticipated.

In less than forty minutes, the door opened, and the little group filed out the door, back toward the van, while additional photos were obtained. Willie noted that the big Haitian apparently ran a tight ship and seemed to have complete control over his little tribe. He also noted that the man had entered the building empty-handed, but he returned carrying a large, oversized manila accordion-type envelope. According to Willie's notes, the group had been in the dental office for a total of thirty-nine minutes, and he recorded the exit time. What Willie was witnessing, in MICI street language, was a Medicaid scam operation referred to as "solicitation," which translated to illegal renumeration to someone in order to seek medically unnecessary medical services. In Miami, this kind of fraudulent activity was rampant.

Once all were deposited back into the van, the driver pulled out and proceeded west. The streets were not crowded, and the van was relatively easy to keep in sight, but opting for caution, Willie signaled the well-rehearsed switch maneuver to his other team to alternate to the primary lead while he and Carlos stayed comfortably back. Twenty minutes later, the van pulled into a parking lot at *La Clinique Famille*, and Willie scrutinized a repeat of the scene he had observed a few minutes earlier at the dental facility.

This time, the kids spent a total of fifty-one minutes inside the facility. For a second time, the driver entered empty-handed, but returned with the same kind of envelope. Once again, the van headed west, turned, and then went back east and finally made a third stop fifteen minutes later at Pronto Diagnostic Imaging Services. For the third time, the same process occurred, only at this particular stop, the kids only spent a grand total of eighteen minutes at the center. Willie once again took note of the envelope retrieved by the driver.

When everyone was back in the van, they headed east again and pulled through a McDonalds drive-through, and the driver apparently retrieved several large takeout sacks. The final leg of the route eventually led them to a parking lot adjacent to a kid's playground. There was a small crowd waiting, obviously a number of whom were parents or relatives awaiting the return of the children.

Willie was also quick to observe that there was another group of children, along with adults, that was definitely separate from the returnees, and once the McDonald's Happy Meals had all been handed out, along with what appeared to be plain white envelopes to the adults, the big driver turned his complete attention to the new group.

The encounters were friendly and informal, yet carried out efficiently and in a businesslike manner. The driver seemed to be collecting slips from each of the adults and then began writing something on the paper after attaching them to a clipboard. Once the organized process was concluded, the new group was herded into the big white van. Neither Willie nor Carlos were surprised at all when they arrived at the familiar spot where they began their surveillance earlier in the morning. The next three stops were exact duplicates of the morning excursion.

Willie and Carlos, as well as the other team, watched the scene play out at the playground, with kids being linked with their retrievers and scattering in various directions. When all was calm, the driver returned to the empty van and headed west. The van stopped three different times, at an Easy Mail, a mail box, etc., and a mail station. At each specific stop, the driver entered the building with two of what was assumed to be the earlier brown manila envelopes and returned immediately with a somewhat smaller dark brown one. After the third and final stop, the van headed back east and eventually entered a neighborhood about ten blocks from the playground that was the staging area for the pickup and delivery of the kiddie cargo.

The last part of the day's surveillance tail appeared to Willie to be somewhat precarious, due to the fact there was little traffic available to assist them in evading detection. Willie's experience told him that the conspicuousness of their vehicles in this kind of neighborhood would uncloak them in a New York minute and aborted the tail immediately, with both vehicles turning in opposite directions. The two teams met at a designated rendezvous spot several blocks away. Willie already had a plan in mind and ran it by the others.

"Listen, I'm pretty sure we are probably real close to where the van will spend the night. Most of the houses in there don't have any semblance of a garage, and I don't think we will have any difficulty locating it. I believe we need to get something like a small moped, something that won't draw any attention and is easy to get around in, and canvas the neighborhood by just crisscrossing the streets in about a five-to-five block area. I believe that ought to get us the final intel we need for today," Willie finished, concluding he had convinced all of them, including himself.

Willie was right; within thirty minutes, the youngest of the group, P. Pee, as he was nicknamed, had secured a moped and had identified the address where the van was located. Within another hour, Willie had ascertained that the address was the current residence of Jacques La France and that his mother and sister resided there with him. Willie filed his report for the day with Mario Diaz and went in search of adult beverages and some long overdue adult entertainment.

Later that evening, after consuming a considerably more than adequate supply of *Cuba Libres* and sampling several exotic, voyeuristic needs, Willie began rehashing the day's events and was wrestling with an unsettling feeling that he had not been able to get a grasp on. All of a sudden, it hit him. He had a hell of a hunch, and tomorrow, he was going to play it!

32

September 14
Through October 14, 1993

Various sites in Dade/Broward Counties in South Florida

Willie had not had much sleep after returning home after his epiphany at the bar earlier in the evening. Upon arrival, he spent considerable time plotting the next day's operations and lining up the resources to pull them off. Two things Willie was not short on was initiative and grandiose interpretations of assignments. From his point of view, there were only three basic criteria; one, it was simply a matter of the risk vs. reward question; two was the pain worth the pleasure; and three, based on prior experience, it is often easier to receive forgiveness than permission. Willie had access to a number of human resources not normally available, or at least, in all probability, would not survive anything resembling even loose vetting scrutiny, to almost any type of legitimate employment. For Willie's purposes, these, for the most part, unsuitable individuals of questionable character were absolutely perfect. There were primarily only two essential criteria for the job; a warm body and an unexpired driver's license.

By 8:30 the next morning, Willie had assembled six two-person teams in addition to himself. He brought his own partner!

The selected cadre rendezvous occurred in a predetermined Walmart parking lot, where assorted makes/models of rental cars had been assembled. The group's visual composition would have, in all likelihood, attracted police attention if there had been any unnecessary loitering whatsoever. Willie was cognizant of this possibility and had prepared extremely simple specific written instructions and protocols, as well as precise contingency options. He provided each of them with a bag phone, along with his number, and commanded them to only call him if anything really unusual occurred. With those orders, he dispensed his little band with the utmost haste and efficiency.

The initial team was sent to the first site confirmed by the previous day's surveillance. They were instructed to stay put and simply observe and under no circumstances attempt to follow any vehicle whatsoever. They were to be on the lookout for any type of vehicle capable of transporting multiple patients simultaneously. If such a vehicle was identified, a tag number was to be obtained in the most discrete manner possible. They were also directed to observe the driver's actions specifically and record anything that he might have in his hands, both entering or leaving the building. Two additional teams were issued similar marching orders. The remaining three groups were assigned to stakeout the mailbox, businesses, and Easy Mail shops that had been established via the previous day's discoveries and to restrain themselves from doing anything illegal while on Willie's clock. Once again, Willie dictated exactly what he expected them to do, which entailed watching for specific vehicles and the actions of the drivers. In addition, although somewhat more difficult, he wanted them to observe individuals entering these establishments with obvious manila envelopes in their hands. In these situations, they were to make every attempt to secure tag numbers. Finally, they were to meet back at this exact location by 6:30 P.M. for a debriefing.

Willie, along with his partner, a voluptuous creature chosen for reasons outside any sleuthing expertise, assigned himself two totally different tasks for the day. The first was to set up at the staging area where the kids were picked up and returned the previous day. The second was an Easy Mail site outside the previous day's concentrated service area. It was apparent at the first stakeout almost immediately that today's routine was not going to duplicate the previous day's activities. Willie aborted his first task and immediately proceeded to the second one. Once in place and the surroundings had been expertly cased, Willie settled into some special surveillance maneuvers that had absolutely nothing to do with observing the comings and goings associated with the Easy Mail establishment. Willie was pretty much convinced that if his hunch was correct, nothing was going to happen for a while, anyway. He was right, almost!

It was at 9:48 A.M. when Willie's bag phone interrupted the first of several activities not necessarily associated with Easy Mail surveillance. The call was from Gonzolo, one of the more intelligent specimens from Willie's human resource inventory.

"What's up?" Willie answered, cutting to the chase.

"Well, just wanted to let you know a van showed up just like you suspected, and the driver came back carrying a large manila envelope." Gonzalo paused.

"And?" Willie waited impatiently.

"Well, I thought you might want to know that we were, for some reason, expecting kids, and all this guy's passengers were old farts. I just thought you might want to know that," Gonzalo finished hesitantly.

"Damn, nice intel my friend! Yep, you did good — really good. Thanks, good fellow," Willie stated sincerely. "Listen, I might have something a little different I want you to do later this afternoon. Just stay where you are and wait for me to call, okay?"

"You got it, boss," concluded Gonzalo.

Willie mulled over this new information only briefly and concluded it was not a game-changer at all, just a potential expander. Without much break in the action, he returned to the immediate business at hand with his partner, alternating the visions of beautiful breasts and dollar signs.

It was just prior to noon, during a mandatory recoupment session from partnering, when Willie noticed a late model Toyota Forerunner park and a man, most likely Cuban, in an embroidered blue guayabera enter the Easy Mail with several small manila envelopes. Without much fanfare, Willie nonchalantly got out of his car, checked his fly, followed the man into the building, and purchased stamps after memorizing the tag number en route. Willie left after purchasing the stamps and returned to his vehicle. After several minutes, his target emerged with several larger envelopes in his possession. "BINGO!" Willie fist pumped. "Oh yeah! Game on!" He congratulated himself.

Willie saw no point in staying on the stakeout any longer and decided to retreat to a more comfortable environment in order that he and his partner might explore some of the subtler nuances of advanced surveillance techniques. Before leaving, he phoned Gonzalo and directed him to tail the next vehicle if it had old farts aboard and ascertain, if at all possible, their final destination.

Willie arrived for the debriefing at 6:15 P.M. absent his partner, who feigned a case of terminal fatigue after what she claimed was an exhausting day of surveillance activities. Willie looked and felt like he was ready for a big night on the town. Each team had pretty much the same report, which was exactly what Willie had anticipated. Gonzalo reported that he had been able to discover the whereabouts of the final destination for at least some of the old farts. He had an address, which he surrendered to Willie. Each team provided Willie with the tag numbers they had obtained. Willie thanked them and gave them each an envelope with cash. He asked if they would all be available for the next day, and they all agreed. Willie had already arranged for the rental cars to be picked up, and they would be substituted with a fleet of replacements the next morning. He watched his motley little troupe as they headed to the closest bus stop less than a block away. Willie was pumped, but he realized he needed to curtail his enthusiasm for a while. He needed to report in, but he didn't need to share everything he knew or suspected at this stage of the game. He wanted to up the ante, and to do so meant gathering additional intel. Everything in due time. He knew his hunch had been right on, and his client was going to be extremely pleased, and now it was gravy time!

33

November 23, 1993

Little Haiti, Miami, Florida

All was well in the world of Jacques LaFrance, at least in his mind, anyway. He was making a lot of cash money, but he was also spending most of it. Jacques kept himself in a euphoric state of "fat, dumb and happy." He had a real good thing going which had been sustained for several months now, and Jacques seemed oblivious to any notion it all might immediately end without warning or that there could conceivably be any real consequences that might in any way reflect negatively on his future wellbeing. He was conducting a well-oiled assembly line operation, and there appeared to be no end in sight from his isolated vantage point. He was on top of the world.

One of the only downsides to Jacques's overnight success was the continuous harassment at one of the everyday drop points by the community's Haitian Vodou priestess Weida's continuous warnings of *"le vent de la mort,"* translated from some version of Creole Patwa to "The Wind of Death" or simply "Death Wind." Although Jacques had heard enough stories during his lifetime of vodou's inexplicable powers, he had become Americanized to the point of eschewing and scoffing at such nonsensical premonitions.

Every now and then, there was a slight hiccup in the day to day operations, but Jacques amazed himself with his own personal initiative and troubleshooting abilities. When Jacques began this operation, the rules were straightforward and very simple; he was to do things in a specific way, and he was not to digress from these strict rules related to the operational plan under any circumstances or for any reason whatsoever. It had been emphasized that there was absolutely no tolerance or margin for deviation whatsoever and that consequences for such collapses in judgment would be swift and beyond serious! For whatever reason, human nature being what it is, "Maslow's hierarchy of needs" often decides to kick in, and people begin to gravitate toward things that spell trouble for them without them ever being conscious that it is happening. It might have been confidence, complacency, greed, status, or some combination of the aforementioned, but for whatever reason, Jacques began exercising independent discretion in ways that went well beyond the boundaries established and decided to enhance and improve on things. Jacques now viewed himself as a natural-born entrepreneur in the rough.

Jacques' first little enterprise was to eliminate the McDonald's Happy Meals and replace them with his own version of kiddie snacks at a significantly reduced price that put his mother and sister in business and allowed him to pocket the change. Next, he discovered that if he rented the van for a month at a time, rather than just a week, he could do so at a discounted rate, which saved him an extra $300 per month.

Jacques was so excited over his various entrepreneurial ventures that he never noticed a black tinted-windowed SUV that maintained surveillance on his activities for a little over a week. Concurrently, along with this undetected surveillance, it insightfully dawned on him that he could set up additional solicitors as personal clones and expand his profits exponentially by delegating adjacent neighborhoods to these additional drivers. He considered this idea as an act of self-employed brilliance.

Jacques found that although it was nice to deal in cash, it was sometimes difficult to use it for certain things. He was streetwise enough to know that large cash transactions brought with them attention, accompanied by, often times, a type of undesirable scrutiny. He was savvy enough to not utilize financial institutions for any type of transaction, but he was at least smart enough to maintain a safety deposit box for his stash.

When word gets around that you deal in cash, you begin to draw the attention of some unsavory types of individuals whose business interests might not pass the smell test. This was, in fact, the case with Jacques, and before he realized it, he was in bed with an organized group of mini-cartel drug distributors. Although reluctant and paranoid initially, the first couple of purchases, along with the instant success, provided an exaggerated sense of confidence and delusions of grandeur. Not realizing he was in well over his head, Jacques decided to go for the home run on his next deal and bet the farm upfront with all the stash he could get his hands on, and credit to boot. Whether it was a set up or whether it was just a simple drug deal gone bad, no one will never know. What it did, however, was put Jacques in a very bad position with some very dangerous people who wanted their money immediately, which he did not possess. Jacques was frightened, under extreme duress, and seemingly without immediate options, resorted to committing the ultimate "cardinal sin;" he took what he needed from the sealed envelopes that he routinely secured and delivered, with every intention of replacing it at the first available opportunity. That opportunity never came. Consequences and retaliation were swift. Within three days, Jacques's body was found in an alley in Little Haiti with a single .22 bullet hole through the center of his temple. There was absolutely no forensic evidence at the scene where the body was discovered. Jacques left this world never having any idea the damage he had brought down on the entire operation. As he faced the horror of his fate, the last thought that entered his mind was the old Vodou priestess Weida's prophesy of "*le vent de la mort.*"

The following Monday, there was a replacement for Jacques LaFrance running his route, with a renewed appreciation that in this kind of business, one does not deviate from the simple and strict rules associated with the terms of employment. The message had been delivered with unmistakable clarity and extreme prejudice. Every other solicitor in South Florida realized it as well with a renewed sense of unadulterated vigor.

34

December 20, 1993

Miami, Florida

Marcus was enjoying a fine, legitimate, black-market Cuban cigar along with an expensive port reserve at an outside café patio in Little Havana. He was awaiting the arrival of Jorge, which was unusual, since ninety-nine plus percent of the time, Jorge was the one who arrived first. He had to chuckle: *"el hombre de la reloj."* The tag was perfect for his old friend.

It was a little early for cocktail hour, but Marcus relished his rare leisure time opportunities. Time for reflection and futuristic thinking regarding personal aspects of his life were mental luxuries not often afforded individuals like Marcus, based on his training and professional orientation. Marcus was never melancholy but was capable of deep self-reflection.

Marcus mulled over his current situation and the overall state of the historical and ongoing operation. Things were going exceptionally well, and there were, at the moment, no unanticipated blips on the horizon. Obviously there had been a hiccup or two, but that was anticipated and inevitable when conducting these kinds of activities. It had been a great run so far, and if, by some strange change of fate, things went south tomorrow, the operation would be judged an overwhelming success by any form of reference. However, Marcus was in no hurry for it to end. The longer it continued, the better his next life would be. He planned to maximize this opportunity to the hilt. This was going to be his swan song of sorts and would set the stage for him to exit his professional career at the top of his game with almost legendary status. He would enjoy a future only few could dream of.

Marcus's thoughts were interrupted by a greeting from Jorge, who had entered the premises via the side door. Marcus held up his glass in mock salute and gestured for Jorge to seat himself. Marcus immediately signaled to the server to attend to his guest. Jorge ordered his trademark *Cuba Libre* with *Brugal Añejo* and fresh lime. The two engaged in pleasantries and general small talk until Jorge's drink arrived. "What were you in such deep thought about when I came in and invaded your stupor?" Jorge questioned good-naturedly. "Oh, not much, really; just pondering the mysteries of a future life without intrigue and complete peace of mind," Marcus replied with a forced laugh.

"You mean you are actually capable of contemplating those kinds of human thoughts? I have kind of begun to think of you as a Mr. Spock-type character," Jorge accused playfully. "Tell you what; let me ask you a question. Where is your favorite place that you've been to in this world?"

"Hmmm, sounds like you might be on a fishing expedition," Marcus suggested in his best clandestine manner. "But, tell you what; I'll play your silly little childish game. Southern Spain for entertainment, New Zealand for beauty, and South Africa for excitement. Go on. I'll let you know if you cross the line," Marcus offered.

"Remember, you're the one that let me get my foot in the door. Always been curious, has there ever been anyone special in your life?" Jorge asked bluntly.

Marcus laughed out loud. "You mean other than you?" he deadpanned and then absolutely howled as a result of the expression on Jorge's reddened face. "Well, that's real close to the line, but what the hell; I'm feeling pretty good at the moment, could be the port, but if anyone in this world is entitled, it certainly has to be you. Yes, twice actually. The first was a young lady from Madrid a number of years ago. She was an artist with all the baggage that comes with such talent. At least, I think she had talent. Keep in mind, that's coming from a person that can't even draw decent stick figures. At any rate, I was quite smitten with her, and I believe the feelings were reciprocal. Her name was, well, maybe it's best not to mention names in this little exercise. Pretty obvious to see now that it was destined not to survive. I wanted it to work, but 20/20 hindsight tells me it never had a real chance. My work, extended absences without legitimate explanations, and her constant demands for more of me than I would ever be able to give were doomsday predictions. She tried, bless her, but ultimately, she had no choice but to break my heart, and I can't blame her for it. I'm sure I'll have feelings for her till I draw my last breath. The second time was a ranger guide I met while I was in South Africa. I was thunderstruck the first time I ever saw her. She was absolute raw beauty, wild and spirited, and smart as they come, too, with a zest for life that was contagious. We had some great times that I'll treasure forever. I'm certain I never had a chance with her. I'm not sure she could have ever been a one-man woman, but I kidded myself into hoping that I might be the one. No such luck. I had to just walk away without explanation. I doubt she worried much about it for more than five minutes or so. Next?" he invited.

"Well, we're on a roll here. Let's go this way. Do you think you will retire any time in the near future and, if so, where do you think you might eventually land, and what do you think you will do with yourself?" Jorge asked directly.

"Excellent question, and one I'm not sure I can answer with absolute certainty. Let me say this; I can essentially retire whenever I choose; however, I am not one to leave unfinished business. That's just not in my DNA. My best guess is one to three years. I'm sure you realize that your family is the closest thing I have to family, and, therefore, I would like to set up my retirement years in close proximity. I might have a couple of roost spots; one in the Keys, definitely, and possibly another somewhere so I can easily get to the Marlins' games during the season. I'll never stop traveling as long as I'm able because there are so many places yet to explore. I would like to try my hand at writing some. As you might imagine, I have an extensive inventory of stories and experiences to draw from, but obviously, I have to be extremely careful in that department. I have never had enough time to read as much as I would have liked, and I can easily be lured into a serious competitive bridge game. Does all that sound laid-back and boring enough for you?" Marcus wrapped up.

"Sounds like an envious plan to me. I like it, especially the part about the Marlins games. Just two more questions and that's it; I promise I'll let it rest," Jorge suggested.

"Let it rip. The port has obviously loosened my tongue to the point that I might yield some of my most closely guarded, surreptitious achievements," Marcus answered, shrugging his shoulders in mock surrender.

"Do you enjoy or do have any regrets related to the kind of work you do or have done during your career?" asked Jorge matter-of-factly.

"Well, I'm not sure if that one crosses the line or not, because it assumes that you have some idea of what I actually do or have done in the past, and I can assure you that you have no clue as to that information whatsoever. However, given your assistance in our current little operational endeavor, I am going to attempt to answer your question in a roundabout way. There are a lot of things you know about me from our early years together. For instance, you know how competitive I've always been. You also know that I live for challenges, and that I'm a sponge when it comes to absorbing something that I am really interested in. I'm not built mentally like most people. I learned in the early stages of my life that I do not seem to react to certain kinds of situations and stimuli in the same manner as others. I believe there were some people that were constantly on the lookout for these atypical characteristics. I can't really explain it or go into details, but let me just say that once these traits are recognized in a human being, they may be significantly enhanced and honed through some extremely sophisticated and extensive training-type regimes. For instance, if you jump out from behind a door and try to scare me, my adrenaline does not kick in like most normal folks' will. I might be instantly distracted as a reflex, but I am not frightened. I seem to be immune to most types of fear and anxiety. It's almost like I'm on a constant internal beta blocker and anti-anxiety medication that is produced within the confines of my own body. In some ways, I am a freakish Mr. Spock. As an example, in stressful situations, most people experience anxiety. Under the same circumstances, I, for some reason, experience eagerness.

247

I relish the opportunity to get to the plate in the bottom of the ninth with two outs and the winning run on third. I live for those kinds of experiences and opportunities. Remember the night the guys tried to rob us in the restaurant parking lot? I welcomed that confrontation. I mean, I was actually eager for the encounter. You would be astonished at what is known about the human brain and what it can be trained to do and feel. Now, you know I'm not sociopathic, because you know I have, and have had, extremely strong feelings for both individuals and groups of people. I also have strong patriotic tendencies and can tear up at "Taps" in a heartbeat. I can get chill bumps like everyone else. However, I also have some type of uncanny ability to compartmentalize certain individuals or groups due to an ingrained, dominating conceptual tunnel vision that yields to the notion that any means justifies a specific end. In other words, individuals or groups that impair my mission are essentially just viewed as things, obstacles, if you will, and are no longer viewed as humans; they are simply obstacles and are, therefore, expendable. I have no control whatsoever over these feelings once I have bought into the mission and have been completely indoctrinated. Another thing: I am capable of real anger, but not normally at others. I can get really angry at myself; I mean, I can throw a real two-year-old, childlike temper tantrum when I do something that I consider really stupid or something that is not logical. A little scary, huh?" Marcus abruptly finished, draining his glass and signaling the server for another.

These revelations were sobering to Jorge, and he came face to face with the realization that he had just learned more about his old friend in the last few minutes than he probably had in his entire lifetime. In some ways, both Marcus and Jorge felt an instant relief, appreciating that a long overdue catharsis had just oc-curred between the two men.

"I believe you indicated you had one more for me," Marcus said as he reached for his refreshed snifter of port.

"Well, I'm not sure what you can do for an encore after that last one, but I'll let you make an attempt. Please don't read any-thing into this, but I'm just curious more than anything else; do you have any knowledge about what actually happened to Jacques La France, one of our Haitian solicitors, who was killed in Little Haiti? The reason I ask is I remember when I told you about it; at the time, you seemed somewhat indifferent and simply asked, "What's the word on the street?" "At the time, it was rumored that it was more than likely a drug deal gone bad. Later, however, it was revealed that when his body was discovered, he had a sig-nificant amount of hard cash still on him, so I believe that blows that motive." Jorge stared at Marcus inquisitively.

Marcus looked directly into Jorge's eyes with only the slightest hint of a smile and responded. "Now, Jorge, my good friend, you know that one goes way over the proverbial line. Let me just say this in the most hypothetical and tactful way possible under the cir-cumstances. Even if I knew the answer to that question, I could never answer it. This might be just about enough of this, don't you think? Let's go have ourselves a culinary climax," Marcus concluded with a mysterious smile as he pushed back from the table, grabbed his remaining port, and ushered Jorge into the main dining room.

As the two friends enjoyed their dinner that evening, Mar-cus had not the faintest idea that his operational horizon was about to be lit up by blips, with a tsunami in tow. A confron-tation was imminent.

35

March 5, 1994

Tallahassee, Florida

M was not smiling! Quite the contrary; she was for the moment singularly focused, confused, apprehensive, and actually frightened for reasons beyond her realm of reckoning. What she was experiencing was something totally foreign to her normal mental state and frame of reference. She had been struggling to contact Webb for the past several hours, but to no avail. She was aware that he was often unreachable for several hours during this time of the year, especially on a Saturday at 4:30 A.M. due to his relentless pursuit of "those gobbling things" that seemed to create an obsession with him, as well as make him passionately angry, as one might feel about a serious enemy. It was imperative that she reach him as soon as possible. She had tried every avenue available to get in touch with him short of jungle telegraph. All she could do now was just wait, which, in M's world, was a torture worse than death.

Emerging from his leisurely morning adventure in pursuit of "those gobbling things" —he actually was not hunting, just scouting, since the season would not open for a couple of weeks — Webb was greeted by a barrage of pager messages from M radiating from every source conceivable, emphasizing an urgency that was totally uncharacteristic of the little wizard. Within minutes of gaining phone access after receiving her frantic messages, he had her on the line, and he quickly assessed that he had never witnessed M in such a state. She said it was urgent, it could not be dealt with over the phone, and she needed to see him immediately. They agreed to meet at the office as soon as they each could get there.

M was waiting outside the office in the parking lot when Webb pulled in. He detected instant relief on her face as he exited the vehicle and headed toward her. Webb dispensed with pleasantries and simply said, "Okay, M, tell me what's going on? I know it's got to be something serious. I can tell from the look on your face."

"Better that I show you, boss," she urged gesturing with a twist of her neck toward the door.

"Let's go to the conference room," suggested Webb.

"Perfect, that way I can spread out a little bit," M suggested.

"Coffee?" questioned Webb rhetorically as he switched on the light as they entered the room.

"Always!" replied M, with the first hint of a smile in hours.

"Something tells me this might go better with coffee," quipped Webb.

"I seriously doubt it," M shot back, with her first real smile of the day. She was in her comfort zone now that Webb was corralled; he was all hers, and she had his complete and undivided attention.

Once the coffee brewed, and they each built themselves a serious cup of real caffeine rivaling anything coming north of Little Havana, Webb finally hitched up his trousers, took a deep breath, and said, "Okay, M, show me what you got." "Well, as you know,

I've been working with three unique and unrelated databases. It's working, but as you are acutely aware, it is extremely slow and has to process the files sequentially. I had a long shot idea of how I might create a shortcut and eliminate a ton of processing time. To make a long story short, I wrote a simple program; well, really not so simple, and it worked even better than I could have ever imagined. As a result, I was able to eliminate a number of filters, unrelated files, and redundant algorithms. Then I made an executive decision to utilize only the critical variables and designated common denominators required for target hits. Rather than separating all the profiles independently, I simply summarized them for the time being. Rather than pulling a year of claims processing history, I only did three months. Once I got those results, I ran a random number generator, created a sample, and extrapolated to the universe. I was conservative at this step and went to the 95% confidence level," M finally paused.

"And?" asked Webb impatiently. "So, is it bad?" Webb continued before M could respond.

"Real bad!" she said with emphasis and arched eyebrows. "Let's put it this way. There are aberrant claims that we know about and do something about, and then there are those that we know about and have in the queue. In addition, there are claims that are aberrant, but we can't do anything with them for one reason or another. Finally, there are obviously aberrant claims that are out there but have not been identified yet." M paused again.

"Go on; you're on a roll. I'm following everything so far," nodded Webb intently.

"Okay, well, for starters, we've always surmised that we ain't hit the tip of the iceberg when it comes to identifying aberrant practices. We've always kind of guessed that if we employed a few of the detection strategies we have blueprinted, we would probably detect more potentially illegitimate practices in a week than we could devote investigative resources to for years. Well, boss, I don't believe we have to guess about that anymore. Based on what ought to be intuitively obvious to the casual observer, that iceberg just exploded out of the water like a freaking volcano," M concluded.

"Whoa, hold on a minute; help me here a little bit more, M. I am pretty sure I follow what you did, but are you telling me that you now have some type of a defensible guesstimate, some kind of a real number that is justifiable?" Webb asked.

"Yes, I feel confident that we do," M stated with stanch conviction. "But you need to remember that was not the objective I was trying to accomplish. A number for whatever it may represent is just a byproduct of this process. What is far more important, at this stage of the game, is that we have a high degree of validity and, I would opine, even a higher degree of probability, in that what we use for justifying our generalized analyses as legitimate investigative tools is on point and completely defensible. It is going to allow us to recover untold millions of dollars and cost-avoid even more. As you indicated earlier; we are going to shock the world!"

Webb reclined his chair, put his hands behind his head, and stared at the ceiling, intensely processing what M had just told him. It was something akin to cognitive overstimulation. There were a number of thoughts and questions bouncing around in his head like a pinball machine.

M had seen Webb in this state on previous occasions and was content to sit back and wait for the interrogation that was sure to be forthcoming. It took about three minutes before Webb asked his first question.

"Give me some numbers, M?"

"Sure, but first, let me throw in a few caveats," she suggested. "First of all, this represented a targeted analysis. The common denominators were limited to specific critical variables. Under most circumstances, the claims associated with these providers would escape detection because they are not egregious. In fact, they are artfully crafted by diagnostic groupings and would not fall outside the established standard deviations utilized for quantitative analyses. We know the claims associated with the providers are aberrant because we now have a history of qualitative review that has established profile billing patterns representing medically unnecessary services. We know that the patterns are consistent throughout the universe because the sample tells us so. It is kind of like predicting an election result when less than 2% of the ballots have been counted." She briefly paused.

"Yeah, I get what you did, but don't have the foggiest how you actually did it. But I'm following you so far," Webb stated thoughtfully.

"When we add this to what we already know, we come up with a number that holds water and is defensible. We have identified almost 3,500 pay-to-providers, with somewhere in the vicinity of 9,200 treating providers. What is apparent is that is that we have a significant number of seemingly independent, non-physician medical company entrepreneurs who have physicians under their employ." M paused briefly to organize her next thought as well as catch her breath.

"M, give me a number, please?" Webb pleaded.

"Are you sure?" M questioned, almost apologetically.

"Dang, M, you're killing me here!" moaned Webb.

"If I told you it knocked a hell of a hole in over three-quarters of a billion, how would you react?" M whispered almost sheepishly.

"I would curse you and your entire genealogy, historically and forevermore!" wailed an agonized Webb as he covered his face with hands while uttering an ongoing plethora of indecipherable expletives.

It was everything M could do to keep from busting out laughing at Webb's dramatic antics. Now that she had confided in him and was no longer the sole knowledge and keeper of the secret, she had relaxed and was almost completely back in her element. M loved Webb in a platonic way, and she knew that what she had just provided him with set the stage for major repercussions. She also knew he would find a way to deal with them appropriately.

Webb eventually emerged from his antics and slowly began: "Well, for starters let's get—",

"Whoa!" M interrupted before he could get started, then continued. "I believe you may be overlooking the obvious, and possibly the most important, part of this situation."

"What do you mean?" quizzed Webb through a puzzled expression.

M never skipped a beat and jumped right in. "This is a huge, well-planned, organized, and orchestrated operation. It's been going on unmolested, for the most part, for several years. It would appear that whoever set this thing up, for whatever reason, had resources out the gazoo. Who is brazen enough to do this kind of thing in the magnitude of this scale and has the ability to pull it off? This can't be just greed. There has to be, there must be, another explanation. And one more thing, whoever is involved or behind this thing ain't going to be happy when you do what I think you're gonna do," she finished.

Webb just stared at her, absorbing the revelation she had just hit him with. Slowly he began nodding his head in acknowledgement and eventually began to speak to her very deliberately. "You are absolutely, 100% right; we could not see the forest for the trees for a moment there. This whole thing is definitely a game changer. Got to have a little time to wrap my head around everything, but in the meantime, if you don't mind, get on the horn and ask Kathryn to peddle on over here ASAP to document what you've done and the preliminary indications. Oh, and if she needs child care, tell her we've got her covered. Really need to do this immediately. Also need to get another couple of folks here that talk your language as witnesses as well. That's your call, but make sure they understand that this is all close to the vest, under my personal threat of being drawn and quartered. Make sure Dick Andrews knows absolutely nothing about this; I mean, seriously, not a whiff. While you're waiting for them to show, how 'bout creating a little cheat sheet for me with just the essentials, you know, the highlights. I'm gonna need them in short order, I suspect. I need to make a few calls," he finished.

"May I ask, what you're going to do with all this?" asked a concerned M, displaying considerable anguish.

"What do you expect me to do?" Webb said, flashing a huge grin. "Listen closely, M; what you have done here is nothing short of a Nobel Prize-winning investigation. You deserve a commendation of the highest order for public service achievement. I really owe you. As far as what I'm going to do, as they say, if you are going to run with the "big dogs," you got to jump off the porch. I am going to do my job. You may or may not appreciate the kind of political fallout this is going to cause, but I need to make sure some folks have a heads up and are not ambushed by what's getting ready to happen. Need to get started on that right now. Thanks again; you got no idea how much I appreciate everything you've done on this thing," Webb concluded.

"Dr. Espy, you are being way too modest about this. This was your original idea, remember?!" M emphasized.

"All I did was provide the germ of an idea. There is no way I have the math skills, systemic insights, and technological abilities to navigate through or operationalize what you just did. If I ever even dreamed I had any idea what you just did, I'd apologize! You are the one that is being overly modest." Webb just smiled at her with awe and genuine appreciation as he turned and headed to his office.

With a tailwind of confidence and pride, M retreated to her office to complete what Webb had requested. There was nothing she wouldn't do for that man. As Webb reached his office, the first call he made was to Mario Diaz, requesting assistance in setting up immediate, around-the-clock security for Peggy Melton. The next call was to David Baswell's personal direct phone. When David answered, Webb just said: "We need to talk ASAP!"

For whatever reason, Webb's overwhelming preoccupation with what had just transpired and the myriad of implications blocked his normal logical processing abilities. The enormity and complexity related to what he had just been faced with were beyond his comprehension and escaped his appreciation of the overall magnitude of the situation. It was almost as if he had just killed a drug lord's only son and had no idea who he was and the perils such an act created. As Webb began preparations for his meeting with David, he had no tangible idea what had just been uncovered, who he was dealing with, or any sense of the actual danger pending.

36

March 5, 1994

Capital City Country Club, Tallahassee, Florida

David Baswell agreed to meet with Webb at 2:30 that afternoon, away from the office, at the old Capital City Country Club. If there was one thing David was positive of, it was that Webb Espy would never have called him on a Saturday requesting a one-on-one, face-to-face, if it was not something extremely important and/or very serious. Webb was already waiting at a secluded table in the dining room when David arrived. The two exchanged greetings, and David deadpanned: "Who have you murdered?"

"Did you bring a shovel with you?" Webb matched David's attempt at wit.

"Well, when I get through with what I'm about to tell you, I'd bet big money you wished it was something as easy to deal with. Seriously, David, as much as I look forward to our little ping pong duels and repartee, as well as sticking it to you, I'm going to dispense with the pleasure because you need to pay real close attention to what I am going to tell you, and I am pretty sure you're not going to be real happy about it when I'm through."

"Okay, Dr. Espy; let's stick to business. I'm all ears; let's get it on. I'm on total listening mode," David relented.

For the next twenty minutes, Webb provided a frame of reference, the process employed that resulted in the findings, as well as the obvious implications, along with a few of his own editorials.

David listened intently and never interrupted once while absorbing it all. When Webb finished the orientation, David did not speak immediately. Webb realized that David had unique problem-solving abilities that incorporated some different priorities and analytical algorithms than others might employ. In addition, his knowledge and appreciation of the political landscape and long-term survival for participants was beyond the comprehension of many seasoned veterans. David appeared in some type of a trance, staring into a void and totally focused. Then, suddenly out of nowhere, the first question surfaced. "How much time we got before the shit hits the fan?" he asked seriously.

"Well, that depends if you want us to take the cowardly way out and send M on an extended sabbatical?" Webb shrugged.

"Let's not even kid about a thing like that." David shook his head. You know that ain't in either of our DNAs. I have a germ of an idea about how we might play this, but timing and offense are essential. What I need from you, at this point, is not to pull punches when I ask you a question. Some might deem that some of my scheming is coming from right field, but trust me, there's a method to my madness." Webb gave a brief nod, then responded. "In that case, I would say two weeks from today, although, in reality, it would be fifteen days. I say this because there is a toll-free number that a provider can call on Sunday by midnight to ascertain what his payment is going to be, either by check or electronic deposit, for the week. It is conceivable that we could put it on a fast track and get it done before next week's billing cycle, but then we take the risk of violating our own safeguards and deviating from our normal MO. I would prefer not to do that because I believe it would be more appropriate that they receive our normal certified letter laying out the reason, or reasons, that their claims have been pended for medical review. It will be a lot cleaner and less complicated if we do it in that manner. The obvious downside is that you and I both know we are allowing several million to go out the door that, in all probability, will never be retrieved."

Before he could continue, David interrupted, "That's my department. I'll relieve you of that one right now. Go ahead and do it the way you feel most comfortable. Just keep me completely in the loop 24/7. Now there's something that's rubbing an old brain cell that is almost *déjà vu*. What you have described is reminiscent of the old Leopard case several years ago. If memory serves me, there was a physician that headed up a Medicare mill of sorts called something like Platinum Plus, I believe, and hit Medicare coffers for a huge ticket, skipped the country, fought extradition, outlasted the statute of limitations, and died on a yacht in Spain. To my knowledge, the money was never recovered."

"That's a pretty remarkable recall, I'd have to say," admitted Webb.

"Yeah, well, the truth is, I was privy to a series of special briefings on the case for a variety of reasons while they were trying to extradite him. Bottom line is, just like this situation, greed does not seem to be the primary motivation. The real question then becomes; if greed is not the motivating factor, what else could it possibly be? Nobody ever came up with an answer that would hold up or make any real sense, and let me tell you, there were some real smart sons of bitches trying to figure that one out. There were some theories that were way out there, Dr. Espy, my friend."

"As I touched on earlier, M and I had the same kind of discussion. I've got a strange kind of hunch that we are not going to get the same kind of reaction for pending these claims that we would from other providers who we pend claims for medical review. I don't pretend to understand what's going on here, but if I'm betting my money, it's on the premise that whoever is behind this is not going to expose themselves and let us get our foot in the door, and that's exactly what will happen if they begin attempting to exercise their legal rights and remedies," Webb offered as a rationalization.

"The thing that a lot of folks don't know about the Leopard case was that there were several rumors as to a mystery accomplice who was practically invisible, operated completely incognito, and was camouflaged beyond recognition. It was alleged that this mysterious phantom was the real brains of the operation. Of course, there was not a shred of reliable evidence or proof that a person such as this ever really existed," concluded David.

"Well, it makes for a great story to mull over at cocktail hour," Webb interjected.

"Maybe it will be the subject for one of your books one day. Let's just refer to it for now as *The Sunshine Shenanigan*," chuckled David.

"Never can tell; if so, I'll give credit where credit is due," Webb sniggered.

"Now, this is what I'm going to do. I need to start pulling rabbits out of a hat and do as much damage control as possible. I've got to put a lot of folks on notice without giving any specifics. I don't want anybody to get politically ambushed or blindsided by this thing. At the same time, there are obvious reasons that we can't be too forthcoming. I believe you are insulated from any repercussions related to whatever happens, but I got your back completely, and I'm not letting you get scapegoated, and don't even think about falling on your sword. I got this, and got a few ideas that I just might be able turn from a liability into an asset. One thing we have going for us is Chapter 409 of the Florida Statutes, which outlines how you are to operate. Although Florida has mandatory government in the sunshine as set forth in Chapter 119 of the Florida Statues, that doesn't really apply here. As a matter of fact, Chapter 409 specifically exempts almost any and all information related to investigations from disclosure until certain criteria have been met. Under the current circumstances, I personally don't see these criteria being met in the foreseeable future, if ever. And always keep in mind what we both know so well: 'If you feed from the public trough,' you got to be prepared to be called a 'pig' every now and then," concluded David.

"You are a quick study and never cease to amaze me, Mr. Sec," Webb said, shaking his head in approval and admiration.

"Listen, when you talk to M, tell her I said thank you. I want you to bring her over to my office as soon as possible because I'd really like to do it personally. She did one hell of a job. Oh, and thank you, too, I guess. I don't know if M and I could have done this without you," David ended, with a legitimate belly laugh.

"Referencing one of your earlier points, let me suggest that you personally brief Senator Arthur St. John and Demetri Lorenzo at TaxWatch," Webb requested.

"Consider it done. Give me a shout if you think any other special touches are required. Now, if that's all you need me for right now, I need to return my shovel to the shed and start making a few calls of my own," said the Secretary as he engaged in a contortionist type of maneuver to untangle his massive frame from underneath the table.

37

March 5 Through March 19, 1993

Tallahassee, Florida

There had been a whirlwind of activity in Medicaid Program Integrity for the past two weeks. Webb had been physically at the helm of the command post, constantly providing both the catalyst and continuity for the entire operation. *Esprit de corps* could not have been higher, and Webb had temporarily displaced the majority of MPI staff from their routine functions and responsibilities and assembled an ad hoc task force in order to deal most efficiently with the deviated business-as-usual norms. It was a flat organizational model; Webb at the top and then everybody else. The model could not be employed for any extended period, but it was, temporally, the most efficient means to get the most accomplished in a short, concentrated time frame. Webb estimated that he only had a brief window of opportunity to maximize the impact of this project, and he wanted to exploit it to the hilt and expose primary operatives before contingency plans might be employed. Webb was in total command of the operation, conducting the orchestra and choreographing the dance troupe.

On the heels of M's innovative discovery, along with expanded due diligence as well as Charlie and Virginia's identification of linked treating providers, there had been two other bombshells that enhanced the target group significantly.

Webb had never met Willie Dozios, the infamous little Miami Cuban Jew, but he decided that when he did — and he intended to do just that as soon as feasible — he was going to kiss him, buy him the best steak dinner in Miami, and give him his choice of the best escort services available. Willie had worked overtime, exercised initiative, and had expanded due diligence far beyond any anticipated expectations. With the intel Willie's operation had provided, which had included a staggering number of new addresses, vehicle license numbers, and actual recipient targets, it was a simple matter for M to link this additional information through MPI's patented "AIM" program, destined evermore to stand for Artificial Intelligence, M's Program, and expand the capture net significantly.

The other major development was a timely and purely coincidental fluke. In the process of reviewing the paper Medicaid provider enrollment applications that had been submitted during the past twenty-four months, it was discovered accidentally, under close scrutiny, that there were a number of applications submitted from an original master application packet which had been copied, completed, and submitted, and which contained an identifying flaw. Unbeknownst to the submitter of these specific applications, there was a crease on the second page of the document, which made it easy to detect the potentially aberrant submissions on the copies. These applications were cherry-picked and immediately feed into AIM, which resulted in the identification of bullpen provider entities that had yet to submit a single claim. These currently dormant billing and pay-to-providers were sitting there, just waiting to be launched as contingencies. Now, that would not happen!

The proverbial operational trigger was set to be pulled during the weekend's last phase of the Claims Processing Subsystem's final run. This part of the automated process cut actual checks, made electronic deposits into provider accounts, and printed the Provider Explanation of Medicaid Benefits for each claim submitted, indicating whether the claim had been paid, denied, or pended and the reasons for each action during the payment cycle. The upcoming anticipated results for numerous providers would yield unparalleled surprises and chaos throughout the Florida Medicaid provider community.

Preparations were also being put in place outside MPI, in anticipation of the avalanche of reactions bound to occur once the provider community was faced with the reality of what had transpired. David Baswell had personally intervened, at Webb's request, to instruct the Medicaid Fiscal Agent to shut down the qualitative component of the Medicaid Hot Line, or, in other words, a caller would not be able to speak with a live representative. As a bonus, MPI decided to capture the phone numbers from calls after midnight on Sunday to feed into AIM as another potential detection strategy.

The Office of Public Information within the Department of Health and Rehabilitative Services had been provided with a courteously worded, tactfully brutal boilerplate response and was strictly prohibited from deviating from this response in any manner whatsoever. Select legislators had received personal calls from Secretary Baswell as a heads up in order to brace for a potential onslaught of constituent demands for answers. His advice to such inquiries was to simply state: "No information is available or can be provided since any such information is related to a formal ongoing investigation."

From Webb's perspective, there would more than likely be two major peaks in the provider community's explosive responses to Medicaid's actions. The first would occur when the providers either checked their electronic deposits or received pended claims notifications, rather than their anticipated paper checks. The second would occur during the following week, when it was discovered that the bullpen providers had been shut down as well. Wagers by MPI staff ran the spectrum. There was the camp which believed that there would be little, if any, response from those that were guilty and had been caught in the net. Others bet on an overwhelming flood of protests. Contrary to most situations, Webb tended to suspect that it would be the truly innocent which made the most noise. Both Webb and M were anxiously curious as to what was about to happen. They really did not know, but one thing was for sure: something!

38

April 5, 1993

Miami, Florida

"SHIT, DAMN, MUTHERFUCKING SON A BITCH," roared a maniacal Manasa as he bounced his Rolex off the opposite bedroom wall with a velocity that would have solicited appreciative drools from Nolan Ryan wannabes. "Mutherfucker!" he echoed again. This kind of emotional outburst would have been shockingly foreign to anyone who had ever known, worked, or had in anyway ever been associated with the traditionally cool and levelheaded Marcus Manasa. Even under the most pressured circumstances, he traditionally demonstrated himself to be stoic, a rock, an oak, always exuding confidence and calmness. This exhibition of intense rage and violence was completely outside the typical boundaries which defined the man or the professional that he was.

Only a week earlier, he had demonstrated a much calmer demeanor when confronted with the initial news that a significant portion of his operation had been stymied and payments delayed, and possibly reduced or eliminated, due to an error message stating simply: "Pended for Medical Review by MPI." The early news, not altogether unanticipated, was more of a nuisance and allowed contingency provider entities to be unleashed into the payment system. The most recent information suggested that contingency strategies had been compromised and, therefore, had failed in almost 85% of the cases. Marcus glared at the telephone, that demonic instrument, the one that had just conveyed the completely unanticipated, game-changing news that would alter his life in the foreseeable future in almost every way imaginable. An objective outsider observing Marcus at this precise instant would, in all likelihood, assume that he seemingly was contemplating the same fate for the phone which had, only seconds earlier, resulted in the watch fatality. As quickly as it had happened, it was over. Marcus was disgusted with his temper tantrum, but the emotion was short-lived as he regained his poise and his brain kicked into warp drive mode. The result was a series of analytics, rationalizations, calculations, contingency strategies, and a reprieve for the phone. What had happened could not have happened, but it had! He had to assume the worst-case scenarios and back into what operational components were absolutely destroyed and what might be potentially salvageable. By any measurable standard, the operation he had been orchestrating for the past several years was a colossal success. He could have folded the tent after eighteen months, and it would have been considered an A-plus operation. This, however, would not have satisfied him in the least. This was not what he had created nor planned. This was to have been his proverbial swan song, setting the bar to a level that others in his profession would set their sights on, yet never be able to attain. Marcus felt that his destiny was to be considered a legend among those peers who operated under the various cloaks of clandestine activities for causes unknown to many, foreign to most and unappreciated by the masses.

Marcus spent the next hour on the phone verifying the details of the devastation, methodically pouring over ingrained cerebral

spreadsheets, cataloging mental notes to himself, and deciphering numerous calculations. The most serious and disconcerting
issue was not the initial shutdown and the immediate revenue
loss from Espy's MPI maneuvers. That had been planned for.
The real problem was that it appeared that the various failsafe
contingency strategies, with only a few exceptions, had also been
completely shut down and effectively compromised. In the final
analysis, for all practical purposes, it appeared to Marcus that his
mainstream operation was currently completely stymied and rendered impotent!

Eventually, Marcus hit a point of diminishing returns in his
analysis of the overall situation. There was no way of getting
around it; things were as bad as he had initially determined. Sensing that reality was what it was, he deposited himself on the sofa,
closed his eyes, and began employing some heuristic exercises in
an attempt to find a legitimate, or for that matter, any path forward. In his mind, questions were emerging that had to be answered prior to being able to proceed. Had he underestimated
Espy that badly? Was there any possible way this could have been
a coincidence? Was it conceivable this might have been some type
of an overall blanket exercise in which his operation had just been
caught in the net, along with other victims?

For the next three hours, Marcus went down a comprehensive
list of algorithmic labyrinths challenging each possible conclusion
until he had exhausted almost every conceivable possibility. Eventually, he reconciled himself to a simple reality; Espy had pulled
something off that was almost virtually impossible, but somehow,
he had managed to do it! He could not have had the resources,
technology, expertise, or proper authorizations to conduct what
amounted to "artificial intelligence." In Marcus's calculated con-

clusion, one thing was absolutely clear — if things had any chance of going forward, Espy had to go. During the next hour, two additional names were added to that list. In Marcus Manasa's world, and the stakes he played for, surgery was the only cure for cancer!

39

April 17, 1994

Apalachicola River Swamps,
south of Chattahoochee, Florida

From out of nowhere, an owl hollered. It was well on up in the morning and unusual for an owl to be on the prowl. Webb recognized this particular owl, however, and answered with a one-note hoot of his own. In less than three minutes, the owl materialized without feathers or wings, disguised as one of his best friends, Max Bloodworth. "Been a tough morning," announced Max as he caught his breath from the climb up the hill.

"Yep, got a T-shirt myself; it's been fun, though! As they say, the worst day in the woods is better than the best day at the office," Webb offhandedly responded. "Well, are you gonna tell me a story or not?" Webb commanded.

"You want the long or short version?" Max grinned as he leaned his gun against a tree, pulled out a Winston, lit it, and took a long drag.

"I'll settle for the short version, because I'm sure they're pretty much the same, knowing your yarns and storytelling proficiencies," Webb said, returning the grin.

Max leaned against the tree. "I got here early and slipped in while it was still dark, so I could get close to where I wanted to set up. I waited until I heard a couple of cardinals wake up and then I owled. He gobbled right back, and he was exactly where I figured he might be. He was probably seventy-five yards down in the head, and I actually moved a little away from him to set up the way I wanted to. I stayed quiet until I heard a low cluck, and he gobbled at that. I went through the routine; a few soft clucks, tree calls, and eventually, a fly-down cackle with wing beats and all. He double gobbled at that. After that, he didn't gobble but a few times; hell, he didn't need to! I heard at least nine young ladies fly down before he just pitched off the roost into the midst of them. I called to him, knowing that was probably useless; of course, you never know. Then I tried calling to the hens, but there is an old boss hen that's running the show and is in complete charge. Every time I called, he gobbled, and she let me have it. You know the drill; she eventually dragged him in the opposite direction. Last time I heard them they were almost to the river. At some time today, he will be in the middle of the power line in one of his strut zones. I've seen him out there with his little harem, and, eventually, once those hens are no longer a factor, he will come a long way to the call," finished Max.

"I've seen him out there myself. Can't see his spurs for the grass, but he has a paint brush for a beard, and his fan looks like a damn golf umbrella. You know, if you really want him, you could just go ahead and get out there with him," Webb suggested, knowing what was coming.

" You know me better than that. I don't want to assassinate him or ambush his ass; hell, anybody can do that. The old bastard deserves a better fate than that," Max declared almost reverently.

"Spoken like a tried and true reformed outlaw," Webb laughed. Although Webb was joking with his buddy, he was also speaking the truth. Max had learned to turkey hunt from his uncles, who, in fact, had been out-and-out outlaws. They learned to hunt turkeys to feed their families in hard times, and there were no rules, seasons, or limits. Max knew all the tricks and shortcuts, and by age eighteen, he ended being even better at it than the best of any of his mentors. Somehow, someway, after returning from his tours in Vietnam, Max went through some type of metamorphosis, resulting in an almost born-again mentality when it came to harvesting turkeys, while rejecting the former hunting methods of his outlaw relatives. Maybe it was his association and friendship with Lovett Williams, renowned wildlife biologist and wild turkey expert, or possibly, it was the realization that the wild turkey in America had been on the verge of extinction until the National Wild Turkey Federation stepped in and turned things around. But for some reason, conservation had suddenly become a fanatical priority and extremely important to him. Along with the reformation, his reverence and respect for America's greatest game bird reached a new pinnacle — the bird had rights that needed to be respected and not infringed upon. Turkey hunting was a calling sport, and it should be honored as such. Max would go livid if he heard about someone shooting a turkey out of a deer stand with a rifle in the fall.

Webb and Max had met some twenty years earlier at an NWTF fundraising banquet event. A mutual admiration began almost immediately, and the two began hunting together immediately, whenever they could. The first time Max heard Webb call, he instantly realized that he was listening to something special. Webb had a rhythm and emotion to his calling that was instinctive and not teachable. Max had never seen anyone do the things on a box call that Webb demonstrated. By the same token, Webb thought Max was the best overall turkey hunter he had ever had the privilege to hunt with, and he had hunted with some of the best in the country. Max's knowledge of the bird, woodsman ship, calling ability, hunting strategies, and improvisation was uncanny. Webb often said if it were a life or death situation, and he needed someone to go with him to take a bird, he would choose Max every time.

The two discovered they had a number of other things in common as well. For starters, they shared the same birthday, with Webb being only about three hours older. They both loved baseball and held a deep appreciation for the detailed nuances of the game. They even stumbled upon the fact that they had played against one another in a couple of Little League All-Star games back in the late fifties. Both joined the military a month apart in early 1966 — Webb to the Air Force and Max to the Marines. Webb was deployed to Japan, South Korea, and England as a training specialist, and Max, after being selected as a Marine Recon after extensive training, went to the jungles of Vietnam as a special services sniper and communications specialist. Max didn't talk much about his time in Vietnam, but on a few occasions, when he and Webb had gone out of state on turkey hunts and the red liquor was flowing, he recounted a few incidents which made Webb aware that he had been in the thick of things and had killed folks, and more than just a few. On one particular occasion, when the two friends had been out of state on a hunting trip, Webb touched a hot coffee pot and joked about a purple heart. As an afterthought, he casually asked Max if he had been awarded "the Purple Heart." After a brief delay in responding,

Max, in a somewhat humorous, thought-provoking manner, simply replied: "No, not unless you consider jungle foot rot, dysentery, and creature bites. Naw, Webb; based on the kind of stuff I did, if I had gotten a purple heart, we probably wouldn't be having this conversation right now."

"Let's hear about your morning, Mr. Turkey Hunter?" probed Max.

"A little different from yours, but obviously, no cigar. Contrary to your situation, the bird I've been chasing was nowhere near where I thought he might be; however, you know me, always the optimist. I figure if he can hear me, I got a chance to call him. Well, I did, but he didn't; however, I did manage to call in those same two-year-old toms for the third time, who I've named Heckle and Jeckle," Webb said, grinning like a Cheshire cat.

Max laughed. "I'm sure they are the same two stooges I called in last week. Full fans, but about nine-inch beards.

"Sounds like you've made their acquaintance as well," Webb stated.

"Listen, Webb, I almost forgot; did you see or hear anyone else in our vicinity this morning?" Max asked seriously.

"No, I don't think I heard anything that would make me suspect anybody else was in the area. I heard a vehicle up on Dolan Road about an hour ago, but I don't think I've heard another human sound other than your owl hooting. Why, what makes you ask such questions, young grasshopper?" Webb said kiddingly.

"Well, when you've been where I've been and done what I've done, you just notice little things and feel things. Something spooked a doe up out of the bottom back behind me this morning, and I don't believe it was a coyote, because I could still hear squirrels running around and playing on the ground. I caught movement later on, only for a split second, but it just didn't feel right. Whatever. I can't imagine what in the world another human being would be doing in these mosquito-infested swamps, unless he is crazy enough to be chasing these fine feathered friends, like me and you," Max laughed. "When can you do it again?" Max asked.

"How about Tuesday?" Webb volunteered.

"That's a roger, then," Max confirmed. "I'm working nights right now, and I'll be getting off at 5:00 A.M., and I'll meet you at McDonald's on Tennessee as soon as I can get there. If you don't mind, let's use your vehicle; I need some new tires, and they are on order and won't be in until Wednesday at the earliest," Max indicated.

"No problem, partner; now let's go get some biscuits," Webb offered as they headed toward their vehicles.

40

The Premeditated Accident April 19, 1994

Tallahassee to Gadsden County

Webb entered the McDonald's parking lot on West Tennessee Street just before 5:00 A.M., and immediately recognized Max's truck parked on the back side of the building. Webb pulled in beside the truck, motioned to Max to roll down his window to let him know he needed to go in to use the facilities, and asked if he needed anything from inside. Max acknowledged he already had coffee by holding up his cup for Webb to see. Webb left the jeep and headed inside, while in the meantime, Max began stowing his gear in the back seat of Webb's jeep. Once everything was in, he deposited himself in the front passenger side, reclined the seat almost horizontally, pulled his cap over his face, and promptly began his nap. When Webb returned to the jeep, Max was snoozing like an infant.

Marcus was several hundred yards behind Webb when he pulled into McDonald's as he had anticipated he would. He saluted himself on his ability to ascertain how predictable Webb Espy appeared to be. Marcus pulled off at a gas station about a quarter of a mile past McDonald's and waited for Webb's vehicle to appear. Marcus wanted Webb well in front of him and was confident of his destination and exactly where he would park once he got there. If that turned out not to be the case, he would simply abort the plan for today. In less than five minutes, Webb's jeep drove by, and Marcus muttered a congratulatory affirmation to himself.

Webb made his way to Interstate 10 and headed west. After about twenty-nine minutes of driving, he got off at the Chattahoochee Exit and, after several turns, eventually took one of several dirt roads that led west, toward the Apalachicola River. The trip had been uneventful, and Max had slept the entire way. About a mile away from the river, Webb turned north onto an old logging road that led toward the high river ridges that overlooked the mud swamps between the bluffs and the river.

Webb parked in his normal spot, which left about another 600-yard walk to the ridge. Max was still asleep when they came to a stop. "Wakeup, Rip Van Winkle," Webb said, giving his buddy a hearty shake.

"I think I may leave it all to you today," groaned Max as Webb got out of the car and began sorting out his gear. Presently, Max finally began to stir and eventually, a human form materialized when his door opened. After going through various superstitious rituals and the usual good-natured badgering, the two started ambling up the gradual incline toward their staging area at the crest of the ridge. Their assent was interrupted by the calls of a whippoorwill close by.

"That's a good sign!" remarked Max.

"Yeah, I love to hear those things. Gives me the warm and fuzzies every time," replied Webb. A few minutes later, the sound of an automobile coming down a parallel road to the east made them exchange quizzical glances. After a brief pause, they simply shrugged at each other and ventured on. The morning was quiet and still, with little or no wind, and the heavy dew allowed walking with almost no sound at all. Although it was cool and in the high thirties, the air was fresh, and the exercise felt invigorating. Arriving at the crest of the hill, they stood together, catching their breath, and took a little respite while listening to the stillness of the woods that had not quite decided to wake up just yet. It was a peaceful feeling shared by both of the men.

Several hundred yards east, Marcus was taking an almost direct route toward where the pair were currently standing. He had already verified that Webb's jeep was parked precisely where he had anticipated it would be. Batting 1000, Marcus thought to himself as he kept buttressing the validity of his all-inclusive plan. The general area had been reconnoitered personally by Marcus over the past several days, and his independent observations had been supplemented with topo maps and enlarged aerial photographs. Marcus knew the lay of the land and, most importantly, he knew the precise spot where Webb Espy's hunting blind was located, and how he needed to approach it. With direct purpose and confidence, Marcus, with the aid of the most sophisticated night vision assistance equipment available, was making rapid progress in the direction of his prey. Everything was absolutely perfect so far.

Max and Webb stood just listening for a few minutes until a cardinal's call brought them out of their trance.

"Guess it's about that time for me to mosey on down and get comfortable," announced Webb, breaking the silence.

"Go get him, partner," responded Max genuinely.

"Ditto, my friend," replied Webb as he threw his shotgun sling over his shoulder and started making his way down the slight slope toward his blind some seventy yards or so below. Max watched his good friend descend in the direction of his predetermined setup. There was one major difference in their hunting styles — Webb's preference was to wait for the bird to come to him, while Max preferred to go to the bird and then set up. Max had already decided that he was going to stay put for a few more minutes because the bird he was after could be in several different places, and there was no sense committing to the wrong direction and then having to backtrack if he guessed wrong. He still had plenty of time, although it was getting light enough to see pretty easily now.

As Max was waiting, he suddenly became aware that the earlier coffee, which he had determined to be inferior, had all of a sudden mysteriously decided to come alive with much vigor and had awakened his sleeping bowels to the state that an immediate constitutional requirement demanded an even more immediate deposit. Max scanned the area for a suitable impromptu toilet facility and spied one under a large magnolia tree a few yards toward Webb's blind down the hill. With more than one might consider slight urgency, Max made it to the tree in less time than most would deem possible for a man of his age and limitations. In a whirlwind of activity, reminiscent of a Tasmanian Devil, Max made it to the tree, shucked laundry, and took his position with TP in hand in just the nick of time. There was instant relief in more ways than one, and Max was praising his good fortune that a serious accident of the nasty variety had been averted by the hair of his chinny chin chin.

Max began finishing up his business and was putting his hunting vest back on when all of a sudden, a turkey began loud clucking about eighty-five yards back to the east, which was beyond the logging road that they had just walked up. The hen gave seven or eight loud, alarm-type clucks, then sailed off the roost, cracking limbs and flapping wings until eventually, she locked her wings and glided out of sight over a small clear cut to the woods beyond.

Max waited to see if other turkeys would follow suit, but apparently this turkey had roosted alone. Max was juggling several thoughts simultaneously. Turkeys often act in strange ways at times; however, they also react in extremely predictable ways, given specific circumstances. A turkey flying off the roost in the dark or poor light is the result of being frightened. Not many things frighten a turkey on the roost at night. Occasionally, an owl might get too close for comfort, and the turkey simply concludes that discretion is the better part of valor and decides to retreat to a more strategic position. Normally, when this occurs, the turkey leaves the roost without much vocalization. When a turkey starts a series of alarm putts, something is upsetting the bird. More often than not, it is a predator and, more often than not, of the two-legged variety! Max began focusing his total attention in the direction that the turkey flew from.

Marcus was pleased with his progress, and he knew that he had made up a great deal of time on Webb. He was actually slightly ahead of schedule and slowed his pace a little. He paused briefly, checked his compass reading, and adjusted his course slightly southwest about three degrees. Based on his estimate, he calculated that he was approximately 175 yards from his predetermined setup point. He no longer required the night vision equipment and took time to remove it and stow it in his fanny pack. He did not want to arrive too early, based on the amount of light he wanted to work with.

Marcus waited a couple of minutes and then began a gradual and steady ascent up the head toward the ridge. He had only taken a few steps when, all of a sudden, a series of loud, sharp staccato notes very close above stopped him in his tracks. The instant effect was like getting precariously close to a rattlesnake, although Marcus would not react to a rattlesnake like most people would. His reaction was more akin to a fleeting split second of confusion. As the turkey flew off the limb, breaking several small branches with wing-beating frenzy, Marcus was instantly amused, and it dawned on him that a wild turkey flying off a roost was a brand-new experience for him. Eventually, he laughed at himself and the incident and did an immediate reassessment of the situation. No harm to the mission, he finally convinced himself. Although he did not know it at the time, this was only one thing he had not planned for, nor anticipated.

As the moments went by, Max became even more curious about what had just occurred. It was simply a strange situation, with not much of any reasonable explanation he could come up with that would justify the turkey's unusual behavior. Whether it was his Vietnam experiences, intuition, a sixth sense, or whatever, Max felt something was strangely amiss. Max sensed the presence of a lifeform before it was visible. He heard distinct little noises, undecipherable to most people, that made him keenly aware that he was not alone, and something was making its way directly towards him. It might be a deer, a hog, a coyote, possibly even a bear, but whatever it was, it was certainly alive, and it was getting closer.

Marcus was approaching his destination and began slowly and stealthily moving toward the specific spot he had previously reconnoitered. Prior to the final leg of his approach, he raised his weapon with the telescope and ascertained that his target was positioned in the blind, exactly as he was supposed to be. With that piece of information confirmed, Marcus immediately negotiated the final few yards of the stalk.

Max kept his eyes focused on the natural funnel area where he anticipated that the thing, whatever it was, would emerge. He was almost relieved when a human form appeared. Initially, he could only see the man from about the waist up due to the fact that he was looking slightly up the hill, and the broom sage hid the bottom part of the man's silhouette. Just about the same time as Max saw him, the man abruptly stopped and appeared to look back the way he had come. Max's initial assessment was that another hunter had, by happenstance or pure coincidence, invaded their hunting setups without any knowledge of their presence whatsoever. The perpetrator had turned slightly to the right, and his body was shielding some activity that was requiring attention and concentration. Max was more curious regarding the man's peculiar actions than anything else at this point. Almost as an afterthought, Max remembered he had not restored the roll of toilet paper into the back sack of his hunting vest, and bent over to pick it up and fumbled momentarily getting it secured in his hunting vest properly.

Marcus had reached the spot; it was exactly sixty yards to the large white oak tree where Webb was currently situated. Marcus wasted no time whatsoever and moved with haste and precision. Marcus wrapped the strap of his customized 300 Win Mag around his elbow, cheeked the rifle, and began moving the crosshairs to the general target area. He found the target easily, and it was completely still. He moved the crosshairs to a spot about the size of a dime, relaxed himself completely, let out a deep breath, and gently began to touch the trigger.

Max finished with his toilet paper rescue diversion and returned his attention to the man in front of him. The scene unfolded as a complete surprise and initially was incomprehensible. The alleged hunter had an obvious sniper's rifle shouldered, with the sling secured around his elbow for steadiness, and was looking through the scope while aiming the weapon in the direction of Webb's blind. Without realizing what was happening, Max's instincts took over and he screamed, "Hey," a hair-split second before the rifle fired. Max's scream was accompanied by automatic movements, resulting in his own weapon, seemingly on autopilot, moving to his own launch position.

As Marcus began the process of gently squeezing the trigger, a sound erupted to his left, soliciting only the slightest reflex response just prior to muzzle blast. Without hesitation, Marcus, through conditioned response, pivoted to his left while simultaneously ejecting the spent hull from the rifle and throwing another round in the chamber. Fate itself must have looked down Max Bloodworth's gun barrel! Marcus's bolt-action sniper rifle with a scope at twenty steps was no match for a specialty-trained, combat-seasoned veteran armed with a three and a half inch Benelli Super Black Eagle with Magnum blend HEVI-shot loads.

Immediately after the rifle fired and the left turn maneuver by the shooter, Max knew he was the intended next target. Preconditioned survival mode kicked in, and Max fired off the first of two rounds. The first caught Marcus in the upper chest, throat, and chin area, the second, as Marcus was staggering backward, was lower in the lungs, abdomen, and groin area. As Max knew from previous combat experience in the jungles of Vietnam, both shots were fatal, and he dismissed the fact that he had just killed another human being as he sprinted toward Webb's blind.

Webb had settled into his blind and was peacefully listening to the woods wake up and come alive. He was totally oblivious to everything that was transpiring behind him. He did come to full alert when he heard a turkey excitedly start clucking back behind him and then fly off the roost. Unlike Max, he dismissed the incident without attaching much significance. A few moments passed, and Webb heard an owl a long distance away, toward the river. Seconds later, someone very close yelled "hey" behind him to his left, and Webb spontaneously jerked his head toward the sound, at which point the tree he was resting his back on exploded, and the world went black.

Max arrived at the blind expecting the worst and found pretty much what he had anticipated. Webb was lying on his left side, with the right side of his head and upper torso exposed. The amount of blood from the head wound made it difficult to believe that he could possibly be alive. Without hesitation, Max immediately went into battlefield protocols. He was able to find a pulse and then began to address the wound and bleeding. No primary entry or exit wound was immediately apparent. Max retrieved the roll of toilet paper and rapidly began wrapping it over the side of the head, over the top, and around the chin. He wrapped until he was out of paper. He next took a roll of duct tape, which he never went into the woods without, and wrapped it tightly over the toilet paper bandage.

Now, Max faced the next major obstacle; how the hell was he going to get him out of here for emergency medical assistance? Max did not have time to dwell on the matter. He needed to go ahead and do something, even if it was wrong. The major issue he faced was getting the vehicle as close as possible. Unfortunately, where Webb's blind had been constructed made it almost impossible to get a vehicle closer than about twenty-five yards. Once he checked Webb's pulse one last time, he started out. His path took him directly past the man he had just shot and killed. The corpse was not a pretty sight. From just slightly below the navel up to the nose looked like jelly, with the esophagus, trachea, and larynx severed and exposed. Other damage was indecipherable due to the massive amount of blood. As an afterthought, Max retraced his steps, bent down, felt the man's pockets, and discovered a set of car keys and slipped them in his pocket. He then started jogging toward the general direction of the vehicle. Max had already calculated and committed to a more direct route to the jeep rather than staying on the logging road, which made a wide, winding arc up the ridge that he and Webb had walked up earlier. The route took him along the same course which Marcus had taken just moments earlier.

Max was already gasping for air, and his lungs felt that they might burst any second, but he still had a long way to go. Every step solicited a renewed curse aimed alternately at Winston cigarettes and then toward himself. Before long, although it seemed like an eternity to Max, he had no alternative but to stop briefly for relief. With his eyes shut and hands on his knees, he sucked large amounts of fresh air into his lungs and continued this respite activity for almost a full minute. Finally, when he was able, he stood up, and as he opened his eyes, he caught an unmistakable reflection from the sun hitting something almost directly in front of him. Max instantly processed what his eyes had relayed, knew what it had to be, and without a second's hesitation, headed directly toward it.

Marcus's GMC SUV was black with dark tinted windows. As Max touched the door handle, the locks automatically opened.

He opened the door and got in. The interior was spotless and immaculately maintained. The first thing he spied was an unusual-looking, small mobile phone. Max, working in the high-tech end of the phone company for many years, was somewhat bewildered, in that he had never seen a prototype of this type of device before. Although anticlimactic, Max was more than elated at his seemingly good fortune with finding a vehicle and a phone. He was cognizant the phone would probably not work well, if at all, in this location, but he was relatively confident it might once he got out of the dead area and reached the main dirt road.

Max cranked the vehicle and drove like a mad man toward Webb's blind. He was now totally preoccupied with the next major challenge, which was extracting Webb from the woods and into the vehicle. By the time Max reached his friend, he was not feeling well at all. His heart was pounding, and he was nauseous and dehydrated. Max surveyed the situation and quickly decided to create a makeshift harness out of duct tape and Webb's belt, as well as his own. Once constructed and attached, Max began the arduous task of dragging Webb's dead weight toward the vehicle. It was slow going, and in Max's physical state, slow was an optimistic exaggeration of progress. Once Max finally got him to the vehicle, it took a Herculean effort of both brain and brawn to eventually succeed in securing Webb in the back seat. Max was completely drained and had long since passed his physical capabilities. He was currently operating on pure adrenaline and hidden reserves. Max checked for a pulse one more time, confirmed its presence, and headed for help.

Max gave a brief thought to checking the corpse, which he could not see from the current vantage point, and quickly decided there was no point in it, anyway. After what seemed like an eternity, he reached the main dirt road leading back to the highway and grabbed for the mobile phone. Overall, the phone was user-friendly, and Max had no difficulty initiating a call. On the first attempt, the call failed, indicating the absence of service, and Max cussed like a drunken sailor. Approximately a quarter of a mile up the road, he tried again, and his relief was overwhelming as the call went through. The voice on the other end was calm and professional. Max was not. He began to talk and realized he could not. His throat was parched, and he could barely utter a sound. What vocal sounds emerged were complete gibberish, while the voice on the other end remained patient and reassuring. Max's mind and his mouth were not in sync, and he was experiencing serious difficulty even breathing. He was having trouble putting thoughts into words and was aware that what was coming out of his mouth was absolutely incoherent. Things like hunting, swamp, buddy, head wound, heart attack, dead man, and help needed immediately were words that were distinctively audible but non-communicative. In pure frustration, Max was eventually able to clearly state: "Emergency! Help required immediately! I-10 at Chattahoochee exit. Meet us there ASAP!"

Max put the hazard flashers on and raced towards the rendezvous. After what, to Max, seemed was an eternity, he eventually arrived at the overpass over I-10. As he slid to a halt and put the vehicle in park, he could see there were blue lights already flashing directly in front of him and a firetruck coming in from behind him. He could also see both blue and red flashing lights on the interstate of at least two approaching emergency vehicles. Oh, thank God, was all that Max could think. He opened the door to greet the paramedics, discovered his legs were rubber, vomited uncontrollably, and collapsed unconsciously face-first to the asphalt below like a felled tree.

41

Later the Same Morning

Apalachicola River swamp area,
South of Chattahoochee, Florida

Within moments after Marcus's fatal encounter with Max Blood-worth, various sensor chips strategically embedded at various points in his body began transmitting signals to automated monitors in a number of surveillance stations around the globe and on satellites as well, which ran continuously, twenty-four hours per day. Beyond basic vital signs, the sensors also captured a variety of other bodily activities. Abnormal transmissions signaled a priority alert status, which brought highly trained human specialists to fail-safe positions. The protocols were precise, extremely simple, and directly straightforward. There was absolutely no room for discretion whatsoever. Depending entirely on the transmissions, there were only three courses of action: assistance, extraction, or eradication.

At least two of Marcus's sensors had become nonfunctional at the onset of the aberrant readings. The others were spiraling downward rapidly. Based on the global readings that pinpointed Marcus's current physical position, the protocols directed that the eradication process should commence within twelve minutes, unless all sensor readings should somehow restore or reverse themselves and begin transmitting normal readings. Twelve minutes later, it was confirmed that the situation had deteriorated and had not reversed itself.

Via technology well beyond the archives and comprehension of the general public, the existing chips remaining within Marcus's corpse were activated, and a chemical compound developed during the NASA program referred to as T-87, approximately 300 times stronger than fluorinated carborane acid, was activated and released into the soft tissue of Marcus's lifeless corpse, eliciting an immediate and incredible chemical reaction. In less than a minute, the tissue, as well as the entire body cavity and anything touching the body, or any object within fifteen yards that had been touched by the body, crystalized, decomposed, formed almost invisible ash particles, and completely vanished from sight, leaving no discernable residue. It was almost as if Marcus Manasa had never existed.

The next thing that the specialty monitors had to assess were items that had been in Marcus's possession that were in close proximity to his body as of the last normal readings. The sniper rifle and night vision equipment were the only items identified. This was an easy fix and, within seconds, subjected the rifle and other personal gear to a similar metamorphosis that had transformed Marcus's corpse to an invisible state only moments earlier.

The vehicle that had been in Marcus's possession was considered an exceptional situation and demanded special qualitative protocols, requiring a direct visual verification in order that collateral damage could be controlled to the extent possible. A verification team had been alerted and had already been deployed. The Special OPS group out of Panama City, Florida, was scheduled to arrive at a staging area within a quarter of a mile from the current vehicle's location inside an estimated twenty-seven minutes. From that point, the vehicle would be visually assessed in concert with its existing surroundings and discretionary options, and actions would be initiated accordingly.

Major Don Spelling was in charge of the Special OPS operation and would be the individual charged with initiating the necessary actions. It did not take long for the major to assess the situation. An immediate reconnaissance revealed the vehicle was wrapped in yellow crime scene tape and being loaded to an AAA tow truck, subcontracted by the Gadsden County Sheriff's Department. Once the tow truck had the vehicle loaded and secured, and the driver had pulled down the east ramp towards I-10, Major Spelling gave the signal. As the tow truck was about halfway down the ramp, the driver glanced in his mirror and, to his horror, saw his cargo totally engulfed in orange-blue flames. Exiting his truck, he was exposed to the most intense heat he had ever felt. It took only an instant for him to realize he was in the wrong place, and he sprinted down the ramp as fast as he could run. It might have been a humorous scene under different circumstances.

Later, when it was safe to gain a closer inspection, there was virtually no evidence that there had ever been a vehicle loaded to the burned-out skeleton of the tow truck. Marcus did not exist, his rifle did not exist, and his vehicle no longer existed. Later that same morning, Deputy Waylan Griggs, who had in his possession Marcus's car keys and cell phone, no longer existed either.

42

Still Later the Same Morning

Tallahassee Memorial Regional Medical Center

It was almost three hours after arriving at the hospital before Webb and Max could be identified. Neither of the men could identify themselves due to the state of their medical conditions. Neither had any identification on their persons, and the vehicle associated with them no longer existed. Fingerprints had, of course, been taken to feed through various data bases, but that process would take a little time. Media reports were sparse and initially speculated on the possibility of a potential hunting accident north of I-10, somewhere in close proximity to Chattahoochee, Florida.

When Webb did not appear for his first meeting of the day and had not contacted her, Marsha Kaye knew something was amiss. Webb was a creature of habit and punctuality; these, along with consideration of others' time, were big things to him. When she heard the sketchy news flash regarding a potential hunting accident, she was immediately alarmed, because she knew Webb had intended to go hunting that morning, and she knew it was somewhere in that general area. Without hesitation, she called Tallahassee Memorial Regional Hospital and spoke with Admissions. She identified herself, provided contact information, and indicated she might possibly have information related to a potential hunting accident hospital admission, or victim, and to please have someone call her as quickly as possible.

In less than five minutes, her phone rang; in less than thirty minutes she had been authenticated, escorted to the hospital, and identified Webb as the accident victim. Although she really did not know Max Bloodworth very well, she suspected that he was potentially the other person receiving treatment and provided this information to the officers as well. Based on the other information she was able to provide, they were able to locate Webb's vehicle within the next hour and a half. Marsha Kaye was provided no information whatsoever related to Webb's medical status, but in the process of identifying him, she knew it was really bad, and she was devastated.

Although she was anxious and worried sick, she realized there were actions she needed to initiate and returned to the workplace. Once she reached the office, the efficiency syndrome kicked in, and she shifted gears. She closed Webb's office door, isolated herself inside, and immediately began going about the things she knew had to be done. She purposefully avoided MPI staff and forwarded all calls to a senior secretary in the SURS Unit. Since Webb had no family, she was a designed surrogate with limited power of attorney for specified emergencies. She was in possession of an unsealed packet of materials, for her eyes only, with instructions to open only in the case of an emergency. The existing situation qualified, and she opened the packet. The first item was a single sheet of letter-size paper with typed instructions. The first item was a direction to immediately, before doing anything else, place a call to Mario Diaz — "(The mysterious 'Phantom Man')" Webb had written in parentheses — an attorney who was in charge of all his affairs and had knowledge of almost every aspect of his life. There were two phone numbers listed next to his name. The second item referenced was "A Living Will (attached)." The next item was the combination to his gun safe. There were also three sets of keys referenced and included with identification tags. Lastly, Webb emphasized that Mario Diaz was in possession of explicit and specific detailed plans and contingency options related to most every conceivable situation that might arise. As a final emphasis, Webb had added: "If he requests your assistance, please cooperate with him to the extent possible as if it was me that was asking. Thank you for everything." It was simply signed: "Webb."

Marsha Kaye decided she had better call Mario Diaz before she began crying her eyes out and dialed his number. He answered on the second ring. She introduced herself and explained the situation. He was calm, focused, and very much to the point. He let her know that he knew exactly who she was and what she meant to Webb. After several brief questions, most related to Webb's medical status, which she could not answer, he indicated that he was on his way and would let her know exactly when he would arrive. He indicated that he would appreciate it if she would go back to the hospital, take M with her, if possible, and wait for his arrival. In the interim, she could call him at the same number she had just called and let him know of any updates related to Webb's condition.

Next, she called David Baswell's office, spoke briefly with Marge, and indicated she needed to speak directly with the Secretary and that it was an emergency. David did not take the news well and was obviously shaken. Finally, she called each of the units and asked for everyone to gather in The Bullpen for a brief announcement. Once the crowd was assembled, she entered the room, told them everything she knew, which was very little, and promised she would keep them updated as she obtained any additional information. She indicated that Charlie was acting Chief until further notice. With that, she grabbed M and asked her to please come with her. All of MPI was in a state of shock.

When the duo returned to the hospital, Marsha Kaye went immediately to the Admissions Office and presented both the Living Will and the Limited Power of Attorney authorization. She asked who the doctor in charge of Webb's case was and when she might speak with him. She was briefed as to the procedures and was sent to the Neuro Intensive Care Unit waiting room on the fourth floor and instructed to sign in as personal representative for Webb Espy. Once she complied with the patient-representative protocols, the two sat down without saying much, and Marsha Kaye unconsciously slipped her arm around M's shoulder and comforted her. Marsha Kaye needed for Mario Diaz to hurry!

Marsha Kaye could not believe how fast the South Florida attorney actually arrived, and once he did, he took over total control of the situation in "spades." Marsha Kaye appreciated efficiency, and she also recognized that when accompanied with power, dangling financial carrots, and charismatic intimidation, things started getting done! Mario Diaz practiced it to perfection. Within forty-five minutes, he had met with the floor nurse, the physician on call, and the hospital administrator and had been briefed in specific detail as to the current medical status of his client. He had also ordered personal, paid-from-pocket, comprehensive consultations from the head of the Neuro Department, as well as the youngest and newest physician member of the practice group, ASAP. He already had prepared a list of specific questions and decision tree options dependent upon what he learned from them.

What Mario had gleaned so far was that the patient was in extremely critical condition. He had lost a massive amount of blood, suffered a severe concussion and cranium fractures, and was hemorrhaging in the brain, which had required life-saving measures to relieve the pressure. In addition, there were fractures in both the right scapula (shoulder blade) and the right clavicle (collarbone). There were multiple external injuries in the form of severe lacerations and abrasions, primarily concentrated on the right portion of the neck and face. Although other, more life-threatening issues were a priority, there was also the secondary reality that hundreds of wood splinters and particles had penetrated deeply into the neck, ear, and facial tissue. Assuming he survived the worse, he was not going to be pretty without extensive work over an extended period of time. Marsha Kaye and M had been privy to the medical update and held out for the most optimistic outcomes. Mario asked to be excused in order that he could take care of a quick errand. He indicated he would return in short order.

Mario had ascertained based on his briefing with the floor physician that Max Bloodworth's status was still designated as critical but would soon be downgraded. The patient was currently located in the regular critical care unit on the third floor of the hospital. Mario took the elevator to the third floor and went directly to the waiting room. He stood just outside the entrance and scanned the various groups and isolated individuals in the room. There were not that many. Mario decided on the simplest and most direct approach. He entered the waiting room and, in a clear and respectful manner, asked: "Is there anyone here from the Max Bloodworth family?"

A lady with salt-and-pepper hair replied apprehensively: "I'm Shirley Bloodworth."

"May I have a brief word with you, Mrs. Bloodworth?" Mario politely insisted rather than asked, gesturing with his shoulder and hand toward the hall outside, indicating a respect for privacy. She immediately followed him, accompanied by a companion who she quickly introduced as her daughter. In the most disarming manner he could muster, Mario began speaking to the two ladies. "My name is Mario Diaz, a close friend for many years of Webb Espy, your husband's friend as well. I just got out of a consultation related to Webb's case and learned inadvertently that Max's condition is shortly to be downgraded from critical to serious. I believe that is good news!"

"Oh, thank God!" she uttered as she hugged her daughter and Mario as well, in obvious relief.

"I thought it might take a little time for the information to trickle down to you through normal channels, so I thought I might just cut through some the red tape. Obviously, what I just said is unofficial, but in my opinion, I think it is a safe bet," Mario opined.

"Thank you so much. That was extremely thoughtful and considerate," Maxine, Max and Shirley's daughter, interjected.

"Let me also say that once he is moved out of the ICU, I have also taken the liberty of arranging for a family suite for the duration of his stay at the hospital. I realize that insurance does not normally cover such accommodations, but that has all been prearranged and taken care of and, obviously, will be of no additional expense to you whatsoever. I am sure this is the way Webb would want it. Let me also say this to you both right now. I don't know exactly what happened out there this morning, but one thing I am confident of is that Max made a heroic effort to save Webb's life. If Webb should manage to pull through this thing, it will be due to Max. Until Max can tell us what actually happened, we can all only speculate, but one thing I am confident of is that Max is not responsible for the injuries to Webb. Webb is not going to be able to tell us anything for several days, if at all. At some point, Max is going to be asked to make a statement. I believe it wise to advise you, as an attorney, not to allow him to do so without legal representation. This is not to suggest that Max is some kind of a suspect or anything, but simply to protect your family's right to privacy and from any potential harassment from the media, insurance representatives, or others. Just as I am doing this for Webb, let me offer myself and my services on an interim basis — absolutely free of charge, let me hasten to add — in order to act on your family's behalf until you can secure your choice of legal representation," Mario finished, with earnest sincerity.

"That is certainly kind and generous, and we thank you for everything you have already done so far," responded an appreciative Shirley Bloodworth.

Glancing quickly at his watch, Mario added presumptively: "I need to go to the business office for a few moments, anyway, to take care of a few housekeeping matters. While I am there, I can ask them to print out one of my 'Authorizations for Representation' and bring it back to you for signature. Once it is filed in the official patient record, and you have a copy in your possession, no one can question or bother Max or any other member of the family without my presence or permission. That work for you all?" Mario concluded, nodding with a reassuring smile.

"Yes, that is perfect, and again, I don't know how we can ever thank you," she emphasized sincerely.

"Let me assure you that no thanks is necessary, and the pleasure is entirely mine," Mario emphasized as he turned and retreated toward the elevator.

Webb's condition remained unchanged for four days. His vitals had improved, and the pressure on the brain had reduced, but he still was in an induced coma. The doctors were realistic with Mario and Marsha Kaye, but they always were careful to provide a hint of optimism to hold on to. From day one, there was always someone in the waiting room. David Baswell had authorized special assignment delegations for selected MPI staff in order to ensure there was always someone there, 24/7, until things sorted themselves out. Marsha Kaye was in charge of coordinating the schedules.

During the interim, Mario had been busy on a number of fronts. At the first opportunity available, he met with Max Bloodworth and listened to every detail of his account of what had happened. He was convinced Max's version was accurate and totally credible. He was present when law enforcement investigators questioned him initially and allowed him to present them with a carefully worded statement that had been prepared in advance. The sworn statement included a comprehensive, specifically crafted question-and-answer section in order to establish, for the record, Max's official responses in a manner that would leave little room for additional clarification or interpretation. Mario also informed law enforcement officials that as soon as Max was physically capable, he would like for officers to accompany them to the site of the incident. He made a point of emphasizing that he did not want for either himself or Max to be accused of contaminating the incident site. Next, Mario contacted Willie Dozios and asked him to put out his antennas throughout his vast informal network for any street talk that, in any stretch of the imagination, might in anyway relate to Webb Espy's alleged accident. He then directed the paralegals in his office to comb the news world for unusual reports of unique healthcare events or anything that might be potentially associated with the interruption of large amounts of cash infusions. Finally, he cornered M and asked her, knowing the request was strictly out of bounds, if she would mind participating in a few secret squirrel activities based on information he might be able to provide for her. She never wavered for an instant and answered in the affirmative. Mario spoke every day with David Baswell at David's request.

On the eighth day of Webb's hospitalization, he apparently turned a medical corner of sorts, and the doctors began to show varying degrees of guarded optimism. By the tenth day, the patient's progress suggested it might not be so much a question of recovery but more of a timetable. Mario had arranged for various medical consultations via telephonic means, in which he was a participant observer. In addition, two on-site, hands-on consultations by physicians from New York and Louisiana had also occurred. Based on the input and an analysis of all the information available related to the best future treatment and medical care required for Webb, Mario ascertained that as soon as medical clearance was provided, Webb would be transported via a privately chartered Medjet Assistance to a specialty clinic in Zurich, Switzerland. Seven days later, under the cloak of darkness, Webb, escorted by Mario, was transported from the hospital via ambulance to Tallahassee International Airport, where they boarded a specially equipped medical transport jet, manned with a full complement of appropriate critical health care staff, and flew nonstop to Switzerland. Webb would not return to the U.S. until fourteen months later.

43

May 19 Through May 29, 1994

Coral Gables, Florida, to Washington D.C

Jorge knew something was terribly wrong. He had used his special mobile phone as instructed, to no avail. It had now been over two weeks since he had been contacted by any means by Marcus. Operational systems had come to an absolute standstill. The tasks required for Jorge to accomplish and oversee each and every day were stymied. Each day, Jorge went through his assigned routines, and each day yielded the same results. Jorge feared the worst for his friend, but held out hope. After another week, he had reconciled himself to the fact all he could do was wait. Marcus had assured him that, eventually, even in the worst-case scenarios, certain things would ultimately reveal themselves.

A month to the day after his last contact with Marcus, a visitor appeared at Jorge's residence. The man was well-dressed in an expensive suit and introduced himself as Colonel Richard Mitchell, Special Envoy Services, U.S. State Department. He projected an undisguised military demeanor and, in a formal, straightforward, well-rehearsed message, informed Jorge that he regretted to inform him that Marcus Manasa had been killed in the line of duty. There would be a formal interment at Arlington National Cemetery the following Saturday, and transport and all accommodations were complimentary in order that he and other immediate family members might attend. Colonel Mitchell then handed Jorge a detailed itinerary, which included a number to call if there should be any questions that were not included or clear with the itinerary. The Colonel offered no additional information and asked if there were any questions. Jorge, in his dazed state, just simply shook his head no, at which point Colonel Mitchell simply said: "I am sorry for your loss, sir." With that said, he abruptly exercised a precise about-face and walked directly to a chauffeured limousine that was parked, with its engine running, at the curb.

Jorge shared with his wife the news that he had just received. She did not take it well. Over the past year, Marcus had been more involved in their lives than he had ever been. She had strong feelings for their friend and deeply appreciated all that he had done for their family over the years. Although Jorge left the choice to her, he strongly suggested that she not accompany him to this emotional ceremony. Ultimately, she agreed with him.

Precisely on cue, in accordance with the itinerary, a limousine arrived at Jorge De Valle's address in Coral Gables, and a young man in a dark suit, with a military bearing, knocked on the door, politely addressed Jorge, took his bag, and ushered him toward the vehicle. Once they arrived, he held the door open until Jorge had entered and was situated. He then closed the door, deposited Jorge's bag in the trunk, and joined the chauffeur in the front seat. The trip to Miami International Airport was uneventful. They arrived at a section of the airport Jorge did not even know existed. They stopped at a checkpoint, handed some sort of sentry an official-looking document, and were immediately waved through the gate. The limousine drove directly into a hangar, where an unmarked, mid-sized jet was waiting. Jorge was escorted into the jet and, once inside, was overwhelmed, since the interior was nothing like what he expected. It was beyond plush. A steward identified himself as Edward, announced he would be attending to his needs for the duration of the flight, and asked if there was anything he might like from the bar. He quickly adlibbed that he had some wonderfully dark *Brugal Añejo Reserva* with fresh limes, and his *Cuba Libres* were quite excellent.

Jorge looked up at him, dumbfounded for a second. It was almost like Marcus was playing a practical joke on him. Jorge flashed a huge smile at Edward and responded: "Absolutely my friend, absolutely, and I suspect you probably have some cashews to go with that concoction too, don't you?"

"Absolutely!" said Edward, laughing out loud.

The itinerary indicated that the interment for Marcus Manasa would take place in the twilight hour on Saturday, which would be precisely at 6:19 P.M., during the twilight hour. Since there was considerable time prior to the ceremony, a special driving tour of the area had been arranged for Jorge, if he should be interested in exercising such an option. Since he had nothing else planned, he elected to see the historical Washington sights. The day went by quickly, and he was glad he had something to do to distract him from the business at hand. When he arrived back at the hotel, he had time for a brief nap before he got himself ready in time to be picked up. At the appointed time, there was a punctual knock at the anticipated time, and *"el hombre de La reloj"* was impressed.

The trip to Arlington National Cemetery did not take long, especially under the mantle of a full military escort contingency. Jorge had really no frame of reference as to what to expect, but somehow, he felt at ease with the situation. The only uneasiness he was experiencing was that he would probably never know what actually happened to his old friend. Not really knowing and the likelihood of probably never knowing produced an anxious form of melancholy.

Upon arrival, Jorge noticed there were two chairs set up, about ten feet apart. His curiosity peaked instantly. The scene was simple, but eloquent. There was an open grave, a casket draped with the flag of the United States of America, a seven-member color guard, and a separate bugler and drummer stationed away from the others. There were two other military officers in attendance, who appeared to be waiting to commence the proceedings.

Presently, another limousine appeared, and a clone that had attended Jorge escorted what appeared to be a middle-aged lady —though it was difficult to determine, as she was wearing a black veil — toward the unoccupied seat. Jorge was totally mystified. Once she was seated, the ceremony began.

It became intuitively obvious that this was intended to be a simple memorial service and not a religious one. References were made to Marcus in only general terms, and there were no personal testimonials as related to deeds or accomplishments. There was only the slightest reference to him as a professional patriot, serving unselfishly in a capacity that could never be honored or recognized appropriately. Once that part of the ceremony was concluded, the second man began reading a somewhat personalized citation that concluded by awarding Marcus Manasa the "Distinguished Service Cross" posthumously.

Once completed, the folded flag process commenced and ended, with the flag presented to the occupant residing in the other chair. Almost simultaneously, another earlier prepared flag was deposited in Jorge's hands. In choreographed synchronization, the honor guard of seven, with military pomp and circumstance, fired three volleys. About thirty yards away, a lone bugler and a drummer with a muffled drum roll played taps. It was almost too emotional for Jorge to take. Tears streamed down his cheeks, and he remembered the remark Marcus had made about taps during his revelations only a few months earlier.

Once the official part of the ceremony was concluded, both of the primary participants came forward and paid their personal condolences to the lady and presented her with a personalized box. They then duplicated the exact ritual for Jorge. Lastly, Jorge was advised that he would be permitted a few minutes alone at the gravesite for private reflection and closure. Jorge stood alone for a couple of minutes and then quietly approached the lady with her head bowed in meditation. Sensing someone in her presence, she looked up at Jorge with a questioning expression.

Jorge immediately attempted to disarm any suspicion or alarm and said: "Please pardon my intrusion, but my name is Jorge De Valle. I am an old friend of Marcus, and I am curious if, by any chance, you might possibly be an artist that once resided in Madrid?" Jorge could see the hint of a sly smile behind the black veil as she responded.

"Yes, I know who you are, although I did not know your name until you just introduced yourself, and yes, I am an artist and once resided in Madrid. I no longer live there and have not for several years. I knew the man you refer to as Marcus Manasa, but at the time, when we were together, he did not go by that name. He claimed to be Martin Maus, and I called him Marty," she offered with a wry smile.

"And may I be permitted to inquire as to your name?" Jorge asked politely.

"By all means," she immediately replied. "My name is Anna Louisa Espaillat, and my friends call me Louanna."

Jorge was now more intrigued and curious than ever and acted on reflex. "Then I will refer to you as Louanna, if I may be granted the privilege?"

"Of course," she responded with a genuine smile.

"I know it might be presumptuous to ask, but if you do not have any previous plans, would you allow me the pleasure of taking you to dinner this evening?" Jorge asked in his most gracious manner.

"I have no specific plans that I cannot alter, and I would be most delighted to accept your invitation. I suspect we might have a lot of things to talk about," she laughed softly as she responded.

"How may I contact you?" asked Jorge politely.

"I believe we may be staying at the same hotel. I saw your limousine leave just prior to mine. I am in room 2218. Is around eight okay?" she replied.

"Perfect, then it's settled. I will call for you at eight."

The two told stories; they laughed, they cried, and they speculated about "Mysterious Marcus," which they mutually settled on the nickname as a handle.

At one point in the conversation, she paused, took a healthy sip of brandy, and declared: "You know, he was the real love of my life. It would have been impossible for a relationship between us to survive. I required more than he would have ever been able to give, and if he had tried, he would have been miserable."

"I suspect you might be right, but I do know this; he was smitten by you, and that was a direct quote," Jorge informed her in all seriousness.

"Thank you, Jorge; I needed to hear that. I can live with that," she sighed.

"When was the last time you were with him?" Jorge questioned.

"The last time I was with him, or the last time I saw him?" she asked nonchalantly.

"Oh, there's a difference?" Jorge inquired respectfully.

"Yes, the last time we spent any time together was in Madrid back in 1982, but I actually saw him briefly, quite by accident, in the summer of 1987 in Valencia. I was attending an art show, had just sold an expensive painting, and bumped into him at a café outdoors. It was a little awkward because I was with a friend of mine, but he was cordial, of course. He still had that hideous cigar," she laughed.

"Yes, it had a rather unpleasant aroma," Jorge admitted with a chuckle. "Are you positive it was in the summer of 1987?" he inquired.

"Definitely, it was early June. I never forget when I sell an expensive piece of art," she laughed out loud.

They both drank more than they should have, but during the process, they both learned a lot about the mutual person they both loved and admired. They finished the evening more than pleased that they had met one another.

One month later, Jorge was at home on a Saturday morning when he was summoned to the front door to sign for a package delivered by special courier service. Inside the package was a letter from Marcus. The rest of the package's contents almost caused Jorge a coronary. At approximately the same time on another continent, the same exact scene was replayed for one Anna Louisa Espaillat.

44

August 20, 1994

Zurich, Switzerland

It was almost four months after Webb had initially been hospitalized and transferred to the facility in Switzerland when Mario
was actually able to meet and converse with him. Part of this was
due to Webb's complicated medical issues, as well as his continued
reliance on pain medications.

Webb's only information related to what had happened to him
was in the form of the sworn statement that Max had supplied
under the tutelage of Mario. For the most part, Max and Mario
had left no stone unturned. What was not on Max's statement
were the things that he could not have had knowledge of at the
time his statement was prepared and had been ascertained sub-
sequently. First and foremost, there was no body discovered at
the scene, and there was no forensic evidence that there ever had
been. There was no rifle, as Max had indicated, and there certainly appeared to be no motive or reasonable explanation for
anything that had happened that morning. The only discoveries
and evidence that lent any credibility to Max's statement were two
ejected shotgun hulls, a spent brass hull from a recently fired 300
Win Mag, and a splintered white oak tree, as well as both a vehicle and the phone, both witnessed and observed, but neither of

which currently existed. The lab team was able to ascertain and verify, as belonging to Max, his waste deposit and associated two-ply Charmin. It would have almost been as if Max had seen and reported a flying saucer, except for the mysterious vehicle, phone, and brass rifle hull.

Webb had absolutely no doubt that what Max had described was exactly what had happened. The question was, who was the person Max had shot, and more importantly, why was this person trying to kill Webb Espy? The mystery of all mysteries was, what had happened to the body? Mario was of the same mind. There were no answers, just questions that could not be answered. Finally, Mario reached the point that some trial lawyers sometimes do. If there are no real answers, then you proceed through a series of mental gymnastics and propose an exhaustive list of hypotheticals. Obviously, somebody did it, and they did it for a reason, and Webb was the intended target. Someone or some entity knew, with some predictable certainty, where Webb was going to be. What they obviously did not know was that Max was going to be an unanticipated intervening variable.

"Let's assume this," stated Mario. "I believe we have to suspect that what happened was the result of something related to work. Now, this question I'm going to ask is extremely important. I want you to think back over the past few weeks or months and try to recall if anything either happened at work or travel that you would consider an anomaly or something that might be considered unusual to norms, something you've never experienced before?"

After pausing for several brief seconds, it hit Webb like a bolt of lightning! "Yes, of course! I am so stupid, and Mario, you are brilliant. Let me tell you. About five weeks before this so-called premeditated accident, Allen and I were in Miami. What started out as joke and a gentleman's bet actually became a routine qualitative detection strategy. Twice a month, we would take a slow drive down the major streets, let's say, for example, Flagler or *Calle Ocho* in Little Havana, and video all the storefronts. We would then compare them to previous videos and target each of the new healthcare clinics and facilities for Medicaid participation levels. At any rate, much to our chagrin, somebody had us under surveillance; they knew we were in Miami and where we were staying. When we arrived at the hotel later that afternoon, there was a message waiting for me at the desk. The message was in an envelope that contained a key for a room at the Embassy Suites. The message indicated that I should come alone and retrieve some very important information that was awaiting me related to what we were working on. I was advised that it would be well worth my time, and I would be extremely pleased."

Allen advised me not to go, and we argued like hell about it, but I insisted. He relented when I told him he could go with me, but just not enter the room. When I arrived at the room and entered, there was no one there. There was a Bass Pro duffle bag. Inside the bag, there were five shoeboxes. I checked in one of them, and there were forty small bank envelopes, containing what I assumed comprised $5,000 each. There could have been a million dollars overall in those boxes. At that point, I put the box back in the bag and left it as I had found it. I went out where I left Allen and shared with him what had happened. We had gotten into the elevator and were about halfway down when Allen bluntly asked me if I realized what I had just done. When I told him no, I really had not had time to think it through, he rather frankly informed me I had just turned down a bribe.

He let me know in no uncertain terms that a million dollars was a lot of money to some people and that it should be intuitively obvious to the casual observer that somebody must want something very badly. He pointed out the obvious; if they could not buy it, they would simply find another way."

"I hate to be the one to tell you, but I believe Allen was right!" reiterated Mario.

"So, you're saying I was the target for assassination?" Webb challenged incredulously.

"Yes, as a matter of fact, I am, and I also suspect that if you think back, you might come to the same conclusion. Let me ask you this; why did you request that I get someone to babysit M when she hit the mother lode?" Mario questioned. Webb appeared befuddled by the question and instantly retreated mentally to be in a deep-thought state of mind. Mario continued: "Webb, I got no idea what you were thinking, which isn't like you, but I can't for the life of me explain how you knew almost instinctively that M required protection, and you didn't? My only explanation is that you had absolutely no frame of reference for how big this thing really was and the danger it potentially posed," he paused briefly.

Mario advised: "Let me keep going down this path for a while. I have more or less already worked my way through this maze, and I'm pretty sure where this is going to end up. I strongly suspect you and M stumbled on to something that was far bigger than either of you could have ever imagined. At first, you were just a nuisance and were treated the way a retail business treats shrinkage. Your interference was just a simple cost of doing business. However, once you guys created "The Perfect Storm" as I refer to it, you hurt them very badly, stymied them, maybe even ruined them. Not only did you guys take out their primary operations, you annihilated their safety nets and contingency options as well. I really don't know if there was anything to salvage, but if there was any chance whatsoever, you in particular had to be eliminated. You know, cut off the head thing. I would not be surprised if M might have been a potential target as well," Mario concluded.

Webb was processing what Mario had been telling him and realized that Mario had thought things through in a thoroughly comprehensive manner and had to admit that it was about the only thing that made any real sense, and for the first time, it frightened him!

"Another thing I need to point out," Mario began again, "Just so you know, M and I, along with Marsha Kaye, of course, by de facto, actually ran MPI in your absence right after your initial hospitalization. If this ever comes to light, I would be disbarred, and all of us would probably be put under the jail. At any rate, based on what I suspected you were up to as a result of my role in being the link pin to some of Willie's surreptitious assignments, as well as what I could pry out of M by employing some of my most devious, unlawyerly methods, I pretty much had a good hunch where you might be headed. Turned out you were right, but not completely right. I detected a flaw in your theory, or rather, the application that you ultimately employed to the theory. For some reason, you directed all your attention toward the hot spots in the South Florida area. I recognized that if your theory was correct, there were a number of additional potential hot spots with large concentrations of Medicaid recipients and providers that had gone unmolested with your initial thrust. I selected three of them as targets: the Hillsborough/Pinellas area, the Duval/St.

Johns area, and the Escambia/Santa Rosa area. Then, employing an absolute stroke of genius, I took a major shortcut. I asked M to identify, in any manner possible, all of the Easy Mails, Mail Box ETCs, and UPS stations that provided private mail box services and ascertain any "pay-to-providers" that listed any of those addresses. As it turned out, she got lots of hits. I then suggested that she have any providers' claims identified on that list to pend for medical review, just like what had been done before. Well, she did, and guess what? Not even so much as a small whimper! I'm not even going to tell you how much money we saved the state Medicaid coffers," he concluded smugly.

Webb simply stared at him in amazement. "You're not kidding; you really did that, didn't you? And you are absolutely right, they would have put every damn one of you under the jail," Webb acknowledged, shaking his head in astonishment.

Mario just chuckled and continued with his premediated confession. "If you get the gist of what we did and think it through, it was kind of like an insurance policy. If it was not the final nail in the coffin, it sent the signal to whomever, that you, Webb Espy specifically, were not required for this thing to continue via autopilot," Mario emphasized triumphally.

Webb paused for a moment and reflected analytically on the information Mario had just provided. After a long pause, Webb looked at Mario and began shaking his head approvingly. "Now that's what they call a real *coup de grace*! Mario, that was absolutely brilliant. Now I know why you make the big bucks. I know where there is a job vacancy if you are interested," he suggested.

"You're kidding! Doesn't pay near enough. Not enough money in state government to lure me away from the gravy train I'm on as your personal Man Friday!" he retorted. "One more final thing related to all this before we move on to the next topic. Since you were hospitalized, I've had feelers out and have had my paralegals on the prowl for anything that, in any way, might even be remotely related to what happened to you. Willie came up with a few plausible leads, but they were either dead ends, real stretches, or things that could not possibly ever be verified. Here's the thing, though; within two weeks after your hospitalization, there were in the area numerous car washes, laundromats, video arcades, and an alleged major embezzlement scam reported at the casino on the reservation. The thing in common with all these entities is that they all deal with significant amounts of cash, and they all have the capability of laundering money." Mario waited for Webb to assimilate this information. Then he continued: "There is also a person of interest, believed to be somehow connected to all of this. We have no idea how, and there are no direct connections or links to him related to anything that has transpired. Willie says it's just word on the street and certainly he can't prove it, but he is sure there is some involvement or connection. His name is Jorge De Valle, a pharmacist, and he heads up the Cuban Pharmacy Association in Exile. He has a nickname, *el hombre de el reloj*, The Clock Man. We have checked him out, down to the number of expressos he has every day, and he runs a squeaky-clean pharmacy operation," Mario finished.

"I actually know this man. My impression of him has always been that he was a real gentleman," Webb admitted in a somewhat disinterested mien.

"There are a couple of other things in that department. You don't know Willie like I do, but when Willie does a job for you, he goes at it with a "baker's dozen" mentality. He's a curious little son of a bitch by nature, and that's why one always needs to be generous with him. Not only is he a sleuth, he's creative, sneaky, and the best I know at connecting the dots.

"I have admired his work from afar, but now I can't wait to meet this character," Webb stated.

"He has networks and resources to draw from that would, in some respects, in all likelihood, dwarf Scotland Yard. Anyway, Willie tells me that according to his sources, Mr. De Valle was witnessed, on multiple occasions, in the company of an unknown person. Based on the sketchy recalled accounts from limited eye-witnesses, this mystery man looked very much like he could possibly be a younger brother or relative, but according to records I've assessed, there is no such potential relative. These same persons, waitresses from three different upscale restaurants in Little Havana, all verified that this mysterious stranger, in the company of Mr. De Valle, drank expensive port wines, smoked Cuban cigars, and always paid in cash. They also mentioned that he was prone to leave generous gratuities. My sources, as well as Willie's, have hit a dead end in trying to actually identify him. Obviously, we have padded some palms for an alert if he should ever reappear, but I am not all that optimistic. In fact, I rather doubt he'll be seen or heard from again."

"Why is that?" Webb questioned.

"Don't know for sure; just a feeling, hunch, whatever you want to call it. We might circle back to that in a little bit." Mario paused.

"Okay, it's your dog and pony show. I'm strictly ears at this stage of the game," Webb conceded.

Mario picked right up again. "Three weeks ago, my paralegals locked on to a brief report in *USA TODAY*. I brought a copy for you to have a look at." Mario produced a copy and handed it to Webb to review.

MEDICAID FUNDS DIVERTED TO POTENTIALLY ARM REBEL FORCES IN CENTRAL AMERICA

The *Associated Press* reported disturbing allegations related to Medicaid/Medicare dollars being routinely siphoned from state and federal coffers over the past few years via various fraud and abuse scams. Although few details are available, there are claims that the U.S. government has been stealing from themselves for years in order to fund illegal covert rebel operations in Central America. At the center of these allegations is Major General Hawkeye West, a top echelon envoy on temporary assignment to the State Department from the National Security Council. There have been no official comments to date related to these allegations.

Webb finished reading the article and glanced up dubiously at Mario. "So, you think this might be it?" he asked, raising his eyebrows.

"Well, let's just say I strongly suspect there's a good chance. Ah, what the hell, yeah, I really think there is more than a real strong possibility," he replied, nodding affirmatively. "Let me add a little perspective, if I may. I think the only way certain things could have happened is if somebody, or some entity that was really big, was involved. That would explain the David Copperfield-type magic of the disappearing corpse, and the batmobile disintegrating into nothing before the naked eye. My take is that you are now safe and no longer a target or even a person of interest. I believe there were two potential motives to go after you. The first was to potentially salvage the operation, the other was simply an act of personal competitive revenge by someone you really pissed off! It's conceivable that it might possibly have been a combination of the two. At any rate, I'm confident you are no longer in harm's way," Mario concluded.

"Well, I'll be damned," mumbled a dazed and confused Webb Espy.

"Here's another tidbit as well. I'm not going to go down this road very far or dig up an old grave because there's really no point. This is mostly conjecture on my part, anyway, and serves no real, useful benefit to anybody. Might even open up an old wound that's best left alone. But I'm gonna say this, just hear me out and then let's just leave it alone and let it lie. You good with that?" Mario asked candidly.

"Under the circumstances and criteria you just set forth, it doesn't seem like you have provided much of a choice," Webb relented.

"Hell, Webb, you know better than that. This is something I even debated with myself about ever even sharing with you," Mario confessed openly.

"Mario, I realize that, and I'm assuming that your reluctance to share whatever it is with me is more than likely based on your belief that my potential safety is involved, should I start some type of Quixotic due diligence. Let me say, once and for all; in my wildest and craziest imagination, I have absolutely no intentions of going down any such road," Webb declared with finality.

"Then here we go. I'm only going to hit the highlights, because it's easy to get bogged down in details and not see the forest for the trees. According to responsible sources within the MJG, there are a number of things that have been going on fast and furious for about a decade or so now."

"Whoa, wait," interrupted Webb. "What's the MJG?"

"It is a slang acronym for 'Miami Jewish Grapevine' and is comprised mainly of old silverbacks who have their fingers on the pulse of pretty much anything of any significance that goes on in South Florida and the international business world in general. Since the early '80s, there has been a cabal with international interests related to the replacement of political regimes in central America. Although the cabal has no official government involvement, it is naive to believe that said governments are without unofficial representation. There have been numerous attempts at *putsches* and *coups* over the years; however, there has been an overall continuous and ongoing disguised strategy for creating chaos, insurrections, and upheaval in certain governments and political interests in Central America over the years. The long-term stakes are extremely high. One of the cabal's top priorities has been an ongoing effort aimed at organizing, supplying, and funding various rebel and guerilla military forces in an effort to overthrow several of the socialist governments in the region." Mario paused.

"Okay, I'm following along so far, and I believe you are following a reasonable trail up to this point. I can't wait to see where you think it eventually leads us," Webb stated solemnly.

"Continuing in the same vein, although initially some of the funding was openly transparent in governmental appropriations, it was gradually reduced and ultimately eliminated once it came to light that some of these efforts were aiding and abetting cartel drug diversions, as well as facilitating gruesome terrorism against the civilian populace. Once that happened, resources had to be forthcoming from other means, if you catch my drift. Ergo, the infamous Hawkeye West. It appears that several of the elder statesmen from the MJG have some direct knowledge of General West and may have even dined with him on occasion in the past. Although absent of fact and purely speculation on my part, I would not be surprised if several of them might not have had in-direct business dealings with the good general in the past." Mario paused once again to collect his thoughts.

"Damn, Mario, you are blowing me away here. As they say, 'truth is sometimes stranger than fiction.' I am fascinated with this story, whether it's true or not," Webb said honestly.

"It gets better, my good friend. It seems as though there were some pretty direct links with our friend Hawkeye to the old 'Leopard Case,' if you happen to recall that little piece of un-solved history," Mario reported.

"Oh yeah, almost anyone in my line of work is familiar with Dr. Renaldo's notorious Medicare heist and disappearing act," Webb confirmed.

"It seems that Hawkeye's operations, or the cabals, or some combination, had invisible echelons in play. To those with some knowledge and appreciation of such things, there were independ-ent claims that there was at least one liaison who pulled a lot of weight and many strings. He was often jokingly referred to as "The Phantom." It has been alleged that he was actually the brains behind The Leopard! Based on what's transpired in your situation and what we know about Dr. Renaldo, it's not a significant leap to grasp the logical implications," Mario finished smugly.

"You mean you believe it was the same individual in both sit-uations?" Webb asked incredulously.

"Let's just put it this way. If I was allowed to gamble on the probability, I would bet the farm!" Mario responded dogmatically.

"So, you must believe this mysterious phantom character was De Valle's mysterious dinner partner, don't you?" Webb suggested insightfully.

"As a matter of fact, I do, but I also have also another piece of the puzzle that you don't have or know about at this stage of the game," Mario offered as he smiled.

"Damn, Mario, you gonna keep me in suspense or tell me what the hell you know, for Christ's sake?" Webb asked in anguish.

"Don't get your dander up. I'm going to tell you, but in doing so, I'm making you an accomplice and accessory, although I'm pretty sure you're not going to mind. As you will recall, it was reported that our mystery man enjoyed Cuban cigars. Well, it so happens that Max discovered a new unsmoked cigar along with the phone when he commandeered the shooter's vehicle. With several other things occupying his mind at the time, he just completely forgot about it initially, but later recalled it sometime after we submitted our statement. We both agreed after the fact not to report that omission to the detectives. I figured it probably disappeared along with everything else that vanished. Well, guess what; it didn't. Someway, somehow, that damn cigar ended up in Max's hunting vest backpack, along with the harness made out of belts and the duct tape. Max apparently just left it at the staging site when he loaded you into the back seat. As you've already guessed, it was an expensive Cuban cigar," Mario concluded.

"Whoa, hold on; so you're telling me that you believe that Max Bloodworth allegedly killed the 'Carlos' of our times?" asked a drained Webb Espy.

"Yes, that's precisely what I'm conveying to you, and based on what I have discerned from certain people who I regard as having insights into such matters, I have little doubt as to the validity of my final supposition. Now, one more thing and I'm done forever with this particular topic. I want you to remember that you are hearing this from both your close friend, as well as from an attorney. Being right is not always legal, and being legal ain't always right. That's all I'm going to say," finished Mario.

"Well, I got to say, that's one hell of a story, my friend. I guess that's a wrap, then, complete with a bow. I'll never be able to ever thank you, Mario," Webb said tearfully.

"Are you crazy, you already have; I'll never be able to repay my debt to you," Mario declared.

"Then it's a standoff, my friend; a mutual admiration society of sorts," stated Webb as the two men made eye contact, then laughed and hugged one another.

Later in the day, once the rehab rituals had been completed, Webb and Mario reconvened their meeting. Webb initiated the conversation. "Mario, there are a number of financial matters I would appreciate if you would take care of. I have a list of sorts," he said as he handed it to Mario.

"I tell you what, let me just go ahead and share my list with you, and let's see if I have the gift of mental telepathy," he playfully grinned at Webb. They both began reviewing one another's lists. Webb snickered first, and Mario followed suit.

"You sure as hell are generous with my resources," Webb laughingly scoffed, looking at Mario in mock disapproval.

"Webb, I know how you think and feel about money and how you choose to use it. Folks have a wide range of perspectives on money. Some don't care about it; they just want to collect it and hoard it; others want to use it to create things just for the fun of it. For some, it is simply a medium of exchange. Then, of course, there are folks who try to buy happiness with it. Finally, there is a category which, in my opinion, I believe you fall into — that you really don't care about it, are generous with it, and use it for the betterment of mankind. You, my friend, ain't never going to be accused of pulling a U-Haul behind the hearse!" Mario decreed, laughing out loud. Webb laughed with him.

"You pretty much have me pegged, I guess. A long time ago, I realized that once you got the basics covered, you can only either enhance them or duplicate them. A couple of things money can do is provide options and diversions. I really get a charge out of giving money away, but I like to do it in more of a qualitative manner. I used to love the show *The Millionaire!* However, you know what I have also discerned; there are those who claim that money can't buy happiness, and that may be true, but I tell you what, I'd rather be unhappy and rich than unhappy and poor! With that little philosophical pearl of wisdom, let me compliment you on anticipating my wishes far better than I had thought them through. Oh, and nice touch with Max Bloodworth and family. He would never have accepted anything from me directly. There were a couple of surprises, but you were well ahead of me. Nice job! Oh, that reminds me, did you take care of my new friend Willie? I believe he requires some very special attention; don't you agree?" Webb suggested.

Mario began laughing and shaking his head. "Let me assure you, Little Willie has been taken care of. I feel sure he may, and in all likelihood will, indulge himself in some of the most perverted sexual fantasies known to man, as well as some that he will no doubt invent," Mario declared with a facial gesture signifying who in the hell in this world knows? The two men laughed together, and then Mario dipped into his repertoire of some of Willie's most infamous exploits, which could go on indefinitely.

On the flight back to Miami, Mario was in a deeply reflective and somber mood. His emotional psyche oscillated the gamut between congratulating and admonishing himsel f as related to his dealings with Webb. His conscience was engaged in a battle royale, with multiple realistic and rational faculties. His state of quandary was based on the basic fact that he had not been completely forthcoming with Webb, and he had done so with premeditated deliberation.

Although, he was confident of the pragmatic consequences of his actions, he nevertheless was entangled in a quagmire of contradictive arguments with himself that incorporated friendship, legal responsibilities, ethical considerations, and various other extenuating circumstances. On the one hand, the results of his initiatives and interventions had resulted in quadrupling Webb's net worth overnight without any additional tax burdens or obligations whatsoever. He did not suspect Webb would have any significant issues with that particular result, albeit it was achieved without specific authorization . Part of Mario's mind games kept reminding him that he was, in fact, Webb's designated legal surrogate, with across-the-board power of attorney for all his business and investment activities, and that during the time period in question, Webb had arguably been legally and medically incapacitated. Now, the material hitch; how it had been accomplished might represent a horse of a slightly different hue! Mario was accustomed and unreservedly comfortable in operating in legally gray areas and did not hesitate to push the envelope toward the most liberal interpretations, assuming it suited or benefited either his legal strategy or his client's best interests. There were even instances, at least, in a hypothetical manner of speaking, that Mario had pondered over the years whether he might even consider jeopardizing or sacrificing his sacrosanct legal career for the sake of justice, if there were obviously egregious gaps in the system of jurisprudence and/or legitimate revelations or knowledge that rendered archaic legal precedents obsolete in today's culture and society.

In explicit ways, Mario held himself to a unique standard of ethical equity, fueled by criteria known only to his subconscious self. Ergo, the proverbial catch-22 he now was wrestling with. He had, in effect, withheld certain information, actions, and specific detailed activities, acts of omissions rather than commissions, from his friend and client that he was not positive that either his friend and client was actually entitled to possess. This was complicated by the notion that he had, and still was, manipulating events and situations which were really none of his business and, in a pure sense, beyond his jurisdictional purview as eit her a friend, attorney, or business confidant. The main dilemma was that Mario realized that he himself was benefiting from these actions, if by nothing other than osmosis.

Finally, Mario reached a point of diminishing returns, at which point he yielded to his fail-safe solution strategy and ordered a Long Island Iced Tea, confident that the resultant nap from the concoction would provide the ultimate clarity he was seeking.

As Mario had anticipated, he awoke from his lethargy, and the demons had deserted him. The cobwebs that existed prior to exiting the world had disappeared entirely. He was of clear mind and purpose and had reconciled the world and possibly even the universe. Reservations had been replaced by optimism. Any earlier sense of guilt had been absorbed by sagacious pride.

Everything was in order, and Mario was in charge. He commanded the chess board, the game, and all the pieces, and was charged with an obligation to do so. In his philosophical wisdom, he had more than convinced himself that everything that had been done up to this point was really nothing more than settlement negotiations on behalf of a client. He was not a social worker; he was an attorney, as well as a friend, and the rights of self-determination and need to know did not apply in this game, based on what had transpired to date. Mario awoke completely relieved from any historical transgressions and was instantly filled with an invigorated sense of resolve. He was in a good place, and there were other chess pieces that required manipulation in an orchestrated and choreographed sequence. He anticipated that the remainder of the trip would now pass by very quickly. As an afterthought, he smiled to himself when he remembered that he was traveling first class in a private jet from the recent acquisition of a fleet of such jets that was part of an entrepreneurial venture with his business partner, Webb Espy. Mario owned a third of the business, with Webb owning the remainder. This new enterprise was henceforth to be known as: "E/D {ESPY/DIAZ) GOLDEN PARACHUTE SVS." Mario loved the logo that was prominently displayed on the tail, which incorporated a highly visible golden parachute. Mario laughed out loud to himself! Hell, he could afford to be generous.

45

June 19, 1995

Zurich, Switzerland

It was less than two weeks until Webb was scheduled to return to the states. He had one more minor procedure to endure, which was scheduled for the next morning, followed by a brief recovery period. Considering the circumstances that had necessitated Webb's interruption from normal life, the fourteen-month hiatus had, overall, been good for him in a number of ways, especially on the mental side of the equation. Never particularly vain about his appearance, Webb was forced to admit that the image he viewed, staring back at him in the mirror, had to be considered somewhat of an improvement. He joked with some of the staff that this place could make a warthog look like a swan!

Almost through an unconscious osmosis, due to the structure and daily regiment of the facility, as well as a rehab therapist's persistent intimidation techniques over him, he had gotten himself into better shape than he had been in years. He almost looked forward to it every day — almost! The major accomplishments, from Webb's perspective, were in his own mind and how his psychiatrist had led him through a grueling gauntlet of insightful admissions that had forced him to deal with repressed emotions going back to the tragedy he had endured with the loss of his family and even earlier.

Through a variety of therapeutic manipulations and interventions, Webb was enticed to create his own individualized comprehension and acceptance of providence and a hybrid form of personalized, philosophical existentialism. Although for several years, Webb had disguised his actions to others and was able to put meaning in his life by pouring himself into challenging endeavors, there had always been an ongoing gnawing under the surface that all was not what it was supposed to be. At the present, Webb was in a good place, completely at peace with himself, and was looking forward to exploring the future with a healthy sense of realism and anticipation.

It was a beautiful day, and Webb had finished his morning workout routines and was enjoying the pleasant weather outside under the covered patio. He had been engrossed in a new novel for about ten minutes when a voice from the past directly behind him invaded the solitude of his literary stupor like a bombshell.

"Well, as I live and breathe, if it's not Dr. Webb Espy, the human Houdini himself." Coming from a voice clearly distinguishable from all others, Webb whirled around and came face to face with the "poet laureate" of MPI, Kathryn Armstrong, who was casually leaning against one of the patio support pillars as if posing for inspection. She was dressed to kill and looked as if she might have just come from a *Vanity Fair* photo op. She adorned a fashionable light beige suit with a rather flattering emerald green blouse, which must have been at the top of her color chart. As the two engaged in a welcoming embrace, Webb could smell a freshness about her and the slight hint of fragrance from expensive cologne. As he held her at arm's length for examination, it was almost as if he wanted to make sure he was not dreaming. Finally, he found his tongue and simply blurted: "If you aren't a sight for sore eyes!"

"I believe that's my line," she teased, and continued. "Well, I'm just here in your part of the world on a little business, was in the neighborhood, thought I might take a potluck and just drop in and check on you. These are quite some digs you have here," she suggested while casting appreciative glances in various directions.

"Business, you say; what kind of business? Come over here; let's sit and tell me all about it. I want to know everything! How long will you be here?" He bombarded her with questions as he ushered her to the patio couch beside him. "Later." She deflected his request as she kept speaking. "Right now, I am your guest, and this is all about you. I want to know everything, and I mean everything, that has been going on in your life so that when I return to my envious MPI playmates, I can share firsthand the things that I have learned from you over here in wonderland," she proclaimed as she sat down easily in the comfort of the patio couch.

"Sounds like a deal, but first, may I offer you some kind of refreshment? This place has an incredible bar, stocked with some of the best brands in the universe and a bartender that can turn ripple into champagne," Webb declared proudly.

"You mean they let you actually imbibe demonic spirits in this place?" Kat questioned with arched eyebrows.

"You would be surprised what they allow and actually encourage you to do in this place. What may I get for you, Kat?" Webb offered in his most hospitable manner.

Kat kind of wrinkled her brow in thought and finally said:

"Well, it's a little early, but alcohol makes me talk better, and I guess as long as you're buying, I believe I'll have, well, let's see; you know, I really don't care for sissy drinks; tell you what, let me have a Bloody Mary, but I wonder if they might substitute tequila for vodka?" she quizzed.

"I believe that may be referred to as a *"Sangre de Maria!"* Sounds like a plan. I believe I'll join you." Webb motioned to one of the attendants and placed their order. While they were waiting for their drinks and engaged in preliminary pleasantries, Kat removed her coat, yielding the totality of her fashionable and complimentary low-cut emerald green blouse, which revealed a distracting amount of abundant cleavage.

Once the drinks arrived pursuant to Kat's ultimatum, Webb set his tongue in perpetual motion, beginning with what he had been told about what had happened to everything he could recall after regaining his senses in the hospital. He tried to describe the intense pain and noticed Kat actually grimace at one of his descriptions. He confessed there were in-and-out voids based on the intense pain as well as the medications required to control the pain. He continued nonstop through the fourteen-month continuum, which included seemingly endless ongoing surgeries, the excruciating rehabilitation tortures under the supervision of a disciple apprentice of Marques de Sade, through the gut-wrenching confrontations with himself via insights provoked by his relentless psychiatrist.

Although oblivious to it while it was happening, Webb exposed vulnerabilities, hidden feelings, and emotions he had shared with no one else, ever. Kat unknowingly served as both a catalyst and human sponge for Webb's outpourings. When he finally finished, she was watching him intently. She was emotionally spent, yet mysteriously fascinated by what by what he had revealed to her.

"Webb, I have no frame of reference for what you've been through, but I have some strange sense that you feel it has somehow been worth it," she stated, with a sincerity that caught him off guard.

"Well, I'm not sure about that," he said with a forced laugh. "But I have to admit that after all is said and done if I had not been forced to go through this process, my future would have been kind of aimless, and I would have probably lived out much of my existence in a rudderless vessel," he confided to her.

"So, have you given much thought as to what you are going to do once you get back?" she asked.

"Oh yeah, you know me. Always plotting and scheming. Got to find new mountains to climb. That's what drives me, you know. I've got ideas out the yazoo that I'm pondering. But hey, let's hold that part for a while. I have been doing all the talking, and at this point, I feel like I have just gone through a mental enema," he suggested somewhat guiltily.

"Well, that that sure conjures up an interesting visual mental image!" she chortled.

"How about another round, and you start bringing me up to speed on our old playmates?" he offered.

"Well, hell, you're buying, I'm not driving, so I really can't think of a legitimate reason why not," she conceded cheerfully.

For the next hour, she told him about everyone she thought he might be interested in hearing about. He was stunned yet inwardly pleased when she informed him that M had been seeing someone for a few months. Apparently, it was some fellow she met at the Math Fair Exposition. Kat said she had met him, and he seemed nice, a little geekish of sorts, but probably a good fit for M. Kat said M spent some time at her house staying with her son, Kenny, on occasion, and he was crazy about her because she would play video games with him for hours. Kat also shared with him that, although there was a difference in age, she and Marsha Kaye had become very good friends and enjoyed spending a good bit of time together. She provided a humorous account of the Sec's Deputy Secretary, Skip, trying an end run in an attempt to assign Dick Andrews to run MPI during Webb's absence. When Marsha Kaye realized what was happening, she had a conversation with Mario Diaz and then made a call to Secretary Baswell. Kat claimed to have no idea what she said to him, but he was not a happy camper. Dick had already brought some of his stuff and was putting it in your office when Deputy Dog himself appeared personally and escorted him out of the building and back to his cubicle, toting a box himself. It was a funny thing to watch," she said, laughing at the image she remembered.

"Sounds like Marsha Kaye must have finally figured out what I had on the Sec," Webb laughed.

"Don't know about that, but what I do know is that when Marsha Kaye and Mario team up, that's a dangerous and powerful combination," she said in all seriousness.

"Yep, you can go to the bank on that one!" Webb agreed.

Kathryn asked to be excused and indicated that when she returned, she wanted to hear about the plans he had dangled in front of her. Webb took the opportunity to visit the facilities and was back at his perch by the time Kat returned.

"Okay, I'm all ears, boss," she claimed as she settled back and began nursing her drink.

"Well, for starters, you can dispense with that "boss" mess.

I'm just Webb from here on out, or whatever handle you want to saddle me with," Webb stated with a stern emphasis.

"How's 'Honey' sound?" she asked, opening her eyes wide in comical fashion. Webb could not hold back a laugh.

"No, really, Kat, I'm not going to be going back to MPI, and I'm not going back to academia, either. I think I'm going to try something new and totally different. What I have in mind is to open a healthcare regulatory and consulting company. I am going to try to set up the whole enchilada. This company is going to provide cafeteria-style services, from provider enrollment services, licensing assistance, billing agent services, quality assurance contracts, qualitative claims resolutions, mediation and settlement representation, and litigation support. The only thing I really don't want to include is a lobbying component, but that's not poured in concrete. In addition, the company will provide consultation and hands-on grant writing for various federal provider services, waivers, and functional equivalents for back-end requirements for certification for the fed's System Performance Requirements. I also plan to explore the opportunity to participate with various vendors, to bid on the back-end requirements associated with the Medicaid fiscal agent contracts. Sound ambitious enough?" Webb asked proudly.

"You betchum, Red Ryder!" she shot back enthusiastically. "Well, just so you know, there is a major role for you that I have in mind, if you are interested, and I really hope you are." He looked questioningly at her. She simply continued to look at him with a strange, unnerving look about her. Sensing a sudden awkwardness he could neither decipher nor comprehend, he continued. "I think Marsha Kaye will serve as Chief Operating Officer and be in charge of running all office support systems; M, of course, will serve as Chief Technical Officer, and what I wanted you to —" He stopped midsentence and looked at her apologetically. "Kat, I'm so sorry; I've been so excited with you being here and all that I forgot that you are here on business, and I had no right whatsoever to assume you are at my beck and call for any of my grandiose future endeavors. That was totally presumptuous on my part, and I regret that I've put you in such a position."

She looked at him for a moment. There was something resembling an emerging mysterious twinkle in her eyes. "Webb," she eventually started, as she scooted over closer to him and grasped his hand. "Yes, I'm here on business. Mario sent me. However, first, before I forget my manners, I need to tell you that I will forever be indebted to you for the generous gesture regarding my son's future educational requirements," she said seriously.

"Well, wait a minute, not so fast; it was not my gesture; that money didn't come from me," Webb confessed in all honesty.

"Webb, I'm not a moron; I know the money came from you," she chided him annoyingly.

"Well, Kat, I hate to tell you, but you are dead wrong! That money did not come from yours truly. As I understand the situation, Mario, after a series of coincidences, learned about the severance package you had received earlier from your previous employer and the circumstances involved with your leaving the firm. He concluded, based on his legal experience, that you had not been dealt with fairly and were entitled to compensation and a settlement commensurate to the actual circumstances of the situation, at which point he contacted certain members of the firm on his client's behalf and, to borrow a phrase, simply made them an offer they could not refuse.

"Webb, I have never engaged Mario to represent me!"

"And he was not representing you. I was his client," Webb confessed as innocently as possible.

"You're a real piece of work, you know that!" she admonished him. Webb simply grinned.

"Now, let's return to the business at hand, which I was beginning to discuss when I went off on a tangent," she continued.

Webb frowned and once again was confused and bewildered. "Yeah, Kat, let's do that! As a matter of fact, let's start where you left off; especially with the part 'Mario sent you!' What in the world are you talking about? I got no clue what you are saying or attempting to convey or how Mario could have anything to do with it," he asked bewilderedly.

"Well, if you give me your undivided attention for a moment, you might be enlightened to some significant degree. I am here on business; it's serious business, and I have thought about nothing else for some time now. I have never been on a more serious business venture in my life! I almost cancelled this trip, but both Mario and Marsha Kaye forced my hand," she confessed, not able to meet his gaze momentarily. Webb was beyond confused.

Drawing upon some intestinal fortitude reserve, she looked up longingly and confidently, directly into his eyes. "Webb, Mario and Marsha Kaye already know this, so let me just tell you how it is; you need companionship; I am more than willing and prepared to provide that companionship. My son needs a man in his life to teach him the things that a single mother simply cannot. I can think of no other man that I've ever met in my life who could fulfill that role better than you. I think Kenny's athletic, but I'm probably not a good judge. I know he needs to have someone to teach him to hunt, fish, play golf, and provide a role model or whatever. I have to confess, I have had feelings for you since shortly after I first met you. I sure as hell hope that surprises you," she demanded. Webb simply stared at her in total bewilderment.

"At any rate, I went well out of my way to stay far away and hide any indication of those feelings," she said tenderly, meeting his eyes.

Webb, for one of the few times in his life, was practically speechless. "Kat, I don't know what to say. I mean, I don't have the words. Forgive me, I never had any idea. My God, I wish I had known. Believe me, I wish I had known! You have no idea what you're saying means to me! Kat, you are drop dead gorgeous and totally out of my league. I just can't even begin to process what you're telling me. Give me a second to take this in, Kat. Hell, and there I was, going on and on about finding new mountains to climb and all that kind of dumb crap," he admonished himself, while shaking his head at his ineptitude.

Kat immediately sensed Webb's overwhelming surprise and legitimate shock to what he had just learned, and she realized exactly how to deal with it and quickly seized upon a brazen strategy to diffuse the awkwardness of the moment and offered enticingly. "Well, how about climbing one of these?" she said tauntingly, dipping her chin and eyes toward her low-cut blouse and then looking up at him seductively. "I've got a couple of wet T-shirt trophies on my resume, and I've kept myself in pretty decent shape over the years."

Although she caught him totally off guard with her tantalizing antics, Webb rebounded somehow by reflex with a witty boomerang retort as he gazed down toward the view afforded and remarked casually: "Why, yes, Kat; I believe I see your point!" She howled in response. They both sat there momentarily, simply staring and assessing one another. They both realized it was going to happen and when they embraced, both knew it was something special. Kat was the first to speak as she looked at him with a distinct haze in her eyes. "I believe we need to get out of here!" she more than suggested. "Kat, it's been a long time. I don't know —"

She never let him finish. "'Spect it's kind of like riding a bicycle, don't you think!" she kidded.

"No, Kat, seriously; I really don't know what to expect," he confessed earnestly.

"Hey, you're in good hands, and I promise to be gentle," she said confidently and reassuringly while flashing a provocatively mischievous grin.

A chauffeured limo from the facility took them to her hotel. En route, Kat talked non-stop; it was like she had been vaccinated with a Victrola needle.

Webb had never seen her in this kind of state and found it quite humorous. Finally, he jokingly remarked that he did not believe he had ever seen her talk as much. She confessed, without reservation, that she always talked excessively when she was excited.

"Hell, if that was my case, under the current circumstances, I'd be spewing gibberish gobbledygook in unknown tongues nonstop, like an erupting volcano!" he declared somewhat seriously.

"You know, Webb, honey, that's just one of the things I really appreciate about you. You know exactly what to say to a girl to make her feel so special," she said as she nestled closer and squeezed him a little tighter.

He pondered her comment and wondered if it was delivered with sincerity or sarcasm. "You don't need to overthink this thing," he chastised himself. For the first time in several years, Webb was really looking forward to the future!

46

Date Unknown

Small Outside Cafe in Little Havana

The formal invitation had been hand delivered by a spiffy-attired young man in a chauffeured limousine to his personal residence and was addressed simply to: My Guest. The invitation included the date, time, address, and that transportation would be provided. It emphasized "Regrets Only!" Although the purpose was vague, the intrigue related to the wording: "Personal/business activities during the past several years and closure" was not! The invitation was simply signed, The Host. The teasing conundrum was effective and there was no way he could not accept and he waited anxiously for the appointed day to finally arrive.

The guest presented himself promptly at the café at the time indicated on the invitation and announced his presence. The maître d', apparently awaiting his entrance, immediately ushered him to an isolated table set for two in a far corner of the terrace under the shade of an open cabana. There was the gentle breeze from an almost noiseless hidden floor fan that was unanticipated, but a welcome accommodation. A cocktail arrived without being ordered and the guest more than approved of its contents. His curiosity was second only to his state of anxiousness. The guest surveyed the other patrons on the terrace level and discovered nothing remarkable, with the lone exception of one specific Latin beauty with attributes that were threatening the integrity of the structure that housed them. With not much else to do, he relaxed as best as he could and began nursing his drink.

The guest noticed the man immediately as he entered the premises. He was tall, with a thick dark mustache, and adorned with an authentic wide brim safari- style Panama hat, dark-tinted Costa sunglasses and a long sleeve embroidered linen guayabera. The man glanced once in the guest's direction and quickly headed directly towards the cabana. The guest could detect a hint of a smile on the man's mouth beneath the distracting sunglasses, which he made no attempt to remove, as he reached the table. When in range the man held out his hand to the guest as he simply stated; "I am your host for this occasion and you are my guest.

The salutation was not what the guest had anticipated and there was a brief awkwardness before the guest found his tongue. "Well, I must admit I'm not accustomed to invitations such as this or mysterious meetings. I live a rather routine and dull kind of existence," he suggested laughing nervously. "I'm not going to lie to you, my curiosity is off the charts at the moment."

The host awarded the guest's confession with a genuine smile and nodded at him almost knowingly as he began to speak. "I'm certain that you have to be curious, but the last thing I want is to make you uncomfortable. My intentions are straightforward, mutually beneficial, I suspect, and easily achievable. Now let me suggest a few protocols in order to proceed with our business in the most expeditious manner possible," he paused momentarily, as the waiter placed a tall fruit filled glass of freshly prepared sangria in front of him.

"First of all, let me alert you to the fact our conversation today is being recorded." The guest reacted immediately with alarm and suspicion. Anticipating the reaction, the host quickly interjected, "No, it's not anything like you might be thinking and let me assure you I am here with you today, heaven forbid, in no official capacity or representing any law enforcement or regulatory or governmental entity. I am here strictly as an individual with a business mission and I assure you there are no clandestine motives whatsoever. I am simply here for a reconciliation in a matter of speaking, as well as reciprocity between, or more aptly, among us going forward. Actually, two recordings are being made, one for each of us. It is kind of like a pact of guaranteed mutual destruction." He laughed genuinely in an attempt to relax the guest. The ploy on the part of the host did not succeed, based on the facial expression registering on the guest.

"Seriously, I sincerely apologize for the surreptitiousness of my actions, but I believe you will comprehend the necessity momentarily. Please allow me to continue. I introduced myself as your host and you are my guest; therefore, hereafter in our conversation today, I will address you as Mr. Guest and you may address me as Mr. Host, if that is acceptable?"

"Well, I have not the foggiest notion of where this is heading, but for some strange reason I, all of a sudden, seem to be sensing an inquiring type of faith in you," the guest stated executing a double reverse.

"Excellent! Now, there really is no need for you to speak and I recommend you allow me to do most of the talking. First of all, I know you and a considerable amount about you. I do not believe we have ever met, but it is possible that we might have. At any rate, I am relatively confident that we have never been formally

345

been introduced. The reason that speaking may be limited is because I have prepared a number of written questions with potential answers on cards. You will simply read the card silently and point to the answer. I believe you will find the questions straightforward as well as extremely simple and the range of potential answers exhaustive. Are you following me so far?"

"Yes, I believe I may be beginning to get your drift and I appreciate the approach."

"Good, then let's proceed, shall we. As a preface let me say that we both share a mutual acquaintance. Truthfully, he is more than an acquaintance for me, but I have no reason to suspect that the two of you are anything more than passing acquaintances. More about that possibly later. The information I am about to share with you is probably going to surprise you, but it will serve notice that I am capable of performing in-depth due diligence and that I know more things about you and your activities than you can possibly imagine. Let me assure you that I have no interest whatsoever in the things you have been involved in with your friend in the past or the motives for any such activities. First of all, I know in considerable detail what you have been doing over the past few years and I know who you have been doing it with," as he flashed a photograph. The guest's facial expression said it all. It was a dead giveaway and the host thought his invitee might become physically ill. He immediately pushed a question card in front of the guest with a simple question and answer card which read:

Do you know this man and do you know his name?

YES   NO

The guest pointed hesitantly to the "YES" answer.

The host continued with a series of question-and-answer cards to which the guest's responses gave the host no reason to hold any reservations or suspicions that his guest had answered any of the questions deceptively or inappropriately. When he had finished the exercise, he signaled the waiter to refresh the guest's drink. Once the drink had been delivered, the host went into a well-rehearsed monologue outlining almost everything he knew about his guest, his friend and the things they had been up to, improvising with several things he had just confirmed via his question/answer strategy. It was obvious that his guest was completely stunned and helplessly overwhelmed at what had just transpired.

The host finished and sat back in his chair without speaking and allowed the information just revealed to sink in. The host waited patiently for a brief while and then sensing the right instant, seized the opportunity and presented his well-orchestrated plan. "I understand that you have recently relinquished yourself of a couple of rather lucrative businesses. My sources also tell me that due to your recent attainment of nouveau-riche status you are in the process of acquiring several international resort property investments. I believe those are shrewd business moves and I have no doubt given your business insights and other intangibles which you obviously possess, that you will do quite well," he stated in a sincere and gentlemanly manner.

"Well, you are smooth, but you are blowing smoke up my ass. You're good at it, but I don't need it. What is it you want?

"Certainly, as I mentioned earlier, I am interested in a final reconciliation and an ongoing reciprocal agreement for our mutual acquaintance that is commensurate with the difficulties and consequences suffered due to the actions related to you and your significant friend. This is a one-time shot and we both will go on with our lives as if we have never held these conversations today. At this point there is really no need for any additional conversation. I am about to give you an envelope. I am going to put your tape in it." At that point the host went through an overly dramatized display of retrieving a mini cassette tape and inserting it into an envelope. Once the tape had been secured and deposited in the envelope the host continued; "Off the record my friend: Mr. Guest, I view you as the partner and a willing accomplice with your estranged friend and based on your less than legitimate activities in which the two of you were engaged, you are therefore considered by default as self-insured. Inside the envelope you will find a piece of paper that contains a number and an account and routing number to an offshore conversion/transmittal intermediary. Based on my overall assessment I believe the amount is actually inadequate and inequitable due to the premeditation involved. In my opinion, it represents a significant discount from what ought to be forthcoming. However, as someone prudently advised me once upon a time under similar circumstances, we must not throw out the baby with the bathwater," he concluded.

"And if for some reason I am unable to meet the requirements?" the guest questioned, regretting such an uttering before it was out of his mouth.

"You will have no problem whatsoever fulfilling the obligations, and based on my resourcefulness which you are aware by now are quite extensive, it will not make a dent in your coffers and overall portfolio," he prophesied, drawing to an inside straight, without any such knowledge. And, as a sidebar, let me just add that having considerable experience in certain situations, I consider you with some degree of impunity related to this situation. I believe you to be an honorable man with integrity and if I had any thoughts that you possessed any foresight or role into was going to happen to our mutual acquaintance, we would be having a very different conversation right now," the host stated with the utmost clarity.

The guest managed the courage to look directly into the sunglasses opposite him and stated as convincingly as he knew how, "Let me assure you that I had no idea what was going down. Looks like you know more about it than I do. I feel almost certain there are things that I know that you did not ask and possibly may not even care about. I have no choice but to trust you. Let me say this. Your presence here today and some of the things you shared through your questions have convinced me that a number of my unvalidated assumptions are now pretty well confirmed and they give me, for obvious reasons, no comfort," the guest surrendered with legitimate humility.

"You are a quick study and in other circumstances we might have a different relationship," stated the host with the utmost sincerity.

"I have to ask hypothetically; what if the demands are beyond the ability to comply?"

Well, that is obviously hypothetical, but let me just say; one plans carefully and executes ruthlessly. You have no idea what happened to your friend, I do," the host stated rather emphatically with a sinister expression on his face that almost magically evolved into a warm and genuine grin.

"Oh, one other thing. Is it possible that you might share with me a copy of the questions and answers?" the guest asked inquisitively?

"Not in a million years, Mr. Guest. Those cards will be shredded and incinerated within the hour, my good friend," the host retorted, laughing out loud. At that point, the two men shook hands and the host took leave indicating in a leave-taking gesture that he had taken the liberty of ordering dinner for his guest.

Both men realized without verification that the aforementioned deal had been consummated.

The host was chauffeured to Miami International Airport and exited the limousine at the departures level. He entered the terminal and proceeded directly to the men's facilities. Once inside he selected a stall and began transforming himself. First, he removed the thick black mustache and gave it a flush. Next, he removed the giant Panama hat and allowed his hair to return to its normal state. From his attaché case, his shirt and sunglasses were replaced with a polo and regular wire framed reading glasses. When he exited the airport to hail a taxi, he was seemingly a totally different human being.

It was all the guest could do to restrain himself from discovering what was contained on the piece of paper inside the envelope. For several minutes after the host had departed, he just sat there and stared at the menacing object. Eventually the suspense overcame his tentativeness and he mustered the courage to face his fate. When he unfolded the paper and viewed the figure his heart almost stopped. The sum was astonishing by any standard and would have probably even forced Warren Buffett to do a double take. The guest, however, was instantly relieved and concluded without the slightest reservation that this was not a game changer in the least and immediately signaled the waiter for another round.

Epilogue

<u>Webb and Kathryn</u> *were married within fourteen months after they returned from his treatment in Switzerland. Their marriage was one of the social events of the year in Tallahassee and was held at the Pebble Hill Plantation with over 400 guests. David Baswell gave away the bride, and Mario Diaz served as best man. Webb and Kathryn embarked on a lifetime of numerous adventures and entrepreneurial enterprises while donating the majority of profits to various causes. They also continued their own version of* The Millionaire Game. *In addition to Kathryn's first child, Kenny, adopted by Webb, who is currently on the PGA Tour, they had a second child, Marsha Kathryn, who became a world-class gymnast and currently is a freelance sports journalist and broadcaster. Although the couple have a home in Tallahassee, they spend a considerable amount of time traveling the globe.*

<u>Marsha Kaye</u> *managed Webb's healthcare regulatory consulting business for almost fifteen years. She continues to reside in Tallahassee and maintains close contact with Webb and Kathryn and considers their children her grandchildren. She is in charge of all their affairs when they are traveling. She lives without any financial worries whatsoever, in part off of dividends from over* *twenty-five shares of Coca Cola stock of the 1930s variety. In the last few years, she has turned into a prissy little old lady and is a serious competitive ballroom dancer.*

David Baswell *died of a massive stroke in 2008 during a bid for the U.S. Senate, which at the time, polls were suggesting his ultimate election was almost something of a guarantee. Webb performed the eulogy. Prior to the Espy wedding, David had confided to Webb that he did not know for sure if Kathryn was his half-sister or a blood cousin, but it was for certain that it was one or the other. There had been, apparently, a series of complicated indiscretions by male members of the Baswell clan prior to early Vietnam deployments. Kathryn was the result. Both Kathryn and her mother had been well provided for under the circumstances, but there was guilt never-theless. When Kathryn's mother died prematurely from a brain aneurysm, David had been the male Baswell designee charged with monitoring Kathryn's overall state of well-being to the extent possible.*

Mario Diaz *continues to serve Webb and Kathryn as their "financial everything" as he always has. Mario never officially "came out of the closet," but he did the next best thing by marrying a lady with a similar persuasion. Her maiden name was Rachel McMann. A number of years ago, they met a couple with comparable needs, became extremely close, and are a compatible quartet. They all have been very happy for a number of years with their openly special arrangement.*

"M" *worked with Webb for over a decade and made a sizable fortune. She sold a detection application to Electronic Data Systems that Mario*

Diaz brokered and is financially set for life. She eventually married her mathematical soulmate, and they had a son who was not geekish in the least and went to Wake Forest on a soccer scholarship. She and her husband currently live on a small acreage farm in southeast Leon County and raise prize "show goats."

__Phyllis Newberry__ eventually was named by David Baswell to head the Medicaid Integrity Office, once Webb make it clear that he had no intentions of returning to public service. Asked to name his replacement, Webb never hesitated. Phyllis Newberry was his only recommendation. With her appointment to Senior Management, she became the highest black female minority ever to join the upper echelons of the Department of Health and Rehabilitative Services.

__Arthur St. John__ tired of state politics and made an unsuccessful run for a congressional seat. With the defeat, his political career ended. Eventually, in a partnership arrangement with Webb and Kathryn, he opened a children's research and teaching hospital in Miami. He and Webb still play golf on occasion.

__Little Willie Diozos__ currently resides in Miami and seems to enjoy his ongoing infamous, legendary status. Willie contracted HIV several years ago, but apparently recovered and is reportedly back to "normal activities."

__Jorge De Valle__ sold his pharmacies in Miami and invested in numerous resort properties throughout Latin America and Spain. He attends the Masters in Augusta every year with complete clubhouse privileges.

Anna Louisa Espaillant *has world-renowned art galleries in Paris, Madrid, Amsterdam, and Manhattan. She also funds multiple full-expense scholarships for the arts and humanities. She spends most of her time on her yacht moorings throughout the Mediterranean and Amalfi Coast. She enjoys a yearly pilgrimage to one of Jorge De Valle's resorts.*

Max Bloodworth *resides on a 600-acre rural estate in Wakulla County, which he inherited from an anonymous relative, along with over half a million of estate benefits. His health has deteriorated over the years due to heart disease and apparent Agent Orange exposure. When he retired from the phone company, he opened a bail bondsman business with his son that was extremely successful and financially lucrative. Max no longer turkey hunts, but on occasion, he and Webb will go red fishing in the flats on Max's converted pontoon party boat.*

Tim Fagan *left the Office of the Inspector General not long after Webb was hospitalized and held a number of senior management positions before his ultimate retirement. He and Webb remain extremely close friends and travel the world in search of feathers.*

Waylon Griggs's *mysterious disappearance was never solved. There was never so much as a clue as to what had happened to either him or his vehicle. They both had simply vanished without a trace. His disappearance became a political issue with racial overtones since a black deputy went missing on a white man's watch and ended up costing the sheriff the next election. It is still considered an open case.*

Acknowledgements

It goes without saying that an endeavor such as this is never accomplished in isolation or in a vacuum. There are many individuals who have influenced or participated in this effort, many unknowingly! Regrettably, there are quite a number of these individuals who are no longer with us and therefore will not physically hoist a celebratory stem to toast the occasion, but somehow I am hopeful their spirits will imbibe the fruits of the festivities somehow via osmosis.

I have been blessed by a various assortment of numerous mentors. Included in such a list are relatives, friends, teachers, authors, actors, bosses, coworkers, philosophers, and drugstore cowboys.

I will forever be indebted to my mother for introducing me to books and reading. She was the first one I ever heard express: "Brains need books like swords need whetstones!" She entertained both my sister and me by reading to us for hours on end, painting amazing visual images, and breathing life into the story characters via expressions, dialects, and impersonations. Both my mother and radio plays share equally for my imagination and embellishments of mundane and ordinary situations. For an individual of her time, especially a female of the south, *she espoused a plethora of eclectic progressive thoughts and views and was whimsically proud of her seemingly eccentric personality,*

I owe my Daddy a debt of gratitude for teaching me that you learn how to do things from the bottom up, and there are usually few real shortcuts to legitimate success. My work ethic and my optimistic approach to most things in my life are due to his patience and encouragement. He was also a gifted storyteller, complete with an excellent repertoire of impersonations. He found real pleasure in the simplest things and was willing to share them.

Major kudos to my sister, Juanita, "Bright Arrow," the legitimate and really gifted writer in the family who set aside sibling rivalry and competitiveness to objectively assess my early trials and flatter me by suggesting I might have stumbled onto something worthwhile while simultaneously offering encouragement, performing multiple reads, suggesting improvements, and some editing expertise.

An extraordinary special credit to Carol Ann Thompson, who performed a yeoman's task by volunteering her time to painstakingly proof the early manuscripts and offer remedial eighth-grade English tutoring. I will forever be indebted and grateful. There are not enough words to thank her.

I have no idea how this attempt at writing a work of fiction will be received, but I know for a fact that it is certainly better than it was due to Jay Ter Louw's review and the various insights, critiques, and suggestions he made. His independent read provided significant encouragement to me. Jay is a serious writer himself!

The facilitator award is for my son, John "Whiddy" Jr., who requested oral recitations and listened intently to the individual chapter drafts and offered thumbs up or downs, along with questions and constructive criticisms.

My daughter, Alexandra, deserves credit for orchestrating the process from initiation to completion of the book jacket, various cover designs, and packaging. She also was one of the primary motivators for authoring this work by encouraging me, since she was just a little girl, to tell my stories.

Barbara Fincher, friend, colleague, neighbor, earth mother, hardest worker I've ever known, and my technical everything; she has participated on so many of my projects and works for wine!

Sincere appreciation is due to the initial guinea pig readers, who plowed through either entire early drafts or selected special sections and offered advice, critiques, and encouragement. These individuals include: Judy Sisk Millspaugh, Kathy Johnson, James Roberts, and Bill Marvin.

The girth of materials accumulated and used for concocting such fiction can rarely be adequately identified, but let it suffice to say that they obviously emerged from associations and acquaintances in my historical wake. I am indebted to my Air Force buddies, Mayo's Barber Shop patrons, graduate school classmates, the ding-a-lings, and Camp Bear Wallow friends. I am especially thankful to my friends and colleagues from Medicaid Program Integrity for providing the seeds that fed the imagination and embellishments for this particular story.

Last, but certainly not least, the inspiration and the motivation for this book, as well as most everything I have ever accomplished, is due to my wife, Carmen. She is the force in my life that has constantly pushed me well beyond my own initiatives.

Printed in the USA
CPSIA information can be obtained
at www.ICGtesting.com
JSHW010715031123
51219JS00005B/16/J